107b

Presented

Winter 1950 for coming second in
the House Quartet singing competition.


D.M.

Jock Alden — Director of Music
Bradfield College until 1955.

# THE THREE HOSTAGES

GLENAICILL FOREST

MACHRAY

HARIPOL FOREST

CNOC GLAS

R. AICILL

CORRIE EALLIN FOREST

FUISGHIN THULA

R. MADDIE

SCORRIE TRINKUE

CEOCILL

CLARE BAN

CLARE STRALN

R. REAUCILL

R. SGURR UICK

CLOU

Mr Machray and Haripol Forests
a diagram of containing chapter

Mr Wм Heinemann's Books

# THE
# THREE HOSTAGES

JOHN BUCHAN

THOMAS NELSON AND SONS LTD
LONDON EDINBURGH PARIS MELBOURNE
TORONTO AND NEW YORK

## THOMAS NELSON AND SONS LTD

Parkside Works Edinburgh 9
3 Henrietta Street London WC2
312 Flinders Street Melbourne C1

THOMAS NELSON AND SONS (CANADA) LTD
91–93 Wellington Street West   Toronto 1

THOMAS NELSON AND SONS
385 Madison Avenue New York 17

SOCIÉTÉ FRANÇAISE D'EDITIONS NELSON
25 rue Henri Barbusse Paris V^e

———

*First published July 1924*
*Reprinted 1924 (eleven times), 1925 (twice), 1926 (t:vice)*
*First published in this edition September 1926*
*Reprinted 1929, 1931, 1935, 1936, 1945, 1946, 1948 (twice)*
    *1949*

HONOURED SIR,

On your last birthday a well-meaning godfather presented you with a volume of mine, since you had been heard on occasion to express approval of my works. The book dealt with a somewhat arid branch of historical research, and it did not please you. You wrote to me, I remember, complaining that I had " let you down," and summoning me, as I valued your respect, to " pull myself together." In particular you demanded to hear more of the doings of Richard Hannay, a gentleman for whom you professed a liking. I too have a liking for Sir Richard, and when I met him the other day (he is now a country neighbour) I observed that his left hand had been considerably mauled, an injury which I knew had not been due to the War. He was so good as to tell me the tale of an unpleasant business in which he had recently been engaged, and to give me permission to re-tell it for your benefit. Sir Richard took a modest pride in the affair, because from first to last it had been a pure contest of wits, without recourse to those more obvious methods of strife with which he is familiar. So I herewith present it to you, in the hope that in the eyes of you and your friends it may atone for certain other writings of mine with which you have been afflicted by those in authority.

J. B.

*June 1924*

# CONTENTS

# NOTE

OCCASIONAL references will be found in this tale to the earlier experiences of Sir Richard Hannay, which are chronicled in *The Thirty-Nine Steps*, *Greenmantle*, and *Mr. Standfast*.

# THE
# THREE HOSTAGES

## CHAPTER I

### DR. GREENSLADE THEORIZES

THAT evening, I remember, as I came up through the Mill Meadow, I was feeling peculiarly happy and contented. It was still mid-March, one of those spring days when noon is like May, and only the cold pearly haze at sunset warns a man that he is not done with winter. The season was absurdly early, for the blackthorn was in flower and the hedge roots were full of primroses. The partridges were paired, the rooks were well on with their nests, and the meadows were full of shimmering grey flocks of fieldfares on their way north. I put up half a dozen snipe on the boggy edge of the stream, and in the bracken in Sturn Wood I thought I saw a woodcock, and hoped that the birds might nest with us this year, as they used to do long ago. It was jolly to see the world coming to life again, and to remember that this patch of England was my own, and all these wild things, so to speak, members of my little household.

As I say, I was in a very contented mood, for I had found something I had longed for all my days. I had bought Fosse Manor just after the War as a wedding present for Mary, and for two and a half years we had been settled there. My son, Peter John, was rising fifteen months, a thoughtful infant, as healthy as a young colt and as comic as a terrier puppy. Even Mary's anxious eye could scarcely detect in him any symptoms of decline. But the place wanted a lot of looking to, for it had run wild during the War, and the woods had to be thinned, gates and fences repaired, new drains laid, a ram put in to supplement the wells, a heap of thatching to be done, and the garden borders to be brought back to cultivation. I had got through the worst of it, and as I came out of the Home Wood on to the lower lawns and saw the old stone gables that the monks had built, I felt that I was anchored at last in the pleasantest kind of harbour.

There was a pile of letters on the table in the hall, but I let them be, for I was not in the mood for any communication with the outer world. As I was having a hot bath Mary kept giving me the news through her bedroom door. Peter John had been raising Cain over a new tooth; the new shorthorn cow was drying off; old George Whaddon had got his granddaughter back from service; there was a new brood of runner-ducks; there was a missel-thrush building in the box hedge by the lake. A chronicle of small beer, you will say, but I was by a long chalk more interested in it than in what might be happening in Parliament or Russia or the Hindu Kush. The fact is I was becoming such a mossback that I had almost stopped reading the papers. Many a day the *Times* would remain unopened, for Mary never looked at anything but the first page to see who was dead or married. Not that I didn't read a lot, for I used to spend my evenings digging into county history, and learning all I could about the old fellows who had been my predecessors. I liked to think that I lived in a place that had been continuously inhabited for a thousand years. Cavalier and Roundhead had fought over the countryside, and I was becoming a considerable authority on their tiny battles. That was about the only interest I had left in soldiering.

As we went downstairs, I remember we stopped to look out of the long staircase window which showed a segment of lawn, a corner of the lake, and through a gap in the woods a vista of green downland. Mary squeezed my arm. " What a blessed country," she said. " Dick, did you ever dream of such peace ? We're lucky, lucky people."

Then suddenly her face changed in that way she has and grew very grave. I felt a little shiver run along her arm.

" It's too good and beloved to last," she whispered. " Sometimes I am afraid."

"Nonsense," I laughed. "What's going to upset it? I don't believe in being afraid of happiness." I knew very well, of course, that Mary couldn't be afraid of anything.

She laughed too. "All the same I've got what the Greek called *aidos*. You don't know what that means, you old savage. It means that you must walk humbly and delicately to propitiate the Fates. I wish I knew how."

She walked too delicately, for she missed the last step, and our descent ended in an undignified shuffle right into the arms of Dr. Greenslade.

Paddock—I had got Paddock back after the War and he was now my butler—was helping the doctor out of his ulster, and I saw by the satisfied look on the latter's face that he was through with his day's work and meant to stay to dinner. Here I had better introduce Tom Greenslade, for of all my recent acquaintances he was the one I had most taken to. He was a long lean fellow with a stoop in his back from bending over the handles of motor-bicycles, with reddish hair, and the greeny-blue eyes and freckled skin that often accompany that kind of hair. From his high cheek-bones and his colouring you would have set him down as a Scotsman, but, as a matter of fact, he came from Devonshire—Exmoor, I think, though he had been so much about the world that he had almost forgotten where he was raised. I have travelled a bit, but nothing to Greenslade. He had started as a doctor in a whaling ship. Then he had been in the South African War, and

afterwards a temporary magistrate up Lyden-
burg way. He soon tired of that, and was for a
long spell in Uganda and German East, where he
became rather a swell on tropical diseases, and
nearly perished through experimenting on himself with fancy inoculations. Then he was in
South America, where he had a good practice in
Valparaiso, and then in the Malay States, where
he made a bit of money in the rubber boom.
There was a gap of three years after that when
he was wandering about Central Asia, partly with
a fellow called Duckett exploring Northern Mon-
golia, and partly in Chinese Tibet hunting for
new flowers, for he was mad about botany. He
came home in the summer of 1914, meaning to do
some laboratory research work, but the War
swept him up and he went to France as M.O.
of a territorial battalion. He got wounded, of
course, and after a spell in hospital went out to
Mesopotamia, where he stayed till the Christmas
of 1918, sweating hard at his job but managing
to tumble into a lot of varied adventures, for he
was at Baku with Dunsterville and got as far as
Tashkend, where the Bolsheviks shut him up for
a fortnight in a bath-house. During the War
he had every kind of sickness, for he missed no
experience, but nothing seemed to damage per-
manently his whipcord physique. He told me
that his heart and lungs and blood pressure were
as good as a lad's of twenty-one, though by this
time he was on the wrong side of forty.

But when the War was over he hankered for a

quiet life, so he bought a practice in the deepest
and greenest corner of England. He said his
motive was the same as that which in the rackety
Middle Ages made men retire into monasteries :
he wanted quiet and leisure to consider his soul.
Quiet he may have found, but uncommon little
leisure, for I never heard of a country doctor that
toiled at his job as he did. He would pay three
visits a day to a panel patient, which shows the
kind of fellow he was ; and he would be out in the
small hours at the birth of a gipsy child under a
hedge. He was a first-class man in his profession,
and kept abreast of it, but doctoring was only one
of a thousand interests. I never met a chap with
such an insatiable curiosity about everything
in heaven and earth. He lived in two rooms
in a farmhouse some four miles from us, and I
daresay he had several thousand books about
him. All day, and often half the night, he would
scour the country in his little run-about car, and
yet, when he would drop in to see me and have a
drink after maybe twenty visits, he was as full of
beans as if he had just got out of bed. Nothing
came amiss to him in talk—birds, beasts, flowers,
books, politics, religion—everything in the world
except himself. He was the best sort of company,
for behind all his quickness and cleverness you
felt that he was solid bar-gold. But for him I
should have taken root in the soil and put out
shoots, for I have a fine natural talent for vege-
tating. Mary strongly approved of him and
Peter John adored him.

(2,745)

He was in tremendous spirits that evening, and for once in a way gave us reminiscences of his past. He told us about the people he badly wanted to see again : an Irish Spaniard up in the north of the Argentine who had for cattlemen a most murderous brand of native from the mountains, whom he used to keep in good humour by arranging fights every Sunday, he himself taking on the survivor with his fists and always knocking him out ; a Scotch trader from Hankow who had turned Buddhist priest and intoned his prayers with a strong Glasgow accent ; and most of all a Malay pirate, who, he said, was a sort of St. Francis with beasts, though a perfect Nero with his fellow-men. That took him to Central Asia, and he observed that if ever he left England again he would make for those parts, since they were the refuge of all the superior rascality of creation. He had a notion that something very odd might happen there in the long run. " Think of it ! " he cried. " All the places with names like spells —Bokhara, Samarkand—run by seedy little gangs of communist Jews. It won't go on for ever. Some day a new Genghis Khan or a Timour will be thrown up out of the maelstrom. Europe is confused enough, but Asia is ancient Chaos."

After dinner we sat round the fire in the library, which I had modelled on Sir Walter Bullivant's room in his place on the Kennet, as I had promised myself seven years ago. I had meant it for my own room where I could write and read and smoke, but Mary would not allow it. She had a jolly panelled sitting-room of her own upstairs, which she rarely entered; but though I chased her away, she was like a hen in a garden and always came back, so that presently she had staked out a claim on the other side of my writing-table. I have the old hunter's notion of order, but it was useless to strive with Mary, so now my desk was littered with her letters and needlework, and Peter John's toys and picture-books were stacked in the cabinet where I kept my fly-books, and Peter John himself used to make a kraal every morning inside an upturned stool on the hearth-rug.

It was a cold night and very pleasant by the fireside, where some scented logs from an old pear-tree were burning. The doctor picked up a detective novel I had been reading, and glanced at the title page.

"I can read most things," he said, "but it beats me how you waste time over such stuff. These shockers are too easy, Dick. You could invent better ones for yourself."

"Not I. I call that a dashed ingenious yarn. I can't think how the fellow does it."

"Quite simple. The author writes the story inductively, and the reader follows it deductively. Do you see what I mean?"

"Not a bit," I replied.

"Look here. I want to write a shocker, so I begin by fixing on one or two facts which have no sort of obvious connection."

"For example?"

" Well, imagine anything you like. Let us take three things a long way apart——" He paused for a second to consider—" say, an old blind woman spinning in the Western Highlands, a barn in a Norwegian *saeter*, and a little curiosity shop in North London kept by a Jew with a dyed beard. Not much connection between the three ? You invent a connection—simple enough if you have any imagination, and you weave all three into the yarn. The reader, who knows nothing about the three at the start, is puzzled and intrigued and, if the story is well arranged, finally satisfied. He is pleased with the ingenuity of the solution, for he doesn't realize that the author fixed upon the solution first, and then invented a problem to suit it."

" I see," I said. " You've gone and taken the gilt off my favourite light reading. I won't be able any more to marvel at the writer's cleverness."

" I've another objection to the stuff—it's not ingenious enough, or rather it doesn't take account of the infernal complexity of life. It might have been all right twenty years ago, when most people argued and behaved fairly logically. But they don't nowadays. Have you ever realized, Dick, the amount of stark craziness that the War has left in the world ? "

Mary, who was sitting sewing under a lamp, raised her head and laughed.

Greenslade's face had become serious. " I can speak about it frankly here, for you two are almost the only completely sane people I know. Well, as a pathologist, I'm fairly staggered. I hardly meet a soul who hasn't got some slight kink in his brain as a consequence of the last seven years. With most people it's rather a pleasant kink—they're less settled in their grooves, and they see the comic side of things quicker, and are readier for adventure. But with some it's *pukka* madness, and that means crime. Now, how are you going to write detective stories about that kind of world on the old lines ? You can take nothing for granted, as you once could, and your argus-eyed, lightning-brained expert has nothing solid with which to build his foundations."

I observed that the poor old War seemed to be getting blamed for a good deal that I was taught in my childhood was due to original sin.

" Oh, I'm not questioning your Calvinism. Original sin is always there, but the meaning of civilization was that we had got it battened down under hatches, whereas now it's getting its head up. But it isn't only sin. It's a dislocation of the mechanism of human reasoning, a general loosening of screws. Oddly enough, in spite of parrot talk about shell shock, the men who fought suffer less from it on the whole than other people. The classes that shirked the War are the worst— you see it in Ireland. Every doctor nowadays has got to be a bit of a mental pathologist. As I say, you can hardly take anything for granted, and if you want detective stories that are not

childish fantasy you'll have to invent a new kind.
Better try your hand, Dick."

" Not I. I'm a lover of sober facts."

" But, hang it, man, the facts are no longer
sober. I could tell you——" He paused and I
was expecting a yarn, but he changed his
mind.

" Take all this chatter about psycho-analysis.
There's nothing very new in the doctrine, but
people are beginning to work it out into details,
and making considerable asses of themselves in
the process. It's an awful thing when a scientific
truth becomes the quarry of the half-baked.
But, as I say, the fact of the subconscious self is
as certain as the existence of lungs and arteries."

" I don't believe that Dick has any subconscious
self," said Mary.

" Oh yes, he has. Only, people who have led
his kind of life have their ordinary self so well
managed and disciplined—their wits so much
about them, as the phrase goes—that the subconscious rarely gets a show. But I bet if Dick
took to thinking about his soul, which he never
does, he would find some queer corners. Take
my own case." He turned towards me so that I
had a full view of his candid eyes and hungry
cheek-bones which looked prodigious in the firelight. " I belong more or less to the same totem
as you, but I've long been aware that I possessed
a most curious kind of subconsciousness. I've a
good memory and fair powers of observation, but
they're nothing to those of my subconscious self.

Take any daily incident. I see and hear, say, about a twentieth part of the details and remember about a hundredth part—that is, assuming that there is nothing special to stimulate my interest. But my subconscious self sees and hears practically everything, and remembers most of it. Only I can't use the memory, for I don't know that I've got it, and can't call it into being when I wish. But every now and then something happens to turn on the tap of the subconscious, and a thin trickle comes through. I find myself sometimes remembering names I was never aware of having heard, and little incidents and details I had never consciously noticed. Imagination, you will say; but it isn't, for everything that that inner memory provides is exactly true. I've tested it. If I could only find some way of tapping it at will, I should be an uncommonly efficient fellow. Incidentally I should become the first scientist of the age, for the trouble with investigation and experiment is that the ordinary brain does not observe sufficiently keenly or remember the data sufficiently accurately."

"That's interesting," I said. "I'm not at all certain I haven't noticed the same thing in myself. But what has that to do with the madness that you say is infecting the world?"

"Simply this. The barriers between the conscious and the subconscious have always been pretty stiff in the average man. But now with the general loosening of screws they are growing shaky and the two worlds are getting mixed. It is like two separate tanks of fluid where the containing wall has worn into holes, and one is percolating into the other. The result is confusion, and, if the fluids are of a certain character, explosions. That is why I say that you can't any longer take the clear psychology of most civilized human beings for granted. Something is welling up from primeval deeps to muddy it."

" I don't object to that," I said. " We've overdone civilization, and personally I'm all for a little barbarism. I want a simpler world."

" Then you won't get it," said Greenslade. He had become very serious now, and was looking towards Mary as he talked. " The civilized is far simpler than the primeval. All history has been an effort to make definitions, clear rules of thought, clear rules of conduct, solid sanctions, by which we can conduct our life. These are the work of the conscious self. The subconscious is an elementary and lawless thing. If it intrudes on life two results must follow. There will be a weakening of the power of reasoning, which, after all, is the thing that brings men nearest to the Almighty. And there will be a failure of nerve."

I got up to get a light, for I was beginning to feel depressed by the doctor's diagnosis of our times. I don't know whether he was altogether serious, for he presently started on fishing, which was one of his many hobbies. There was very fair dry-fly fishing to be had in our little river, but I had taken a deer-forest with Archie Roylance for the season, and Greenslade was coming up with me to try his hand at salmon. There had been no sea-trout the year before in the West Highlands, and we fell to discussing the cause. He was ready with a dozen theories, and we forgot about the psychology of mankind in investigating the uncanny psychology of fish. After that Mary sang to us, for I considered any evening a failure without that, and at half-past ten the doctor got into his old ulster and departed.

As I smoked my last pipe I found my thoughts going over Greenslade's talk. I had found a snug harbour, but how yeasty the waters seemed to be outside the bar and how erratic the tides! I wondered if it wasn't shirking to be so comfortable in a comfortless world. Then I reflected that I was owed a little peace, for I had had a roughish life. But Mary's words kept coming back to me about "walking delicately." I considered that my present conduct filled that bill, for I was mighty thankful for my mercies and in no way inclined to tempt Providence by complacency.

Going up to bed, I noticed my neglected letters on the hall table. I turned them over and saw that they were mostly bills and receipts or tradesmen's circulars. But there was one addressed in a handwriting that I knew, and as I looked at it I experienced a sudden sinking of the heart. It was from Lord Artinswell—Sir Walter Bullivant, as was—who had now retired from the Foreign Office, and was living at his place on the Kennet. He and I occasionally corresponded about farming and fishing, but I had a premonition that this was something different. I waited for a second or two before I opened it.

"MY DEAR DICK,
        "This note is in the nature of a warning. In the next day or two you will be asked. nay pressed, to undertake a troublesome piece of business. I am not responsible for the request, but I know of it. If you consent, it will mean the end for a time of your happy vegetable life. I don't want to influence you one way or another; I only give you notice of what is coming in order that you may adjust your mind and not be taken by surprise. My love to Mary and the son.
                                    "Yours ever,
                                        "A."

That was all. I had lost my trepidation and felt very angry. Why couldn't the fools let me alone? As I went upstairs I vowed that not all the cajolery in the world would make me budge an inch from the path I had set myself. I had done enough for the public service and other people's interests, and it was jolly well time that I should be allowed to attend to my own.

# CHAPTER II

## I HEAR OF THE THREE HOSTAGES

THERE is an odour about a country house which I love better than any scent in the world. Mary used to say it was a mixture of lamp and dog and wood smoke, but at Fosse, where there was electric light and no dogs indoors, I fancy it was wood smoke, tobacco, the old walls, and wafts of the country coming in at the windows. I liked it best in the morning, when there was a touch in it of breakfast cooking, and I used to stand at the top of the staircase and sniff it as I went to my bath. But on the morning I write of I could take no pleasure in it; indeed it seemed to tantalize me with a vision of country peace which had somehow got broken. I couldn't get that confounded letter out of my head. When I read it I had torn it up in disgust, but I found myself going down in my dressing-gown, to the surprise of a housemaid, piecing together the fragments from the waste-paper basket, and reading it again. This time I flung the bits into the new-kindled fire.

I was perfectly resolved that I would have nothing to do with Bullivant or any of his designs, but all the same I could not recapture the serenity which yesterday had clothed me like a garment. I was down to breakfast before Mary, and had finished before she appeared. Then I lit my pipe and started on my usual tour of my domain, but nothing seemed quite the same. It was a soft, fresh morning with no frost, and the scillas along the edge of the lake were like bits of summer sky. The moor-hens were building, and the first daffodils were out in the rough grass below the clump of Scotch firs, and old George Whaddon was nailing up rabbit wire and whistling through his two remaining teeth, and generally the world was as clean and jolly as spring could make it. But I didn't feel any more that it was really mine, only that I was looking on at a pretty picture. Something had happened to jar the harmony between it and my mind, and I cursed Bullivant and his intrusions.

I returned by the front of the house, and there at the door, to my surprise, stood a big touring Rolls-Royce. Paddock met me in the hall and handed me a card, on which I read the name of Mr. Julius Victor.

I knew it, of course, for the name of one of the richest men in the world—the American banker who had done a lot of Britain's financial business in the War, and was in Europe now at some international conference. I remembered that Blenkiron, who didn't like his race, had once described him to me as "the whitest Jew since the Apostle Paul."

In the library I found a tall man standing by the window looking out at our view. He turned as I entered, and I saw a thin face with a neatly trimmed grey beard, and the most worried eyes I have ever seen in a human countenance. Everything about him was spruce and dapper—his beautifully-cut grey suit, his black tie and pink pearl pin, his blue-and-white linen, his exquisitely polished shoes. But the eyes were so wild and anxious that he looked dishevelled.

"General," he said, and took a step towards me.

We shook hands and I made him sit down.

"I have dropped the 'General,' if you don't mind," I said. "What I want to know is, have you had breakfast?"

He shook his head. "I had a cup of coffee on the road. I do not eat in the morning."

"Where have you come from, sir?" I asked.

"From London."

Well, London is seventy-six miles from us, so he must have started early. I looked curiously at him, and he got out of his chair and began to stride about.

"Sir Richard," he said, in a low, pleasant voice which I could imagine convincing any man he tried it on, "you are a soldier and a man of the world and will pardon my unconventionality. My business is too urgent to waste time on apologies. I have heard of you from common friends as a man of exceptional resource and courage. I have been told in confidence something of your

record.    I have come to implore your help in a
desperate emergency."

I passed him a box of cigars, and he took one
and lit it carefully.   I could see his long slim
fingers trembling as he held the match.

" You may have heard of me," he went on.    " I
am a very rich man, and my wealth has given
me power, so that Governments honour me with
their confidence.   I am concerned in various important affairs, and it would be false modesty
to deny that my word is weightier than that
of many Prime Ministers.   I am labouring, Sir
Richard, to secure peace in the world, and consequently I have enemies, all those who would
perpetuate anarchy and war.   My life has been
more than once attempted, but that is nothing.
I am well guarded.   I am not, I think, more of a
coward than other men, and I am prepared to take
my chance.   But now I have been attacked by a
subtler weapon, and I confess I have no defence.
I had a son, who died ten years ago at college.
My only other child is my daughter, Adela, a girl
of nineteen.   She came to Europe just before
Christmas, for she was to be married in Paris in
April.   A fortnight ago she was hunting with
friends in Northamptonshire—the place is called
Rushford Court.   On the morning of the 8th of
March she went for a walk to Rushford village to
send a telegram, and was last seen passing through
the lodge gates at twenty minutes past eleven.
She has not been seen since."

" Good God ! " I exclaimed, and rose from my

chair. Mr. Victor was looking out of the window, so I walked to the other end of the room and fiddled with the books on a shelf. There was silence for a second or two, till I broke it.

"Do you suppose it is loss of memory?" I asked.

"No," he said. "It is not loss of memory. I know—we have proof—that she has been kidnapped by those whom I call my enemies. She is being held as a hostage."

"You know she is alive?"

He nodded, for his voice was choking again. "There is evidence which points to a very deep and devilish plot. It may be revenge, but I think it more likely to be policy. Her captors hold her as security for their own fate."

"Has Scotland Yard done nothing?"

"Everything that man could do, but the darkness only grows thicker."

"Surely it has not been in the papers. I don't read them carefully, but I could scarcely miss a thing like that."

"It has been kept out of the papers—for a reason which you will be told."

"Mr. Victor," I said, "I'm most deeply sorry for you. Like you, I've just the one child, and if anything of that kind happened to him I should go mad. But I shouldn't take too gloomy a view. Miss Adela will turn up all right, and none the worse, though you may have to pay through the nose for it. I expect it's ordinary blackmail and ransom."

" No," he said very quietly. " It is not black-mail, and if it were, I would not pay the ransom demanded. Believe me, Sir Richard, it is a very desperate affair. More, far more, is involved than the fate of one young girl. I am not going to touch on that side, for the full story will be told you later by one better equipped to tell it. But the hostage is my daughter, my only child. I have come to beg your assistance in the search for her."

" But I'm no good at looking for things," I stammered. " I'm most awfully sorry for you, but I don't see how I can help. If Scotland Yard is at a loss, it's not likely that an utter novice like me would succeed."

" But you have a different kind of imagination and a rarer kind of courage. I know what you have done before, Sir Richard. I tell you you are my last hope."

I sat down heavily and groaned. " I can't begin to explain to you the bottomless futility of your idea. It is quite true that in the War I had some queer jobs and was lucky enough to bring some of them off. But, don't you see, I was a soldier then, under orders, and it didn't greatly signify whether I lost my life from a crump in the trenches or from a private bullet on the back-stairs. I was in the mood for any risk, and my wits were strung up and unnaturally keen. But that's all done with. I'm in a different mood now and my mind is weedy and grass-grown. I've settled so deep into the country that I'm just an

ordinary hay-seed farmer. If I took a hand—
which I certainly won't—I'd only spoil the game."

Mr. Victor stood looking at me intently. I
thought for a moment he was going to offer me
money, and rather hoped he would, for that would
have stiffened me like a ramrod, though it would
have spoiled the good notion I had of him. The
thought may have crossed his mind, but he was
clever enough to reject it.

"I don't agree with a word you say about
yourself, and I'm accustomed to size up men. I
appeal to you as a Christian gentleman to help
me to recover my child. I am not going to press
that appeal, for I have already taken up enough
of your time. My London address is on my card.
Good-bye, Sir Richard, and believe me, I am very
grateful to you for receiving me so kindly."

In five minutes he and his Rolls-Royce had gone,
and I was left in a miserable mood of shamefaced
exasperation. I realized how Mr. Julius Victor
had made his fame. He knew how to handle
men, for if he had gone on pleading he would
only have riled me, whereas he had somehow
managed to leave it all to my honour, and thoroughly unsettle my mind.

I went for a short walk, cursing the world at
large, sometimes feeling horribly sorry for that
unfortunate father, sometimes getting angry because he had tried to mix me up in his affairs.
Of course I would not touch the thing ; I couldn't ;
it was manifestly impossible ; I had neither the
capacity nor the inclination. I was not a pro-

fessional rescuer of distressed ladies whom I did not know from Eve.

A man, I told myself, must confine his duties to his own circle of friends, except when his country has need of him. I was over forty, and had a wife and a young son to think of ; besides, I had chosen a retired life, and had the right to have my choice respected. But I can't pretend that I was comfortable. A hideous muddy wave from the outer world had come to disturb my little sheltered pool. I found Mary and Peter John feeding the swans, and couldn't bear to stop and play with them. The gardeners were digging in sulphates about the fig trees on the south wall, and wanted directions about the young chestnuts in the nursery ; the keeper was lying in wait for me in the stable-yard for instructions about a new batch of pheasants' eggs, and the groom wanted me to look at the hocks of Mary's cob. But I simply couldn't talk to any of them. These were the things I loved, but for a moment the gilt was off them, and I would let them wait till I felt better. In a very bad temper I returned to the library.

I hadn't been there two minutes when I heard the sound of a car on the gravel. " Let 'em all come," I groaned, and I wasn't surprised when Paddock entered, followed by the spare figure and smooth keen face of Macgillivray.

I don't think I offered to shake hands. We were pretty good friends, but at that moment there was no one in the world I wanted less to see.

(2,745)

3

"Well, you old nuisance," I cried, "you're the second visitor from town I've had this morning. There 'll be a shortage of petrol soon."

"Have you had a letter from Lord Artinswell?" he asked.

"I have, worse luck," I said.

"Then you know what I've come about. But that can keep till after luncheon. Hurry it up, Dick, like a good fellow, for I'm as hungry as a famished kestrel."

He looked rather like one, with his sharp nose and lean head. It was impossible to be cross for long with Macgillivray, so we went out to look for Mary. "I may as well tell you," I told him, "that you've come on a fool's errand. I'm not going to be jockeyed by you or any one into making an ass of myself. Anyhow, don't mention the thing to Mary. I don't want her to be worried by your nonsense."

So at luncheon we talked about Fosse and the Cotswolds, and about the deer-forest I had taken —Machray they called it—and about Sir Archibald Roylance, my co-tenant, who had just had another try at breaking his neck in a steeplechase. Macgillivray was by way of being a great stalker and could tell me a lot about Machray. The crab of the place was its neighbours, it seemed; for Haripol on the south was too steep for the lessee, a middle-aged manufacturer, to do justice to it, and the huge forest of Glenaicill on the east was too big for any single tenant to shoot, and the Machray end of it was nearly thirty miles by road from the lodge. The result was, said Macgillivray, that Machray was surrounded by unauthorized sanctuaries, which made the deer easy to shift. He said the best time was early in the season when the stags were on the upper ground, for it seemed that Machray had uncommonly fine high pastures. . . . Mary was in good spirits, for somebody had been complimentary about Peter John, and she was satisfied for the moment that he wasn't going to be cut off by an early consumption. She was full of housekeeping questions about Machray, and revealed such spacious plans that Macgillivray said that he thought he would pay us a visit, for it looked as if he wouldn't be poisoned, as he usually was in Scotch shooting-lodges. It was a talk I should have enjoyed if there had not been that uneasy morning behind me and that interview I had still to get over.

There was a shower after luncheon, so he and I settled ourselves in the library. " I must leave at 3.30," he said, " so I have got just a little more than an hour to tell you my business in."

" Is it worth while starting ? " I asked. " I want to make it quite plain that under no circumstances am I open to any offer to take on any business of any kind. I'm having a rest and a holiday. I stay here for the summer, and then I go to Machray."

" There's nothing to prevent your going to Machray in August," he said, opening his eyes. " The work I am going to suggest to you must be finished long before then."

I suppose that surprised me, for I did not stop him as I had meant to. I let him go on, and before I knew I found myself getting interested. I have a boy's weakness for a yarn, and Macgillivray knew this and played on it.

He began by saying very much what Dr. Greenslade had said the night before. A large part of the world had gone mad, and that involved the growth of inexplicable and unpredictable crime. All the old sanctities had become weakened, and men had grown too well accustomed to death and pain. This meant that the criminal had far greater resources at his command, and, if he were an able man, could mobilize a vast amount of utter recklessness and depraved ingenuity. The moral imbecile, he said, had been more or less a sport before the War; now he was a terribly common product, and throve in batches and battalions. Cruel, humourless, hard, utterly wanting in sense of proportion, but often full of a perverted poetry and drunk with rhetoric—a hideous, untamable breed had been engendered. You found it among the young Bolshevik Jews, among the young entry of the wilder Communist sects, and very notably among the sullen murderous hobbledehoys in Ireland.

"Poor devils," Macgillivray repeated. "It is for their Maker to judge them, but we who are trying to patch up civilization have to see that they are cleared out of the world. Don't imagine that they are devotees of any movement, good or bad. They are what I have called them, moral imbeciles, who can be swept into any movement by those who understand them. They are the neophytes and hierophants of crime, and it is as criminals that I have to do with them. Well, all this desperate degenerate stuff is being used by a few clever men who are not degenerates or anything of the sort, but only evil. There has never been such a chance for a rogue since the world began."

Then he told me certain facts, which must remain unpublished, at any rate during our lifetimes. The main point was that there were sinister brains at work to organize for their own purposes the perilous stuff lying about. All the contemporary anarchisms, he said, were interconnected, and out of the misery of decent folks and the agony of the wretched tools certain smug *entrepreneurs* were profiting. He and his men, and indeed the whole police force of civilization —he mentioned especially the Americans—had been on the trail of one of the worst of these combines, and by a series of fortunate chances had got their hand on it. Now at any moment they could stretch out that hand and gather it in.

But there was one difficulty. I learned from him that this particular combine was not aware of the danger in which it stood, but that it realized that it must stand in some danger, so it had taken precautions. Since Christmas it had acquired hostages.

Here I interrupted, for I felt rather incredulous about the whole business. " I think since the

War we're all too ready to jump at grandiose explanations of simple things. I'll want a good deal of convincing before I believe in your international clearing-house for crime."

"I guarantee the convincing," he said gravely. "You shall see all our evidence, and, unless you have changed since I first knew you, your conclusion won't differ from mine. But let us come to the hostages."

"One I know about," I put in. "I had Mr. Julius Victor here after breakfast."

Macgillivray exclaimed. "Poor soul! What did you say to him?"

"Deepest sympathy, but nothing doing."

"And he took that answer?"

"I won't say he took it. But he went away. What about the others?"

"There are two more. One is a young man, the heir to a considerable estate, who was last seen by his friends in Oxford on the 17th day of February, just before dinner. He was an undergraduate of Christ Church, and was living out of college in rooms in the High. He had tea at the Gridiron and went to his rooms to dress, for he was dining that night with the Halcyon Club. A servant passed him on the stairs of his lodgings, going up to his bedroom. He apparently did not come down, and since that day has not been seen. You may have heard his name—Lord Mercot."

I started. I had indeed heard the name, and knew the boy a little, having met him occasionally at our local steeplechases. He was the grandson and heir of the old Duke of Alcester, the most respected of the older statesmen of England.

"They have picked their bag carefully," I said. "What is the third case?"

"The cruellest of all. You know Sir Arthur Warcliff. He is a widower—lost his wife just before the War, and he has an only child, a little boy about ten years old. The child—David is his name—was the apple of his eye, and was at a preparatory school near Rye. The father took a house in the neighbourhood to be near him, and the boy used to be allowed to come home for luncheon every Sunday. One Sunday he came to luncheon as usual, and started back in the pony-trap. The boy was very keen about birds, and used to leave the trap and walk the last half-mile by a short cut across the marshes. Well, he left the groom at the usual gate, and, like Miss Victor and Lord Mercot, walked into black mystery."

This story really did horrify me. I remembered Sir Arthur Warcliff—the kind, worn face of the great soldier and administrator, and I could imagine his grief and anxiety. I knew what I should have felt if it had been Peter John. A much-travelled young woman and an athletic young man were defenceful creatures compared to a poor little round-headed boy of ten. But I still felt the whole affair too fantastic for real tragedy.

"But what right have you to connect the three cases?" I asked. "Three people disappear within a few weeks of each other in widely separated

parts of England.  Miss Victor may have been
kidnapped for ransom, Lord Mercot may have lost
his memory, and David Warcliff may have been
stolen by tramps.  Why should they be all part
of one scheme ?  Why, for that matter, should
any one of them have been the work of your
criminal combine ?  Have you any evidence for
the hostage theory ? "

"Yes."  Macgillivray took a moment or two
to answer.  "There is first the general probability.
If a band of rascals wanted three hostages they
could hardly find three better—the daughter of
the richest man in the world, the heir of our
greatest dukedom, the only child of a national
hero.  There is also direct evidence."  Again he
hesitated.

"Do you mean to say that Scotland Yard has
not a single clue to any one of these cases ? "

"We have followed up a hundred clues, but
they have all ended in dead walls.  Every detail,
I assure you, has been gone through with a fine
comb.  No, my dear Dick, the trouble is not that
we're specially stupid on this side, but that there
is some superlative cunning on the other.  That
is why I want *you*.  You have a kind of knack of
stumbling on truths which no amount of ordinary
reasoning can get at.  I have fifty men working
day and night, and we have mercifully kept all
the cases out of the papers, so that we are not
hampered by the amateur.  But so far it's a
blank.  Are you going to help ? "

"No, I'm not.  But supposing I were, I don't

see that you've a scrap of proof that the three cases are connected, or that any one of them is due to the criminal gang that you say you've got your hand on. You've only given me presumptions, and precious thin at that. Where's your direct evidence ? "

Macgillivray looked a little embarrassed. " I've started you at the wrong end," he said. " I should have made you understand how big and desperate the thing is that we're out against, and then you'd have been in a more receptive mood for the rest of the story. You know as well as I do that cold blood is not always the most useful accompaniment in assessing evidence. I said I had direct evidence of connection, and so I have, and the proof to my mind is certain."

" Well, let's see it."

" It's a poem. On Wednesday of last week, two days after David Warcliff disappeared, Mr. Julius Victor, the Duke of Alcester, and Sir Arthur Warcliff received copies of it by the first post. They were typed on bits of flimsy paper, the envelopes had the addresses typed, and they had been posted in the West Central district of London the afternoon before."

He handed me a copy, and this was what I read :

> " Seek where under midnight's sun
> Laggard crops are hardly won ;—
> Where the sower casts his seed in
> Furrows of the fields of Eden ;—
> Where beside the sacred tree
> Spins the seer who cannot see."

I burst out laughing, for I could not help it—
the whole thing was too preposterous. These six
lines of indifferent doggerel seemed to me to put
the coping-stone of nonsense on the business.
But I checked myself when I saw Macgillivray's
face. There was a slight flush of annoyance on his
cheek, but for the rest it was grave, composed, and
in deadly earnest. Now Macgillivray was not a fool,
and I was bound to respect his beliefs. So I pulled
myself together and tried to take things seriously.

"That's proof that the three cases are linked
together," I said. "So much I grant you. But
where's the proof that they are the work of the
great criminal combine that you say you have got
your hand on?"

Macgillivray rose and walked restlessly about
the room. "The evidence is mainly presumptive,
but to my mind it is certain presumption. You
know as well as I do, Dick, that a case may be
final and yet very difficult to set out as a series of
facts. My view on the matter is made up of a
large number of tiny indications and cross-bear-
ings, and I am prepared to bet that if you put
your mind honestly to the business you will take
the same view. But I'll give you this much by
way of direct proof—in hunting the big show we
had several communications of the same nature
as this doggerel, and utterly unlike anything else
I ever struck in criminology. There's one of the
miscreants who amuses himself with sending useless clues to his adversaries. It shows how secure
the gang thinks itself."

" Well, you've got that gang anyhow. I don't quite see why the hostages should trouble you. You'll gather them in when you gather in the malefactors."

" I wonder. Remember we are dealing with moral imbeciles. When they find themselves cornered they won't play for safety. They'll use their hostages, and when we refuse to bargain they'll take their last revenge on them."

I suppose I stared unbelievingly, for he went on. " Yes. They'll murder them in cold blood—three innocent people—and then swing themselves with a lighter mind. I know the type. They've done it before." He mentioned one or two recent instances.

" Good God ! " I cried. " It's a horrible thought ! The only thing for you is to go canny, and not strike till you have got the victims out of their clutches."

" We can't," he said solemnly. " That is precisely the tragedy of the business. We must strike early in June. I won't trouble you with the reasons, but, believe me, they are final. There is just a chance of a settlement in Ireland, and there are certain events of the first importance impending in Italy and America, and all depend upon the activities of the gang being at an end by midsummer. Do you grasp that ? By midsummer we must stretch out our hand. By midsummer, unless they are released, the three hostages will be doomed. It is a ghastly dilemma, but in the public interest there is only one way out. I ought to say that Victor and the Duke and Warcliff are aware of this fact, and accept the situation. They are big men, and will do their duty even if it breaks their hearts."

There was silence for a minute or two, for I did not know what to say. The whole story seemed to me incredible, and yet I could not doubt a syllable of it when I looked at Macgillivray's earnest face. I felt the horror of the business none the less because it seemed also partly unreal ; it had the fantastic grimness of a nightmare. But most of all I realized that I was utterly incompetent to help, and as I understood that I could honestly base my refusal on incapacity and not on disinclination I began to feel more comfortable.

" Well," said Macgillivray, after a pause, " are you going to help us ? "

" There's nothing doing with that Sunday-paper acrostic you showed me. That's the sort of riddle that's not meant to be guessed. I suppose you are going to try to work up from the information you have about the combine towards a clue to the hostages."

He nodded.

" Now, look here," I said ; " you've got fifty of the quickest brains in Britain working at the job. They've found out enough to put a lasso round the enemy which you can draw tight whenever you like. They're trained to the work and I'm not. What on earth would be the use of an amateur like me butting in ? I wouldn't be half as good as any one of the fifty. I'm not an expert, I'm not quick-witted, I'm a slow, patient fellow, and this job, as you admit, is one that has to be done against time. If you think it over, you'll see that it's sheer nonsense, my dear chap."

" You've succeeded before with worse material."

" That was pure luck, and it was in the War when, as I tell you, my mind was morbidly active. Besides, anything I did then I did in the field, and what you want me to do now is office work. You know I'm no good at office work—Blenkiron always said so, and Bullivant never used me on it. It isn't because I don't want to help, but because I can't."

" I believe you can. And the thing is so grave that I daren't leave any chance unexplored. Won't you come ? "

" No. Because I could do nothing."

" Because you haven't a mind for it."

" Because I haven't the right kind of mind for it."

He looked at his watch and got up smiling rather ruefully.

" I've had my say, and now you know what I want of you. I'm not going to take your answer as final. Think over what I've said, and let me hear from you within the next day or two."

But I had lost all my doubts, for it was very clear to me that on every ground I was doing the right thing.

" Don't delude yourself with thinking that I'll change my mind," I said, as I saw him into his car. "Honestly, old fellow, if I could be an atom of use I'd join you, but for your own sake you've got to count me out this time."

Then I went for a walk, feeling pretty cheerful. I settled the question of the pheasants' eggs with the keeper, and went down to the stream to see if there was any hatch of fly. It had cleared up to a fine evening, and I thanked my stars that I was out of a troublesome business with an easy conscience, and could enjoy my peaceful life again. I say "with an easy conscience," for though there were little dregs of disquiet still lurking about the bottom of my mind, I had only to review the facts squarely to approve my decision. I put the whole thing out of my thoughts and came back with a fine appetite for tea.

There was a stranger in the drawing-room with Mary, a slim, oldish man, very straight and erect, with one of those faces on which life has written so much that to look at them is like reading a good book. At first I didn't recognize him when he rose to greet me, but the smile that wrinkled the corners of his eyes and the slow deep voice brought back the two occasions in the past when I had run across Sir Arthur Warcliff. . . . My heart sank as I shook hands, the more as I saw how solemn was Mary's face. She had been hearing the story which I hoped she would never hear.

I thought it best to be very frank with him. "I can guess your errand, Sir Arthur," I said, "and I'm extremely sorry that you should have come this long journey to no purpose." Then I told him of the visits of Mr. Julius Victor and Macgillivray, and what they had said, and what had been my answer. I think I made it as clear as day that I could do nothing, and he seemed to assent. Mary, I remember, never lifted her eyes.

Sir Arthur had also looked at the ground while I was speaking, and now he turned his wise old face to me, and I saw what ravages his new anxiety had made in it. He could not have been much over sixty and he looked a hundred.

"I do not dispute your decision, Sir Richard," he said. "I know that you would have helped me if it had been possible. But I confess I am sorely disappointed, for you were my last hope. You see—you see—I had nothing left in the world but Davie. If he had died I think I could have borne it, but to know nothing about him and to imagine terrible things is almost too much for my fortitude."

I have never been through a more painful experience. To hear a voice falter that had been used to command, to see tears in the steadfastest eyes that ever looked on the world, made me want to howl like a dog. I would have given a thousand pounds to be able to bolt into the library and lock the door.

Mary appeared to me to be behaving very oddly. She seemed to have the deliberate purpose of probing the wound, for she encouraged Sir Arthur to speak of his boy. He showed us a miniature he carried with him—an extraordinarily handsome child with wide grey eyes and his head most

nobly set upon his shoulders. A grave little boy,
with the look of utter trust which belongs to
children who have never in their lives been un-
fairly treated. Mary said something about the
gentleness of the face.

"Yes, Davie was very gentle," his father said.
"I think he was the gentlest thing I have ever
known. That little boy was the very flower of
courtesy. But he was curiously stoical, too.
When he was distressed, he only shut his lips
tight, and never cried. I used often to feel
rebuked by him."

And then he told us about Davie's performances
at school, where he was not distinguished, except
as showing a certain talent for cricket. "I am
very much afraid of precocity," Sir Arthur said,
with the ghost of a smile. "But he was always
educating himself in the right way, learning to
observe and think." It seemed that the boy was
a desperately keen naturalist, and would be out
at all hours watching wild things. He was a
great fisherman too, and had killed a lot of trout
with the fly on hill burns in Galloway. And as
the father spoke I suddenly began to realize the
little chap, and to think that he was just the
kind of boy I wanted Peter John to be. I liked
the stories of his love of nature and trout streams.
It came on me like a thunderclap that if I were in
his father's place I should certainly go mad, and
I was amazed at the old man's courage.

"I think he had a kind of genius for animals,"
Sir Arthur said. "He knew the habits of birds

by instinct, and used to talk of them as other people talk of their friends. He and I were great cronies, and he would tell me long stories in his little quiet voice of birds and beasts he had seen on his walks. He had odd names for them too. . . ."

The thing was almost too pitiful to endure. I felt as if I had known the child all my life, I could see him playing, I could hear his voice, and as for Mary she was unashamedly weeping.

Sir Arthur's eyes were dry now, and there was no catch in his voice as he spoke. But suddenly a sharper flash of realization came on him and his words became a strained cry : " Where is he now ? What are they doing to him ? O God ! My beloved little man—my gentle little Davie ! "

That fairly finished me. Mary's arm was round the old man's neck, and I saw that he was trying to pull himself together, but I didn't see anything clearly. I only know that I was marching about the room, scarcely noticing that our guest was leaving. I remember shaking hands with him, and hearing him say that it had done him good to talk to us. It was Mary who escorted him to the car, and when she returned it was to find me blaspheming like a Turk at the window. I had flung the thing open, for I felt suffocated, though the evening was cool. The mixture of anger and disgust and pity in my heart nearly choked me.

" Why the devil can't I be left alone ? " I cried. " I don't ask for much—only a little peace. Why

in Heaven's name should I be dragged into other
people's business ?  Why on earth——"

Mary was standing at my elbow, her face rather
white and tear-stained.

" Of course you are going to help," she said.

Her words made clear to me the decision which
I must have taken a quarter of an hour before,
and all the passion went out of me like wind out
of a pricked bladder.

" Of course," I answered.  " By the way, I had
better telegraph to Macgillivray.  And Warcliff
too.  What's his address ? "

" You needn't bother about Sir Arthur," said
Mary.  " Before you came in—when he told me
the story—I said he could count on you.  Oh,
Dick, think if it had been Peter John ! "

# CHAPTER III

## RESEARCHES IN THE SUBCONSCIOUS

I WENT to bed in the perfect certainty that I wouldn't sleep. That happened to me about once a year, when my mind was excited or angry, and I knew no way of dodging it. There was a fine moon, and the windows were sheets of opal cut by the dark jade limbs of trees ; light winds were stirring the creepers ; owls hooted like sentries exchanging passwords, and sometimes a rook would talk in its dreams ; the little odd squeaks and rumbles of wild life came faintly from the woods ; and I lay staring at the ceiling with my thoughts running round about in a futile circus. Mary's even breathing tantalized me, for I never knew any one with her perfect gift for slumber. I used to say that if her pedigree could be properly traced it would be found that she descended direct from one of the Seven Sleepers of Ephesus who married one of the Foolish Virgins.

What kept me wakeful was principally the thought of that poor little boy, David Warcliff. I was sorry for Miss Victor and Lord Mercot, and desperately sorry for the parents of all three, but what I could not stand was the notion of the innocent little chap, who loved birds and fishing and the open air, hidden away in some stuffy den by the worst kind of blackguards. The thing preyed on me till I got to think it had happened to us and that Peter John was missing. I rose and prowled about the windows, looking out at the quiet night, and wondering how the same world could contain so much trouble and so much peace.

I laved my face with cold water and lay down again. It was no good letting my thoughts race, so I tried to fix them on one point in the hope that I would get drowsy. I endeavoured to recapitulate the evidence which Macgillivray had recited, but only made foolishness of it, for I simply could not concentrate. I saw always the face of a small boy, who bit his lips to keep himself from tears, and another perfectly hideous face that kept turning into one of the lead figures in the rose garden. A ridiculous rhyme, too, ran in my head—something about the "midnight sun" and the "fields of Eden." By-and-by I got it straightened out into the anagram business Macgillivray had mentioned. I have a fly-paper memory for verse when there is no reason why I should remember it, and I found I could repeat the six lines of the doggerel.

After that I found the lines mixing themselves up, and suggesting all kinds of odd pictures to my brain. I took to paraphrasing them—" Under

the midnight sun, where harvests are poor "—
that was Scandinavia anyhow, or maybe Iceland
or Greenland or Labrador.  Who on earth was
the sower who sowed in the fields of Eden ?
Adam, perhaps, or Abel, who was the first farmer ?
Or an angel in heaven ?  More like an angel, I
thought, for the line sounded like a hymn.  Anyhow it was infernal nonsense.

The last two lines took to escaping me, and
that made me force my mind out of the irritable
confusion in which it was bogged.  Ah !  I had
them again :

> " Where beside the sacred tree
> Spins the seer who cannot see."

The sacred tree was probably Yggdrasil and the
spinner one of the Norns.  I had once taken an
interest in Norse mythology, but I couldn't
remember whether one of the Norns was blind.
A blind woman spinning.  Now where had I
heard something like that ?  Heard it quite
recently, too ?

The discomfort of wakefulness is that you are
not fully awake.  But now I was suddenly in full
possession of my senses, and worrying at that
balderdash like a dog at a bone.  I had been
quite convinced that there was a clue in it, but
that it would be impossible to hit on the clue.
But now I had a ray of hope, for I seemed to feel
a very faint and vague flavour of reminiscence.

Scandinavian harvests, the fields of Eden, the

blind spinner—oh, it was maddening, for every time I repeated them the sense of having recently met with something similar grew stronger. The North—Norway—surely I had it there! Norway —what was there about Norway?—Salmon, elk, reindeer, midnight sun, *saeters*—the last cried out to me. And the blind old woman that spun!

I had it. These were two of the three facts which Dr. Greenslade had suggested the night before as a foundation for his imaginary "shocker." What was the third? A curiosity shop in North London kept by a Jew with a dyed beard. That had no obvious connection with a sower in the fields of Eden. But at any rate he had got two of them identical with the doggerel. . . . It was a clue. It must be a clue. Greenslade had somewhere and somehow heard the jingle or the substance of it, and it had sunk into the subconscious memory he had spoken of, without his being aware of it. Well, I had got to dig it out. If I could discover where and how he had heard the thing, I had struck a trail.

When I had reached this conclusion, I felt curiously easier in my mind, and almost at once fell asleep. I awoke to a gorgeous spring morning, and ran down to the lake for my bath. I felt that I wanted all the freshening and screwing up I could get, and when I dressed after an icy plunge I was ready for all comers.

Mary was down in time for breakfast, and busy with her letters. She spoke little, and seemed to be waiting for me to begin; but I didn't want to raise the matter which was uppermost in our minds till I saw my way clearer, so I said I was going to take two days to think things over. It was Wednesday, so I wired to Macgillivray to expect me in London on Friday morning, and I scribbled a line to Mr. Julius Victor. By half-past nine I was on the road making for Greenslade's lodgings.

I caught him in the act of starting on his rounds, and made him sit down and listen to me. I had to give him the gist of Macgillivray's story, with extracts from those of Victor and Sir Arthur. Before I was half-way through he had flung off his overcoat, and before I had finished he had lit a pipe, which was a breach of his ritual not to smoke before the evening. When I stopped he had that wildish look in his light eyes which you see in a cairn terrier's when he is digging out a badger.

"You've taken on this job?" he asked brusquely.

I nodded.

"Well, I shouldn't have had much respect for you if you had refused. How can I help? Count on me, if I'm any use. Good God! I never heard a more damnable story."

"Have you got hold of the rhyme?" I repeated it, and he said it after me.

"Now, you remember the talk we had after dinner the night before last. You showed me how a ' shocker ' was written, and you took at random three facts as the foundation. They were, you remember, a blind old woman spinning in the Western Highlands, a *saeter* in Norway, and a curiosity shop in North London, kept by a Jew with a dyed beard. Well, two of your facts are in that six-line jingle I have quoted to you."

"That is an odd coincidence. But is it anything more ? "

"I believe that it is. I don't hold with coincidences. There's generally some explanation which we're not clever enough to get at. Your inventions were so odd that I can't think they were mere inventions. You must have heard them somehow and somewhere. You know what you said about your subconscious memory. They're somewhere in it, and, if you can remember just how they got there, you'll give me the clue I want. That six-line rhyme was sent in by people who were so confident that they didn't mind giving their enemies a clue—only it was a clue which they knew could never be discovered. Macgillivray and his fellows can make nothing of it—never will. But if I can start from the other end I'll get it on their rear. Do you see what I mean ? I'm going to make you somehow or other dig it out."

He shook his head. "It can't be done, Dick. Admitting your premise—that I heard the nonsense and didn't invent it—the subconscious can't be handled like a business proposition. I remember unconsciously and I can't recall consciously. . . . But I don't admit your premise. I think the whole thing is common coincidence."

" I don't," I said stubbornly, " and even if I did I'm bound to assume the contrary, for it's the only card I possess. You've got to sit down, old chap, and do your damnedest to remember. You've been in every kind of odd show, and my belief is that you *heard* that nonsense. Dig it out of your memory and we've a chance to win. Otherwise, I see nothing but tragedy."

He got up and put on his overcoat. " I've got a long round of visits which will take me all day. Of course I'll try, but I warn you that I haven't the ghost of a hope. These things don't come by care and searching. I'd better sleep at the Manor to-night. How long can you give me ? "

" Two days—I go up to town on Friday morning. Yes, you must take up your quarters with us. Mary insists on it."

There was a crying of young lambs from the meadow, and through the open window came the sound of the farm carts jolting from the stack-yard into the lane. Greenslade screwed up his face and laughed.

" A nasty breach in your country peace, Dick. You know I'm with you if there's any trouble going. Let's get the thing clear, for there's a lot of researching ahead of me. My three were an old blind woman spinning in the Western Highlands—Western Highlands, was it ?—a *saeter* barn, and a Jew curiosity shop. The other three were a blind spinner under a sacred tree, a *saeter* of sorts, and a sower in the fields of Eden—Lord, such rot ! Two pairs seem to coincide, the other

pair looks hopeless. Well, here goes for fortune!
I'm going to break my rule and take my pipe with
me, for this business demands tobacco."

I spent a busy day writing letters and making
arrangements about the Manor, for it looked as if
I might be little at home for the next month.
Oddly enough, I felt no restlessness or any particular anxiety. That would come later; for the
moment I seemed to be waiting on Providence in
the person of Tom Greenslade. I was trusting
my instinct, which told me that in those random
words of his there was more than coincidence, and
that with luck I might get from them a line on
our problem.

Greenslade turned up about seven in the evening, rather glum and preoccupied. At dinner he
ate nothing, and when we sat afterwards in the
library he seemed to be chiefly interested in reading the advertisements in the *Times*. When I
asked "What luck?" he turned on me a dis-
consolate face.

"It is the most futile job I ever took on," he
groaned. "So far it's an absolute blank, and
anyhow I've been taking the wrong line. I've
been trying to *think* myself into recollection, and,
as I said, this thing comes not by searching, nor
yet by prayer and fasting. It occurred to me
that I might get at something by following up
the differences between the three pairs. It's a
familiar method in inductive logic, for differences
are often more suggestive than resemblances. So
I worried away at the 'sacred tree' as contrasted

with the 'Western Highlands' and the 'fields of Eden' as set against the curiosity shop. No earthly good. I gave myself a headache, and I daresay I've poisoned half my patients. It's no use, Dick, but I'll peg away for the rest of the prescribed two days. I'm letting my mind lie fallow now and trusting to inspiration. I've got two faint glimmerings of notions. First, I don't believe I said 'Western Highlands.' "

" I'm positive those were your words. What did you say, then ? "

" Hanged if I know, but I'm pretty certain it wasn't that. I can't explain properly, but you get an atmosphere about certain things in your mind, and that phrase somehow jars with the atmosphere. Different key. Wrong tone. Second, I've got a hazy intuition that the thing, if it is really in my memory, is somehow mixed up with a hymn tune. I don't know what tune, and the whole impression is as vague as smoke, but I tell it you for what it is worth. If I could get the right tune, I might remember something."

" You've stopped thinking ? "

" Utterly. I'm an Æolian harp to be played on by any wandering wind. You see, if I did hear these three things there is no conscious rational clue to it. They were never part of my workaday mind. The only chance is that some material phenomenon may come along and link itself with them and so rebuild the scene where I heard them. A scent would be best, but a tune

might do. Our one hope—and it's about as
strong as a single thread of gossamer on the grass
—is that that tune may drift into my head. You
see the point, Dick? Thought won't do, for the
problem doesn't concern the mind, but some tiny
physical sensation of nose, ear, or eye might
press the button. Now, it may be hallucination,
but I've a feeling that the three facts I thought
I invented were in some infinitely recondite way
connected with a hymn tune."

He went to bed early, while I sat up till nearly
midnight writing letters. As I went upstairs, I
had a strong sense of futility and discouragement.
It seemed the merest trifling to be groping among
these spectral unrealities, while tragedy, as big
and indisputable as a mountain, was overhang-
ing us. I had to remind myself how often the
trivial was the vital before I got rid of the prick
in my conscience. I was tired and sleepy, and
as I forced myself to think of the immediate
problem, the six lines of the jingle were all blurred.
While I undressed I tried to repeat them, but
could not get the fourth to scan. It came out as
" fields of Erin," and after that " the green fields
of Erin." Then it became " the green fields of
Eden."

I found myself humming a tune.

It was an old hymn which the Salvation Army
used to play in the Cape Town streets when I
was a schoolboy. I hadn't heard it or thought of
it for thirty years. But I remembered the tune
very clearly, a pretty, catchy thing like an early

Victorian drawing-room ballad, and I remembered
the words of the chorus—

> " On the other side of Jordan
> In the green fields of Eden,
> Where the Tree of Life is blooming,
> There is rest for you."

I marched off to Greenslade's room and found
him lying wide awake staring at the ceiling, with
the lamp by his bedside lit. I must have broken
in on some train of thought, for he looked at me
crossly.

" I've got your tune," I said, and I whistled it,
and then quoted what words I remembered.

" Tune be blowed," he said. " I never heard
it before." But he hummed it after me, and
made me repeat the words several times.

" No good, I'm afraid. It doesn't seem to hank
on to anything. Lord, this is a fool's game. I'm
off to sleep."

But three minutes later came a knock at my
dressing-room door, and Greenslade entered. I
saw by his eyes that he was excited.

" It's the tune all right. I can't explain why,
but those three blessed facts of mine fit into it
like prawns in an aspic. I'm feeling my way
towards the light now. I thought I'd just tell
you, for you may sleep better for hearing it."

I slept like a log, and went down to breakfast
feeling more cheerful than I had felt for several
days. But the doctor seemed to have had a poor
night. His eyes looked gummy and heavy, and

he had ruffled his hair out of all hope of order. I knew that trick of his ; when his hair began to stick up at the back he was out of sorts either in mind or body. I noticed that he had got himself up in knickerbockers and thick shoes.

After breakfast he showed no inclination to smoke. " I feel as if I were going to be beaten on the post," he groaned. " I'm a complete convert to your view, Dick. I *heard* my three facts and didn't invent them. What's more, my three are definitely linked with the three in those miscreants' doggerel. That tune proves it, for it talks about the ' fields of Eden,' and yet is identified in my memory with my three which didn't mention Eden. That's a tremendous point, and proves we're on the right road. But I'm hanged if I can get a step farther. Wherever I heard the facts I heard the tune, but I'm no nearer finding out that place. I've got one bearing, and I need a second to give me the point of intersection I want, and how the deuce I'm to get it I don't know."

Greenslade was now keener even than I was on the chase, and indeed his lean anxious face was uncommonly like an old hound's. I asked him what he was going to do.

" At ten o'clock precisely I start on a walk— right round the head of the Windrush and home by the Forest. It's going to be a thirty-mile stride at a steady four and a half miles an hour, which, with half an hour for lunch, will get me back here before six. I'm going to drug my body and mind into apathy by hard exercise. Then I shall have a hot bath and a good dinner, and after that, when I'm properly fallow, I may get the revelation. The mistake I made yesterday was in trying to *think*."

It was a gleamy, blustering March morning, the very weather for a walk, and I would have liked to accompany him. As it was I watched his long legs striding up the field we call Big Pasture, and then gave up the day to the job of putting Loch Leven fry into one of the ponds—a task so supremely muddy and wet that I had very little leisure to think of other things. In the afternoon I rode over to the market town to see my builder, and got back only just before dinner to learn that Greenslade had returned. He was now wallowing in a hot bath, according to his programme.

At dinner he seemed to be in better spirits. The wind had heightened his colour, and given him a ferocious appetite, and the 1906 Clicquot, which I regard as the proper drink after a hard day, gave him the stimulus he needed. He talked as he had talked three nights ago, before this business got us in its clutches. Mary disappeared after dinner, and we sat ourselves in big chairs before the library fire, like two drowsy men who have had a busy day in the open air. I thought I had better say nothing till he chose to speak.

He was silent for a long time, and then he laughed, not very mirthfully.

" I'm as far off it as ever. All day I've been

letting my mind wander and measuring off miles with my two legs like a pair of compasses. But nothing has come to me. No word yet of that confounded cross-bearing I need. I might have heard that tune in any one of a thousand parts of the globe. You see, my rackety life is a disadvantage—I've had too many different sorts of experience. If I'd been a curate all my days in one village it would have been easier."

I waited, and he went on, speaking not to me but to the fire.

"I've got an impression so strong that it amounts to certainty that I never heard the words 'Western Highlands.' It was something like it, but not that."

"Western Islands," I suggested.

"What could they be?"

"I think I've heard the phrase used about the islands off the west coast of Ireland. Does that help you?"

He shook his head. "No good. I've never been in Ireland."

After that he was silent again, staring at the fire, while I smoked opposite him, feeling pretty blank and dispirited. I realized that I had banked more than I knew on this line of inquiry which seemed to be coming to nothing. . . .

Then suddenly there happened one of those trivial things which look like accidents, but I believe are part of the reasoned government of the universe.

I leaned forward to knock out the ashes of my

pipe against the stone edge of the hearth. I hammered harder than I intended, and the pipe, which was an old one, broke off at the bowl. I exclaimed irritably, for I hate to lose an old pipe, and then pulled up sharp at the sight of Greenslade.

He was staring open-mouthed at the fragments in my hand, and his eyes were those of a man whose thoughts are far away. He held up one hand, while I froze into silence. Then the tension relaxed, and he dropped back into his chair with a sigh.

" The cross-bearing ! " he said. " I've got it. . . . Medina."

Then he laughed at my puzzled face.

" I'm not mad, Dick. I once talked to a man, and as we talked he broke the bowl of his pipe as you have just done. He was the man who hummed the hymn tune, and though I haven't the remotest recollection of what he said, I am as certain as that I am alive that he gave me the three facts which sunk into the abyss of my subconscious memory. Wait a minute. Yes. I see it as plain as I see you. He broke his pipe just as you have done, and some time or other he hummed that tune."

" Who was he ? " I asked, but Greenslade disregarded the question. He was telling his story in his own way, with his eyes still abstracted as if he were looking down a long corridor of memory.

" I was staying at the Bull at Hanham—shooting wildfowl on the sea marshes. I had the place to myself, for it wasn't weather for a country pub, but late one night a car broke down outside, and the owner and his chauffeur had to put up at the Bull. Oddly enough I knew the man. He had been at one of the big shoots at Rousham Thorpe and was on his way back to London. We had a lot to say to each other and sat up into the small hours. We talked about sport, and the upper glens of the Yarkand River, where I first met him. I remember quite a lot of our talk, but not the three facts or the tune, which made no appeal to my conscious memory. Only, of course, they must have been there."

" When did this happen ? "

" Early last December, the time we had the black frost. You remember, Dick, how I took a week's holiday and went down to Norfolk after duck."

" You haven't told me the man's name."

" I have. Medina."

" Who on earth is Medina ? "

" O Lord ! Dick. You're overdoing the rustic. You've heard of Dominick Medina."

I had, of course, when he mentioned the Christian name. You couldn't open a paper without seeing something about Dominick Medina, but whether he was a poet or a politician or an actor-manager I hadn't troubled to inquire. There was a pile of picture-papers on a side-table, and I fetched them and began to turn them over. Very soon I found what I wanted. It was a photograph of a group at a country-house party for some steeplechase, the usual "reading-from-left-to-right" business, and there between a Duchess and a foreign Princess was Mr. Dominick Medina. The poverty of the photograph could not conceal the extraordinary good looks of the man. He had the kind of head I fancy Byron had, and I seemed to discern, too, a fine, clean, athletic figure.

"If you had happened to look at that rag you might have short-circuited your inquiry."

He shook his head. "No. It doesn't happen that way. I had to get your broken pipe and the tune, or I would have been stuck."

"Then I suppose I have to get in touch with this chap and find where he picked up the three facts and the tune. But how if he turns out to be like you, another babbler from the subconscious?"

"That is the risk you run, of course. He may be able to help you, or more likely he may prove only another dead wall."

I felt suddenly an acute sense of the difficulty of the job I had taken on, and something very near hopelessness.

"Tell me about this Medina. Is he a decent fellow?"

"I suppose so. Yes, I should think so. But he moves in higher circles than I'm accustomed to, so I can't judge. But I'll tell you what he is beyond doubt—he's rather a great man. Hang it, Dick, you must have heard of him. He's one of the finest shots living, and he's done some tall things in the exploration way, and he was the devil of a fellow as a partisan leader in South

Russia. Also—though it may not interest you—
he's an uncommon fine poet."

" I suppose he's some sort of a Dago."

" Not a bit of it. Old Spanish family settled
here for three centuries. One of them rode with
Rupert. Hold on ! I rather believe I've heard
that his people live in Ireland, or did live, till life
there became impossible."

" What age ? "

" Youngish. Not more than thirty-five. Oh !
and the handsomest thing in mankind since the
Greeks."

" I'm not a flapper," I said impatiently. " Good
looks in a man are no sort of recommendation to
me. I shall probably take a dislike to his face."

" You won't. From what I know of him and
you you'll fall under his charm at first sight. I
never heard of a man that didn't. He has a
curious musical voice and eyes that warm you—
glow like sunlight. Not that I know him well,
but I own I found him extraordinarily attractive.
And you see from the papers what the world thinks
of him."

" All the same I'm not much nearer my goal.
I've got to find out where he heard those three
blessed facts and that idiotic tune. He'll probably send me to blazes, and, even if he's civil,
he'll very likely be helpless."

" Your chance is that he's a really clever man,
not an old blunderer like me. You'll get the help
of a first-class mind, and that means a lot. Shall
I write you a line of introduction ? "

He sat down at my desk and wrote. "I'm saying nothing about your errand—simply that I'd like you to know each other—common interest in sport and travel—that sort of thing. You're going to be in London, so I had better give your address as your Club."

Next morning Greenslade went back to his duties and I caught the early train to town. I was not very happy about Mr. Dominick Medina, for I didn't seem able to get hold of him. *Who's Who* only gave his age, his residence—Hill Street —his clubs, and the fact that he was M.P. for a South London division. Mary had never met him, for he had appeared in London after she had stopped going about, but she remembered that her Wymondham aunts raved about him, and she had read somewhere an article on his poetry. As I sat in the express, I tried to reconstruct what kind of fellow he must be—a mixture of Byron and Sir Richard Burton and the young political high-brow. The picture wouldn't compose, for I saw only a figure like a waxwork, with a cooing voice and a shopwalker's suavity. Also his name kept confusing me, for I mixed him up with an old ruffian of a Portugee I once knew at Beira.

I was walking down St. James's Street on my way to Whitehall, pretty much occupied with my own thoughts, when I was brought up by a hand placed flat on my chest, and lo and behold! it was Sandy Arbuthnot.

## CHAPTER IV

### I MAKE THE ACQUAINTANCE OF A POPULAR MAN

YOU may imagine how glad I was to see old Sandy again, for I had not set eyes on him since 1916. He had been an Intelligence Officer with Maude, and then something at Simla, and after the War had had an administrative job in Mesopotamia, or, as they call it nowadays, Iraq. He had written to me from all kinds of queer places, but he never appeared to be coming home, and, what with my marriage and my settling in the country, we seemed to be fixed in ruts that were not likely to intersect. I had seen his elder brother's death in the papers, so he was now Master of Clanroyden and heir to the family estates, but I didn't imagine that that would make a Scotch laird of him. I never saw a fellow less changed by five years of toil and travel. He was desperately slight and tanned—he had always been that—but the contours of his face were still soft like a girl's, and his brown eyes were merry as ever.

We stood and stared at each other.

" Dick, old man," he cried, " I'm home for

good. Yes—honour bright. For months and months, if not years and years. I've got so much to say to you I don't know where to begin. But I can't wait now. I'm off to Scotland to see my father. He's my chief concern now, for he's getting very frail. But I'll be back in three days. Let's dine together on Tuesday."

We were standing at the door of a club—his and mine—and a porter was stowing his baggage into a taxi. Before I could properly realize that it was Sandy, he was waving his hand from the taxi window and disappearing up the street.

The sight of him cheered me immensely, and I went on along Pall Mall in a good temper. To have Sandy back in England and at call made me feel somehow more substantial, like a commander who knows his reserves are near. When I entered Macgillivray's room I was smiling, and the sight of me woke an answering smile on his anxious face. "Good man!" he said. "You look like business. You're to put yourself at my disposal while I give you your bearings."

He got out his papers and expounded the whole affair. It was a very queer story, yet the more I looked into it the thinner my scepticism grew. I am not going to write it all down, for it is not yet time; it would give away certain methods which have not yet exhausted their usefulness; but before I had gone very far, I took off my hat to these same methods, for they showed amazing patience and ingenuity. It was an odd set of links that made up the chain. There was an

importer of Barcelona nuts with a modest office
near Tower Hill. There was a copper company,
purporting to operate in Spain, whose shares
were not quoted on the Stock Exchange, but
which had a fine office in London Wall, where you
could get the best luncheon in the City. There
was a respectable accountant in Glasgow, and a
French count, who was also some kind of Highland
laird and a great supporter of the White Rose
League. There was a country gentleman living
in Shropshire, who had bought his place after the
War and was a keen rider to hounds and a very
popular figure in the county. There was a little
office not far from Fleet Street, which professed
to be the English agency of an American religious
magazine; and there was a certain publicist,
who was always appealing in the newspapers for
help for the distressed populations of Central
Europe. I remembered his appeals well, for I
had myself twice sent him small subscriptions.
The way Macgillivray had worked out the connection between these gentry filled me with
awe.

Then he showed me specimens of their work.
It was sheer unmitigated crime, a sort of selling
a bear on a huge scale in a sinking world. The
aim of the gang was money, and already they had
made scandalous profits. Partly their business
was mere conscienceless profiteering well inside
the bounds of the law, such as gambling in falling
exchanges and using every kind of brazen and
subtle trick to make their gamble a certainty.

Partly it was common fraud of the largest size. But there were darker sides—murder when the victim ran athwart their schemes, strikes engineered when a wrecked industry somewhere or other in the world showed symptoms of reviving, shoddy little outbursts in shoddy little countries which increased the tangle. These fellows were wreckers on the grand scale, merchants of pessimism, giving society another kick downhill whenever it had a chance of finding its balance, and then pocketing their profits.

Their motive, as I have said, was gain, but that was not the motive of the people they worked through. Their cleverness lay in the fact that they used the fanatics, the moral imbeciles as Macgillivray called them, whose key was a wild hatred of something or other, or a reasoned belief in anarchy. Behind the smug exploiters lay the whole dreary wastes of half-baked craziness. Macgillivray gave me examples of how they used these tools, the fellows who had no thought of profit, and were ready to sacrifice everything, including their lives, for a mad ideal. It was a masterpiece of cold-blooded, devilish ingenuity. Hideous, and yet comic too ; for the spectacle of these feverish cranks toiling to create a new heaven and a new earth and thinking themselves the leaders of mankind, when they were dancing like puppets at the will of a few scoundrels engaged in the most ancient of pursuits, was an irony to make the gods laugh.

I asked who was their leader.

Macgillivray said he wasn't certain. No one of the gang seemed to have more authority than the others, and their activities were beautifully specialized. But he agreed that there was probably one master mind, and said grimly that he would know more about that when they were rounded up. " The dock will settle that question."

" How much do they suspect ? " I asked.

" Not much. A little, or they would not have taken hostages. But not much, for we have been very careful to make no sign. Only, since we became cognizant of the affair, we have managed very quietly to put a spoke in the wheels of some of their worst enterprises, though I am positive they have no suspicion of it. Also we have put the brake on their propaganda side. They are masters of propaganda, you know. Dick, have you ever considered what a diabolical weapon that can be—using all the channels of modern publicity to poison and warp men's minds ? It is the most dangerous thing on earth. You can use it cleanly —as I think on the whole we did in the War— but you can also use it to establish the most damnable lies. Happily in the long run it defeats itself, but only after it has sown the world with mischief. Look at the Irish ! They are the cleverest propagandists extant, and managed to persuade most people that they were a brave, generous, humorous, talented, warm-hearted race, cruelly yoked to a dull mercantile England, when God knows they were exactly the opposite."

Macgillivray, I may remark, is an Ulsterman, and has his prejudices.

"About the gang—I suppose they're all pretty respectable to outward view ?"

"Highly respectable," he said. "I met one of them at dinner the other night at ——'s "—he mentioned the name of a member of the Government. "Before Christmas I was at a covert shoot in Suffolk, and one of the worst had the stand next me—an uncommonly agreeable fellow."

Then we sat down to business. Macgillivray's idea was that I should study the details of the thing and then get alongside some of the people. He thought I might begin with the Shropshire squire. He fancied that I might stumble on something which would give me a line on the hostages, for he stuck to his absurd notion that I had a special *flair* which the amateur sometimes possessed and the professional lacked. I agreed that that was the best plan, and arranged to spend Sunday in his room going over the secret *dossiers*. I was beginning to get keen about the thing, for Macgillivray had a knack of making whatever he handled as interesting as a game.

I had meant to tell him about my experiments with Greenslade ; but after what he had shown me I felt that that story was absurdly thin and unpromising. But as I was leaving, I asked him casually if he knew Mr. Dominick Medina.

He smiled. "Why do you ask ? He's scarcely your line of country."

"I don't know. I've heard a lot about him,

and I thought I would rather like to meet him."

"I barely know him, but I must confess that the few times I've met him I was enormously attracted. He's the handsomest being alive."

"So I'm told, and it's the only thing that puts me off."

"It wouldn't if you saw him. He's not in the least the ordinary matinée idol. He is the only fellow I ever heard of who was adored by women and also liked by men. He's a first-class sportsman and said to be the best shot in England after His Majesty. He's a coming man in politics, too, and a most finished speaker. I once heard him, and, though I take very little stock in oratory, he almost had me on my feet. He has knocked a bit about the world, and he is also a very pretty poet, though that wouldn't interest you."

"I don't know why you say that," I protested. "I'm getting rather good at poetry."

"Oh, I know. Scott and Macaulay and Tennyson. But that is not Medina's line. He is a deity of *les jeunes* and a hardy innovator. Jolly good, too. The man's a fine classical scholar."

"Well, I hope to meet him soon, and I'll let you know my impression."

I had posted my letter to Medina, enclosing Greenslade's introduction, on my way from the station, and next morning I found a very civil reply from him at my Club. Greenslade had talked of our common interest in big-game shooting, and he professed to know all about me, and to be anxious to make my acquaintance.  He was out of town unfortunately for the week-end, he said, but he suggested that I should lunch with him on the Monday.  He named a club, a small, select, old-fashioned one, of which most of the members were hunting squires.

I looked forward to meeting him with a quite inexplicable interest, and on Sunday, when I was worrying through papers in Macgillivray's room, I had him at the back of my mind.  I had made a picture of something between a Ouida guards-man and the Apollo Belvedere and rigged it out in the smartest clothes.  But when I gave my name to the porter at the club door, and a young man who was warming his hands at the hall fire came forward to meet me, I had to wipe that picture clean off my mind.

He was about my own height, just under six feet, and at first sight rather slightly built, but a hefty enough fellow to eyes which knew where to look for the points of a man's strength.  Still he appeared slim, and therefore young, and you could see from the way he stood and walked that he was as light on his feet as a rope-dancer. There is a horrible word in the newspapers, "well-groomed," applied to men by lady journalists, which always makes me think of a glossy horse on which a stable-boy has been busy with the brush and curry-comb.  I had thought of him as "well-groomed," but there was nothing glossy about his appearance.  He wore a rather old well-cut brown tweed suit, with a soft shirt and collar, and a russet tie that matched his complexion. His get-up was exactly that of a country squire who has come up to town for a day at Tattersall's.

I find it difficult to describe my first impression of his face, for my memory is all overlaid with other impressions acquired when I looked at it in very different circumstances. But my chief feeling, I remember, was that it was singularly pleasant. It was very English, and yet not quite English; the colouring was a little warmer than sun or weather would give, and there was a kind of silken graciousness about it not commonly found in our countrymen. It was beautifully cut, every feature regular, and yet there was a touch of ruggedness that saved it from conventionality. I was puzzled about this, till I saw that it came from two things, the hair and the eyes. The hair was a dark brown, brushed in a wave above the forehead, so that the face with its strong fine chin made an almost perfect square. But the eyes were the thing. They were of a startling blue, not the pale blue which is common enough and belongs to our Norse ancestry, but a deep dark blue, like the colour of a sapphire. Indeed if you think of a sapphire with the brilliance of a diamond, you get a pretty fair notion of those eyes. They would have made a plain-headed woman lovely, and in a man's face, which had not a touch of the feminine, they were startling. Startling—I stick to that word—but also entrancing.

He greeted me as if he had been living for this

hour, and also with a touch of the deference due to a stranger.

"This is delightful, Sir Richard. It was very good of you to come. We've got a table to ourselves by the fire. I hope you're hungry. I've had a devilish cold journey this morning and I want my luncheon."

I was hungry enough, and I never ate a better meal. He gave me burgundy on account of the bite in the weather, and afterwards I had a glass of the Bristol Cream for which the Club was famous; but he drank water himself. There were four other people in the room, all of whom he appeared to call by their Christian names, and these lantern-jawed hunting fellows seemed to cheer up at the sight of him. But they didn't come and stand beside him and talk, which is apt to happen to your popular man. There was that about Medina which was at once friendly and aloof, the air of a simple but tremendous distinction.

I remember we began by talking about rifles. I had done a good deal of shikar in my time, and I could see that this man had had a wide experience and had the love of the thing in his bones. He never bragged, but by little dropped remarks showed what a swell he was. We talked of a new ·240 bore which had remarkable stopping power, and I said I had never used it on anything more formidable than a Scotch stag. "It would have been a godsend to me in the old days on the Pungwe where I had to lug about a ·500 express that broke my back."

He grinned ruefully. " The old days ! " he said. " We've all had 'em, and we're all sick to get 'em back. Sometimes I'm tempted to kick over the traces and be off to the wilds again. I'm too young to settle down. And you, Sir Richard— you must feel the same. Do you never regret that that beastly old War is over ? "

" I can't say I do. I'm a middle-aged man now and soon I'll be stiff in the joints. I've settled down in the Cotswolds, and though I hope to get a lot of sport before I die I'm not looking for any more wars. I'm positive the Almighty meant me for a farmer."

He laughed. " I wish I knew what He meant me for. It looks like some sort of politician."

" Oh, you ! " I said. " You're the fellow with twenty talents. I've only got the one, and I'm jolly well going to bury it in the soil."

I kept wondering how much help I would get out of him. I liked him enormously, but somehow I didn't yet see his cleverness. He was just an ordinary good fellow of my own totem—just such another as Tom Greenslade. It was a dark day, and the firelight silhouetted his profile, and as I stole glances at it I was struck by the shape of his head. The way he brushed his hair front and back made it look square, but I saw that it was really round, the roundest head I have ever seen except in a Kaffir. He was evidently conscious of it and didn't like it, so took some pains to conceal it.

All through luncheon I was watching him

covertly, and I could see that he was also taking stock of me. Very friendly these blue eyes were, but very shrewd. He suddenly looked me straight in the face.

" You won't vegetate," he said. " You needn't deceive yourself. You haven't got the kind of mouth for a rustic. What is it to be ? Politics ? Business ? Travel ? You're well off ? "

" Yes. For my simple tastes I'm rather rich. But I haven't the ambition of a maggot."

" No. You haven't." He looked at me steadily. " If you don't mind my saying it, you have too little vanity. Oh, I'm quick at detecting vanity, and anyhow it's a thing that defies concealment. But I imagine—indeed I know—that you can work like a beaver, and that your loyalty is not the kind that cracks. You won't be able to help yourself, Sir Richard. You'll be caught up in some machine. Look at me. I swore two years ago never to have a groove, and I'm in a deep one already. England is made up of grooves, and the only plan is to select a good one."

" I suppose yours is politics," I said.

" I suppose it is. A dingy game as it's played at present, but there are possibilities. There is a mighty Tory revival in sight, and it will want leading. The newly enfranchised classes, especially the women, will bring it about. The suffragists didn't know what a tremendous force of conservatism they were releasing when they won the vote for their sex. I should like to talk to you about these things some day."

In the smoking-room we got back to sport, and he told me the story of how he met Greenslade in Central Asia. I was beginning to realize that the man's reputation was justified, for there was a curious mastery about his talk, a careless power as if everything came easily to him and was just taken in his stride. I had meant to open up the business which had made me seek his acquaintance, but I did not feel the atmosphere quite right for it. I did not know him well enough yet, and I felt that if I once started on those ridiculous three facts, which were all I had, I must make a clean breast of the whole thing and take him fully into my confidence. I thought the time was scarcely ripe for that, especially as we would meet again.

" Are you by any chance free on Thursday ? " he asked as we parted. " I would like to take you to dine at the Thursday Club. You're sure to know some of the fellows, and it's a pleasant way of spending an evening. That's capital ! Eight o'clock on Thursday. Short coat and black tie."

As I walked away, I made up my mind that I had found the right kind of man to help me. I liked him, and the more I thought of him the more the impression deepened of a big reservoir of power behind his easy grace. I was completely fascinated, and the proof of it was that I went off to the nearest bookseller's and bought his two slim volumes of poems. I cared far more about poetry than Macgillivray imagined—Mary had done a lot to educate me—but I hadn't been very fortunate in my experiments with the new people. But I understood Medina's verses well enough. They were very simple, with a delicious subtle tune in them, and they were desperately sad. Again and again came the note of regret and transience and disillusioned fortitude. As I read them that evening I wondered how a man, who had apparently such zest for life and got so much out of the world, should be so lonely at heart. It might be a pose, but there was nothing of the conventional despair of the callow poet. This was the work of one as wise as Ulysses and as far-wandering. I didn't see how he could want to write anything but the truth. A pose is a consequence of vanity, and I was pretty clear that Medina was not vain.

Next morning I found his cadences still running in my head and I could not keep my thoughts off him. He fascinated me as a man is fascinated by a pretty woman. I was glad to think that he had taken a liking for me, for he had done far more than Greenslade's casual introduction demanded. He had made a plan for us to meet again, and he had spoken not as an acquaintance but as a friend. Very soon I decided that I would get Macgillivray's permission and take him wholly into our confidence. It was no good keeping a man like that at arm's length and asking him to solve puzzles presented as meaninglessly as an acrostic in a newspaper. He must be told all or nothing, and I was certain that if he were told all

he would be a very tower of strength to me.  The
more I thought of him the more I was convinced
of his exceptional brains.

I lunched with Mr. Julius Victor in Carlton
House Terrace.  He was carrying on his ordinary
life, and when he greeted me he never referred to
the business which had linked us together.  Or
rather he only said one word.  " I knew I could
count on you," he said.  " I think I told you
that my daughter was engaged to be married this
spring.  Well, her fiancé has come over from
France and will be staying for an indefinite time
with me.  He can probably do nothing to assist
you, but he is here at your call if you want him.
He is the Marquis de la Tour du Pin."

I didn't quite catch the name, and, as it was a
biggish party, we had sat down to luncheon before
I realized who the desolated lover was.  It was
my ancient friend Turpin, who had been liaison
officer with my old division.  I had known that
he was some kind of grandee, but as everybody
went by nicknames I had become used to think
of him as Turpin, a version of his title invented,
I think, by Archie Roylance.  There he was, sitting opposite me, a very handsome pallid young
man, dressed with that excessive correctness found
only among Frenchmen who get their clothes in
England.  He had been a tremendous swash-
buckler when he was with the division, unbridled
in speech, volcanic in action, but always with a
sad gentleness in his air.  He raised his heavy-
lidded eyes and looked at me, and then, with a

word of apology to his host, marched round the table and embraced me.

I felt every kind of a fool, but I was mighty glad all the same to see Turpin. He had been a good pal of mine, and the fact that he had been going to marry Miss Victor seemed to bring my new job in line with other parts of my life. But I had no further speech with him, for I had conversational women on both sides of me, and in the few minutes while the men were left alone at table I fell into talk with an elderly man on my right, who proved to be a member of the Cabinet. I found that out by a lucky accident, for I was lamentably ill-informed about the government of our country.

I asked him about Medina, and he brightened up at once.

" Can you place him ? " he asked. " I can't. I like to classify my fellow-men, but he is a new specimen. He is as exotic as the young Disraeli and as English as the late Duke of Devonshire. The point is, has he a policy, something he wants to achieve, and has he the power of attaching a party to him ? If he has these two things, there is no doubt about his future. Honestly, I'm not quite certain. He has very great talents, and I believe if he wanted he would be in the front rank as a public speaker. He has the ear of the House, too, though he doesn't often address it. But I am never sure how much he cares about the whole business, and England, you know, demands whole-heartedness in her public men. She will follow

blindly the second-rate if he is in earnest, and
reject the first-rate if he is not."

I said something about Medina's view of a great
Tory revival, based upon the women. My neighbour grinned.

"I daresay he's right, and I daresay he could
whistle women any way he pleased. It's extraordinary the charm he has for them. That handsome face of his and that melodious voice would
enslave anything female from a charwoman to a
Cambridge intellectual. Half his power of course
comes from the fact that they have no charm for
*him*. He's as aloof as Sir Galahad from any
interest in the sex. Did you ever hear his name
coupled with a young woman's? He goes everywhere and they would give their heads for him,
and all the while he is as insensitive as a nice
Eton boy whose only thought is of getting into
the Eleven. You know him?"

I told him, very slightly.

"Same with me. I've only a nodding acquaintance, but one can't help feeling the man everywhere and being acutely interested. It's lucky
he's a sound fellow. If he were a rogue he could
play the devil with our easy-going society."

That night Sandy and I dined together. He
had come back from Scotland in good spirits, for
his father's health was improving, and when
Sandy was in good spirits it was like being on the
Downs in a south-west wind. We had so much
to tell each other that we let our food grow cold.
He had to hear all about Mary and Peter John,

and what I knew of Blenkiron and a dozen other old comrades, and I had to get a sketch—the merest sketch—of his doings in the East since the Armistice. Sandy for some reason was at the moment disinclined to speak of his past, but he was as ready as an undergraduate to talk of his future. He meant to stay at home now, for a long spell at any rate ; and the question was how he should fill up his time. "Country life's no good," he said. "I must find a profession or I'll get into trouble."

I suggested politics, and he rather liked the notion.

"I might be bored in Parliament," he reflected, "but I should love the rough-and-tumble of an election. I only once took part in one, and I discovered surprising gifts as a demagogue, and made a speech in our little town which is still talked about. The chief row was about Irish Home Rule, and I thought I'd better have a whack at the Pope. Has it ever struck you, Dick, that ecclesiastical language has a most sinister sound ? I knew some of the words, though not their meaning, but I knew that my audience would be just as ignorant. So I had a magnificent peroration. 'Will you, men of Kilclavers,' I asked, 'endure to see a chasuble set up in your market-place ? Will you have your daughters sold into simony ? Will you have celibacy practised in the public streets ? ' Gad, I had them all on their feet bellowing ' Never ! ' "

He also rather fancied business. He had a

notion of taking up civil aviation, and running a special service for transporting pilgrims from all over the Moslem world to Mecca. He reckoned the present average cost to the pilgrim at not less than £30, and believed that he could do it for an average of £15 and show a handsome profit. Blenkiron, he thought, might be interested in the scheme and put up some of the capital.

But later, in a corner of the upstairs smoking-room, Sandy was serious enough when I began to tell him the job I was on, for I didn't need Mac-gillivray's permission to make a confidant of him. He listened in silence while I gave him the main lines of the business that I had gathered from Mac-gillivray's papers, and he made no comment when I came to the story of the three hostages. But, when I explained my disinclination to stir out of my country rut, he began to laugh.

"It's a queer thing how people like us get a sudden passion for cosiness. I feel it myself coming over me. What stirred you up in the end ? The little boy ? "

Then very lamely and shyly I began on the rhymes and Greenslade's memory. That inter-ested him acutely. "Just the sort of sensible-nonsensical notion you'd have, Dick. Go on. I'm thrilled."

But when I came to Medina he exclaimed sharply.

" You've met him ? "

" Yesterday at luncheon."

" You haven't told him anything ? "

" No.   But I'm going to."

Sandy had been deep in an armchair with his legs over the side, but now he got up and stood with his arms on the mantelpiece looking into the fire.

" I'm going to take him into my full confidence," I said, " when I've spoken to Macgillivray."

" Macgillivray will no doubt agree ? "

" And you ?   Have you ever met him ? "

" Never.   But of course I've heard of him. Indeed I don't mind telling you that one of my chief reasons for coming home was a wish to see Medina."

" You'll like him tremendously.   I never met such a man."

" So every one says."   He turned his face and I could see that it had fallen into that portentous gravity which was one of Sandy's moods, the complement to his ordinary insouciance.   " When are you going to see him again ? "

" I'm dining with him the day after to-morrow at a thing called the Thursday Club."

" Oh, he belongs to that, does he ?   So do I. I think I'll give myself the pleasure of dining also."

I asked about the Club, and he told me that it had been started after the War by some of the people who had had queer jobs and wanted to keep together.   It was very small, only fifteen members. There were Collatt, one of the Q-boat V.C.'s, and Pugh of the Indian Staff Corps, and the Duke of Burminster, and Sir Arthur Warcliff, and several soldiers all more or less well known. "They elected me in 1919," said Sandy, "but of course I've never been to a dinner. I say, Dick, Medina must have a pretty strong pull here to be a member of the Thursday. Though I says it as shouldn't, it's a show most people would give their right hand to be in."

He sat down again and appeared to reflect, with his chin on his hand.

"You're under the spell, I suppose," he said.

"Utterly. I'll tell you how he strikes me. Your ordinary very clever man is apt to be a bit bloodless and priggish, while your ordinary sportsman and good fellow is inclined to be a bit narrow. Medina seems to me to combine all the virtues and none of the faults of both kinds. Anybody can see he's a sportsman, and you've only to ask the swells to discover how high they put his brains."

"He sounds rather too good to be true." I seemed to detect a touch of acidity in his voice. "Dick," he said, looking very serious, "I want you to promise to go slow in this business—I mean about telling Medina."

"Why?" I asked. "Have you anything against him?"

"No—o—o," he said. "I haven't anything against him. But he's just a little incredible, and I would like to know more about him. I had a friend who knew him. I've no right to say this, and I haven't any evidence, but I've a sort of feeling that Medina didn't do him any good."

"What was his name?" I asked, and was told

"Lavater"; and when I inquired what had become of him Sandy didn't know. He had lost sight of him for two years.

At that I laughed heartily, for I could see what was the matter. Sandy was jealous of this man who was putting a spell on everybody. He wanted his old friends to himself. When I taxed him with it he grinned and didn't deny it.

# CHAPTER V

## THE THURSDAY CLUB

WE met in a room on the second floor of a little restaurant in Mervyn Street, a pleasant room, panelled in white, with big fires burning at each end. The Club had its own cook and butler, and I swear a better dinner was never produced in London, starting with preposterously early plovers' eggs and finishing with fruit from Burminster's houses. There were a dozen present including myself, and of these, besides my host, I knew only Burminster and Sandy. Collatt was there, and Pugh, and a wizened little man who had just returned from bird-hunting at the mouth of the Mackenzie. There was Palliser-Yeates, the banker, who didn't look thirty, and Fulleylove, the Arabian traveller, who was really thirty and looked fifty. I was specially interested in Nightingale, a slim peering fellow with double glasses, who had gone back to Greek manuscripts and his Cambridge fellowship after captaining a Bedouin tribe. Leithen was there, too, the Attorney-General, who had been a private in the Guards at the start of the War and had finished up a G.S.O.I., a toughly built man, with a pale face and very keen quizzical eyes. I should think there must have been more varied and solid brains in that dozen than you would find in an average Parliament.

Sandy was the last to arrive, and was greeted with a roar of joy. Everybody seemed to want to wring his hand and beat him on the back. He knew them all except Medina, and I was curious to see their meeting. Burminster did the introducing, and Sandy for a moment looked shy. "I've been looking forward to this for years," Medina said, and Sandy, after one glance at him, grinned sheepishly and stammered something polite.

Burminster was chairman for the evening, a plump, jolly little man, who had been a pal of Archie Roylance in the Air Force. The talk to begin with was nothing out of the common. It started with horses and the spring handicaps, and then got on to spring salmon fishing, for one man had been on the Helmsdale, another on the Naver, and two on the Tay. The fashion of the Club was to have the conversation general, and there was very little talking in groups. I was next to Medina, between him and the Duke, and Sandy was at the other end of the oval table. He had not much to say, and more than once I caught his eyes watching Medina.

Then by-and-by, as was bound to happen, reminiscences began. Collatt made me laugh with a story of how the Admiralty had a notion that sea-lions might be useful to detect submarines. A number were collected, and trained to swim after submarines to which fish were attached as bait, the idea being that they would come to associate the smell of submarines with food, and go after a stranger. The thing shipwrecked on the artistic temperament. The beasts all came from the music-halls and had names like Flossie and Cissie, so they couldn't be got to realize that there was a war on, and were always going ashore without leave.

That story started the ball rolling, and by the time we had reached the port the talk was like what you used to find in the smoking-room of an East African coastal steamer, only a million times better. Everybody present had done and seen amazing things, and moreover they had the brains and knowledge to orientate their experiences. It was no question of a string of yarns, but rather of the best kind of give-and-take conversation, when a man would buttress an argument by an apt recollection. I especially admired Medina. He talked little, but he made others talk, and his keen interest seemed to wake the best in everybody. I noticed that, as at our luncheon three days before, he drank only water.

We talked, I remember, about the people who had gone missing, and whether any were likely still to turn up. Sandy told us about three British officers who had been in prison in Turkestan since the summer of '18 and had only just started home. He had met one of them at Marseilles, and thought there might be others tucked away in those parts. Then some one spoke of how it was possible to drop off the globe for a bit and miss all that was happening. I said I had met an old prospector in Barberton in 1920 who had come down from Portuguese territory, and when I asked him what he had been doing in the War he said, "What war?" Pugh said a fellow had just turned up in Hong Kong who had been a captive of Chinese pirates for eight years and had never heard a word of our four years' struggle, till he said something about the Kaiser to the skipper of the boat that picked him up.

Then Sandy, as the new-comer, wanted news about Europe. I remember that Leithen gave him his views on the *malaise* that France was suffering from, and that Palliser-Yeates, who looked exactly like a Rugby three-quarter back, enlightened him—and incidentally myself—on the matter of German reparations. Sandy was furious about the muddle in the Near East and the mis-handling of Turkey. His view was that we were doing our best to hammer a much-divided Orient into a hostile unanimity.

"Lord!" he cried, "how I loathe our new manners in foreign policy. The old English way was to regard all foreigners as slightly childish and rather idiotic, and ourselves as the only grown-ups in a kindergarten world. That meant that we had a cool detached view and did even-handed unsympathetic justice. But now we have got into the nursery ourselves and are bear-fighting on the floor. We take violent sides, and make pets, and of course if you are *-phil* something or

other you have got to be *-phobe* something else.
It is all wrong. We are becoming Balkanized."

We would have drifted into politics if Pugh
had not asked him his opinion of Gandhi. That
led him into an exposition of the meaning of the
fanatic, a subject on which he was well qualified
to speak, for he had consorted with most varieties.

" He is always in the technical sense mad—that
is, his mind is tilted from its balance, and since we
live by balance he is a wrecker, a crowbar in the
machinery. His power comes from the appeal he
makes to the imperfectly balanced, and as these
are never the majority his appeal is limited. But
there is one kind of fanatic whose strength comes
from balance, from a lunatic balance. You cannot say that there is any one thing abnormal
about him, for he is all abnormal. He is as
balanced as you or me, but, so to speak, in a fourth-
dimensional world. That kind of man has no
logical gaps in his creed. Within his insane
postulates he is brilliantly sane. Take Lenin for
instance. That's the kind of fanatic I'm afraid
of."

Leithen asked how such a man got his influence.
" You say that there is no crazy spot in him
which appeals to a crazy spot in other people."

" He appeals to the normal," said Sandy
solemnly, " to the perfectly sane. He offers
reason, not visions—in any case his visions are
reasonable. In ordinary times he will not be
heard, because, as I say, his world is not our
world. But let there come a time of great suffer-

ing or discontent, when the mind of the ordinary man is in desperation, and the rational fanatic will come by his own. When he appeals to the sane and the sane respond, revolutions begin."

Pugh nodded his head, as if he agreed. "Your fanatic of course must be a man of genius."

"Of course. And genius of that kind is happily rare. When it exists, its possessor is the modern wizard. The old necromancer fiddled away with cabalistic signs and crude chemicals and got nowhere; the true wizard is the man who works by spirit on spirit. We are only beginning to realize the strange crannies of the human soul. The real magician, if he turned up to-day, wouldn't bother about drugs and dopes. He would dabble in far more deadly methods, the compulsion of a fiery nature over the limp things that men call their minds."

He turned to Pugh. "You remember the man we used to call Ram Dass in the War—I never knew his right name?"

"Rather," said Pugh. "The fellow who worked for us in San Francisco. He used to get big sums from the agitators and pay them into the British Exchequer, less his commission of ten per cent."

"Stout fellow!" Burminster exclaimed approvingly.

"Well, Ram Dass used to discourse to me on this subject. He was as wise as a serpent and as loyal as a dog, and he saw a lot of things coming that we are just beginning to realize. He said

(2,745)

7

that the great offensives of the future would be
psychological, and he thought the Governments
should get busy about it and prepare their defence.
What a jolly sight it would be—all the high
officials sitting down to little primers! But there
was sense in what he said. He considered that
the most deadly weapon in the world was the
power of mass-persuasion, and he wanted to meet
it at the source, by getting at the mass-persuader.
His view was that every spell-binder had got
something like Samson's hair which was the key
of his strength, and that if this were tampered
with he could be made innocuous. He would have
had us make pets of the prophets and invite them
to Government House. You remember the winter
of 1917 when the Bolsheviks were making trouble
in Afghanistan and their stuff was filtering through
into India. Well, Ram Dass claimed the credit of
stopping that game by his psychological dodges."

He looked across suddenly at Medina. "You
know the Frontier. Did you ever come across
the *guru* that lived at the foot of the Shansi pass
as you go over to Kaikand?"

Medina shook his head. "I never travelled
that way. Why?"

Sandy seemed disappointed. "Ram Dass used
to speak of him. I hoped you might have met
him."

The Club madeira was being passed round, and
there was a little silence while we sipped it. It
was certainly a marvellous wine, and I noticed
with pain Medina's abstinence.

"You really are missing a lot, you know," Burminster boomed in his jolly voice, and for a second all the company looked Medina's way.

He smiled and lifted his glass of water.

"*Sit vini abstemius qui hermeneuma tentat aut hominum petit dominatum*," he said.

Nightingale translated. "Meaning that you must be pussyfoot if you would be a big man."

There was a chorus of protests, and Medina again lifted his glass.

"I'm only joking. I haven't a scrap of policy or principle in the matter. I don't happen to like the stuff—that's all."

I fancy that the only two scholars among us were Nightingale and Sandy. I looked at the latter and was surprised by the change in his face. It had awakened to the most eager interest. His eyes, which had been staring at Medina, suddenly met mine, and I read in them not only interest but disquiet.

Burminster was delivering a spirited defence of Bacchus, and the rest joined in, but Sandy took the other side.

"There's a good deal in that Latin tag," he said. "There are places in the world where total abstinence is reckoned a privilege. Did you ever come across the Ulai tribe up the Karakoram way?" He was addressing Medina. "No? Well, the next time you meet a man in the Guides ask him about them, for they're a curiosity. They're Mohammedan and so should by rights be abstainers, but they're a drunken set of sweeps and the most priest-ridden community on earth. Drinking is not only a habit among them, it's an obligation, and their weekly *tamasha* would make Falstaff take the pledge. But their priests—they're a kind of theocracy—are strict teetotal. It is their privilege and the secret of their power. When one of them has to be degraded he is filled compulsorily full of wine. That's your—how does the thing go ?—your '*hominum dominatus.*'"

From that moment I found the evening go less pleasantly. Medina was as genial as ever, but something seemed to have affected Sandy's temper and he became positively grumpy. Now and then he contradicted a man too sharply for good manners, but for the most part he was silent, smoking his pipe and answering his neighbours in monosyllables. About eleven I began to feel it was time to leave, and Medina was of the same opinion. He asked me to walk with him, and I gladly accepted, for I did not feel inclined to go to bed.

As I was putting on my coat, Sandy came up. "Come to the Club, Dick," he said. "I want to talk to you." His manner was so peremptory that I opened my eyes.

"Sorry," I said. "I've promised to walk home with Medina."

"Oh, damn Medina!" he said. "Do as I ask or you'll be sorry for it."

I wasn't feeling very pleased with Sandy, especially as Medina was near enough to hear what he said. So I told him rather coldly that

I didn't intend to go back on my arrangement. He turned and marched out, cannoning at the doorway into Burminster, to whom he did not apologize. That nobleman rubbed his shoulder ruefully. "Old Sandy hasn't got used to his corn yet," he laughed. "Looks as if the madeira had touched up his liver."

It was a fine still March night with a good moon, and as we walked along Piccadilly I was feeling cheerful. The good dinner I had eaten and the good wine I had drunk played their part in this mood, and there was also the satisfaction of having dined with good fellows and having been admitted into pretty select company. I felt my liking for Medina enormously increase, and I had the unworthy sense of superiority which a man gets from seeing an old friend whom he greatly admires behave rather badly. I was considering what had ailed Sandy when Medina raised the subject.

"A wonderful fellow Arbuthnot," he said. "I have wanted to meet him for years, and he is certainly up to my expectations. But he has been quite long enough abroad. A mind as keen as his, if it doesn't have the company of its equals, is in danger of getting viewy. What he said to-night was amazingly interesting, but I thought it a little fantastic."

I agreed, but the hint of criticism was enough to revive my loyalty. "All the same there's usually something in his most extravagant theories. I've seen him right when all the sober knowledgeable people were wrong."

"That I can well believe," he said. "You know him well ? "

"Pretty well. We've been in some queer places together."

The memory of those queer places came back to me as we walked across Berkeley Square. The West End of London at night always affected me with a sense of the immense solidity of our civilization. These great houses, lit and shuttered and secure, seemed the extreme opposite of the world of half-lights and perils in which I had sometimes journeyed. I thought of them as I thought of Fosse Manor, as sanctuaries of peace. But to-night I felt differently towards them. I wondered what was going on at the back of those heavy doors. Might not terror and mystery lurk behind that barricade as well as in tent and slum ? I suddenly had a picture of a plump face all screwed up with fright muffled beneath the bed-clothes.

I had imagined that Medina lived in chambers or a flat, but we stopped before a substantial house in Hill Street.

"You're coming in ? The night's young and there's time for a pipe."

I had no wish to go to bed, so I followed him as he opened the front door with a latch-key. He switched on a light, which lit the first landing of the staircase but left the hall in dusk. It seemed to be a fine place full of cabinets, the gilding of which flickered dimly. We ascended thickly carpeted stairs, and on the landing he switched off the first light and switched on another which lit a further flight. I had the sensation of mounting to a great height in a queer shadowy world.

" This is a big house for a bachelor," I observed.

" I've a lot of stuff, books and pictures and things, and I like it round me."

He opened a door and ushered me into an enormous room, which must have occupied the whole space on that floor. It was oblong, with deep bays at each end, and it was lined from floor to ceiling with books. Books, too, were piled on the tables, and sprawled on a big flat couch which was drawn up before the fire. It wasn't an ordinary gentleman's library, provided by the bookseller at so much a yard. It was the working collection of a scholar, and the books had that used look which makes them the finest tapestry for a room. The place was lit with lights on small tables, and on a big desk under a reading-lamp were masses of papers and various volumes with paper slips in them. It was workshop as well as library.

A servant entered, unsummoned, and put a tray of drinks on a side-table. He was dressed like an ordinary butler, but I guessed that he had not spent much of his life in service. The heavy jowl, the small eyes, the hair cut straight round the nape of the neck, the swollen muscles about the shoulder and upper arm told me the profession he had once followed. The man had been in the ring, and not so very long ago. I wondered at Medina's choice, for a pug is not the kind of servant I would choose myself.

" Nothing more, Odell," said Medina. " You can go to bed. I will let Sir Richard out."

He placed me in a long armchair, and held the siphon while I mixed myself a very weak whisky-and-soda. Then he sat opposite me across the hearth-rug in a tall old-fashioned chair which he pulled forward from his writing-table. The servant in leaving had turned out all the lights except one at his right hand, which vividly lit up his face, and which, since the fire had burned low, made the only bright patch in the room.

I stretched my legs comfortably and puffed at my pipe, wondering how I would have the energy to get up and go home. The long dim shelves, where creamy vellum and morocco ran out of the dusk into darkness, had an odd effect on me. I was visited again by the fancies which had occupied me coming through Berkeley Square. I was inside one of those massive sheltered houses, and lo and behold! it was as mysterious as the aisles of a forest. Books—books—old books full of forgotten knowledge! I was certain that if I had the scholarship to search the grave rows I would find out wonderful things.

I was thirsty, so I drank off my whisky-and-soda, and was just adding a little more soda-water from the siphon at my elbow, when I looked towards Medina. There was that in his appearance which made me move my glass so that a thin stream of liquid fell on my sleeve. . . . The patch was still damp next morning.

His face, brilliantly lit up by the lamp, seemed to be also lit from within. It was not his eyes or any one feature that enthralled me, for I did not notice any details. Only the odd lighting seemed to detach his head from its environment so that it hung in the air like a planet in the sky, full of intense brilliance and power.

It is not very easy to write down what happened. For twelve hours afterwards I remembered nothing—only that I had been very sleepy, and must have been poor company and had soon got up to go. . . . But that was not the real story: it was what the man had willed that I should remember, and because my own will was not really mastered I remembered other things in spite of him; remembered them hazily, like a drunkard's dream.

The head seemed to swim in the centre of pale converging lines. These must have been the bookshelves, which in that part of the room were full of works bound in old vellum. My eyes were held by two violet pin-points of light which were so bright that they hurt me. I tried to shift my gaze, but I could only do that by screwing round my head towards the dying fire. The movement demanded a great effort, for every muscle in my body seemed drugged with lethargy.

As soon as I looked away from the light I regained some possession of my wits. I felt that I must be in for some sickness, and had a moment of bad fright. It seemed to be my business to keep my eyes on the shadows in the hearth, for where darkness was there I found some comfort. I was as afraid of the light before me as a child of a bogy. I thought that if I said something I should feel better, but I didn't seem to have the energy to get a word out. Curiously enough, I felt no fear of Medina; he didn't seem to be in the business; it was that disembodied light that scared me.

Then I heard a voice speaking, but still I didn't think of Medina.

"Hannay," it said. "You are Richard Hannay?"

Against my will I slewed my eyes round, and there hung that intolerable light burning into my eyeballs and my soul. I found my voice now, for it seemed to be screwed out of me, and I said "Yes" like an automaton.

I felt my wits and my senses slipping away under that glare. But my main discomfort was physical, the flaming control of the floating brightness—not face, or eyes, but a dreadful overmastering aura. I thought — if at that moment you could call any process of my mind thought—that if I could only link it on to some material thing I should find relief. With a desperate effort I seemed to make out the line of a man's shoulder and the back of a chair. Let me repeat that I never thought of Medina, for he had been wiped clean out of my world.

"You are Richard Hannay," said the voice. "Repeat, 'I am Richard Hannay.'"

The words came out of my mouth involuntarily.

I was concentrating all my wits on the comforting outline of the chair-back, which was beginning to be less hazy.

The voice spoke again.

"But till this moment you have been nothing. There was no Richard Hannay before. Now, when I bid you, you begin your life. You remember nothing. You have no past."

"I remember nothing," said my voice, but as I spoke I knew I lied, and that knowledge was my salvation.

I have been told more than once by doctors who dabbled in the business that I was the most hopeless subject for hypnotism that they ever struck. One of them once said that I was about as unsympathetic as Table Mountain. I must suppose that the intractable bedrock of commonplaceness in me now met the something which was striving to master me and repelled it. I felt abominably helpless, my voice was not my own, my eyes were tortured and aching, but I had recovered my mind.

I seemed to be repeating a lesson at some one's dictation. I said I was Richard Hannay, who had just come from South Africa on his first visit to England. I knew no one in London, and had no friends. Had I heard of a Colonel Arbuthnot? I had not. Or the Thursday Club? I had not. Or the War? Yes, but I had been in Angola most of the time and had never fought. I had money? Yes, a fair amount, which was in such-and-such a bank and such-and-such investments.

. . . I went on repeating the stuff as glibly as a parrot, but all the while I knew I lied. Something deep down in me was insisting that I was Sir Richard Hannay, K.C.B., who had commanded a division in France, and was the squire of Fosse Manor, the husband of Mary, and the father of Peter John.

Then the voice seemed to give orders. I was to do this and that, and I repeated them docilely. I was no longer in the least scared. Some one or something was trying to play monkey-tricks with my mind, but I was master of that, though my voice seemed to belong to an alien gramophone, and my limbs were stupidly weak. I wanted above all things to be allowed to sleep. . . .

I think I must have slept for a little, for my last recollection of that queer sederunt is that the unbearable light had gone, and the ordinary lamps of the room were switched on. Medina was standing by the dead fire, and another man beside him—a slim man with a bent back and a lean grey face. The second man was only there for a moment, but he looked at me closely and I thought Medina spoke to him and laughed. . . . Then I was being helped by Medina into my coat, and conducted downstairs. There were two bright lights in the street which made me want to lie down on the kerb and sleep. . . .

.   .   .   .   .   .   .

I woke about ten o'clock next morning in my bedroom at the Club, feeling like nothing on earth. I had a bad headache, my eyes seemed to be backed with white fire, and my legs were full of weak pains as if I had influenza. It took me several minutes to realize where I was, and when I wondered what had brought me to such a state I could remember nothing. Only a preposterous litany ran in my brain—the name "Dr. New-hover," and an address in Wimpole Street. I concluded glumly that that for a man in my condition was a useful recollection, but where I had got it I hadn't an idea.

The events of the night before were perfectly clear. I recalled every detail of the Thursday Club dinner, Sandy's brusqueness, my walk back with Medina, my admiration of his great library. I remembered that I had been drowsy there and thought that I had probably bored him. But I was utterly at a loss to account for my wretched condition. It could not have been the dinner ; or the wine, for I had not drunk much, and in any case I have a head like cast iron ; or the weak whisky-and-soda in Medina's house. I staggered to my feet and looked at my tongue in the glass. It was all right, so there could be nothing the matter with my digestion.

You are to understand that the account I have just written was pieced together as events came back to me, and that at 10 a.m. the next morning I remembered nothing of it—nothing but the incidents up to my sitting down in Medina's library, and the name and address of a doctor I had never heard of. I concluded that I must have got some infernal germ, probably botulism, and

was in for a bad illness. I wondered dismally
what kind of fool I had made of myself before
Medina, and still more dismally what was going
to happen to me. I decided to wire for Mary
when I had seen a doctor, and to get as soon as
possible into a nursing home. I had never had
an illness in my life, except malaria, and I was
as nervous as a cat.

But after I had had a cup of tea I felt a little
better, and inclined to get up. A cold bath
relieved my headache, and I was able to shave and
dress. It was while I was shaving that I observed
the first thing which made me puzzle about the
events of the previous evening. The valet who
attended to me had put out the contents of my
pockets on the dressing-table—my keys, watch,
loose silver, note-case, and my pipe and pouch.
Now I carry my pipe in a little leather case, and,
being very punctilious in my habits, I invariably
put it back in the case when it is empty. But
the case was not there, though I remembered
laying it on the table beside me in Medina's room,
and moreover the pipe was still half full of un-
smoked tobacco. I rang for the man, and learned
that he had found the pipe in the pocket of my
dinner jacket, but no case. He was positive, for
he knew my ways and had been surprised to find
my pipe so untidily pocketed.

I had a light breakfast downstairs, and as
I ate it I kept wondering as to what exactly
I had been doing the night before. Odd little
details were coming back to me ; in particular, a

recollection of some great effort which had taken all the strength out of me. Could I have been drugged ? Not the Thursday Club madeira. Medina's whisky-and-soda ? The idea was nonsense ; in any case a drugged man does not have a clean tongue the next morning.

I interviewed the night porter, for I thought he might have something to tell me.

" Did you notice what hour I came home last night ? " I asked.

" It was this morning, Sir Richard," the man replied, with the suspicion of a grin. " About half-past three it would be, or twenty minutes to four."

" God bless my soul ! " I exclaimed. " I had no notion it was so late. I sat up talking with a friend."

" You must have been asleep in the car, Sir Richard, for the chauffeur had to wake you, and you were that drowsy I thought I'd better take you upstairs myself. The bedrooms on the top floor is not that easy found."

" I didn't drop a pipe-case ? " I asked.

" No, sir." The man's discreet face revealed that he thought I had been dining too well but was not inclined to blame me for it.

By luncheon-time I had decided that I was not going to be ill, for there was no longer anything the matter with my body except a certain stiffness in the joints and the ghost of a headache behind my eyes. But my mind was in a precious confusion. I had stayed in Medina's room till after

three, and had not been conscious of anything
that happened there after, say, half-past eleven.
I had left finally in such a state that I had forgotten my pipe-case, and had arrived at the Club
in somebody's car—probably Medina's—so sleepy
that I had to be escorted upstairs, and had awoke
so ill that I thought I had botulism. What in
Heaven's name had happened ?

I fancy that the fact that I had resisted the
influence brought to bear on me with my *mind*,
though tongue and limbs had been helpless,
enabled me to remember what the wielder of the
influence had meant to be forgotten. At any
rate bits of that strange scene began to come
back. I remembered the uncanny brightness—
remembered it not with fear but with acute
indignation. I vaguely recalled that I had repeated nonsense to somebody's dictation, but
what it was I could not yet remember. The more
I thought of it the angrier I grew. Medina must
have been responsible, though to connect him
with it seemed ridiculous when I thought of what
I had seen of him. Had he been making me the
subject of some scientific experiment ? If so, it
was infernal impertinence. Anyhow it had failed
—that was a salve to my pride—for I had kept
my head through it. The doctor had been right
who had compared me to Table Mountain.

I had got thus far in my reflections, when I
recollected that which put a different complexion
on the business. Suddenly I remembered the circumstances in which I had made Medina's acquaint-

ance.  From him Tom Greenslade had heard the
three facts which fitted in with the jingle which
was the key to the mystery that I was sworn to
unravel.  Hitherto I had never thought of this
dazzling figure except as an ally.  Was it possible
that he might be an enemy ?  The turn-about
was too violent for my mind to achieve it in one
movement.  I swore to myself that Medina was
straight, that it was sheer mania to believe that
a gentleman and a sportsman could ever come
within hailing distance of the hideous underworld
which Macgillivray had revealed to me. . . . But
Sandy had not quite taken to him. . . . I thanked
my stars that anyhow I had said nothing to him
about my job.  I did not really believe that
there was any doubt about him, but I realized
that I must walk very carefully.

And then another idea came to me.  Hypnotism had been tried on me, and it had failed.
But those who tried it must believe from my
behaviour that it had succeeded.  If so, somehow
and somewhere they would act on that belief.
It was my business to encourage it.  I was sure
enough of myself to think that, now I was forewarned, no further hypnotic experiments could
seriously affect me.  But let them show their
game, let me pretend to be helpless wax in their
hands.  Who " they " were I had still to find
out.

I had a great desire to get hold of Sandy and
talk it over, but though I rung up several of his
lairs I could not find him.  Then I decided to see

Dr. Newhover, for I was certain that that name had come to me out of the medley of last night. So I telephoned and made an appointment with him for that afternoon, and four o'clock saw me starting out to walk to Wimpole Street.

# CHAPTER VI

## THE HOUSE IN GOSPEL OAK

IT was a dry March afternoon, with one of those fantastic winds which seem to change their direction hourly, and contrive to be in a man's face at every street corner. The dust was swirling in the gutters, and the scent of hyacinth and narcissus from the flower-shops was mingled with that bleak sandy smell which is London's foretaste of spring. As I crossed Oxford Street, I remember thinking what an odd pointless business I had drifted into. I saw nothing for it but to continue drifting and see what happened. I was on my way to visit a doctor of whom I knew nothing, about some ailment which I was not conscious of possessing. I didn't even trouble to make a plan, being content to let chance have the guiding of me.

The house was one of those solid dreary erections which have usually the names of half a dozen doctors on their front doors. But in this case there was only one—Dr. M. Newhover. The parlour-maid took me into the usual drab waiting-room furnished with Royal Academy engravings,

115

fumed oak, and an assortment of belated picture-papers, and almost at once she returned and ushered me into the consulting-room. This again was of the most ordinary kind—glazed bookcases, wash-hand basin in a corner, roll-top desk, a table with a medical journal or two and some leather cases. And Dr. Newhover at first sight seemed nothing out of the common. He was a youngish man, with high cheek-bones, a high forehead, and a quantity of blond hair brushed straight back from it. He wore a *pince-nez*, and when he removed it showed pale prominent blue eyes. From his look I should have said that his father had called himself Neuhofer.

He greeted me with a manner which seemed to me to be at once patronizing and dictatorial. I wondered if he was some tremendous swell in his profession, of whom I ought to have heard. " Well, Mr. Hannay, what can I do for you ? " he said. I noticed that he called me " Mr." though I had given " Sir Richard " both on the telephone and to the parlour-maid. It occurred to me that some one had already been speaking of me to him, and that he had got the name wrong in his memory.

I thought I had better expound the alarming symptoms with which I had awakened that morning.

" I don't know what's gone wrong with me," I said. " I've a pain behind my eyeballs, and my whole head seems muddled up. I feel drowsy and slack, and I've got a weakness in my legs and back like a man who has just had 'flu."

He made me sit down and proceeded to catechize me about my health. I said it had been good enough, but I mentioned my old malaria and several concussions, and I pretended to be pretty nervous about my condition. Then he went through the whole bag of tricks—sounding me with a stethoscope, testing my blood pressure, and hitting me hard below the knee to see if I reacted. I had to play up to my part, but upon my soul I came near reacting too vigorously to some of his questions and boxing his ears. Always he kept up that odd, intimate, domineering, rather offensive manner.

He made me lie down on a couch while he fingered the muscles of my neck and shoulder and seemed to be shampooing my head with his long chilly hands. I was by this time feeling rather extra well, but I managed to invent little tendernesses here and there and a lot of alarming mental aberrations. I wondered if he were not getting suspicious, for he asked abruptly : " Have you had these symptoms long ? " so I thought it better to return to the truth, and told him " only since this morning."

At last he bade me get up, took off the tortoise-shell spectacles he had been wearing and resumed his *pince-nez*, and while I was buttoning my collar seemed to be sunk in reflection. He made me sit in the patient's chair, and stood up and looked down on me with a magisterial air that made me want to laugh.

" You are suffering," he said, " from a somewhat

abnormal form of a common enough complaint. Just as the effects of a concussion are often manifest only some days after the blow, so the results of nervous strain may take a long time to develop. I have no doubt that in spite of your good health you have during recent years been working your mind and body at an undue pressure, and now this morning quite suddenly you reap the fruits. I don't want to frighten you, Mr. Hannay, but neurosis is so mysterious a disease in its working that we must take it seriously, especially at its first manifestations. There are one or two points in your case which I am not happy about. There is, for example, a certain congestion—or what seems to me a congestion—in the nerve centres of the neck and head. That may be induced by the accidents—concussion and the like—which you have told me of, or it may not. The true cure must, of course, take time, and rest and change of scene are obligatory. You are fond of sport ? A fisherman ? "

I told him I was.

" Well, a little later I may prescribe a salmon river in Norway. The remoteness of the life from ordinary existence and the contemplation of swift running water have had wonderful results with some of my patients. But Norway is not possible till May, and in the meantime I am going to order you specific treatment. Yes. I mean massage, but by no means ordinary massage. That science is still in its infancy, and its practitioners are only fumbling at the doorway. But now and then we

find a person, man or woman, with a kind of extra
sense for disentangling and smoothing out muscular and nervous abnormalities. I am going to
send you to such a one. The address may surprise you, but you are man of the world enough
to know that medical skill is not confined to the
area between Oxford Street and the Marylebone
Road." He took off his glasses, and smiled.

Then he wrote something on a slip of paper and
handed it to me. I read "Madame Breda, 4 Palmyra Square, N.W."

"Right!" I said. "Much obliged to you. I
hope Madame Breda will cure this infernal headache. When can I see her?"

"I can promise you she will cure the headache.
She is a Swedish lady who has lived in London
since the War, and is so much an enthusiast in her
art that she will only now and then take a private
patient. For the most part she gives her skill free
to the children's hospitals. But she will not
refuse me. As for beginning, I should lose no
time for the sake of your own comfort. What
about to-morrow morning?"

"Why not to-night? I have nothing to do,
and I want to be quit of my headache before bed-
time. Why shouldn't I go on there now?"

"No reason in the world. But I must make
an appointment. Madame is on the telephone.
Excuse me a moment."

He left the room, and returned in a few minutes
to say that he had made an appointment for seven
o'clock. "It is an outlandish place to get to, but

most taxi-drivers know it. If your man doesn't, tell him to drive to Gospel Oak, and then any policeman will direct you."

I had my cheque-book with me, but he didn't want his fee, saying that he was not done with me. I was to come back in a week and report progress. As I left I had a strong impression of a hand as cold as a snake, pale bulging eyes, and cheek-bones like a caricature of a Scotsman. An odd but rather impressive figure was Dr. Newhover. He didn't look a fool, and if I hadn't known the un-common toughness of my constitution I might have been unsettled by his forebodings.

I walked down to Oxford Street and had tea in a tea-shop. As I sat among the chattering typists and shop-boys I kept wondering whether I was not wasting my time and behaving like a jackass. Here was I, as fit as a hunter, consult-ing specialists and visiting unknown masseuses in North London, and all with no clear purpose. In less than twenty-four hours I had tumbled into a perfectly crazy world, and for a second I had a horrid doubt whether the craziness was not inside my mind. Had something given in my brain last night in Medina's room, so that now I was what people call " wanting " ? I went over the sequence of events again, and was reassured by remembering that in it all I had kept my head. I had not got to the stage of making theories ; I was still only waiting on developments, and I couldn't see any other way before me. I must, of course, get hold of Sandy ; but first let me see what this massage business meant. It might all be perfectly square ; I might have remembered Dr. Newhover's name by a queer trick of memory—heard it, perhaps, from some friend—and that remarkable practitioner might be quite honest. But then I remembered the man's manner—I was quite clear that he knew something of me, that some one had told him to expect me. Then it occurred to me that I might be doing a rash thing in going off to an unknown house in a seedy suburb. So I went into a public telephone-booth, rang up the Club, and told the porter that, if Colonel Arbuthnot called, I was at 4 Palmyra Square, N.W.—I made him write down the address—and would be back before ten o'clock.

I was rather short of exercise, so I decided to walk, since I had plenty of time. Strangely enough, the road was pretty much that which I had taken on that June day of 1914 when I had been waiting on Bullivant and the Black Stone gentry, and had walked clean out of London to pass the time.* Then, I remembered, I had been thrilling with wild anticipation, but now I was an older and much wiser man, and though I was sufficiently puzzled I could curb my restlessness with philosophy. I went up Portland Place, past the Regent's Park, till I left the houses of the well-to-do behind me, and got into that belt of mean streets which is the glacis of the northern heights. Various policemen directed me, and I enjoyed the walk as if I had been exploring, for London is

* See *The Thirty-nine Steps.*

always to me an undiscovered country. I passed yards which not so long ago had been patches of market-garden, and terraces, sometime pretentious, and now sinking into slums; for London is like the tropical bush—if you don't exercise constant care the jungle, in the shape of the slums, will break in. The streets were full of clerks and shop-girls waiting for buses, and workmen from the St. Pancras and Clerkenwell factories going home. The wind was rising, and in the untidy alleys was stirring up a noisome dust; but as the ground rose it blew cleaner and seemed to bring from Kentish fields and the Channel the tonic freshness of spring. I stopped for a little and watched behind me the plain of lights, which was London, quivering in the dark-blue windy dusk.

It was almost dark when at last, after several false casts, I came into Palmyra Square. It was a square only in name, for one side was filled with a warehouse of sorts, and another straggled away in nests of small brick houses. One side was a terrace of artisans' dwellings, quite new, each with a tiny bow-window and names like " Chatsworth " and " Kitchener Villa." The fourth side, facing south, had once had a certain dignity, and the builder who had designed the place seventy years ago had thought, no doubt, that he was creating a desirable residential quarter. There the houses stood apart, each in a patch of garden, which may at one time have had lawns and flowers. Now these gardens were mere dusty yards, the refuge of tin cans and bits of paper, and only a blackened elm, an ill-grown privet hedge, and some stunted lilacs told of the more cheerful past. On one house was the brass plate of a doctor, on another that of 'a teacher of music; several advertised lodgings to let; the steps were untidy, the gates askew on their hinges, and over everything was written the dreary legend of a shabby gentility on the very brink of squalor.

No. 4 was smarter than the others, and its front door had been newly painted a vivid green. I rang the bell, which was an electric one, and the door was opened by a maid who looked sufficiently respectable. When I entered I saw that the house was on a more generous scale than I had thought, and had once, no doubt, been the home of some comfortable citizen. The hall was not the tank-like thing of the small London dwelling, and the room into which I was ushered, though small, was well furnished and had an electric fire in the grate. It seemed to be a kind of business room, for there was a telephone, a big safe, and on the shelves a line of lettered boxes for papers. I began to think that Madame Breda, whoever she might be, must be running a pretty prosperous show on ordinary business lines.

I was presently led by the maid to a room on the other side of the hall, where I was greeted by a smiling lady. Madame was a plump person in the early forties, with dark hair and a high colour, who spoke English almost without an accent. "Dr. Newhover has sent you. So? He has

told me. Will you please go in there and take
off your coat and waistcoat? Your collar, too,
please."

I did as I was bid, and in a little curtained
cubicle divested myself of these garments and
returned in my shirt-sleeves. The room was a
very pleasant one, with folding doors at one end,
furnished like an ordinary drawing-room, with
flowers in pots, and books, and what looked like
good eighteenth-century prints. Any suspicion I
may have had of the *bona fides* of the concern
received a rude shock. Madame had slipped over
her black dress a white linen overall, such as
surgeons wear, and she had as her attendant a
thin, odd-looking little girl, who also wore an
overall, and whose short hair was crowned with
a small white cap.

" This is Gerda," Madame said. " Gerda helps
me. She is very clever." She smiled on Gerda,
and Gerda smiled back, a limp little contortion of
a perfectly expressionless face.

Madame made me lie down on a couch. " You
have a headache?"

I mendaciously said that I had.

" That I can soon cure. But there are other
troubles? So? These I must explore. But first
I will take away the pain."

I felt her light firm fingers playing about my
temples and the base of my skull and my neck
muscles. A very pleasant sensation it was, and
I am certain that if I had been suffering from the
worst headache in the world it would have been

spirited away. As it was, being in excellent health, I felt soothed and freshened.

"So," she said, beaming down on me. "You are better? You are so beeg that it is not easy to be well all over at once. Now, I must look into more difficult things. You are not happy in your nerves—not altogether. Ah! these nerves! We do not quite know what they are, except that they are what you call the devil. You are very wakeful now. Is it not so? Well, I must put you to sleep. That is necessary, if you are willing."

"Right-o," I answered; but inwardly I said to myself, "No, my woman, I bet you don't." I was curious to see if, now that I was forewarned, I could resist any hypnotic business, as I believed I could.

I imagined that she would try to master me with her eyes, which were certainly remarkable orbs. But her procedure was the very opposite, for the small girl brought some things on a tray, and I saw that they were bandages. First of all, with a fine cambric handkerchief, she swathed my eyes, and then tied above it another of some heavy opaque material. They were loosely bound, so that I scarcely felt them, but I was left in the thickest darkness. I noticed that she took special pains so to adjust them that they should not cover my ears.

"You are not wakeful," I heard her voice say; "I think you are sleepy. You will sleep now."

I felt her fingers stray over my face, and the sensation was different, for whereas, when she had

treated my headache, they had set up a delicious
cool tingling of the skin, now they seemed to
induce wave upon wave of an equally pleasant
languor. She pressed my forehead, and my
senses seemed to be focused there and to be
lulled by that pressure. All the while she was
cooing to me in a voice which was like the drowsy
swell of the sea. If I had wanted to go to sleep
I could have dropped off easily, but, as I didn't
want to, I had no difficulty in resisting the gentle
coercion. That, I fancy, is my position about
hypnotism. I am no kind of use under compulsion, and for the thing to affect me it has to
have the backing of my own will. Anyhow, I
could appreciate the pleasantness of it and yet
disregard it. But it was my business to be a good
subject, so I pretended to drift away into slumber.
I made my breath come slowly and softly, and let
my body relax into impassivity.

Presently she appeared to be satisfied. She
said a word to the child, whose feet I could hear
cross the room. There was a sound of opening
doors—my ears, remember, were free of the bandages and my hearing is acute—and then it seemed
to me that the couch on which I lay began slowly
to move. I had a moment of alarm and nearly
gave away the show by jerking up my head. The
couch seemed to travel very smoothly on rails, and
I was conscious that I had passed through the
folding doors and was now in another room.
Then the movement stopped, and I realized that
I was in an entirely different atmosphere. I

realized, too, that a new figure had come on the scene.

There was no word spoken, but I had the queer inexplicable consciousness of human presences which is independent of sight and hearing. I have said that the atmosphere of the place had changed. There was a scent in the air which anywhere else I would have sworn was due to peat smoke, and mixed with it another intangible savour which I could not put a name to, but which did not seem to belong to London at all, or to any dwelling, but to some wild out-of-doors. . . . And then I was aware of noiseless fingers pressing my temples.

They were not the plump capable hands of Madame Breda. Nay, they were as fine and tenuous as a wandering wind, but behind their airy lightness was a hint of steel, as if they could choke as well as caress. I lay supine, trying to keep my breathing regular, since I was supposed to be asleep, but I felt an odd excitement rising in my heart. And then it quieted, for the fingers seemed to be smoothing it away. . . . A voice was speaking in a tongue of which I knew not a word, not speaking to me, but repeating, as it were, a private incantation. And the touch and voice combined to bring me nearer to losing my wits than even on the night before, nearer than I have ever been in all my days.

The experience was so novel and overpowering that I find it hard to give even a rough impression of it. Let me put it this way. A man at my time of life sees old age not so very far distant, and the nearer he draws to the end of his journey the more ardently he longs for his receding youth. I do not mean that, if some fairy granted him the gift, he would go back to boyhood; few of us would choose such a return; but he clothes all his youth in a happy radiance and aches to recapture the freshness and wonder with which he then looked on life. He treasures, like a mooning girl, stray sounds and scents and corners of landscape, which for a moment push the door ajar. . . . As I lay blindfolded on that couch I felt mysterious hands and voices plucking on my behalf at the barrier of the years and breaking it down. I was escaping into a delectable country, the Country of the Young, and I welcomed the escape. Had I been hypnotized, I should beyond doubt have moved like a sheep whithersoever this shepherd willed.

But I was awake, and, though on the very edge of surrender, I managed to struggle above the tides. Perhaps to my waking self the compulsion was too obvious and aroused a faint antagonism. Anyhow I had already begun a conscious resistance when the crooning voice spoke in English.

"You are Richard Hannay," it said. "You have been asleep, but I have wakened you. You are happy in the world in which you have wakened?"

My freedom was now complete, for I had begun to laugh, silently, far down at the bottom of my heart. I remembered last night, and the performance in Medina's house which had all day been growing clearer in my memory. I saw it as farce, and this as farce, and at the coming of humour the spell died. But it was up to me to make some kind of an answer, if I wanted to keep up the hoax, so I did my best to screw out an eerie sleepwalker's voice.

" I am happy," I said, and my pipe sounded like the twittering of sheeted ghosts.

" You wish to wake often in this world ? "

I signified by a croak that I did.

" But to wake you must first sleep, and I alone can make you sleep and wake. I exact a price, Richard Hannay. Will you pay my price ? "

I was puzzled about the voice. It had not the rich foreign tones of Madame Breda, but it had a very notable accent, which I could not place. At one moment it seemed to have the lilt which you find in Wester Ross, but there were cadences in it which were not Highland. Also, its *timbre* was curious—very light and thin like a child's. Was it possible that the queer little girl I had seen was the sibyl ? No, I decided ; the hands had not been a child's hands.

" I will pay any price," I said, which seemed to be the answer required of me.

" Then you are my servant when I summon you. Now, sleep again."

I had never felt less like being any one's servant. The hands fluttered again around my temples, but they had no more effect on me than the buzzing of flies. I had an insane desire to laugh, which I repressed by thinking of the idiotic pointlessness

(2,745)

9

of my recent doings. . . . I felt my couch slide backwards, and heard the folding doors open again and close. Then I felt my bandages being deftly undone, and I lay with the light on my closed eye-lids, trying to look like a sleeping warrior on a tomb. Some one was pressing below my left ear, and I recognized the old hunter's method of bring-ing a man back gently from sleep to consciousness, so I set about the job of making a workmanlike awaking. I hope I succeeded. Anyhow I must have looked dazed enough, for the lamps hurt my eyes after the muffled darkness.

I was back in the first room, with only Madame beside me. She beamed on me with the friendliest eyes, and helped me on with my coat and collar. "I have had you under close observation," she said, "for sleep often reveals where the ragged ends of the nerves lie. I have made certain de-ductions, which I will report to Dr. Newhover. . . . No, there is no fee. Dr. Newhover will make arrangements." She bade me good-bye in the best professional manner, and I descended the steps into Palmyra Square as if I had been spend-ing a commonplace hour having my back massaged for lumbago.

Once in the open air I felt abominably tired and very hungry. By good luck I hadn't gone far when I picked up a taxi and told it to drive to the Club. I looked at my watch and saw that it was later than I thought—close on ten o'clock. I had been several hours in the house, and small wonder I was weary.

I found Sandy wandering restlessly about the hall. "Thank God," he said when he saw me. "Where the devil have you been, Dick? The porter gave me a crazy address in North London. You look as if you wanted a drink."

"I feel as if I wanted food," I said. "I have a lot to tell you, but I must eat first. I've had no dinner."

Sandy sat opposite me while I fed, and forbore to ask questions.

"What put you in such a bad humour last night?" I asked.

He looked very solemn. "Lord knows. No, that's not true. I know well enough. I didn't take to Medina."

"Now I wonder why?"

"I wonder too. But I'm just like a dog: I take a dislike to certain people at first sight, and the queer thing is that my instinct isn't often wrong."

"Well, you're pretty well alone in your opinion. What sets you against him? He is well-mannered, modest, a good sportsman, and you can see he's as clever as they make."

"Maybe. But I've got a notion that the man is one vast lie. However, let's put it that I reserve my opinion. I have various inquiries to make."

We found the little back smoking-room on the first floor empty, and when I had lit my pipe and got well into an armchair, Sandy drew up another at my elbow. "Now, Dick," he said.

" First," I said, " it may interest you to learn that Medina dabbles in hypnotism."

" I know that," he said, " from his talk last night."

" How on earth——? "

" Oh, from a casual quotation he used. It's a longish story, which I'll tell you later. Go on."

I began from the break-up of the Thursday Club dinner, and told him all I could remember of my hours in Medina's house. As a story it met with an immense success. Sandy was so interested that he couldn't sit in his chair, but must get up and stand on the hearth-rug before me. I told him that I had wakened up feeling uncommonly ill, with a blank mind except for the address of a doctor-man in Wimpole Street, and how during the day recollection had gradually come back to me. He questioned me like a cross-examining counsel.

" Bright light—ordinary hypnotic property. Face, which seemed detached—that's a common enough thing in Indian magic. You say you must have been asleep, but were also in a sense awake and could hear and answer questions, and that you felt a kind of antagonism all the time which kept your will alive. You're probably about the toughest hypnotic proposition in the world, Dick, and you can thank God for that. Now, what were the questions ? A summons to forget your past and begin as a new creature, subject to the authority of a master. You assented, making private reservations of which the hypnotist knew nothing. If you had not kept your head and made those reservations, you would have remembered nothing at all of last night, but there would have been a subconscious bond over your will. As it is, you're perfectly free; only the man who tried to monkey with you doesn't know that. Therefore you begin by being one up on the game. You know where you are and he doesn't know where he is."

"What do you suppose Medina meant by it? It was infernal impertinence anyhow. But was it Medina? I seem to remember another man in the room before I left."

"Describe him."

"I've only a vague picture—a sad grey-faced fellow."

"Well, assume for the present that the experimenter was Medina. There's such a thing, remember, as spiriting away a man's recollection of his past, and starting him out as a waif in a new world. I've heard in the East of such performances, and of course it means that the memory-less being is at the mercy of the man who has stolen his memory. That is probably not the intention in your case. They wanted only to establish a subconscious control. But it couldn't be done at once with a fellow of your antecedents, so they organized a process. They suggested to you in your trance a doctor's name, and the next stage was his business. You woke feeling very seedy and remembering a doctor's address, and they argued that you would think that you had been advised about the fellow and make a bee-line for him. Remember, they would assume that you had no recollection of anything else from the night's doings. Now go ahead and tell me about the chirurgeon. Did you go to see him ? "

I continued my story, and at the Wimpole Street episode Sandy laughed long and loud.

" Another point up in the game. You say you think the leech had been advised of your coming and not by you ? By the way, he seems to have talked fairly good sense, but I'd as soon vet a hippopotamus for nerves as you." He wrote down Dr. Newhover's address in his pocket-book. " *Continuez.* You then proceeded, I take it, to 4 Palmyra Square."

At the next stage in my narrative he did not laugh. I daresay I told it better than I have written it down here, for I was fresh from the experience, and I could see that he was a good deal impressed.

" A Swedish masseuse and an odd-looking little girl. She puts you to sleep, or thinks she has, and then, when your eyes are bandaged, some one else nearly charms the soul out of you. That sounds big magic. I see the general lines of it, but it is big magic, and I didn't know that it was practised on these shores. Dick, this is getting horribly interesting. You kept wide awake—you are an old buffalo, you know—but you gave the impression of absolute surrender. Good for you— you are now three points ahead in the game."

" Well, but what is the game ? I'm hopelessly puzzled."

" So am I, but we must work on assumptions.

Let us suppose Medina is responsible. He may be only trying to find out the extent of his powers, and selects you as the most difficult subject to be found. You may be sure he knows all about your record. He may be only a vain man experimenting."

"In which case," I said, "I propose to punch his head."

"In which case, as you justly observe, you will give yourself the pleasure of punching his head. But suppose that he has got a far deeper purpose, something really dark and damnable. If by his hypnotic power he could make a tool of you, consider what an asset he would have found. A man of your ability and force. I have always said, you remember, that you had a fine natural talent for crime."

"I tell you, Sandy, that's nonsense. It's impossible that there's anything wrong—badly wrong —with Medina."

"Improbable, but not impossible. We're taking no chances. And if he were a scoundrel, think what a power he might be with all his talents and charm and popularity."

Sandy flung himself into a chair and appeared to be meditating. Once or twice he broke silence.

"I wonder what Dr. Newhover meant by talking of a salmon river in Norway. Why not golf at North Berwick?"

And again:

"You say there was a scent like peat in the room? Peat! You are certain?"

Finally he got up. "To-morrow," he said, "I think I will have a look round the house in Gospel Oak. Gospel Oak, by the way, is a funny name, isn't it ? You say it has electric light. I will visit it as a man from the corporation to see about the meter. Oh, that can easily be managed. Macgillivray will pass the word for me."

The mention of Macgillivray brought me to attention. "Look here," I said, "I'm simply wasting my time. I got in touch with Medina in order to ask his help, and now I've been landed in a set of preposterous experiences which have nothing to do with my job. I must see Macgillivray to-morrow about getting alongside his Shropshire squire. For the present there can be nothing doing with Medina."

"Shropshire squire be hanged ! You're an old ass, Dick. For the present there's everything doing with Medina. You wanted his help. Why ? Because he was the next stage in the clue to that nonsensical rhyme. Well, you've discovered that there may be odd things about him. You can't get his help, but you may get something more. You may get the secret itself. Instead of having to burrow into his memory, as you did with Greenslade, you may find it sticking out of his life."

"Do you really believe that ? " I asked in some bewilderment.

"I believe nothing as yet. But it is far the most promising line. He thinks that from what happened last night *plus* what happened two hours ago you are under his influence, an acolyte, possibly a tool. It may be all quite straight, or it may be most damnably crooked. You have got to find out. You must keep close to him, and foster his illusions, and play up to him for all you're worth. He is bound to show his hand. You needn't take any steps on your own account. He'll give you the lead all right."

I can't say I liked the prospect, for I have no love for play-acting, but I am bound to admit that Sandy talked sense. I asked him about himself, for I counted on his backing more than I could say.

" I propose to resume my travels," he said. " I wish to pursue my studies in the Bibliothèque Nationale of France."

" But I thought you were with me in this show."

" So I am. I go abroad on your business, as I shall explain to you some day. Also I want to see the man whom we used to call Ram Dass. I believe him to be in Munich at this moment. The day after to-morrow you will read in the *Times* that Colonel the Master of Clanroyden has gone abroad for an indefinite time on private business."

" How long will you be away ? " I groaned.

" A week perhaps, or a fortnight—or more. And when I come back it may not be as Sandy Arbuthnot."

## CHAPTER VII

### SOME EXPERIENCES OF A DISCIPLE

I DIDN'T see Sandy again, for he took the night train for Paris next evening, and I had to go down to Oxford that day to appear as a witness in a running-down case. But I found a note for me at the Club when I got back the following morning. It contained nothing except these words : "*Coverts drawn blank, no third person in house.*" I had not really hoped for anything from Sandy's expedition to Palmyra Square, and thought no more about it.

He didn't return in a week, nor yet in a fortnight, and, realizing that I had only a little more than two months to do my job in, I grew very impatient. But my time was pretty well filled with Medina, as you shall hear.

While I was reading Sandy's note Turpin turned up and begged me to come for a drive in his new Delage and talk to him. The Marquis de la Tour du Pin was, if possible, more pallid than before, his eyelids heavier, and his gentleness more silken. He drove me miles into the country, away through Windsor Forest, and as we raced at sixty miles an hour he uncovered his soul. He was going mad, it seemed; was, indeed, already mad, and only a slender and doubtless ill-founded confidence in me prevented him shooting himself. He was convinced that Adela Victor was dead, and that no trace of her would ever be found. "These policemen of yours—bah!" he moaned. "Only in England can people vanish." He concluded, however, that he would stay alive till he had avenged her, for he believed that a good God would some day deliver her murderer into his hands. I was desperately sorry for him, for behind his light gasconading manner there were marks of acute suffering, and indeed in his case I think I should have gone crazy. He asked me for hope, and I gave him it, and told him what I did not believe —that I saw light in the business, and had every confidence that we would restore him his sweetheart safe and sound. At that he cheered up and wanted to embrace me, thereby jolly nearly sending the Delage into a ditch and us both into eternity. He was burning for something to do, and wanted me to promise that as soon as possible I would inspan him into my team. That made me feel guilty, for I knew I had no team, and nothing you could call a clue; so I talked hastily about Miss Victor, lest he should ask me more.

I had her portrait drawn for me in lyric prose. She was slight, it seemed, middling tall, could ride like Diana and dance like the nymphs. Her colouring and hair were those of a brunette, but her eyes were a deep grey, and she had the soft voice which commonly goes with such eyes. Turpin, of course, put all this more poetically, relapsing frequently into French. He told me all kinds of things about her—how she was crazy about dogs, and didn't fear anything in the world, and walked with a throw-out, and lisped delightfully when she was excited. Altogether at the end of it I felt I had a pretty good notion of Miss Victor, especially as I had studied about fifty photographs of her in Macgillivray's room.

As we were nearing home again it occurred to me to ask him if he knew Medina. He said no, but that he was dining at the Victors' that evening—a small dinner-party, mostly political. "He is wonderful, that Mr. Victor. He will not change his life, and his friends think Adela is in New York for a farewell visit. He is like the Spartan boy with the fox."

"Tell Mr. Victor, with my compliments," I said, "that I would like to dine there to-night. I have a standing invitation. Eight-fifteen, isn't it?"

It turned out to be a very small and select party—the Foreign Secretary, Medina, Palliser-Yeates, the Duke of Alcester, Lord Sunningdale the ex-Lord Chancellor, Levasseur the French Minister, besides Turpin and myself. There were no women present. The behaviour of the Duke and Mr. Victor was a lesson in fortitude, and you would never have guessed that these two men were living with a nightmare. It was not a talkative assembly, though Sunningdale had a good deal to say to the table about a new book that a

German had written on the mathematical conception of infinity, a subject which even his brilliant exposition could not make clear to my thick wits. The Foreign Secretary and Levasseur had a *tête-à-tête*, with Turpin as a hanger-on, and the rest of us would have been as dull as sticks if it had not been for Medina. I had a good chance of observing his quality, and I must say I was astonished at his skill. It was he who by the right kind of question turned Sunningdale's discourse on infinity, which would otherwise have been a pedantic monologue, into good conversation. We got on to politics afterwards, and Medina, who had just come from the House, was asked what was happening.

"They had just finished the usual *plat du jour*, the suspension of a couple of Labour mountebanks," he said.

This roused Sunningdale, who rather affected the Labour party, and I was amused to see how Medina handled the ex-Chancellor. He held him in good-humoured argument, never forsaking his own position, but shedding about the whole subject an atmosphere of witty and tolerant understanding. I felt that he knew more about the business than Sunningdale, that he knew so much he could afford to give his adversary rope. Moreover, he never forgot that he was at a dinner-table, the pitch and key of his talk were exactly right, and he managed to bring every one into it.

To me he was extraordinarily kind. Indeed he treated me like a very ancient friend, bantering and affectionate and yet respectful, and he forced me to take a full share in the conversation. Under his stimulus, I became quite intelligent, and amazed Turpin, who had never credited me with any talents except for fighting. But I had not forgotten what I was there for, and if I had been inclined to, there were the figures of Victor and the Duke to remind me. I watched the two, the one thin, grey-bearded, rather like an admiral with his vigilant dark eyes, the other heavy-jowled, rubicund, crowned with fine silver hair ; in both I saw shadows of pain stealing back to the corners of lip and eye, whenever the face was in repose. And Medina—the very *beau ideal* of a courteous, kindly, open-air Englishman. I noted how in his clothes he avoided any touch of overdressing, no fancifully-cut waistcoat or too-smartly-tied tie. In manner and presence he was the perfection of un-self-conscious good breeding. It was my business to play up to him, and I let my devotion be pretty evident. The old Duke, whom I now met for the first time, patted my shoulder as we left the dining-room. "I am glad to see that you and Medina are friends, Sir Richard. Thank God that we have a man like him among the young entry. They ought to give him office at once, you know, get him inside the shafts of the coach. Otherwise he'll find something more interesting to do than politics."

By tacit consent we left the house together, and I walked the streets by his side, as I had done three nights before. What a change, I reflected, in my point of view !   Then I had been blind, now I was acutely watchful.   He slipped an arm into mine as we entered Pall Mall, but its pressure did not seem so much friendly as possessive.

" You are staying at your Club ? " he said. " Why not take up your quarters with me while you are in town ?   There's ample room in Hill Street."

The suggestion put me into a fright.   To stay with him at present would wreck all my schemes ; but, supposing he insisted, could I refuse, if it was my rôle to appear to be under his domination ? Happily he did not insist.   I made a lot of excuses —plans unsettled, constantly running down to the country, and so on.

" All right.   But some day I may make the offer again, and then I'll take no refusal."

They were just the kind of words a friend might have used, but somehow, though the tone was all right, they slightly grated on me.

" How are you ? " he asked.   " Most people who have led your life find the English spring trying.   You don't look quite as fit as when I first saw you."

" No.   I've been rather seedy this past week —headachy, loss of memory, stuffed-up brain and that sort of thing.   I expect it's the spring fret. I've seen a doctor and he doesn't worry about it."

" Who's your man ? "

" A chap Newhover in Wimpole Street."

He nodded.   " I've heard of him.   They tell me he's good."

" He has ordered me massage," I said boldly.
" That cures the headaches anyway."

" I'm glad to hear it."

Then he suddenly released my arm.

" I see Arbuthnot has gone abroad."

There was a coldness in his voice to which I
hastened to respond.

" So I saw in the papers," I said carelessly.
" He's a hopeless fellow. A pity, for he's able
enough ; but he won't stay put, and that makes
him pretty well useless."

" Do you care much for Arbuthnot ? "

" I used to," I replied shamelessly. " But till
the other day I hadn't seen him for years, and I
must say he has grown very queer. Didn't
you think he behaved oddly at the Thursday
dinner ? "

He shrugged his shoulders. " I wasn't much
taken by him. He's too infernally un-English. I
don't know how he got it, but there seems to be a
touch of the shrill Levantine in him. Compare
him with those fellows to-night. Even the Frenchmen—even Victor, though he's an American and
a Jew—are more our own way of thinking."

We were at the Club door, and as I stopped he
looked me full in the face.

" If I were you I wouldn't have much to do
with Arbuthnot," he said, and his tone was a
command. I grinned sheepishly, but my fingers
itched for his ears.

I went to bed fuming. This new possessory
attitude, this hint of nigger-driving, had suddenly

made me hate Medina. I had been unable to set down the hypnotist business clearly to his account, and, even if I had been certain, I was inclined to think it only the impertinent liberty of a faddist— a thing which I hotly resented but which did not arouse my serious dislike. But now—to feel that he claimed me as his man, because he thought, no doubt, that he had established some unholy power over me—that fairly broke my temper. And his abuse of Sandy put the lid on it—abuse to which I had been shamefully compelled to assent. Levantine, by gad! I swore that Sandy and I would make him swallow that word before he was much older. I couldn't sleep for thinking about it. By this time I was perfectly willing to believe that Medina was up to any infamy, and I was resolved that in him and him alone lay the key to the riddle of the three hostages. But all the time I was miserably conscious that if I suggested such an idea to any one except Sandy I should be set down as a lunatic. I could see that the man's repute was as solidly planted as the British Constitution.

Next morning I went to see Macgillivray. I explained that I had not been idle, that I had been pursuing lines of my own, which I thought more hopeful than his suggestion of getting alongside the Shropshire squire. I said I had nothing as yet to report, and that I didn't propose to give him the faintest notion of what I was after till I had secured some results. But I wanted his help, and I wanted his very best men.

"Glad to see you've got busy, Dick," he said. "I await your commands."

"I want a house watched. No. 4 Palmyra Square, up in North London. So far as I know it is occupied by a woman, who purports to be a Swedish masseuse and calls herself Madame Breda, one or more maids, and an odd-looking little girl. I want you to have a close record kept of the people who go there, and I want especially to know who exactly are the inmates of the house and who are the most frequent visitors. It must be done very cautiously, for the people must have no suspicion that they are being spied on."

He wrote down the details.

"Also I want you to find out the antecedents of Medina's butler."

He whistled. "Medina. Dominick Medina, you mean?"

"Yes. Oh, I'm not suspecting *him*." We both laughed, as if at a good joke. "But I should like to hear something about his butler, for reasons which I'm not yet prepared to give you. He answers to the name of Odell, and has the appearance of an inferior prize-fighter. Find out all you can about his past, and it mightn't be a bad plan to have him shadowed. You know Medina's house in Hill Street. But for Heaven's sake, let it be done tactfully."

"I'll see to that for my own sake. I don't want head-lines in the evening papers—'House of Member of Parliament Watched. Another Police Muddle.'"

"Also, could you put together all you can get about Medina? It might give me a line on Odell."

"Dick," he said solemnly, "are you growing fantastic?"

"Not a bit of it. You don't imagine I'm ass enough to think there's anything shady about Medina. He and I have become bosom friends, and I like him enormously. Everybody swears by him, and so do I. But I have my doubts about Mr. Odell, and I would like to know just how and where Medina picked him up. He's not the ordinary stamp of butler." It seemed to me very important to let no one but Sandy into the Medina business at present, for our chance lay in his complete confidence that all men thought well of him.

"Right," said Macgillivray. "It shall be done. Go your own way, Dick. I won't attempt to dictate to you. But remember that the thing is desperately serious, and that the days are slipping past. We're in April now, and you have only till midsummer to save three innocent lives."

I left his office feeling very solemn, for I had suddenly a consciousness of the shortness of time and the magnitude of the job which I had not yet properly begun. I cudgelled my brains to think of my next step. In a few days I should again visit Dr. Newhover, but there was not likely to be much assistance there. He might send me back to Palmyra Square, or I might try to make an appointment with Madame Breda myself, invent-

ing some new ailment ; but I would only find the
same old business, which would get me no further
forward. As I viewed it, the Newhover and
Palmyra Square episodes had been used only to
test my submission to Medina's influence, and it
was to Medina that I must look for further light.
It was a maddening job to sit and wait and tick
off the precious days on the calendar, and I longed
to consult with Sandy. I took to going down to
Fosse for the day, for the sight of Mary and Peter
John somehow quieted my mind and fixed my
resolution. It was a positive relief when at the
end of the week Medina rang me up and asked me
to luncheon.

We lunched at his house, which, seen on a
bright April day, was a wonderful treasury of
beautiful things. It was not the kind of house I
fancied myself, being too full of museum pieces,
and all the furniture strictly correct according to
period. I like rooms in which there is a pleasant
jumble of things, and which look as if homely
people had lived in them for generations. The
dining-room was panelled in white, with a Vandyck
above the mantelpiece and a set of gorgeous
eighteenth-century prints on the walls. At the
excellent meal Medina as usual drank water, while
I obediently sampled an old hock, an older port,
and a most prehistoric brandy. Odell was in
attendance, and I had a good look at him—his
oddly shaped head, his flat sallow face, the bunches
of black eyebrow above his beady eyes. I calculated that if I saw him again I would not fail to

recognize him. We never went near the library on the upper floor, but sat after luncheon in a little smoking-room at the back of the hall, which held my host's rods and guns in glass cabinets, and one or two fine heads of deer and ibex.

I had made up my mind, as I walked to Hill Street, that I was going to convince Medina once and for all of the abjectness of my surrender. He should have proof that I was clay in his hands, for only that way would he fully reveal himself. I detested the job, and as I walked through the pleasant crisp noontide I reflected with bitterness that I might have been fishing for salmon in Scotland, or, better still, cantering with Mary over the Cotswold downs.

All through luncheon I kept my eyes fixed on him like a dog's on his master. Several times I wondered if I were not overdoing it, but he seemed to accept my homage as quite natural. I had thought when I first met him that the man had no vanity ; now I saw that he had mountains of it, that he was all vanity, and that his public modesty was only a cloak to set off his immense private conceit. He unbent himself, his whole mind was in undress, and behind the veneer of good-fellowship I seemed to see a very cold arrogant soul. Nothing worse, though that was bad enough. He was too proud to boast in words, but his whole attitude was one long brag. He was cynical about everything, except, as I suspected, his private self-worship. The thing would have been monstrously indecent, if it had not been done with such con-

summate skill.  Indeed I found my part easy to
play, for I was deeply impressed and had no
difficulty in showing it.

The odd thing was that he talked a good deal
about myself.  He seemed to take pains to rout
out the codes and standards, the points of honour
and points of conduct, which somebody like me
was likely to revere, and to break them down with
his cynicism.  I felt that I was looking on at an
attempt, which the Devil is believed to specialize in,
to make evil good and good evil. . . . Of course
I assented gladly.  Never had master a more
ready disciple. . . . He broke down, too, my
modest ambitions.  A country life, a wife and
family—he showed that they were too trivial for
more than a passing thought.  He flattered me
grossly, and I drank it all in with a silly face.  I
was fit for bigger things, to which he would show
me the way.  He sketched some of the things—
very flattering they were and quite respectable,
but somehow they seemed out of the picture when
compared to his previous talk.  He was clearly
initiating me step by step into something for which
I was not yet fully ready. . . . I wished Sandy
could have seen me sitting in Medina's armchair,
smoking one of his cigars, and agreeing to everything he said like a schoolgirl who wants to keep
on the good side of her schoolmistress.  And yet
I didn't find it difficult, for the man's talk was
masterly and in its way convincing, and, while
my mind repudiated it, it was easy for my tongue
to assent.  He was in a prodigious good-humour,

and he was kindly, as a keeper is kind to a well-broken dog.

On the doorstep I stammered my thanks. " I wish I could tell you what knowing you means to me. It's—it's far the biggest thing in my life. What I mean to say is——" the familiar patois of the tongue-tied British soldier.

He looked at me with those amazing eyes of his, no kindness in them, only patronage and proprietorship. I think he was satisfied that he had got some one who would serve him body and soul.

I, too, was satisfied, and walked away feeling more cheerful than I had done for days. Surely things would begin to move now, I thought. At the Club, too, I got encouragement in the shape of a letter from Sandy. It bore a French postmark which I could not decipher, and it was the merest scribble, but it greatly heartened me.

" I have made progress," it ran, " but I have still a lot to do and we can't talk to each other yet awhile. But I shall have to send you letters occasionally, which you must burn on receipt. I shall sign them with some letter of the Greek alphabet— no, you wouldn't recognize that—with the names of recent Derby winners. Keep our affair secret as the grave—don't let in a soul, not even Mac. And for God's sake stick close to M. and serve him like a slave."

There wasn't much in it, but it was hopeful, though the old ruffian didn't seem in a hurry to come home. I wondered what on earth he had found out—something solid, I judged, for he didn't talk lightly of making progress.

That evening I had nothing to do, and after dinner I felt too restless to sit down to a pipe and book. There was no one in the Club I wanted to talk to, so I sallied forth to another pot-house to which I belonged, where there was a chance of finding some of the younger and cheerier generation. Sure enough the first man I saw there was Archie Roylance, who greeted me with a whoop and announced that he was in town for a couple of days to see his doctor. He had had a bad fall steeplechasing earlier in the year, when he had all but broken his neck, but he declared that he was perfectly fit again except for some stiffness in his shoulder muscles. He was as lame as a duck from his flying smash just before the Armistice, but all the same he got about at a surprising pace. Indeed, out of cussedness he walked more than he used to do in the old days, and had taken to deer-stalking with enthusiasm. I think I have mentioned that he was my partner in the tenancy of Machray forest.

I proposed that we should go to a music-hall or cut into the second act of some play, but Archie had another idea. One of his fads was to be an amateur of dancing, though he had never been a great performer before his smash and would never dance again. He said he wanted to see the latest fashions, and suggested that we should go for an hour to a small (and he added, select) club somewhere in Marylebone, of which he believed he was a member. It bore an evil reputation, he said, for there was a good deal of high play, and the licensing laws were not regarded, but it was the place to see the best dancing. I made no objection, so we strolled up Regent Street in that season of comparative peace when busy people have gone home and the idle are still shut up in theatres and restaurants.

It was a divine April night, and I observed that I wished I were in a better place to enjoy spring weather. " I've just come from a Scotch moor," said Archie. " Lord ! the curlews are makin' a joyful noise. That is the bird for my money. Come back with me, Dick, on Friday and I'll teach you a lot of things. You're a wise man, but you might be a better naturalist."

I thought how much I would have given to be able to accept, as the light wind blew down Langham Place. Then I wished that this job would take me out of town into fresh air, where I could get some exercise. The result was that I was in a baddish temper when we reached our destination, which was in one of the streets near Fitzroy Square. The place proved to be about as hard to get into as the Vatican. It took a long harangue and a tip from Archie to persuade the doorkeeper that we were of the right brand of disreputability to be admitted. Finally we found ourselves in a room with sham Chinese decorations, very garishly lit, with about twenty couples dancing, and about twenty more sitting drinking at little tables.

We paid five shillings apiece for a liqueur, found a table and took notice of the show. It seemed to me a wholly rotten and funereal business. A nigger band, looking like monkeys in uniform, pounded out some kind of barbarous jingle, and sad-faced marionettes moved to it. There was no gaiety or devil in that dancing, only a kind of bored perfection. Thin young men with rabbit heads and hair brushed straight back from their brows, who I suppose were professional dancing partners, held close to their breasts women of every shape and age, but all alike in having dead eyes and masks for faces, and the *macabre* procession moved like automata to the niggers' rhythm. I daresay it was all very wonderful, but I was not built by Providence to appreciate it.

" I can't stand much more of this," I told Archie.

" It's no great shakes. But there are one or two high-class performers. Look at that girl dancing with the young Jew—the one in green."

I looked and saw a slim girl, very young apparently, who might have been pretty but for the way her face was loaded with paint and the preposterous style in which her hair was dressed. Little though I know of dancing, I could see that she was a mistress of the art, for every motion was a delight to watch, and she made poetry out of that hideous ragtime. But her face shocked me. It was *blind*, if you understand me, as expressionless as a mummy, a kind of awful death-in-life. I wondered what kind of experience that poor soul had gone through to give her the stare of a sleep-walker.

As my eyes passed from her they fell on another figure that seemed familiar. I saw that it was Odell the butler, splendidly got up for his night out in dress clothes, white waistcoat, and diamond studs. There was no mistaking the pugilistic air of the fellow, now I saw him out of service; I had seen a dozen such behind the bars of sporting public-houses. He could not see me, but I had a fair view of him, and I observed that he also was watching the girl in green.

" Do you know who she is ? " I asked.

" Some professional. Gad, she can dance, but the poor child looks as if she found it a hard life. I'd rather like to talk to her."

But the music had stopped, and I could see that Odell had made a sign to the dancer. She came up to him as obediently as a dog, he said something to another man with him, a man with a black beard, and the three passed out at the farther door. A moment later I caught a glimpse of her with a cloak round her shoulders passing the door by which we had entered.

Archie laughed. "That big brute is probably her husband. I bet she earns the living of both by dancing at these places, and gets beaten every night. I would say my prayers before taking on that fellow in a scrap."

# CHAPTER VIII

## THE BLIND SPINNER

I LOOK back upon those days of waiting as among the beastliest of my life. I had the clearest conviction now that Medina was the key of the whole puzzle, but as yet I had found out nothing worth mentioning, and I had to wait like the sick folk by the pool of Bethesda till something troubled the waters. The only thing that comforted me was the fine old-fashioned dislike to the man which now possessed me. I couldn't pretend to understand more than a fragment of him, but what I understood I detested. I had been annexed by him as a slave, and every drop of free blood in my veins was in revolt; but I was also resolved to be the most docile slave that ever kissed the ground before a tyrant. Some day my revenge would come, and I promised myself that it would be complete. Meantime I thanked Heaven that he had that blind spot of vanity which would prevent him seeing the cracks in my camouflage.

For the better part of a week we were very little separate. I lunched with him two days out of three, and we motored more than once down to

Brighton for fresh air. He took me to a dinner he gave at the House of Commons to a Canadian statesman who was over on a visit, and he made me accompany him to a very smart dance at Lady Amysfort's, and he got me invited to a week-end party at Wirlesdon because he was going there. I went through the whole programme dutifully and not unpleasurably. I must say he treated me admirably in the presence of other people—with a jolly affectionate friendliness, constantly asking for my opinion, and deferring to me and making me talk, so that the few people I met whom I had known before wondered what had come over me. Mary had a letter from a cousin of hers, who reported that I seemed to have got into society and to be making a big success of it—a letter she forwarded to me with a pencilled note of congratulation at the end. On these occasions I didn't find my task difficult, for I fell unconsciously under the man's spell and could easily play up to him. . . . But when we were alone his manner changed. Iron crept into his voice, and, though he was pleasant enough, he took a devil of a lot for granted, and the note of authority grew more habitual. After such occasions I used to go home grinding my teeth. I never had a worse job than to submit voluntarily to that insolent protection.

Repeatedly in my bedroom at the Club I tried to put together the meagre handful of ascertained facts, but they were like a lot of remnants of different jig-saw puzzles and nothing fitted in to

anything else. Macgillivray reported that so far
he had drawn a blank in the case of Odell; and
that the watchers at Palmyra Square had noted
very few visitors except tradesmen and organ-
grinders. Nothing resembling a gentleman had
been seen to enter or leave, so it appeared that my
estimate of Madame Breda's flourishing business
was wrong. A woman frequently went out and
returned, never walking but always in a taxi or
a motor-car—probably the same woman, but so
hooded and wrapped up as to make details difficult
to be clear about. There were a host of little
notes—coal or firewood had been delivered one
day; twice the wrapped-up lady had gone out in
the evening, to come back in a couple of hours,
but mostly she made her visits abroad in daylight;
the household woke late and retired to bed early;
once or twice a sound like weeping had been
heard, but it might have been the cat. Altogether
it was a poor report, and I concluded that I was
either barking up the wrong tree, or that Macgillivray's agents were a pretty useless crowd.

For the rest, what had I? A clear and well-
founded suspicion of Medina. But of what?
Only that he was behaving towards me in a way
that I resented, that he dabbled in an ugly brand
of hypnotism, and that the more I saw of him the
less I liked him. I knew that his public repute
was false, but I had no worse crime to accuse him
of than vanity. He had a butler who had been a
prize-fighter, and who had a taste for night clubs.
I remember I wrote all this down, and sat staring

blankly at it, feeling how trivial it was. Then I wrote down the six-line jingle and stared at that too, and I thought of the girl, and the young man, and the small boy who liked birds and fishing. I hadn't a scrap of evidence to link up Medina with that business, except that Tom Greenslade believed that he had got from him the three facts which appeared more or less in the rhyme; but Tom might be mistaken, or Medina might have learned them in some perfectly innocent way. I hadn't enough evidence to swing a cat on. But yet—the more I thought of Medina the more dark and subtle his figure loomed in my mind. I had a conviction, on which I would have staked my life, that if I stuck to him I would worry out some vital and damning truth; so, with no very lively or cheerful hope, but with complete certainty, I resolved for the hundredth time to let logic go and back my fancy.

As in duty bound I paid another visit to Dr. Newhover. He received me casually, and appeared to have forgotten about my case till he looked up his diary.

"Ah yes, you saw Madame Breda," he said. "I have her report. Your headaches are cured but you are still a little shaky? Yes, please. Take off your coat and waistcoat."

He vetted me very thoroughly, and then sat down in his desk-chair and tapped his eyeglasses on his knee.

"You are better, much better, but you are not cured. That will take time and care. and lies, of course, in your own hands. You are leading a quiet life ? Half town, half country—it is probably the best plan. Well, I don't think you can improve on that."

"You said something about fishing in Norway when I was here last."

"No, on the whole I don't recommend it. Your case is slightly different from what I at first supposed."

"You are a fisherman yourself ? " I said.

He admitted that he was, and for a minute or two spoke more like a human being. He always used a two-piece Castle-Connell rod, though he granted it was a cumbrous thing to travel with. For flies he swore by Harlows—certainly the best people for Norwegian flies. He thought that there was a greater difference between Norwegian rivers than most people imagined, and Harlows understood that.

He concluded by giving me some simple instructions about diet and exercise.

"If my headaches return, shall I go back to Madame Breda ? " I asked.

He shook his head. "Your headaches won't return."

I paid him his fee, and, as I was leaving, I asked if he wanted to see me again.

"I don't think it necessary. At any rate not till the autumn. I may have to be out of London myself a good deal this summer. Of course if you should find the *malaise* recurring, which I do not anticipate, you must come and see me. If I am out of town, you can see my colleague." He scribbled a name and address on a sheet of paper.

I left the house feeling considerably puzzled. Dr. Newhover, who on my first visit had made a great to-do about my health, seemed now to want to be quit of me. His manner was exactly that of a busy doctor dealing with a *malade imaginaire*. The odd thing was that I was really beginning to feel rather seedy, a punishment for my former pretence. It may have been the reaction of my mental worry, but I had the sort of indefinite out-of-sorts feeling which I believe precedes an attack of influenza. Only I had hitherto been immune from influenza.

That night I had another of Sandy's communications, a typed half-sheet with a Paris postmark. "*Keep close to M.*," it ran. "*Do everything he wants. Make it clear that you have broken for ever with me. This is desperately important.*" It was signed "Buchan," a horse which Sandy seemed to think had been a Derby winner. He knew no more about racing than I knew of Chinese.

Next morning I woke with a bad taste in my mouth and a feeling that I had probably a bout of malaria due me. Now I had had no malaria since the autumn of '17, and I didn't like the prospect of the revisitation. However, as the day wore on, I felt better, and by midday I concluded I was not going to be ill. But all the same I was as jumpy as a cat in a thunderstorm. I had the odd sense of anticipation which I used to have before a battle, a lurking excitement by no means pleasant,—not exactly apprehension, but first cousin to it. It made me want to see Medina, as if there was something between him and me that I ought to get over.

All afternoon this dentist-anteroom atmosphere hung about me, and I was almost relieved when about five o'clock I got a telephone message from Hill Street asking me to come there at six. I went round to the Bath Club and had a swim and a shampoo, and then started for the house. On the way there I had tremors in my legs and a coldness in the pit of the stomach which brought back my childish toothaches. Yes, that was it. I felt exactly like a small boy setting off with dreadful anticipation to have a tooth drawn, and not all my self-contempt could cure me of my funk. The house when I reached it seemed larger and lonelier than ever, and the April evening had darkened down to a scurry of chill dusty winds under a sky full of cloud.

Odell opened the door to me, and took me to the back of the hall, where I found a lift which I had not known existed. We went up to the top of the house, and I realized that I was about to enter again the library where before I had so strangely spent the midnight hours.

The curtains were drawn, shutting out the bleak spring twilight, and the room was warmed by, and had for its only light, a great fire of logs. I smelt more than wood smoke; there was peat burning among the oak billets. The scent recalled, not

the hundred times when I had sniffed peat-reek
in happy places, but the flavour of the room in
Palmyra Square when I had lain with bandaged
eyes and felt light fingers touch my face. I had
suddenly a sense that I had taken a long stride
forward, that something fateful was about to
happen, and my nervousness dropped from me
like a cloak.

Medina was standing before the hearth, but his
was not the figure that took my eyes. There was
another person in the room, a woman. She sat
in the high-backed chair which he had used on the
former night, and she sat in it as if it were a
throne. The firelight lit her face, and I saw that
it was very old, waxen with age, though the glow
made the wax rosy. Her dress was straight and
black like a gaberdine, and she had thick folds of
lace at her wrists and neck. Wonderful hair,
masses of it, was piled on her head, and it was
snow-white and fine as silk. Her hands were laid
on the arms of the chair, and hands more delicate
and shapely I have never seen, though they had
also the suggestion of a furious power, like the
talons of a bird of prey.

But it was the face that took away my breath.
I have always been a great admirer of the beauty
of old age, especially in women, but this was a
beauty of which I had never dreamed. It was a
long face, and the features were large, though
exquisitely cut and perfectly proportioned. Usually in an old face there is a certain loosening of
muscles or blurring of contours, which detracts

from sheer beauty but gives another kind of
charm.  But in this face there was no blurring or
loosening ; the mouth was as firm, the curve of
the chin as rounded, the arch of the eyes as triumphant as in some proud young girl.

And then I saw that the eyes which were looking
at the fire were the most remarkable things of all.
Even in that half-light I could see that they were
brightly, vividly blue.  There was no film or
blearing to mar their glory.  But I saw also that
they were sightless.   How I knew it I do not know,
for there was no physical sign of it, but my conviction was instantaneous and complete.  These
starlike things were turned inward.  In most blind
people the eyes are like marbles, dead windows in
an empty house ; but—how shall I describe it ?—
these were blinds drawn in a room which was full
of light and movement, stage curtains behind
which some great drama was always set.  Blind
though they were, they seemed to radiate an
ardent vitality, to glow and flash like the soul
within.

I realized that it was the most wonderful face
of a woman I had ever looked on.  And I realized
in the same moment that I hated it, that the
beauty of it was devilish, and the soul within was
on fire with all the hatred of Hell.

"Hannay," I heard Medina's voice, "I have
brought you here because I wish to present you to
my mother."

I behaved just like somebody in a play.  I
advanced to her chair, lifted one of the hands, and

put it to my lips. That seemed to me the right thing to do. The face turned towards me, and broke into a smile, the kind of smile you may see on the marble of a Greek goddess.

The woman spoke to Medina in a tongue which was strange to me, and he replied. There seemed to be many questions and answers, but I did not trouble to try to catch a word I knew. I was occupied with the voice. I recognized in it those soft tones which had crooned over me as I lay in the room in Palmyra Square. I had discovered who had been the third person in that scene.

Then it spoke to me in English, with that odd lilting accent I had tried in vain to trace.

" You are a friend of Dominick, and I am glad to meet you, Sir Richard Hannay. My son has told me about you. Will you bring a chair and sit close to me ? "

I pulled up a long low armchair, so long and low that the sitter was compelled almost to recline. My head was on a level with the hand which lay on the arm of her chair. Suddenly I felt that hand laid on my head, and I recognized her now by touch as well as voice.

" I am blind, Sir Richard," she said, " so I cannot see my son's friends. But I long to know how they look, and I have but one sense which can instruct me. Will you permit me to pass my hands over your face ? "

" You may do what you please, Madame," I said. " I would to God I could give you eyes."

" That is a pretty speech," she said. " You

might be one of my own people." And I felt the light fingers straying over my brow.

I was so placed that I was looking into the red heart of the fire, the one patch of bright light in the curtained room. I knew what I was in for, and, remembering past experience, I averted my eyes to the dark folios on the lowest shelves beyond the hearth. The fingers seemed to play a gentle tattoo on my temples, and then drew long soft strokes across my eyebrows. I felt a pleasant languor beginning to creep down my neck and spine, but I was fully prepared, and without much trouble resisted it. Indeed my mind was briskly busy, for I was planning how best to play my game. I let my head recline more and more upon the cushioned back of my chair, and I let my eyelids droop.

The gentle fingers were very thorough, and I had let myself sink back beyond their reach before they ceased.

" You are asleep," the voice said. " Now wake."

I was puzzled to know how to stage-manage that wakening, but she saved me the trouble. Her voice suddenly hissed like a snake's. " Stand up ! " it said. " Quick—on your life."

I scrambled to my feet with extreme energy, and stood staring at the fire, wondering what to do next.

" Look at your master," came the voice again, peremptory as a drill-sergeant's.

That gave me my cue. I knew where Medina was standing, and, in the words of the Bible, my eyes regarded him as a handmaiden regards her mistress.  I stood before him, dumb and dazed and obedient.

"Down," he cried.  "Down, on all-fours."

I did as I was bid, thankful that my job was proving so easy.

"Go to the door—no, on all-fours—open it twice, shut it twice, and bring me the paper-knife from the far table in your mouth."

I obeyed, and a queer sight I must have presented prancing across the room, a perfectly sane man behaving like a lunatic.

I brought the paper-knife, and remained dog-wise.  "Get up," he said, and I got up.

I heard the woman's voice say triumphantly, "He is well broken," and Medina laughed.

"There is yet the last test," he said.  "I may as well put him through it now.  If it fails, it means only that he needs more schooling.  He cannot remember, for his mind is now in my keeping.  There is no danger."

He walked up to me, and gave me a smart slap in the face.

I accepted it with Christian meekness.  I wasn't even angry.  In fact, I would have turned the other cheek in the Scriptural fashion, if it hadn't occurred to me that it might be over-acting.

Then he spat in my face.

That, I admit, tried me pretty high.  It was such a filthy Kaffir trick that I had some trouble in taking it resignedly.  But I managed it.  I kept my eyes on the ground, and didn't even get out my handkerchief to wipe my cheek till he had turned away.

"Well broken to heel," I heard him say. "It is strange how easily these flat tough English natures succumb to the stronger spirit. I have got a useful weapon in him, mother mine."

They paid no more attention to me than if I had been a piece of furniture, which, indeed, in their eyes I was. I was asleep, or rather awake in a phantasmal world, and I could not return to my normal life till they bade me. I could know nothing—so they thought—and remember nothing, except what they willed. Medina sat in my chair, and the woman had her hand on his head, and they talked as if they were alone in the desert. And all the while I was standing sheepishly on the rug, not daring to move, scarcely to breathe, lest I should give the show away.

They made a pretty picture—" The Prodigal's Return " or " The Old Folks at Home," by Simpkins, R.A., Royal Academy, 1887. No, by Heaven, there was no suggestion of that. It was a marvellous and tragic scene that I regarded. The fitful light of the fire showed figures of an antique beauty and dignity. The regal profile of the woman, her superb pose, and the soft eerie music of her voice were a world removed from vulgarity, and so was the lithe vigour and the proud face of the man. They were more like a king and queen in exile, decreeing the sea of blood which was to wash them back again. I realized for the first time that Medina might be damnable, but was also great. Yes, the man who had spat on me like a stable-boy had also something of the prince. I realized another thing. The woman's touch had flattened down the hair above his forehead, which he brushed square, and his head, outlined in the firelight against the white cushion, was as round as a football. I had suspected this when I first saw him, and now I was certain. What did a head like that portend? I had a vague remembrance that I had heard somewhere that it meant madness—at any rate degeneracy.

They talked rapidly and unceasingly, but the confounded thing was that I could hear very little of it. They spoke in low tones, and I was three yards off and daren't for my life move an inch nearer. Also they spoke for the most part in a language of which I did not know a word—it may have been Choctaw, but was probably Erse. If I had only comprehended that tongue I might there and then have learned all I wanted to know. But sometimes Medina talked English, though it seemed to me that the woman always tried to bring him back to the other speech. All I heard were broken sentences that horribly tantalized me.

My brain was cool and very busy. This woman was the Blind Spinner of the rhymes. No doubt of it. I could see her spinning beside a peat fire, nursing ancient hate and madness, and crooning forgotten poetry. "*Beside the Sacred Tree.*" Yggdrasil be hanged! I had it, it was Gospel Oak. Lord, what a fool I had been not to guess it before ! The satisfaction of having got one of the three conundrums dead right made me want to shout. These two harpies held the key to the whole riddle, and I had only to keep up my present character to solve it. They thought they were dealing with a hypnotized fool, and instead they had a peculiarly wide-awake, if rather slow and elderly, Englishman. I wished to Heaven I knew what they were saying. Sluicing out malice about my country, no doubt, or planning the ruin of our civilization for the sake of a neurotic dream.

Medina said something impatiently about "danger," as if his purpose were to reassure. Then I caught nothing for several minutes, till he laughed and repeated the word "*secundus*." Now I was looking for three people, and if there was a "*secundus*" there must have been a "*primus*," and possibly a "*tertius*."

"He is the least easy to handle," he said. "And it is quite necessary that Jason should come home. I have decided that the doctor must go out. It won't be for long—only till midsummer."

The date interested me acutely. So did what followed, for he went on :

"By midsummer they liquidate and disband. There is no fear that it won't succeed. We have the whip hand, remember. Trust me, all will go smoothly, and then we begin a new life. . . ."

I thought she sighed, and for the first time she spoke in English :

"I fear sometimes that you are forgetting your own land, Dominick."

He put up an arm and drew her head to his.

"Never, mother mine. It is our strength that we can seem to forget and still remember."

I was finding my stand on that hearth-rug extraordinarily trying. You see I had to keep perfectly rigid, for every now and then Medina would look towards me, and I knew that the woman had an ear like a hound. But my knees were beginning to shake with fatigue and my head to grow giddy, and I feared that, like the soldiers who stand guard round a royal bier, I might suddenly collapse. I did my best to struggle against the growing weakness, and hoped to forget it by concentrating all my attention on the fragments of talk.

"I have news for you," Medina was saying. "Kharama is in Europe and proposes to come to England."

"You will see him ? " I thought her voice had a trace of alarm in it.

"Most certainly. I would rather see him than any living man."

"Dominick, be careful. I would rather you confined yourself to our old knowledge. I fear these new things from the East."

He laughed. "They are as old as ours—older. And all knowledge is one. I have already drunk of his learning, and I must have the whole cup."

That was the last I heard, for at that moment I made my exit from the scene in a way which I could not have bettered by much cogitation. My legs suddenly gave under me, the room swam round, and I collapsed on the floor in a dead faint. I must have fallen heavily, for I knocked a leg off one of the little tables.

When I came to—which I suppose was a minute or two later—Odell was bathing my face, and Medina with a grave and concerned air was standing by with a brandy decanter.

"My dear fellow, you gave me a bad fright," he said, and his manner was that of the considerate friend. "You're not feeling ill?"

"I haven't been quite fit all day, and I suppose the hot room knocked me out. I say, I'm most awfully sorry for playing the fool like this. I've damaged your furniture, I'm afraid. I hope I didn't scare the lady."

"What lady?"

"Your mother."

He looked at me with a perfectly blank face, and I saw I had made a mistake.

"I beg your pardon—I'm still giddy. I've been dreaming."

He gave me a glass of brandy and tucked me into a taxi. Long before I got to the Club I was feeling all right, but my mind was in a fine turmoil. I had stumbled at last upon not one clue but many, and though they were confused enough, I hoped with luck to follow them out. I could hardly eat any dinner that night, and my brain was too unsettled to do any serious thinking. So I took a taxi up to Gospel Oak, and, bidding it wait for me, had another look at Palmyra Square. The place seemed to have been dead and decaying for centuries, seen in that windy moonless dark, and No. 4 was a shuttered tomb. I opened the gate and, after making sure that the coast was clear, stole round to the back-door where tradesmen called. There were some dilapidated outhouses, and the back garden, with rank grasses and obscene clothes-posts, looked like nothing so much as a neglected graveyard. In that house was the terrible blind Fate that span. As I listened, I heard from somewhere inside the sound of slow heart-broken sobs. I wondered if they came from the queer-looking little girl.

## CHAPTER IX

### I AM INTRODUCED TO STRONG MAGIC

THE first thing I did when I got up next morning was to pay a visit to Harlows, the fishing-tackle people. They knew me well enough, for I used to buy my rods there, and one of the assistants had been down to Fosse to teach Mary how to use a light split-cane. With him I embarked on a long talk about Norwegian rivers and their peculiarities, and very soon got his views on the best flies. I asked which river was considered to be the earliest, and was told in an ordinary season the Nirdal and the Skarso. Then I asked if he knew my friend Dr. Newhover. "He was in here yesterday afternoon," I was told. "He is going to the Skarso this year, and hopes to be on the water in the last week of April. Rather too soon in our opinion, though salmon have been caught in it as early as April 17th. By the end of the first week of May it should be all right." I asked a good deal more about the Skarso, and was told that it was best fished from Merdal at the head of the Merdalfjord. There were only about three miles of fishable water before the big foss, but every yard of it was good. I told him I had hoped to get a beat on the Leardal for June, but had had to give up the notion this year and intended to confine myself to Scotland. I bought a new reel, a quantity of sea-trout flies, and a little book about Norwegian fishing.

Then I went on to see Macgillivray, with whom I had made an appointment by telephone.

"I've come to ask your help," I told him. "I'm beginning to get a move on, but it's a ticklish business, and I must walk very warily. First of all, I want you to find out the movements of a certain Dr. Newhover of Wimpole Street. He is going to Norway some time in the next fortnight, to the Skarso to fish, and his jumping-off place will be Stavanger. Find out by which boat he takes a passage, and book me a berth in it also. I'd better have my old name, Cornelius Brand."

"You're not thinking of leaving England just now ?" he asked reproachfully.

"I don't know. I may have to go or I may not, but in any case I won't be long away. Anyhow, find out about Dr. Newhover. Now for the more serious business. Just about when have you settled to round up the gang ?"

"For the reasons I gave you it must be before midsummer. It is an infernally complicated job and we must work to a time-table. I had fixed provisionally the 20th of June."

"I think you'd better choose an earlier date."

"Why ?"

" Because the gang are planning themselves to liquidate by midsummer, and, if you don't hurry, you may draw the net tight and find nothing in it."

" Now how on earth did you find that out ? " he asked, and his usually impassive face was vivid with excitement.

" I can't tell you.  I found it out in the process of hunting for the hostages, and I give you my word it's correct."

" But you must tell me more.  If you have fresh lines on what you call my ' gang,' it may be desperately important for me to know."

" I haven't.  I've just the one fact, which I have given you.  Honestly, old man, I can't tell you anything more till I tell you everything. Believe me, I'm working hard."

I had thought the thing out, and had resolved to keep the Medina business to myself and Sandy. Our one chance with him was that he should be utterly unsuspecting, and even so wary a fellow as Macgillivray might, if he were told, create just that faint breath of suspicion that would ruin all.

He grunted, as if he were not satisfied.  " I suppose you must have it your own way.  Very well, we'll fix the 10th of June for *Der Tag*.  You realize, of course, that the round-up of all must be simultaneous—that's why it takes such a lot of *bandobast*.  By the way, you've got the same problem with the hostages.  You can't release one without the others, or the show is given away— not your show only, but mine.  You realize that ? "

" I do," I said, " and I realize that the moving

forward of your date narrows my time down to less than two months. If I succeed, I must wait till the very eve of your move. Not earlier, I suppose, than June 9th ? Assume I only find one of the three ? I wait till June 9th before getting him out of their clutches. Then you strike, and what happens to the other two ? "

He shrugged his shoulders. " The worst, I fear. You see, Dick, the gang I mean to crush and the people who hold the hostages are allied, but I take it they are different sets. I may land every member of my gang, and yet not come within speaking distance of the other lot. I don't know, but I'm pretty certain that even if we found the second lot we'd never be able to prove complicity between the two. The first are devilish deep fellows, but the second are great artists."

" All the same," I said, " I'm in hopes of finding at least one of the hostages, and that means some knowledge of the kidnappers."

" I must not ask, but I'd give my head to know how and where you're working. More power to you ! But I wonder if you'll ever get near the real prime fountain of iniquity."

" I wonder," I said, and took my leave.

I had been playing with sickness, and now it looked as if I was going to be punished by getting the real thing. For all the rest of that day I felt cheap, and in the evening I was positive I had a temperature. I thought I might have 'flu, so I went round after dinner to see a doctor whom I had known in France. He refused to admit the temperature. "What sort of life have you been leading these last weeks?" he asked; and when I told him that I had been hanging round London waiting on some tiresome business developments, he said that that was the whole trouble. "You're accustomed to an active life in fresh air and you've been stuffing in town, feeding too well and getting no exercise. Go home to-morrow and you'll be as right as a trivet."

"It would rather suit me to be sick for a spell —say a week."

He looked puzzled and then laughed.

"Oh, if you like I'll give you a chit to say you must go back to the country at once or I won't answer for the consequences."

"I'd like that, but not just yet. I'll ring you up when I want it. Meantime I can take it that there's nothing wrong with me?"

"Nothing that a game of squash and a little Eno won't cure."

"Well, when you send me that chit, say I've got to have a quiet week in bed at home—no visitors—regular rest cure."

"Right," he said. "It's a prescription that every son of Adam might follow with advantage four times a year."

When I got back to the Club I found Medina waiting for me. It was the first time he had visited me there, and I pretended to be delighted to see him—almost embarrassed with delight—and took him to the back smoking-room where I had talked with Sandy  I told him that I was out of sorts, and he was very sympathetic. Then, with a recollection of Sandy's last letter, I started out to blaspheme my gods. He commented on the snugness and seclusion of the little room, which for the moment we had to ourselves.

"It wasn't very peaceful when I was last in it," I said. "I had a row here with that lunatic Arbuthnot before he went abroad."

He looked up at the name.

"You mean you quarrelled. I thought you were old friends."

"Once we were. Now I never want to see the fellow again." I thought I might as well do the job thoroughly, though the words stuck in my throat.

He seemed pleased.

"I told you," he said, "that he didn't attract me."

"Attract!" I cried. "The man has gone entirely to the devil. He has forgotten his manners, his breeding, and everything he once possessed. He has lived so long among cringing Orientals that his head is swollen like a pumpkin. He wanted to dictate to me, and I said I would see him farther —and—oh well, we had the usual row. He's gone back to the East, which is the only place for him, and—no! I never want to clap eyes on him again."

There was a purr of satisfaction in his voice, for he believed, as I meant him to, that his influence over me had been strong enough to shatter an ancient friendship. "I am sure you are wise.

I have lived in the East and know something of its ways. There is the road of knowledge and the road of illusion, and Arbuthnot has chosen the second. . . . We are friends, Hannay, and I have much to tell you some day—perhaps very soon. I have made a position for myself in the world, but the figure which the world sees is only a little part of me. The only power is knowledge, and I have attained to a knowledge compared with which Arbuthnot's is the merest smattering."

I noticed that he had dropped the easy, well-bred, deprecating manner which I had first noted in him. He spoke to me now magisterially, arrogantly, almost pompously.

"There has never been a true marriage of East and West," he went on. "To-day we incline to put a false interpretation on the word Power. We think of it in material terms like money, or the control of great patches of inanimate nature. But it still means, as it has always meant, the control of human souls, and to him who acquires that everything else is added. How does such control arise? Partly by knowledge of the intricacies of men's hearts, which is a very different thing from the stock platitudes of the professional psychologists. Partly by that natural dominion of spirit which comes from the possession of certain human qualities in a higher degree than other men. The East has the secret knowledge, but, though it can lay down the practice, it cannot provide the practitioners. The West has the tools, but not the science of their use. There has never, as I have said, been a true marriage of East and West, but when there is, its seed will rule the world."

I was drinking this in with both ears, and murmuring my assent. Now at last I was to be given his confidence, and I prayed that he might be inspired to go on. But he seemed to hesitate, till a glance at my respectful face reassured him.

"The day after to-morrow a man will be in London, a man from the East, who is a great master of this knowledge. I shall see him, and you will accompany me. You will understand little, for you are only at the beginning, but you will be in the presence of wisdom."

I murmured that I should feel honoured.

"You will hold yourself free for all that day. The time will probably be the evening."

After that he left with the most perfunctory good-bye. I congratulated myself on having attained to just the kind of position I wanted—that of a disciple whose subjection was so much taken for granted that he was treated like a piece of furniture. From his own point of view Medina was justified; he must have thought the sub-conscious control so strong, after all the tests I had been through, that my soul was like putty in his hands.

Next day I went down to Fosse and told Mary to expect me back very soon for a day or two. She had never plagued me with questions, but something in my face must have told her that I was hunting a trail, for she asked me for news and looked as if she meant to have it. I admitted

that I had found out something, and said I would
tell her everything when I next came back. That
would only have been prudent, for Mary was a
genius at keeping secrets, and I wanted some
repository of my knowledge in case I got knocked
on the head.

When I returned to town I found another note
from Sandy, also from France, signed "Alan
Breck"—Sandy was terribly out with his Derby
winners. It was simply two lines imploring me
again to make Medina believe I had broken with
him and that he had gone east of Suez for good.

There was also a line from Macgillivray, saying
that Dr. Newhover had taken a passage on the
*Gudrun*, leaving Hull at 6.30 p.m. on the 21st,
and that a passage had been booked for C. Brand,
Esqre, by the same boat. That decided me, so
I wrote to my own doctor, asking for the chit he
had promised, to be dated the 19th. I was busy
with a plan, for it seemed to me that it was my
duty to follow up the one trail which presented
itself, though it meant letting the rest of the
business sleep. I longed more than I could say
for a talk with Sandy, who was now playing the
fool in France and sending me imbecile notes. I
also rang up Archie Roylance, and found to my
delight that he had not left town, for I ran him to
ground at the Travellers', and fixed a meeting for
next morning.

"Archie," I said, when we met, "I want to ask
a great favour from you. Are you doing anything
special in the next fortnight?"

He admitted that he had thought of getting back to Scotland to watch a pair of nesting green-shanks.

"Let the greenshanks alone, like a good fellow. I've probably got to go to Norway on the 21st, and I shall want to get home in the deuce of a hurry. The steamer's far too slow."

"Destroyer," he suggested.

"Hang it, this is not the War. Talk sense. I want an aeroplane, and I want you to fetch me."

Archie whistled long and loud.

"You're a surprisin' old bird, Dick. It's no joke bein' a pal of yours. . . . I daresay I could raise a bus all right. But you've got to chance the weather. And my recollection of Norway is that it's not very well provided with landin' places. What part do you favour?"

I told him the mouth of the Merdalfjord.

"Lord! I've been there," he said. "It's all as steep as the side of a house."

"Yes, but I've been studying the map, and there are some eligible little islands off the mouth, which look flattish from the contouring. I'm desperately serious, old man. I'm engaged on a job where failure means the loss of innocent lives. I'll tell you all about it soon, but meantime you must take my word for it."

I managed to get Archie suitably impressed, and even to interest him in the adventure, for he was never the man to lag behind in anything that included risk and wanted daring. He promised to see Hansen, who had been in his squadron and was believed to have flown many times across the North Sea.  As I left him I could see that he was really enormously cheered by the prospect, for if he couldn't watch his blessed birds, the next best thing was to have a chance of breaking his neck.

I had expected to be bidden by Medina to meet his necromancer in some den in the East End or some Bloomsbury lodging-house.  Judge of my surprise, then, when I was summoned to Claridge's for nine-thirty that evening.  When I got to the hotel it was difficult to believe that a place so bright and commonplace could hold any mystery. There was the usual dancing going on, and squads of people who had dined well were sitting around watching.  Medina was standing by a fireplace talking to a man who wore a long row of miniature medals and a star, and whom I recognized as Tom Machin, who had commanded a cavalry brigade in France.  Medina nodded casually to me, and Tom, whom I had not seen for years, made a great fuss.

" Regimental dinner," he explained.  " Came out for a moment to give instructions about my car.  Been telling Medina here of the dirty trick the Government have played on my old crowd. I say it's up to the few sahibs like him in that damned monkey-house at Westminster to make a row about it.  You back me up, Hannay.  What I say is . . ." and so on with all the eternal itera- tion of " abso-lutely " and " If you follow me " and " You see what I mean " of the incoherent British regular.

Medina gently disengaged himself. "Sorry, Tom, but I must be off now. You're dining with Burminster on Thursday, aren't you? We'll talk about that business then. I agree it's an infernal shame."

He signed to me and we went together to the lift. On the first floor, where the main suites are, a turbaned Indian waited for us in the corridor. He led us into a little anteroom, and then disappeared through big folding-doors. I wondered what kind of swell this Oriental necromancer must be who could take rooms like these, for the last time I had been in them was when they were occupied by a Crown Prince who wanted to talk to me about a certain little problem in Anatolia.

"You are about to see Kharama," Medina whispered, and there was an odd exaltation in his voice. "You do not know his name, but there are millions in the East who reverence it like that of a god. I last saw him in a hut in the wildest pass in the Karakoram, and now he is in this gilded hotel with the dance-music of the West jigging below. It is a parable of the unity of all Power."

The door was opened, and the servant beckoned us to enter. It was a large room furnished with the usual indifferent copies of French furniture—very hot and scented, just the kind of place where international financiers make their deals over liqueur brandy and big cigars, or itinerant stars of the cinema world receive their friends. Bright, hard, and glossy, you would have said that no vulgarer environment could be found. . . . And yet after the first glance I did not feel its commonness, for it was filled with the personality of the man who sat on a couch at the far end. I realized that here was one who carried with him his own prepotent atmosphere, and who could transform his surroundings, whether it was a Pamir hut or a London restaurant.

To my surprise he was quite young. His hair was hidden by a great turban, but the face was smooth and hairless, and the figure, so far as I could judge, had not lost the grace of youth. I had imagined some one immensely venerable and old with a beard to his girdle, or, alternately, an obese babu with a soft face like a eunuch. I had forgotten that this man was of the hills. To my amazement he wore ordinary evening dress, well-cut, too, I thought, and over it a fine silk dressing-gown. He had his feet tucked up on the couch, but he did not sit cross-legged. At our entrance he slightly inclined his head, while we both bowed. Medina addressed him in some Indian tongue, and he replied, and his voice was like the purr of a big cat.

He motioned us to sit down, looking not so much at us as through us, and while Medina spoke I kept my eyes on his face. It was the thin, high-boned, high-bred face of the hillman; not the Mongolian type, but that other which is like an Arab, the kind of thing you can see in Pathan troops. And yet, though it was as hard as flint and as fierce as Satan, there was a horrid feline softness in it, like that of a man who would never need to strike a blow in anger, since he could win his way otherwise. The brow was straight and heavy, such as I had always associated with mathematical talent, and broader than is common with Orientals. The eyes I could not see, for he kept them half shut, but there was something uncanny in the way they were chased in his head, with an odd slant the opposite from what you see in the Chinaman. His mouth had a lift at each corner as if he were perpetually sneering, and yet there was a hint of humour in the face, though it was as grave as a stone statue.

I have rarely seen a human being at once so handsome and so repulsive, but both beauty and horror were merged in the impression of ruthless power. I had been sceptical enough about this Eastern mage, as I had been sceptical about Medina's arts, because they had failed with me. But as I looked on that dark countenance I had a vision of a world of terrible knowledge, a hideousness like an evil smell, but a power like a blasting wind or a pestilence. . . . Somehow Sandy's talk at the Thursday Club dinner came back to me, about the real danger to the world lying in the constraint of spirit over spirit. This swarthy brute was the priest of that obscene domination, and I had an insane desire there and then to hammer him into pulp.

He was looking at me, and seemed to be asking a question to which Medina replied. I fancy he was told that I was a *chela*, or whatever was the right name, a well-broken and submissive disciple.

Then to my surprise he spoke in English—good English, with the *chi-chi* accent of the Indian.

" You have followed far in the path of knowledge, brother. I did not think a son of the West could have travelled so far and so soon. You have won two of the three keys to Mastery, if you can make a man forget his past, and begin life anew subject to your will. But what of the third key ? "

I thought Medina's voice had a tinge of disappointment. " It is the third key which I look for, master. What good is it to wipe out the past and establish my control if it is only temporary ? I want the third key, to lock the door, so that I have my prisoner safe for ever. Is there such a key ? "

" The key is there, but to find it is not easy. All control tends to grow weak and may be broken by an accident, except in the case of young children, and some women, and those of feeble mind."

" That I know," said Medina almost pettishly. " But I do not want to make disciples only of babes, idiots, and women."

" Only some women, I said. Among our women perhaps all, but among Western women, who are hard as men, only the softer and feebler."

" That is my trouble. I wish to control for ever, and to control without constant watching on my part. I have a busy life and time is precious. Tell me, master, is there a way ? "

I listened to this conversation with feelings of genuine horror. Now I saw Medina's plans, and

I realized that he and he alone was at the bottom of the kidnapping. I realized, too, how he had dealt with the three hostages, and how he proposed to deal. Compared to him a murderer was innocent, for a murderer only took life, while he took the soul. I hated him and that dark scoundrel more intensely than I think I have ever hated man; indeed it was only by a great effort that I checked myself from clutching the two by the throat. The three stories, which had been half forgotten and overlaid by my recent experiences, returned sharp and clear to my memory. I saw again Victor's haggard face, I heard Sir Arthur Warcliff's voice break; and my wrath rose and choked me. This stealing of souls was the worst infamy ever devised by devils among mankind. I must have showed my emotion, but happily the two had no eyes for me.

"There is a way, a sure way," the Indian was saying, and a wicked half-smile flitted over his face. "But it is a way which, though possible in my own country, may be difficult in yours. I am given to understand that your police are troublesome, and you have a public repute which it is necessary to cherish. There is another way which is slower, but which is also sure, if it is boldly entered upon."

The sage seemed to open his half-shut eyes, and I thought I saw the opaque brightness which comes from drug-taking.

"Him whom you would make your slave," he said, "you first strip of memory, and then attune

to your own will.   To keep him attuned you must
be with him often and reinforce the control.   But
this is burdensome, and if the slave be kept apart
and seen rarely the influence will ebb—except, as
I have said, in the case of a young child.   There
is a way to rivet the bondage, and it is this.   Take
him or her whom you govern into the same life
as they have been accustomed to live before, and
there, among familiar things, assert your control.
Your influence will thus acquire the sanction of
familiarity—for though the conscious memory has
gone, the unconscious remains—and presently will
be a second nature."

"I see," said Medina abstractedly.   "I had
already guessed as much.   Tell me, master, can
the dominion, once it is established, be shaken
off ? "

"It cannot save by the will of him who exer-
cises it.   Only the master can release."

After that they spoke again in the foreign tongue
of I know not what devilry.   It seemed to me that
the sage was beginning to tire of the interview, for
he rang a bell and when the servant appeared gave
him some rapid instructions.   Medina rose, and
kissed the hand which was held out to him, and I,
of course, followed suit.

"You stay here long, master ? " he asked.

"Two days.   Then I have business in Paris and
elsewhere.   But I return in May, when I will
summon you again.   Prosper, brother.   The God
of wisdom befriend you."

We went downstairs to the dancing and the

supper parties. The regimental dinner was breaking up, and Tom Machin was holding forth in the hall to a knot of be-medalled friends. I had to say something to Medina to round off the evening, and the contrast of the two scenes seemed to give me a cue. As we were putting on our coats I observed that it was like coming from light to darkness. He approved. "Like falling from a real world into shadows," he said.

He evidently wished to follow his own thoughts, for he did not ask me to walk home with him. I, too, had a lot to think about. When I got back to the Club I found a note signed "Spion Kop," and with an English postmark. "*Meet me*," it said, "*on the 21st for breakfast at the inn called 'The Silent Woman' on the Fosse Way as you go over from Colne to Windrush. I have a lot to tell you.*"

I thanked Heaven that Sandy was home again, though he chose fantastic spots for his assignations. I, too, had something to say to him. For that evening had given me an insight into Medina's mind, and, what was more, the glimmerings of a plan of my own.

# CHAPTER X

## CONFIDENCES AT A WAYSIDE INN

MY first impulse was to go to Macgillivray about this Kharama fellow, who I was certain was up to mischief. I suspected him of some kind of political intrigue ; otherwise what was he doing touring the capitals of Europe and putting up at expensive hotels ? But on second thoughts I resolved to let the police alone. I could not explain about Kharama without bringing in Medina, and I was determined to do nothing which would stir a breath of suspicion against him. But I got the chit from my doctor, recommending a week's rest, and I went round to see Medina on the morning of the 19th. I told him I had been feeling pretty cheap for some days, and that my doctor ordered me to go home and go to bed. He didn't look pleased, so I showed him the doctor's letter, and made a poor mouth, as if I hated the business, but was torn between my inclinations and my duty. I think he liked my producing that chit, like a second-lieutenant asking for leave ; anyhow he made the best of it, and was quite sympathetic.

"I'm sorry you're going out of town," he said, "for I want you badly. But it's as well to get quite fit, and to lie up for a week ought to put you all right. When am I to expect you back?" I told him that without fail I would be in London on the 29th. "I'm going to disappear into a monastery," I said. "Write no letters, receive none, not at home to visitors, only sleep and eat. I can promise you that my wife will watch me like a dragon."

Then I hunted up Archie Roylance, whom I found on the very top of his form. He had seen Hansen, and discovered that on the island of Flacksholm, just off the mouth of the Merdalfjord, there was good landing. It was a big flattish island with a loch in the centre, and entirely un-inhabited except for a farm at the south end. Archie had got a machine, a Sopwith, which he said he could trust, and I arranged with him to be at Flacksholm not later than the 27th, and to camp there as best he could. He was to keep watch by day for a motor-boat from the Merdal-fjord, and at night if he saw a green light he was to make for it. I told him to take ample supplies, and he replied that he wasn't such a fool as to neglect the commissariat. He said he had been to Fortnum and Mason and was going to load up with liqueurs and *delicatessen*. "Take all the clothes you've got, Dick," he added. "It will be perishing cold in those parts at this time of year." He arranged, too, to cable through Hansen for a motor-launch to be ready at Stavanger for a Mr.

Brand who was due by the Hull steamer on the morning of the 23rd. If I had to change my plans I was to wire him at once.

That evening I went down to Fosse a little easier in my mind. It was a blessed relief to get out of London and smell clean air, and to reflect that for a week at any rate I should be engaged in a more congenial job than loafing about town. I found Peter John in the best of health and the Manor garden a glory of spring flowers.

I told Mary that I was ordered by my doctor to go to bed for a week and take a rest cure.

" Dick," she asked anxiously, " you're not ill, are you ? "

" Not a bit, only a trifle stale. But officially I'm to be in bed for a week and not a blessed soul is to be allowed to come near me. Tell the servants, please, and get the cook on to invalid dishes. I'll take Paddock into my confidence, and he'll keep up a show of waiting on me."

" A show ? "

" Yes ; for, you see, I'm going to put in a week in Norway—that is, unless Sandy has anything to say against it."

" But I thought Colonel Arbuthnot was still abroad ? "

" So he is—officially. But I'm going to break-fast with him the day after to-morrow at ' The Silent Woman '—you remember, the inn we used to have supper at last summer when I was fishing the Colne."

" Dick," she said solemnly, " isn't it time

you told me a little more about what you're doing ? "

" I think it is," I agreed, and that night after dinner I told her everything.

She asked a great many questions, searching questions, for Mary's brain was about twice as good as mine. Then she sat pondering for a long time with her chin on her hand.

" I wish I had met Mr. Medina," she said at last. " Aunt Claire and Aunt Doria know him. . . . I am afraid of him, terribly afraid, and I think I should be less afraid if I could just see him once. It is horrible, Dick, and you are fighting with such strange weapons. Your only advantage is that you're such a gnarled piece of oak. I wish I could help. It's dreadful to have to wait here and be tortured by anxiety for you, and to be thinking all the time of those poor people. I can't get the little boy out of my head. I often wake in a terror, and have to go up to the night-nursery to hug Peter John. Nanny must think I'm mad. . . . I suppose you're right to go to Norway ? "

" I see no other way. We have a clue to the whereabouts of one of the hostages—I haven't a notion which. I must act on that, and besides, if I find one it may give me a line on the others."

" There will still be two lost," she said, " and the time grows fearfully short. You are only one man. Can you not get helpers ? Mr. Macgilli-vray ? "

" No. He has his own job, and to let him into mine would wreck both."

"Well, Colonel Arbuthnot? What is he doing?"

"Oh, Sandy's busy enough, and, thank God! he's back in England. I'll know more about his game when I see him, but you may be sure it's a deep one. While I'm away Sandy will be working all the time."

"Do you know, I have never met him. Couldn't I see him some time when you're away? It would be a great comfort to me. And, Dick, can't I help somehow? We've always shared everything, even before we were married, and you know I'm dependable."

"Indeed I do, my darling," I said. "But I can't see how you can help—yet. If I could, I would inspan you straight off, for I would rather have you with me than a regiment."

"It's the poor little boy. I could endure the rest, but the thought of him makes me crazy. Have you seen Sir Arthur?"

"No, I have avoided him. I can stand the sight of Victor and the Duke, but I swear I shall never look Sir Arthur in the face unless I can hand him over his son."

Then Mary got up and stood over me like a delivering angel.

"It is going to be done," she cried. "Dick, you must never give up. I believe in my heart we shall win. We must win or I shall never be able to kiss Peter John again with a quiet mind. Oh, I wish—I wish I could do something!"

I don't think Mary slept that night, and next

morning she was rather pale and her eyes had that funny long-sighted look that they had had when I said good-bye to her at Amiens in March '18, before going up to the line.

I spent a blissful day with her and Peter John wandering round our little estate. It was one of those April days which seem to have been borrowed from late May, when you have the warmth of summer joined with the austerity and fresh colouring of spring. The riot of daffodils under the trees was something to thank God for, the banks of the little lake were one cascade of grape hyacinths, blue and white, and every dell in the woods was bright with primroses. We occupied the morning deepening the pools in a tiny stream which was to be one of the spawning-grounds for the new trout in the lake, and Peter John showed conspicuous talent as a hydraulic engineer. His nurse, who was a middle-aged Scotswoman from the Cheviots, finally carried him off for his morning rest, and, when he had gone, Mary desisted from her watery excavations and sat down on a bank of periwinkles.

"What do you really think of Nanny?" she asked.

"About as good as they make," I replied.

"That's what I think too. You know, Dick, I feel I'm far too fussy about Peter John. I give hours of my time to him, and it's quite unnecessary. Nanny can do everything better than I can. I scarcely dare let him out of my sight, and yet I'm certain that I could safely leave him for weeks with

Nanny and Paddock—and Dr. Greenslade within call."

" Of course you could," I agreed, " but you'd miss him, as I do, for he's jolly good company."

" Yes, he's jolly good company, the dear fellow," she said.

In the afternoon we went for a canter on the downs, and I came back feeling as fit as a race-horse and keyed up for anything. But that evening, as we walked in the garden before dinner, I had another fit of longing to be free of the business, and to return to my quiet life. I realized that I had buried my heart in my pleasant acres, and the thought of how much I loved them made me almost timid. I think Mary understood what I was feeling, for she insisted on talking about David Warcliff, and before I went to bed had worked me into that honest indignation which is the best stiffener of resolution. She went over my plans with me very carefully. On the 28th, if I could manage it, I was to come home, but if I was short of time I was to send her a wire and go straight to London. The pretence of my being in bed was to be religiously kept up. For safety's sake I was to sign every wire with the name of Cornelius.

Very early next morning, long before any one was stirring, I started the big Vauxhall with Paddock's assistance, and, accompanied by a very modest kit, crept down the avenue. Paddock, who could drive a car, was to return to the house about ten o'clock, and explain to my chauffeur that by my orders he had taken the Vauxhall over to Oxford as a loan for a week to a friend of mine. I drove fast out of the silent hill roads and on to the great Roman way which lay like a strap across the highlands. It was not much after six o'clock when I reached "The Silent Woman," which sat like an observation post on a ridge of down, at a junction of four roads. Smoke was going up from its chimneys, so I judged that Sandy had ordered early breakfast. Presently, as I was garaging the car in an outhouse, Sandy appeared in flannel bags and a tweed jacket, looking as fresh as paint and uncommonly sunburnt.

"I hope you're hungry," he said. "Capital fellow the landlord! He knows what a man's appetite is. I ordered eggs, kidneys, sausages and cold ham, and he seemed to expect it. Yes. These are my headquarters for the present, though Advanced G.H.Q. is elsewhere. By-the-bye, Dick, just for an extra precaution, my name's Thomson —Alexander Thomson—and I'm a dramatic critic taking a belated Easter holiday."

The breakfast was as good as Sandy had promised, and what with the run in the fresh air and the sight of him opposite me I began to feel light-hearted.

"I got your letters," I said; "but, I say, your knowledge of Derby winners is pretty rocky. I thought that was the kind of information no gentleman was without."

"I'm the exception. Did you act on them ? "

"I told Medina I had broken with you for good

and never wanted to see your face again. But why did you make such a point of it ? "

" Simply because I wanted to be rid of his attentions, and I reckoned that if he thought we had quarrelled and that I had gone off for good, he might let me alone. You see he has been trying hard to murder me."

" Good Lord ! " I exclaimed. " When ? "

" Four times," said Sandy calmly, counting on his fingers. " Once before I left London. Oh, I can tell you I had an exciting departure. Three times in Paris, the last time only four days ago. I fancy he's off my trail now, for he really thinks I sailed from Marseilles the day before yesterday."

" But why on earth ? "

" Well, I made some ill-advised remarks at the Thursday Club dinner. He believes that I'm the only man alive who might uncover him, and he won't sleep peacefully till he knows that I am out of Europe and is convinced that I suspect nothing. I sent you those letters because I wanted to be let alone, seeing I had a lot to do, and nothing wastes time like dodging assassins. But my chief reason was to protect *you*. You mayn't know it, Dick, but you've been walking for three weeks on the edge of a precipice with one foot nearly over. You've been in the most hideous danger, and I was never more relieved in my life than when I saw your solemn old face this morning. You were only safe when he regarded our friendship as broken and me out of the way and you his blind and devoted slave."

"I'm that all right," I said. "There's been nothing like it since Uncle Tom's Cabin."

"Good. That's the great thing, for it gives us a post in the enemy's citadel. But we're only at the beginning of a tremendous fight, and there's no saying how it will go. Have you sized up Medina?"

"Only a little bit. Have you?"

"I'm on the road. He's the most complex thing I've ever struck. But now we've got to pool our knowledge. Shall I start?"

"Yes. Begin at the Thursday dinner. What started you off then? I could see that something he said intrigued you."

"I must begin before that. You see, I'd heard a good deal about Medina up and down the world, and couldn't for the life of me place him. Everybody swore by him, but I had always a queer feeling about the man. I told you about Lavater. Well, I had nothing to go upon there except the notion that his influence upon my friend had been bad. So I began making inquiries, and, as you know, I've more facilities than most people for finding things out. I was curious to know what he had been doing during the War. The ordinary story was that he had been for the first two years pretty well lost in Central Asia, where he had gone on a scientific expedition, and that after that he had been with the Russians, and had finished up by doing great work with Denikin. I went into that story and discovered that he had been in Central Asia all right, but had never been near any fighting front, and had never been within a thousand miles of Denikin. That's what I meant when I told you that I believed the man was one vast lie."

"He made everybody believe it."

"That's the point. He made the whole world believe what he wanted. Therefore he must be something quite out of the common—a propagandist of genius. That was my first conclusion. But how did he work ? He must have a wonderful organization, but he must have something more —the kind of personality which can diffuse itself like an atmosphere, and which, like an electric current, is not weakened by distance. He must also have unique hypnotic powers. I had made a study of that in the East, and had discovered how little we know here about the compulsion of spirit by spirit. That, I have always believed, is to-day, and ever has been, the true magic. You remember I said something about that at the Thursday dinner ? "

I nodded. " I suppose you did it to try him ? "

"Yes. It wasn't very wise, for I might easily have frightened him. But I was luckier than I deserved, and I drew from him a tremendous confession."

"The Latin quotation ? "

"The Latin quotation. *Sit vini abstemius qui hermeneuma tentat aut hominum petit dominatum.* I nearly had a fit when I heard it. Listen, Dick. I've always had a craze for recondite subjects, and when I was at Oxford I wasted my time on them when I should have been working for my schools.

I only got a third in Greats, but I acquired a lot of unusual information. One of my subjects was Michael Scott. Yes—the wizard, only he wasn't a wizard, but a very patient and original thinker. He was a Borderer like me, and I started out to write a life of him. I kept up the study, and when I was at the Paris Embassy I spent my leisure tracking him through the libraries of Europe. Most of his works were published in the fifteenth and sixteenth centuries, and mighty dull they are, but there are some still in manuscript, and I had always the hope of discovering more, for I was positive that the real Michael Scott was something far bigger than the translator and commentator whom we know. I believed that he taught the mad Emperor Ferdinand some queer things, and that the centre of his teaching was just how one human soul could control another. Well, as it turned out, I was right. I found some leaves of manuscript in the Bibliothèque Nationale, which I was certain were to be attributed to Michael. One of his best-known works, you remember, is the *Physionomia,* but that is only a version of Aristotle. This, too, was part of a *Physionomia,* and a very different thing from the other, for it purported to give the essence of the *Secreta Secretorum*—it would take too long to explain about that—and the teaching of the Therapeutae, with Michael's own comments. It is a manual of the arts of spiritual control—oh, amazingly up-to-date, I assure you, and a long way ahead of our foolish psycho-analysts. Well, that quotation of Medina's comes from that fragment—the rare word ' hermeneuma ' caught my attention as soon as he uttered it. That proved that Medina was a student of Michael Scott, and showed me what was the bent of his mind."

" Well, he gave himself away then, and you didn't."

" Oh yes, I did. You remember I asked him if he knew the *guru* who lived at the foot of the Shansi pass as you go over to Kaikand ? That was a bad blunder, and it is on account of that question that he has been trying to remove me from the earth. For it was from that *guru* that he learned most of his art."

" Was the *guru's* name Kharama ? " I asked.

Sandy stared as if he had seen a ghost.

" Now how on earth do you know that ? "

" Simply because I spent an hour with him and Medina a few nights ago."

" The devil you did ! Kharama in London ! Lord, Dick, this is an awesome business. Quick, tell me every single thing that passed."

I told him as well as I remembered, and he seemed to forget his alarm and to be well satisfied. " This is tremendously important. You see the point of Medina's talk ? He wants to rivet his control over those three unfortunate devils, and to do that he is advised to assert it in some environment similar to that of their past lives. That gives us a chance to get on their track. And the control can only be released by him who first imposed it ! I happened to know that, but I was not sure that Medina knew it. It is highly important to have found this out."

"Finish your story," I begged him. "I want to know what you have been doing abroad."

"I continued my studies in the Bibliothèque Nationale, and I found that, as I suspected, Medina, or somebody like him, had got on to the Michael Scott MS. and had had a transcript made of it. I pushed my researches further, for Michael wasn't the only pebble on the beach, though he was the biggest. Lord, Dick, it's a queer business in a problem like ours to have to dig for help in the débris of the Middle Ages. I found out something—not much, but something."

"And then?"

"Oh, all the time I was making inquiries about Medina's past—not very fruitful—I've told you most of the results. Then I went to see Ram Dass—you remember my speaking about him. I thought he was in Munich, but I found him in Westphalia, keeping an eye on the German industrials. Don't go to Germany for a holiday, Dick; it's a sad country and a comfortless. I had to see Ram Dass, for he happens to be the brother of Kharama."

"What size of a fellow is Kharama?" I asked.

Sandy's reply was: "For knowledge of the theory unequalled, but only a second-class practitioner "—exactly what Medina had said.

"Ram Dass told me most of what I wanted to know. But he isn't aware that his brother is in Europe. I rather fancy he thinks he is dead. . . .

That's all I need tell you now. Fire away, Dick, and give me an exact account of your own doings."

I explained as best I could the gradual change in Medina's manner from friendship to proprietorship. I told how he had begun to talk freely to me, as if I were a disciple, and I described that extraordinary evening in Hill Street when I had met his mother."

"His mother!" Sandy exclaimed, and made me go over every incident several times—the slap in the face, the spitting, my ultimate fainting. He seemed to enjoy it immensely. "Good business," he said. "You never did a better day's work, old man."

"I have found the Blind Spinner at any rate," I said.

"Yes. I had half guessed it. I didn't mention it, but when I got into the house in Gospel Oak as the electric-light man, I found a spinning-wheel in the back room, and they had been burning peat on the hearth. Well, that's Number One."

"I think I am on my way to find Number Two," I said, and I told him of the talk I had overheard between the two about *secundus* and sending "the doctor" somewhere, and of how I had discovered that Dr. Newhover was starting this very day for the Skarso. "It's the first clear clue," I said, "and I think I ought to follow it up."

"Yes. What do you propose to do?"

"I am travelling this evening on the *Gudrun*, and I'm going to trail the fellow till I find out his game. I'm bound to act upon what little information we've got."

"I agree. But this means a long absence from London, and *secundus* is only one of three."

"Just a week," I said. "I've got sick leave from Medina for a week, and I'm supposed to be having a rest cure at Fosse, with Mary warding off visitors. I've arranged with Archie Roylance to pick me up in an aeroplane about the 28th and bring me back. It doesn't allow me much time, but an active man can do the deuce of a lot in a week."

"Bravo!" he cried. "That's your old moss-trooping self!"

"Do you approve?"

"Entirely. And, whatever happens, you present yourself to Medina on the 29th? That leaves us about six weeks for the rest of the job."

"More like five," I said gloomily, and I told him how I had learnt that the gang proposed to liquidate by midsummer, and that Macgillivray had therefore moved the date when he would take action ten days forward. "You see how we are placed. He must collect all the gang at the same moment, and we must release all three hostages, if we can, at the same time. The releasing mustn't be done too soon or it will warn the gang. Therefore if Macgillivray strikes on the 10th of June, we must be ready to strike not earlier than the 9th, and, of course, not later."

"I see," he said, and was silent for a little. "Have you anything more to tell me?"

I ransacked my memory and remembered about Odell. He wrote down the name of the dancing club where I had seen that unprepossessing butler. I mentioned that I had asked Macgillivray to get on to his *dossier*.

"You haven't told Macgillivray too much?" he inquired anxiously, and seemed relieved when I replied that I had never mentioned the Medina business.

"Well, here's the position," he said at last. "You go off for a week hunting Number Two. We are pretty certain that we have got Number One. Number Three—that nonsense about the fields of Eden and the Jew with a dyed beard in a curiosity shop in Marylebone—still eludes us. And of course we have as yet no word of any of the three hostages. There's a terrible lot still to do. How do you picture the thing, Dick? Do you think of the three, the girl, the young man, and the boy, shut up somewhere and guarded by Medina's minions? Do you imagine that if we find their places of concealment we shall have done the job?"

"That was my idea."

He shook his head. "It is far subtler than that. Did no one ever tell you that the best way of hiding a person is to strip him of his memory? Why is it that when a man loses his memory he is so hard to find? You see it constantly in the newspapers. Even a well-known figure, if he loses his memory and wanders away, is only discovered by accident. The reason is that the human personality is identified far less by appearance than by its habits and mind. Loss of memory means the loss of all true marks of identification, and the physical look alters to correspond. Medina has stolen these three poor souls' memories and set them adrift like waifs. David Warcliff may at this moment be playing in a London gutter along with a dozen guttersnipes, and his own father could scarcely pick him out from the rest. Mercot may be a dock labourer or a deck hand, whom you wouldn't recognize if you met him, though you had sat opposite him in a college hall every night for a year. And Miss Victor may be in a gaiety chorus or a milliner's assistant or a girl in a dancing saloon. . . . Wait a minute. You saw Odell at a dance-club ? There may be something in that." I could see his eyes abstracted in thought.

"There's another thing I forgot to mention," I said. "Miss Victor's fiancé is over here, staying in Carlton House Terrace. He is old Turpin, who used to be with the division—the Marquis de la Tour du Pin."

Sandy wrote the name down. "Her fiancé. He may come in useful. What sort of fellow ? "

"Brave as a lion, but he'll want watching, for he's a bit of a gascon."

We went out after breakfast and sat in an arbour looking down a shallow side-valley to the upper streams of the Windrush. The sounds of morning were beginning to rise from the little village far away in the bottom—the jolt of a wagon, the

14

" clink-clenk " from the smithy, the babble of children at play. In a fortnight the may-fly would be here, and every laburnum and guelder rose in bloom. Sandy, who had been away from England for years, did not speak for a long time, but drank in the sweet-scented peace of it. " Poor devil," he said at last, " he has nothing like this to love. He can only hate."

I asked whom he was talking about, and he said " Medina."

" I'm trying to understand him. You can't fight a man unless you understand him, and in a way sympathize with him."

" Well, I can't say I sympathize with him, and I most certainly don't understand him."

" Do you remember once telling me that he had no vanity ? You were badly out there. He has a vanity which amounts to delirium."

" This is how I read him," he went on. " To begin with, there's a far-away streak of the Latin in him, but he is mainly Irish, and that never makes a good cross. He's the *déraciné* Irish, such as you find in America. I take it that he imbibed from that terrible old woman—I've never met her, but I see her plainly and I know that she is terrible —he imbibed that venomous hatred of imaginary things—an imaginary England, an imaginary civilization, which they call love of country. There is no love in it. They think there is, and sentimentalize about an old simplicity, and spinning wheels and turf fires and an uncouth language, but it's all hollow. There's plenty of decent plain folk in Ireland, but his kind of *déraciné* is a ghastly throw-back to something you find in the dawn of history, hollow and cruel like the fantastic gods of their own myths. Well, you start with this ingrained hate."

"I agree about the old lady. She looked like Lady Macbeth."

"But hate soon becomes conceit. If you hate, you despise, and when you despise you esteem inordinately the self which despises. This is how I look at it, but remember, I'm still in the dark and only feeling my way to an understanding. I see Medina growing up—I don't know in what environment—conscious of great talents and immense good looks, flattered by those around him till he thinks himself a god. His hatred does not die, but it is transformed into a colossal egotism and vanity, which, of course, is a form of hate. He discovers quite early that he has this remarkable hypnotic power—— Oh, you may laugh at it, because you happen to be immune from it, but it is a big thing in the world for all that. He discovers another thing—that he has an extraordinary gift of attracting people and making them believe in him. Some of the worst scoundrels in history have had it. Now, remember his vanity. It makes him want to play the biggest game. He does not want to be a king among pariahs; he wants to be the ruler of what is most strange to him, what he hates and in an unwilling bitter way admires. So he aims at conquering the very heart, the very soundest part of our society. Above all, he wants to be admired by men and admitted into the innermost circle."

" He has succeeded all right," I said.

" He has succeeded, and that is the greatest possible tribute to his huge cleverness. Everything about him is dead right—clothes, manner, modesty, accomplishments. He has made himself an excellent sportsman. Do you know why he shoots so well, Dick ? By faith—or fatalism, if you like. His vanity doesn't allow him to believe that he could miss. . . . But he governs himself strictly. In his life he is practically an ascetic, and though he is adored by women he doesn't care a straw for them. There are no lusts of the flesh in that kind of character. He has one absorbing passion which subdues all others—what our friend Michael Scott called ' hominum dominatus.' "

" I see that. But how do you explain the other side ? "

" It is all the ancestral hate. First of all, of course, he has got to have money, so he gets it in the way Macgillivray knows about. Second, he wants to build up a regiment of faithful slaves. That's where you come in, Dick. There is always that inhuman hate at the back of his egotism. He wants to conquer in order to destroy, for destruction is the finest meat for his vanity. You'll find the same thing in the lives of Eastern tyrants, for when a man aspires to be like God he becomes an incarnate devil."

" It is a tough proposition," I observed dismally.

" It would be an impossible proposition, but

for one thing. He is always in danger of giving himself away out of sheer arrogance. Did you ever read the old Irish folk-lore? Very beautiful it is, but there is always something fantastic and silly which mars the finest stories. They lack the grave good-sense which you find in the Norse sagas and, of course, in the Greek. Well, he has this freakish element in his blood. That is why he sent out that rhyme about the three hostages, which by an amazing concatenation of chances put you on to his trail. Our hope is—and, mind you, I think it is a slender hope—that his vanity may urge him to further indiscretions."

"I don't know how you feel about it," I said, "but I've got a pretty healthy hatred for that lad. I'm longing for a quiet life, but I swear I won't settle down again till I've got even with him."

"You never will," said Sandy solemnly. "Don't let's flatter ourselves that you and I are going to down Medina. We are not. A very wise man once said to me that in this life you could often get success, if you didn't want victory. In this case we're out for success only. We want to release the hostages. Victory we can never hope for. Why, man, supposing we succeed fully, we'll never be able to connect Medina with the thing. His tools are faithful, because he has stolen their souls and they work blindly under him. Supposing Macgillivray rounds up all the big gang and puts the halter round their necks. There will be none of them to turn King's evidence and give Medina away. Why? Because none of them *know* anything against him. They're his unconscious agents, and very likely most have never seen him. And you may be pretty sure that his banking accounts are too skilfully arranged to show anything."

"All the same," I said stubbornly, "I have a notion that I'll be able to put a spoke in his wheel."

"Oh, I daresay we can sow suspicion, but I believe he'll be too strong for us. He'll advance in his glorious career, and may become Prime Minister —or Viceroy of India—what a chance the second would be for him!—and publish exquisite little poetry books, as finished and melancholy as *The Shropshire Lad*. Pessimism, you know, is often a form of vanity."

At midday it was time for me to be off, if I was to be at Hull by six o'clock. I asked Sandy what he proposed to do next, and he said he was undecided. "My position," he said, "badly cramps my form. It would be ruination if Medina knew I was in England—ruination for both you and me. Mr. Alexander Thomson must lie very low. I must somehow get in touch with Mac-gillivray to hear if he has anything about Odell. I rather fancy Odell. But there will probably be nothing doing till you come back, and I think I'll have a little fishing."

"Suppose I want to get hold of you?"

"Suppose nothing of the kind. You mustn't make any move in my direction. That's our only safety. If I want you I'll come to you."

As I was starting he said suddenly : "I've never

met your wife, Dick. What about my going over to Fosse and introducing myself ? "

" The very thing," I cried. " She is longing to meet you. But remember that I'm supposed to be lying sick upstairs."

As I looked back he was waving his hand, and his face wore its familiar elfish smile.

# CHAPTER XI

HOW A GERMAN ENGINEER FOUND STRANGE
FISHING

I GOT to Hull about six o'clock, having left my car at a garage in York, and finished the journey by train. I had my kit in a small suit-case and rucksack, and I waited on the quay till I saw Dr. Newhover arrive with a lot of luggage and a big rod-box. When I reckoned he would be in his cabin arranging his belongings, I went on board myself, and went straight to my own cabin, which was a comfortable two-berthed one well forward. There I had sandwiches brought me, and settled myself to doze and read for thirty-six hours.

All that night and all next day it blew fairly hard, and I remained quietly in my bunk, trying to read Boswell's *Life of Johnson*, and thanking my stars that I hadn't lived a thousand years earlier and been a Viking. I didn't see myself ploughing those short steep seas in an open galley. I woke on the morning of the 23rd to find the uneasy motion at an end, and, looking out of my port-hole, saw a space of green sunlit water, a rocky beach, and the white and red of a little town. The *Gudrun* waited about an hour at Stavanger, so I gave Dr. Newhover time to get on shore, before I had a hurried breakfast in the saloon and followed him. I saw him go off with two men, and get on board a motor-launch which was lying beside one of the jetties. The coast was now clear, so I went into the town, found the agents to whom Archie Roylance had cabled, and learned that my own motor-launch was ready and waiting in the inner harbour where the fishing-boats lie. A clerk took me down there, and introduced me to Johan, my skipper, a big, cheerful, bearded Norwegian, who had a smattering of English. I bought a quantity of provisions, and by ten o'clock we were on the move. I asked Johan about the route to Merdal, and he pointed out a moving speck a couple of miles ahead of us. " That is Kristian Egge's boat," he said. " He carries an English fisherman to Merdal, and we follow." I got my glasses on the craft, and made out Newhover smoking in the stern.

It was a gorgeous day, with that funny northern light which makes noon seem like early morning. I enjoyed every hour of it, partly because I had now a definite job before me, and partly because I was in the open air to which I properly belonged. I got no end of amusement watching the wild life— the cormorants and eider-duck on the little islands, and the seals, with heads as round as Medina's, that slipped off the skerries at our approach. The air was chilly and fresh, but when we turned the corner of the Merdalfjord out of the sea-wind and the sun climbed the sky it was as warm as June. A big flat island we passed, all short turf and rocky outcrops, was pointed out to me by Johan as Flacksholm. Soon we were shaping due east in an inlet which was surrounded by dark steep hills, with the snow lying in the gullies. I had Boswell with me in two volumes ; the first I had read in the steamer, and the second I was now starting on, when it fell overboard, through my getting up in a hurry to look at a flock of duck. So I presented the odd volume to Johan, and surrendered myself to tobacco and meditation.

In the afternoon the inlet narrowed to a fjord, and the walls of hill grew steeper. They were noble mountains, cut sharp like the edge of the Drakensberg, and crowned with a line of snow, so that they looked like a sugar-coated cake that had been sliced. Streams came out of the upper snow-wreaths and hurled themselves down the steeps—above a shimmering veil of mist, and below a torrent of green water tumbling over pebbles to the sea. The landscape and the weather lulled me into a delectable peace which refused to be disturbed by any " looking before or after," as some poet says. Newhover was ahead of me— we never lost track of his launch—and it was my business to see what he was up to and to keep myself out of his sight. The ways and means of it I left to fortune to provide.

By-and-by the light grew dimmer, and the fjord grew narrower, so that dusk fell on us, though,

looking back down the inlet, we could see a bright
twilight. I assumed that Newhover would go on
to Merdal and the fjord's head, where the Skarso
entered the sea, and had decided to stop at Hauge,
a village two miles short of it, on the south shore.
We came to Hauge about half-past eight, in a
wonderful purple dusk, for the place lay right
under the shadow of a great cliff. I gave Johan
full instructions : he was to wait for me and
expect me when I turned up, and to provision himself from the village. On no account must he
come up to Merdal, or go out of sight or hail of
the boat. He seemed to relish the prospect of a
few days' idleness, for he landed me at a wooden
jetty in great good-humour, and wished me sport.
What he thought I was after I cannot imagine,
for I departed with a rucksack on my back and a
stout stick in my hand, which scarcely suggested
the chase.

I was in good spirits myself as I stretched my
legs on the road which led from Hauge to Merdal.
The upper fjord lay black on my left hand, the
mountains rose black on my right, but though I
walked in darkness I could see twilight ahead of
me, where the hills fell back from the Skarso valley,
that wonderful apple-green twilight which even in
spring is all the northern night. I had never seen
it before, and I suppose something in my blood
answered to the place—for my father used to say
that the Hannays came originally from Norse
stock. There was a jolly crying of birds from the
waters, ducks and geese and oyster-catchers and

sandpipers, and now and then would come a great splash as if a salmon were jumping in the brackish tides on his way to the Skarso. I was thinking longingly of my rods left behind, when on turning a corner the lights of Merdal showed ahead, and it seemed to me that I had better be thinking of my next step.

I knew no Norwegian, but I counted on finding natives who could speak English, seeing so many of them have been in England or America. Newhover, I assumed, would go to the one hotel, and it was for me to find lodgings elsewhere. I began to think this spying business might be more difficult than I had thought, for if he saw me he would recognize me, and that must not happen. I was ready, of course, with a story of a walking tour, but he would be certain to suspect, and certain to let Medina know. . . . Well, a lodging for the night was my first business, and I must start inquiries. Presently I came to the little pier of Merdal, which was short of the village itself. There were several men sitting smoking on barrels and coils of rope, and one who stood at the end looking out to where Kristian Egge's boat, which had brought Newhover, lay moored. I turned down the road to it, for it seemed a place to gather information.

I said good-evening to the men, and was just about to ask them for advice about quarters, when the man who had been looking out to sea turned round at the sound of my voice. He seemed an oldish fellow, with rather a stoop in his back, wearing an ancient shooting-jacket. The light was bad, but there was something in the cut of his jib that struck me as familiar, though I couldn't put a name to it.

I spoke to the Norwegians in English, but it was obvious that I had hit on a bunch of indifferent linguists. They shook their heads, and one pointed to the village, as if to tell me that I would be better understood there. Then the man in the shooting-jacket spoke.

"Perhaps I can help," he said. "There is a good inn in Merdal, which at this season is not full."

He spoke excellent English, but it was obvious that he wasn't an Englishman. There was an unmistakable emphasis of the gutturals.

"I doubt the inn may be too good for my purse," I said. "I am on a walking-tour and must lodge cheaply."

He laughed pleasantly. "There may be accommodation elsewhere. Peter Bojer may have a spare bed. I am going that way, sir, and can direct you."

He had turned towards me, and his figure caught the beam of the riding-light of the motor-launch. I saw a thin sunburnt face with a very pleasant expression, and an untidy grizzled beard. Then I knew him, and I could have shouted with amazement at the chance which had brought us two together again.

We walked side by side up the jetty road and on to the highway.

" I think," I said, " that we have met before,
Herr Gaudian."

He stopped short. "That is my name—but I do
not—I do not think——"

" Do you remember a certain Dutchman called
Cornelius Brandt, whom you entertained at your
country house one night in December '15 ? "

He looked searchingly in my face.

" I remember," he said. " I also remember a
Mr. Richard Hanau, one of Guggenheim's engineers,
with whom I talked at Constantinople."

" The same," I said. For a moment I was not
clear how he was going to take the revelation, but
his next action reassured me, and I saw that I
had not been wrong in my estimate of the one
German I have ever whole-heartedly liked. He
began to laugh, a friendly, tolerant laugh.

" *Kritzi Turken !* " he cried. " It is indeed
romantic. I have often wondered whether I
should see or hear of you again, and behold ! you
step out of the darkness on a Norwegian fjord."

" You bear no malice ? " I said. " I served
my country as you served yours. I played fair,
as you played fair."

" Malice ! " he cried. " But we are gentlemen ;
also we are not children. I rejoice to see that
you have survived the War. I have always wished
you well, for you are a very bold and brave man."

" Not a bit of it," I said—" only lucky."

" By what name shall I call you now—Brandt
or Hanau ? "

" My name is Richard Hannay, but for the

present I am calling myself Cornelius Brand—for a reason which I am going to tell you." I had suddenly made up my mind to take Gaudian into my full confidence. He seemed to have been sent by Providence for that purpose, and I was not going to let such a chance slip.

But at my words he stopped short.

"Mr. Hannay," he said, "I do not want your confidence. You are still engaged, I take it, in your country's service ? I do not question your motive, but remember I am a German, and I cannot be party to the pursuit of one of my country-men, however base I may think him."

I could only stare. "But I am not in my country's service," I stammered. "I left it at the Armistice, and I'm a farmer now."

"Do English farmers travel in Norway under false names ? "

"That's a private business which I want to explain to you. I assure you there is no German in it. I want to keep an eye on the doings of a fashionable English doctor."

"I must believe you," he said, after a pause. "But two hours ago a man arrived in the launch you see anchored out there. He is a fisherman, and is now at the inn. That man is known to me—too well known. He is a German, who during the War served Germany in secret ways, in America and elsewhere. I did not love him, and I think he did my country grievous ill, but that is a matter for us Germans to settle, and not for foreigners."

" I know your man as Dr. Newhover of Wimpole Street."

" So ? " he said. " He has taken again his father's name, which was Neuhofer. We knew him as Kristoffer. What do you want with him ? "

" Nothing that any honest German wouldn't approve," and there and then I gave him a sketch of the Medina business. He exclaimed in horror.

" Mr. Hannay," he said hesitatingly, " you are being honest with me ? "

" I swear by all that's holy I am telling you the plain truth, and the full truth. Newhover may have done anything you jolly well like in the War. That's all washed out. I'm after him to get a line on a foul business which is English in origin. I want to put a spoke in the wheel of English criminals, and to save innocent lives. Besides, Newhover is only a subordinate. I don't propose to raise a finger against him, only to find out what he is doing."

He held out his hand. " I believe you," he said, " and if I can I will help you."

He conducted me through the long street of the village, past the inn, where I supposed Newhover was now going to bed, and out on to the road which ran up the Skarso valley. We came in sight of the river, a mighty current full of melted snow, sweeping in noble curves through the meadowland in that uncanny dusk. It appeared that he lodged with Peter Bojer, who had a spare bed, and when we reached the cottage, which stood a hundred yards from the highway on the very brink of the stream, Peter was willing to let me have it. His wife gave us supper—an omelette, smoked salmon, and some excellent Norwegian beer—and after it I got out my map and had a survey of the neighbourhood.

Gaudian gave me a grisly picture of the condition of his own country. It seemed that the downfall of the old régime had carried with it the decent wise men like himself, who had opposed its follies, but had lined up with it on patriotic grounds when the War began. He said that Germany was no place for a moderate man, and that the power lay with the bloated industrials, who were piling up fortunes abroad while they were wrecking their country at home. The only opposition, he said, came from the communists, who were half-witted, and the monarchists, who wanted the impossible. " Reason is not listened to, and I fear there is no salvation till my poor people have passed through the last extremity. You foreign Powers have hastened our destruction, when you had it in your hands to save us. I think you have meant well, but you have been blind, for you have not supported our moderate men and have by your harshness played the game of the wreckers among us."

It appeared that he was very poor now, like all the professional classes. I thought it odd that this man, who had a world-wide reputation as an engineer, couldn't earn a big income in any country he chose. Then I saw that it was because he had lost the wish to make money. He had seen too deep into the vanity of human wishes to have any

ambition left. He was unmarried, with no near
relations, and he found his pleasure in living
simply in remote country places and watching
flowers and beasts. He was a keen fisherman,
but couldn't afford a good beat, so he leased a few
hundred yards from a farmer, who had not enough
water to get a proper rent for it, and he did a lot
of trout fishing in the tarns high up in the hills
and in the Skarso above the foss. As he sat facing
me beyond the stove, with his kind sad brown eyes
and his rugged face, I thought how like he was to a
Scottish moorland shepherd. I had liked him when
I first saw him in Stumm's company, but now I
liked him so much that because of him I was prepared to think better of the whole German race.

I asked him if he had heard of any other Englishman in the valley—any one of the name of Jason,
for instance. He said no ; he had been there for
three weeks, but the fishing did not begin for
another fortnight, and foreign visitors had not yet
arrived. Then I asked him about the *saeter* farms,
and he said that few of these were open yet, since
the high pastures were not ready. One or two
on the lower altitudes might be already inhabited,
but not many, though the winter had been a mild
one and the spring had come early. "Look at
the Skarso," he said. "Usually in April it is
quite low, for the snowfields have not begun to
melt. But to-day it is as brimming as if it were
the middle of May."

He went over the map with me—an inch-to-a-
mile one I had got in London—and showed me

the lie of the land. The *saeters* were mostly
farther up the river, reached by paths up the tributary glens. There was a good road running the
length of the valley, but no side roads to connect
with the parallel glens, the Uradal and the Bre-
mendal. I found indeed one track marked on the
map, which led to the Uradal by a place called
Snaasen. "Yes," said Gaudian, "that is the
only thing in the way of what you soldiers would
call lateral communications. I've walked it, and
I'm sorry for the man who tries the road in bad
weather. You can see the beginning of the track
from this house; it climbs up beside the torrent
just across the valley. Snaasen is more or less
inhabited all the year round, and I suppose you
would call it a kind of *saeter*. It is a sort of shelter
hut for travellers taking that road, and in summer
it is a paradise for flowers. You would be surprised at the way the natives can cross the hills
even in winter. Snaasen belongs to the big farm
two miles up-stream, which carries with it the best
beat on the Skarso. Also there is said to be first-
class ryper-shooting later in the year, and an
occasional bear. By the way, I rather fancy
some one told me that the whole thing was owned
by, or had been leased to, an Englishman. . . .
You are rich, you see, and you do not leave much
in Norway for poor people."

I slept like a log on a bed quite as hard as a log,
and woke to a brilliant blue morning, with the
birds in the pine-woods fairly riotous, and snipe
drumming in the boggy meadows, and the Skarso

coming down like a sea. I could see the water almost up to the pathway of a long wooden bridge that led to the big farm Gaudian had spoken of. I got my glass on the torrent opposite, and saw the track to Snaasen winding up beside it till it was lost in a fold of the ravine. Above it I scanned the crown of the ridge, which was there much lower than on the sides of the fjord. There was no snow to be seen, and I knew by a sort of instinct that if I got up there I should find a broad tableland of squelching pastures with old snow-drifts in the hollows and tracts of scrubby dwarf birch.

While I was waiting for breakfast I heard a noise from the highroad, and saw a couple of the little conveyances they call *stolkjaeres* passing. My glass showed me Dr. Newhover in the first and a quantity of luggage in the second. They took the road across the wooden bridge to the big farm, and I could see the splash of their wheels at the far end of it, where the river was over the road. So Dr. Newhover, or some friend of his, was the lessee of this famous fishing, which carried with it the shooting on the uplands behind it. I rather thought I should spend the day finding out more about Snaasen, and I counted myself lucky to have got quarters in such an excellent observation-post as Peter Bojer's cottage.

I wouldn't go near the track to Snaasen till I saw what Newhover did, so Gaudian and I sat patiently at Peter Bojer's window. About ten o'clock a couple of ponies laden with kit in charge

of a tow-headed boy appeared at the foot of the
track and slowly climbed up the ravine. An hour
later came Dr. Newhover, in a suit that looked
like khaki, and wearing a long mackintosh cape.
He strode out well and breasted the steep path like
a mountaineer. I wanted to go off myself in
pursuit of him, keeping well behind, but Gaudian
very sensibly pointed out how sparse the cover
was, and that if he saw a man on that lonely road
he would certainly want to know all about him.

We sat out-of-doors after luncheon in a pleasant
glare of sun, and by-and-by were rewarded by the
sight of the pack-ponies returning, laden with a
different size and shape of kit. They did not stop
at the big farm, but crossed the wooden bridge
and took the highroad for Merdal. I concluded
that this was the baggage of the man whom Newhover had replaced, and that he was returning to
Stavanger in Kristian Egge's boat. About tea-
time the man himself appeared—Jason, or whatever his name was. I saw two figures come down
the ravine by the Snaasen road, and stop at the
foot and exchange farewells. One of them turned
to go back, and I saw that this was Newhover,
climbing with great strides like a man accustomed
to hills. The other crossed the bridge, and passed
within hail of us—a foppish young man, my glass
told me, wearing smart riding-breeches and with
an aquascutum slung over his shoulder.

I was very satisfied with what I had learned. I
had seen Newhover relieve his predecessor, just as
Medina had planned, and I knew where he was

lodged. Whatever his secret was it was hidden in Snaasen, and to Snaasen I would presently go. Gaudian advised me to wait till after supper, when there would be light enough to find the way and not too much to betray us. So we both lay down and slept for four hours, and took the road about ten-thirty as fresh as yearlings.

It was a noble night, windless and mild, and, though darkness lurked in the thickets and folds of hill, the sky was filled with a translucent amethyst glow. I felt as if I were out on some sporting expedition, and enjoyed every moment of the walk with that strung-up expectant enjoyment which one gets in any form of chase. The torrent made wild music on our left hand, grumbling in pits and shooting over ledges with a sound like a snowslip. There was every kind of bird about, but I had to guess at them by their sounds and size, for there was no colour in that shadowy world.

By-and-by we reached the top and had a light cold wind in our faces blowing from the snowy mountains to the north. The place seemed a huge broken tableland, and every hollow glistened as if filled with snow or water. There were big dark shapes ahead of us which I took to be the hills beyond the Uradal. Here it was not so easy to follow the track, which twined about in order to avoid the boggy patches, and Gaudian and I frequently strayed from it and took tosses over snags of juniper. Once I was up against an iron pole, and to my surprise saw wires above. Gaudian nodded. " Snaasen is on the telephone," he said.

I had hoped to see some light in the house, so as to tell it from a distance. But we did not realize its presence till we were close upon it, standing a little back from the path, as dark as a tombstone. The inhabitants must have gone early to bed, for there was no sign of life within. It was a two-storied erection of wood, stoutly built, with broad eaves to the roof. Adjacent there stood a big barn or hayshed, and behind it some other outbuildings which might have been byres or dairies. We walked stealthily round the place, and were amazed at its utter stillness. There was no sound of an animal moving in the steading, and when a brace of mallards flew overhead we started at the noise like burglars at the creaking of a board.

Short of burglary there was nothing further to be done, so we took the road home and scrambled at a great pace down the ravine, for it was chilly on the tableland. Before we went to bed we had settled that next day Gaudian should go up to Snaasen like an ordinary tourist and make some excuse to get inside, while I would take a long tramp over the plateau, keeping well away from the house, in case there might be something ado in that barren region.

Next morning saw the same cloudless weather, and we started off about ten o'clock. I had a glorious but perfectly futile day. I went up the Skarso to well above the foss, and then climbed the north wall of the valley by a gully choked with brushwood, which gave out long before the top and left me to finish my ascent by way of some very loose screes and unpleasant boiler-plates. I reached the plateau much farther to the east, where it was at a greater altitude, so that I looked down upon the depression where ran the track to Uradal. I struck due north among boggy meadows and the remains of old snowdrifts, through whose fringes flowers were showing, till I was almost on the edge of Uradal, and looked away beyond it to a fine cluster of rock peaks streaked and patched with ice. The Uradal glen was so deep cut that I could not see into it, so I moved west and struck the Merdal track well to the north of Snaasen. After that I fetched a circuit behind Snaasen, and had a good view of the house from the distance of about half a mile. Two of its chimneys were smoking, and there were sounds of farm work from the yard. There was no sign of live stock, but it looked as if some one was repairing the sheds against the summer season. I waited for more than an hour, but I saw no human being, so I turned homeward, and made a careful descent by the ravine, reconnoitring every corner in case I should run into Newhover.

I found that Gaudian had returned before me. When I asked him what luck he had had he shook his head.

"I played the part of a weary traveller, and asked for milk. An ugly woman gave me beer. She said she had no milk, till the cattle came up from the valleys. She would not talk and she was deaf. She said an English Herr had the ryper-shooting, but lived at Tryssil. That is the name of the big farm by the Skarso. She would tell me no more, and I saw no other person. But I observed that Snaasen is larger than I thought. There are rooms built out at the back, which we thought were barns. There is ample space there for a man to be concealed."

I asked him if he had any plan, and he said he thought of going boldly up next day and asking for Newhover, whom he could say he had seen passing Peter Bojer's cottage. He disliked the man, but had never openly quarrelled with him. I approved of that, but in the meantime I resolved to do something on my own account that night. I was getting anxious, for I felt that my time was growing desperately short; it was now the 25th of April and I was due back in London on the 29th, and, if I failed to turn up, Medina would make inquiries at Fosse Manor and suspect. I had made up my mind to go alone that night to Snaasen and do a little pacific burgling.

I set out about eleven, and I put my pistol in my pocket, as well as my flask and sandwiches and electric torch, for it occurred to me that anything might happen. I made good going across the bridge and up the first part of the track, for I wanted to have as much time as possible for my job. My haste was nearly my undoing, for, instead of reconnoitring and keeping my ears open, I strode up the hill as if I had been walking to make a record. It was by the mercy of Heaven that I was at a point where an outjutting boulder made a sharp corner when I was suddenly aware that some one was coming down the road. I flattened myself into the shadow, and saw Newhover.

He did not see or hear me, for he, too, was pre-occupied. He was descending at a good pace, and he must have started in a hurry, for he had no hat. His longish blond locks were all touzled, and his face seemed sharper than usual with anxiety.

I wondered what on earth had happened, and my first notion was to follow him downhill. And then it occurred to me that his absence gave me a sovereign chance at Snaasen. But if the house-hold was astir there might be other travellers on the road, and it behoved me to go warily. Now, near the top of the ravine, just under the edge of the tableland, there was a considerable patch of wood—birches, juniper, and wind-blown pines—for there the torrent flowed in a kind of cup, after tumbling off the plateau and before hurling itself down to the valley. Here it was possible to find an alternative road to the path, so I dived in among the matted whortleberries and moss-covered boulders.

I had not gone ten yards before I realized that there was somebody or something else in the thicket. There was a sound of plunging ahead of me, then the crack of a rotten log, then the noise of a falling stone. It might be a beast, but it struck me that no wild thing would move so awkwardly. Only human boots made that kind of clumsy slipping.

If this was somebody from Snaasen, what was he doing off the track ? Could he be watching me ? Well, I proposed to do a little stalking on my own account. I got down on all-fours and crawled in cover in the direction of the sound. It was very dark there, but I could see a faint light where the scrub thinned round the stream.

Soon I was at the edge of the yeasty water. The sounds had stopped, but suddenly they began again a little farther up, and there was a scuffle as if part of the bank had given way. The man, whoever he was, seemed to be trying to cross. That would be a dangerous thing to do, for the torrent was wide and very strong. I crawled a yard or two up-stream, and then in an open patch saw what was happening.

A fallen pine made a crazy bridge to a great rock, from which the rest of the current might conceivably be leaped. A man was kneeling on the trunk and beginning to move along it. . . . But as I looked the rotten thing gave way, and the next I saw he was struggling in the foam. It was all the matter of a fraction of a second, and before I knew I was leaning over the brink and clutching at an arm. I gripped it, braced one leg against a rock, and hauled the owner close into the edge out of the main current. He seemed to have taken no hurt, for he found a foothold, and scarcely needed my help to scramble up beside me.

Then to my surprise he went for me tooth and

nail. It was like the assault of a wild beast, and its suddenness rolled me on my back. I felt hands on my throat, and grew angry, caught the wrists and wrenched them away. I flung a leg over his back and got uppermost, and after that he was at my mercy. He seemed to realize it, too, for he lay quite quiet and did not struggle.

"What the devil do you mean?" I said angrily. "You'd have been drowned but for me, and then you try to throttle me."

I got out my torch and had a look at him. It was the figure of a slight young man, dressed in rough homespun such as Norwegian farm lads wear. His face was sallow and pinched, and decorated with the most preposterous wispish beard, and his hair was cut roughly as if with garden shears. The eyes that looked up at me were as scared and wild as a deer's.

"What the devil do you mean?" I repeated, and then to my surprise he replied in English.

"Let me up," he said, "I'm too tired to fight. I'll go back with you."

Light broke in on me.

"Don't you worry, old chap," I said soothingly. "You're going back with me, but not to that infernal *saeter*. We've met before, you know. You're Lord Mercot, and I saw you ride Red Prince last year at the 'House' Grind."

He was sitting up, staring at me like a ghost.

"Who are you? Oh, for God's sake, who are you?"

"Hannay's my name. I live at Fosse Manor

in the Cotswolds. You once came to dine with us before the Heythrop Ball."

"Hannay!" He repeated stumblingly—"I remember—I think—remember—remember Lady Hannay. Yes—and Fosse. It's on the road between——"

He scrambled to his feet.

"Oh, sir, get me away. He's after me—the new devil with the long face, the man who first brought me here. I don't know what has happened to me, but I've been mad a long time, and I've only got sane in the last days. Then I remembered —and I ran away. But they're after me. Oh, quick, quick! Let's hide."

"See here, my lad," I said, and I took out my pistol. "The first man that lays a hand on you I shoot, and I don't miss. You're as safe now as if you were at home. But this is no place to talk, and I've the devil of a lot to tell you. I'm going to take you down with me to my lodging in the valley. But they're hunting you, so we've got to go cannily. Are you fit to walk? Well, do exactly as I tell you, and in an hour you'll be having a long drink and looking up time-tables."

I consider that journey back a creditable piece of piloting. The poor boy was underfed and shaking with excitement, but he stepped out gallantly, and obeyed me like a lamb. We kept off the track so as to muffle our steps in grass, and took every corner like scouts in a reconnaissance. We met Newhover coming back, but we heard him a long way off, and were in good cover when he passed.

He was hurrying as furiously as ever, and I could hear his laboured breathing. After that we had a safe road over the meadow, but we crossed the bridge most circumspectly, making sure that there was no one in the landscape. About half-past one I pushed open Gaudian's bedroom window, woke him, and begged him to forage for food and drink.

"Did you get into Snaasen?" he asked sleepily.

"No, but I've found what we've been looking for. One of the three hostages is at this moment sitting on your cabin-box."

# CHAPTER XII

## I RETURN TO SERVITUDE

WE fed Mercot with tinned meats and biscuits and bottled beer, and he ate like a famished schoolboy. The odd thing was that his terror had suddenly left him. I suppose the sight of me, which had linked him up definitely with his past, had made him feel a waif no more, and, once he was quite certain who he was, his natural courage returned. He got great comfort from looking at Gaudian, and indeed I could not imagine a better sedative than a sight of that kind, wise old face. I lent him pyjamas, rubbed him down to prevent a chill from his ducking, put him in my bed, and had the satisfaction of seeing him slip off at once into deep slumber.

Next morning Gaudian and I interviewed Peter Bojer and explained that a young English friend of ours had had an accident while on a walking tour, and might be with us for a day or two. It was not likely that Newhover would advertise his loss, and in any case Peter was no gossip, and Gaudian, who had known him for years, let him see that we wanted the fact of a guest being with us kept as quiet as possible. The boy slept till nearly midday, while I kept a watch on the road. Newhover appeared early, and went down to Merdal village, where he spent the better part of the forenoon. He was probably making inquiries, but they were bound in his own interest to be discreet ones. Then he returned to Tryssil, and later I saw a dejected figure tramping up the Snaasen track. He may have thought that the body of the fugitive was in some pool of the torrent or being swirled down by the Skarso to the sea, and I imagined that that scarcely fitted in with his instructions.

When Mercot awoke at last and had his breakfast he looked a different lad. His eyes had lost their fright, and though he stuttered badly and seemed to have some trouble in collecting his wits, he had obviously taken hold of himself. His great desire was to get clean, and that took some doing, for he could not have had a bath for weeks. Then he wanted to borrow my razor and shave his beard, but I managed to prevent him in time, for I had been thinking the thing out, and I saw that that would never do. So far as I could see, he had recovered his memory, but there were still gaps in it ; that is to say, he remembered all his past perfectly well till he left Oxford on February 17th, and he remembered the events of the last few days, but between the two points he was still hazy.

On returning to his rooms that February evening he had found a note about a horse he was trying to buy, an urgent note asking him to come round at once to certain stables.  He had just time for this before dressing for dinner, so he dashed out of the house—meeting nobody, as it chanced, on the stairs, and, as the night was foggy, being seen by no one in the streets.  After that his memory was a blank.  He had wakened in a room in London, which he thought was a nursing home, and had seen a doctor—I could picture that doctor—and had gone to sleep again.  After that his recollection was like a black night studded with little points of light which were physical sensations.  He remembered being very cold and sometimes very tired, he recollected the smell of paraffin, and of mouldy hay, and of a treacly drink which made him sick.  He remembered faces, too, a cross old woman who cursed him, a man who seemed to be always laughing, and whose laugh he feared more than curses. . . .

I suppose that Medina's spell must have been wearing thin during these last days, and that the keeper, Jason, or whoever he was, could not revive it.  For Mercot had begun to see Jason no longer as a terror but as an offence—an underbred young bounder whom he detested.  And with this clearing of the foreground came a lightening of the background.  He saw pictures of his life at Alcester, at first as purely objective things, but soon as in some way connected with himself.  Then longing started, passionate longing for something which he knew was his own. . . . It was a short step from that to the realization that he was Lord Mercot, though he happened to be clad like a tramp and was as dirty as a stoker. And then he proceeded to certain halting deductions. Something bad had happened to him : he was in a foreign land—which land he didn't know : he was being ill-treated and kept prisoner ; he must escape and get back to his old happy world. He thought of escape quite blindly, without any plan ; if only he could get away from that accursed *saeter*, he would remember better, things would happen to him, things would come back to him.

Then Jason went and Newhover came, and Newhover drove him half crazy with fear, for the doctor's face was in some extraordinary way mixed up with his confused memory of the gaps between the old world and the new. He was mad to escape now, but rather to escape from Newhover than to reach anywhere. He watched for his chance, and found it about eight o'clock the evening before, when the others in the house were at supper. Some instinct had led him towards Merdal. He had heard footsteps behind him and had taken to the thicket. . . . I appeared, an enemy as he thought, and he had despairingly flung himself on me. Then I had spoken his name, and that fixed the wavering panorama of his memory. He "came to himself" literally, and was now once more the undergraduate of Christ Church, rather shell-shocked and jumpy, but quite sane.

The question which worried me was whether the cure was complete, whether Newhover could act as Medina's deputy and resurrect the spell.

I did not believe that he could, but I wasn't certain. Anyhow it had to be risked.

Mercot repeated his request for the loan of my razor. He was smoking a Turkish cigarette as if every whiff took him nearer Elysium. Badly shorn, ill-clad, and bearded as he was, he had still the ghost of the air of the well-to-do, sporting young men. He wanted to know when the steamer sailed, but there seemed no panic now in his impatience.

"Look here," I said. "I don't think you can start just yet. There's a lot I want to tell you now you're able to hear it."

I gave him a rough summary of Macgillivray's story, and the tale of the three hostages. I think he found it comforting to know that there were others in the same hole as himself. "By Jove!" he said, "what a damnable business! And I'm the only one you've got on the track of. No word of the girl and the little boy?"

"No word!"

"Poor devils," he said, but I do not think he really took in the situation.

"So you see how we are placed. Macgillivray's round-up is fixed for the 10th of June. We daren't release the hostages till the 9th, for otherwise the gang would suspect. They have everything ready, as I've told you, for their own liquidation. Also, we can't release one without the others, unless by the 9th of June we have given up hope of the others. Do you see what I mean?"

He didn't. "All I want is to get home in double-quick time," he said.

"I don't wonder. But you must see that that is impossible, unless we chuck in our hand."

He stared at me, and I saw fright beginning to return to his eyes.

"Do you mean that you want me to go back to that bloody place ?"

"That's what I mean. If you think it out, you'll see it's the only way. We must do nothing to spoil the chances of the other two. You're a gentleman, and are bound to play the game."

"But I can't," he cried. "Oh, my God, you can't ask me to." There were tears in his voice. and his eyes were wild.

"It's a good deal to ask, but I know you will do it. There's not a scrap of danger now, for you have got back your memory, and you know where you are. It's up to you to play a game with your gaoler. He is the dupe now. You fill the part of the half-witted farm-boy and laugh at him all the time in your sleeve. Herr Gaudian will be waiting down here to keep an eye on you, and when the time is ripe—and it won't be more than five weeks—I give you full permission to do anything you like with Dr. Newhover."

"I can't, I can't," he wailed, and his jaw dropped like a scared child's.

Then Gaudian spoke. "I think we had better leave the subject for the present. Lord Mercot will do precisely what he thinks right. You have sprung the thing on him too suddenly. I think it might be a good plan if you went for a walk, Hannay. Try the south side of the foss—there's some very pretty scrambling to be had there."

He spoke to me at the door. "The poor boy is all in pieces. You cannot ask him for a difficult decision when his nerves are still raw. Will you leave him with me? I have had some experience in dealing with such cases."

When I got back for supper, after a climb which exercised every muscle in my body, I found Gaudian teaching Mercot a new patience game. We spent a very pleasant evening, and I noticed that Gaudian led the talk to matters in which the boy could share, and made him speak of himself. We heard about his racing ambitions, his desire to ride in the Grand National, his hopes for his polo game. It appeared that he was destined for the Guards, but he was to be allowed a year's travel when he left the 'Varsity, and we planned out an itinerary for him. Gaudian, who had been almost everywhere in the world, told him of places in Asia where no tourist had ever been and where incredible sport was to be had in virgin forest, and I pitched him some yarns about those few districts of Africa which are still unspoiled. He got very keen, for he had a bit of the explorer in him, and asked modestly if we thought he could pull off certain plans we had suggested. We told him there was no doubt about it. "It's not as tough a proposition as riding in the National," I said.

When we had put him to bed, Gaudian smiled

as if well pleased. "He has begun to get back his confidence," he said.

He slept for twelve hours, and when he woke I had gone out, for I thought it better to leave him in Gaudian's hands. I had to settle the business that day, for it was now the 27th. I walked down the fjord to Hauge, and told Johan to be ready to start next morning. I asked him about the weather, which was still cloudless, and he stared at the sky and sniffed, and thought it would hold for a day or two. "But rain is coming," he added, "and wind. The noise of the foss is too loud."

When I returned Gaudian met me at the door. "The boy has recovered," he said. "He will speak to you himself. He is a brave boy and will do a hard task well."

It was a rather shy and self-conscious Mercot that greeted me.

"I'm afraid I behaved rather badly yesterday, sir. I was feeling a bit rattled, and I'm ashamed of myself, for I've always rather fancied my nerve."

"My dear chap," I said, "you've been through enough to crack the nerve of a buffalo."

"I want to say that of course I'll do what you want. I must play the game by the others. That poor little boy! And I remember Miss Victor quite well—I once stayed in the same house with her. I'll go back to the *saeter* when you give the word. Indeed, I'm rather looking forward to it. I promise to play the half-wit so that Dr. Newhover will think me safe in the bag.

All I ask is that you let me have my innings with him when the time comes. I've a biggish score to settle."

"Indeed I promise that. Look here, Mercot, if you don't mind my saying it, I think you're behaving uncommonly well. You're a gallant fellow."

"Oh, that's all right," he said, blushing. "When do you want me to start ? If it's possible, I'd like another night in a decent bed."

"You shall have it. Early to-morrow morning we'll accompany you to the prison door. You've got to gibber when you see Newhover, and pretend not to be able to give any account of your doings. I leave you to put up a camouflage. The next five weeks will be infernally dull for you, but you must just shut your teeth and stick it out. Remember, Gaudian will be down here all the time and in touch with your friends, and when the day comes you will take your instructions from him. And, by the way, I'm going to leave you my pistol. I suppose you can keep it concealed, for Newhover is not likely to search your pockets. Don't use it, of course, but it may be a comfort to you to know that you have it."

He took it gladly. "Don't be afraid I'll use it. What I'm keeping for Newhover is the best hiding man ever had. He's a bit above my weight, but I don't mind that."

Very early next morning we woke Mercot, and, while the sky was turning from sapphire to turquoise, took our way through the hazy meadows and up the Snaasen track. We left it at the summit, and fetched a circuit round by the back of the *saeter*, but first we made Mercot roll in the thicket till he had a very grubby face and plenty of twigs and dust in his untidy hair. Then the two of us shook hands with him, found a lair in a patch of juniper, and watched him go forward.

A forlorn figure he looked in that cold half-light as he approached the *saeter* door. But he was acting his part splendidly, for he stumbled with fatigue, dropped heavily against the door, and beat on it feebly. It seemed a long time till it opened, and then he appeared to shrink back in terror. The old woman cried out shrilly to summon some one from within, and presently Newhover came out in a dressing-gown. He caught Mercot by the shoulder and shook him, and that valiant soul behaved exactly like a lunatic, shielding his head and squealing like a rabbit. Finally we saw him dragged indoors. . . . It was horrible to leave him like that, but I comforted myself with the thought of what Newhover would be like in five weeks' time.

We raced back to Peter Bojer's, and after a hasty breakfast started off for Hauge. I settled with Gaudian that he was to report any developments to me by cable, and I was to do the same to him. When the day of release was fixed, he was to go boldly up to Snaasen and deal with the doctor as he liked, making sure that he could not communicate with Medina for a day or two. A motor-launch would be waiting at Merdal to take the two to Stavanger, for I wanted him to see Mercot on board the English steamer. I arranged, too, that he should be supplied with adequate funds, for Mercot had not a penny.

We pushed off at once, for I had to be at Flacksholm in good time, and as the morning advanced I did not feel so sure of the weather. What wind we had had these last days had been mild breezes from the west, but now it seemed to be shifting more to the north, and increasing in vehemence. Down in that deep-cut fjord it was calm enough, but up on the crest of the tableland on the northern shore I could see that it was blowing hard, for my glass showed me little *tourmentes* of snow. Also it had suddenly got much colder. I made Johan force the pace, and early in the afternoon we were out of the shelter of the rock walls in the inlet into which the fjord broadened. Here it was blowing fairly hard, and there was a stiff sea running. Flying squalls of rain beat down on us from the north, and for five minutes or so would shut out the view. It was a regular gusty April day, such as you find in spring salmon-fishing in Scotland, and had my job been merely to catch the boat at Stavanger I should not have minded it at all. But there was no time for the boat, for in little more than twenty-four hours I had to meet Medina. I wondered if Archie Roylance had turned up. I wondered still more how an aeroplane was to make the return journey over these stormy leagues of sea.

Presently the low green lines of Flacksholm

showed through the spray, and when Johan began
to shape his course to the south-west for Stavanger,
I bade him go straight forward and land me on the
island. I told him I had a friend who was camp-
ing there, and that we were to be picked up in a
day or two by an English yacht. Johan obviously
thought me mad, but he did as he was told.
"There will be no one on the island yet," he said.
"The farmer from Rosmaer does not come till
June, when the haymaking begins. The winter
pasture is poor and sour." That was all to the
good, for I did not want any spectator of our
madness.

As we drew nearer I could see no sign of life on
the low shore, except an infinity of eider-ducks,
and a fine osprey which sat on a pointed rock like
a heraldic griffin. I was watching the bird, for I
had only seen an osprey twice before, when Johan
steered me into a creek, where there was deep
water alongside a flat reef. This, he told me, was
the ordinary landing-place from the mainland. I
flung my suit-case and rucksack on shore, said
good-bye to Johan and tipped him well, and
watched the little boat ploughing south till it was
hidden by a squall. Then, feeling every kind of
a fool, I seized my baggage and proceeded, like
Robinson Crusoe, into the interior.

It was raining steadily, a fine thin rain, and
every now and then a squall would burst on me
and ruffle the sea. Jolly weather for flying, I
reflected, especially for flying over some hundreds
of miles of ocean! . . . I found the farm, a few

rough wooden buildings and a thing like a stone
cattle-pen, but there was no sign of human life
there. Then I got out my map, and concluded
that I had better make for the centre of the
island, where there seemed to be some flat ground
at one end of the loch. I was feeling utterly
depressed, walking like a bagman with my kit in
my hand in an uninhabited Norwegian isle, and
due in London the next evening. London seemed
about as inaccessible in the time as the moon.

When I got to the rim of the central hollow there
was a brief clearing of the weather, and I looked
down on a little grey tarn set in very green meadows. In the meadows at the north end I saw to
my joy what looked like an aeroplane picketed
down, and a thing like a small tent near it. Also
I could see smoke curling up from a group of
boulders adjoining. The gallant Archie had
arrived, and my spirits lightened. I made good
going down the hill, and, as I shouted, a figure
like an Arctic explorer crawled out of the tent.

" Hullo, Dick," it cried. " Any luck ? "

" Plenty," I said. " And you ? "

" Famous. Got here last night after a clinkin'
journey, with the bus behavin' like a lamb. Had
an interestin' evenin' with the birds—Lord ! such
a happy huntin'-ground for 'em. I've been doin'
sentry-go on the tops all mornin' lookin' for you,
but the weather got dirty, so I returned to the
wigwam. Lunch is nearly ready."

" What about the weather ? " I asked anxiously.

" *Pas si bête*," he said, sniffing. " The wind is

pretty sure to go down at sunset. D'you mind a night journey?"

Archie's imperturbable good-humour cheered me enormously. I must say he was a born campaigner, for he had made himself very snug, and gave me as good a meal as I have ever eaten—a hot stew of tinned stuff and curry, a plum-pudding, and an assortment of what he called *delicatessen*. To keep out the cold we drank benedictine in horn mugs. He could talk about nothing but his blessed birds, and announced that he meant to come back to Flacksholm and camp for a week. He had seen a special variety—some kind of phalarope—that fairly ravished his heart. When I asked questions about the journey ahead of us, he scarcely deigned to answer, so busy he was with speculations on the feathered fauna of Norway.

"Archie," I said, "are you sure you can get me across the North Sea?"

"I won't say 'sure.' There's always a lottery in this game, but with any luck we ought to manage it. The wind will die down, and besides it's a ground wind, and may be quiet enough a few hundred feet up. We'll have to shape a compass course anyhow, so that darkness won't worry us."

"What about the machine?" I asked. I don't know why, but I felt horribly nervous.

"A beauty. But of course you never know. If we were driven much out of a straight course, our petrol might run short."

"What would that mean?"

"Forced landin'."

" But supposing we hadn't reached land ? "

" Oh, then we'd be for it," said Archie cheerfully. He added, as if to console me : " We might be picked up by a passin' steamer or a fishin' smack. I've known fellows that had that luck."

" What are the chances of our getting over safely ? "

" Evens. Never better or worse than evens in this flyin' business. But it will be all right. Dash it all, a woodcock makes the trip constantly in one flight."

After that I asked no more questions, for I knew I could not get him past the woodcock. I was not feeling happy, but Archie's calm put me to shame. We had a very good tea, and then, sure enough, the wind began to die down, and the clouds opened to show clear sky. It grew perishing cold, and I was glad of every stitch of clothing, and envied Archie his heavy skin coat. We were all ready about nine, and in a dead calm cast loose, taxied over a stretch of turf, rose above the loch so as to clear the hill, and turned our faces to the west, which was like a shell of gold closing down upon the molten gold of the sea.

Luck was with us that night, and all my qualms were belied. Apart from the cold, which was savage, I enjoyed every moment of the trip, till in the early dawn we saw a crawling black line beneath us which was the coast of Aberdeen. We filled up with petrol at a place in Kincardine, and had an enormous breakfast at the local hotel. Everything went smoothly, and it was still early in the day when I found we were crossing the Cheviots. We landed at York about noon, and, while Archie caught the London train, I got my car from the garage and started for Oxford. But first I wired to Mary asking her to wire to Medina in my name that I would reach London by the 7.15. I had a pleasant run south, left the car at Oxford, and duly emerged on the platform at Paddington to find Medina waiting for me.

His manner was almost tender.

" My dear fellow, I do hope you are better ? "

" Perfectly fit again, thank you. Ready for anything."

" You look more sunburnt than when you left town."

" It's the wonderful weather we've had. I've been lying basking on the veranda."

# CHAPTER XIII

## I VISIT THE FIELDS OF EDEN

THERE was a change in Medina. I noticed it the following day when I lunched with him, and very particularly at the next dinner of the Thursday Club, to which I went as his guest. It was a small change, which nobody else would have remarked, but to me, who was watching him like a lynx, it was clear enough. His ease of manner towards the world was a little less perfect, and when we were alone he was more silent than before. I did not think that he had begun to suspect any danger to his plans, but the day for their consummation was approaching, and even his cold assurance may have been flawed by little quivers of nervousness. As I saw it, once the big liquidation took place and he realized the assets which were to be the foundation of his main career, it mattered little what became of the hostages. He might let them go; they would wander back to their old world unable to give any account of their absence, and, if the story got out, there would be articles in the medical journals about these unprecedented cases of lost memory. So far I was certain that they had taken no lasting harm. But if the liquidation failed, God knew what their fate would be. They would never be seen again, for if his possession of them failed to avert disaster to his plans, he would play for safety, and, above all, for revenge. Revenge to a mind like his would be a consuming passion.

The fact that I had solved one conundrum and laid my hand on one of the hostages put me in a perfect fever of restlessness. Our time was very short, and there were still two poor souls hidden in his black underworld. It was the little boy I thought most of, and perhaps my preoccupation with him made me stupid about other things. My thoughts were always on the Blind Spinner, and there I could not advance one single inch. Macgillivray's watchers had nothing to report. It was no use my paying another visit to Madame Breda, and going through the same rigmarole. I could only stick to Medina and pray for luck. I had resolved that if he asked me again to take up my quarters with him in Hill Street I would accept, though it might be hideously awkward in a score of ways.

I longed for Sandy, but no word came from him, and I had his strict injunctions not to try to reach him. The only friend I saw in those early days of May was Archie Roylance, who seemed to have forgotten his Scotch greenshanks and settled down in London for the season. He started playing polo, which was not a safe game for a man with a crocked leg, and he opened his house in Grosvenor

Street and roosted in a corner of it.  He knew I was busy in a big game, and he was mad to be given a share in it, but I had to be very careful with Archie.  He was the best fellow alive, but discretion had never been his strong point.  So I refused to tell him anything at present, and I warned Turpin, who was an ancient friend of his, to do the same.  The three of us dined together one night, and poor old Turpin was rallied by Archie on his glumness.

"You're a doleful bird, you know," he told him.  "I heard somewhere you were goin' to be married, and I expect that's the cause.  What do you call it—*ranger* yourself?  Cheer up, my son. It can't be as bad as it sounds.  Look at Dick there."

I switched him on to other subjects, and we got his opinion on the modern stage.  Archie had been doing a course of plays, and had very strong views on the drama.  Something had got to happen, he said, or he fell asleep in the first act, and something very rarely happened, so he was left to slumber peacefully till he was awakened and turned out by the attendants.  He liked plays with shooting in them, and knockabout farce— anything indeed with a noise in it.  But he had struck a vein of serious drama which he had found soporific.  One piece in especial, which showed the difficulties of a lady of fifty who fell in love with her stepson, he seriously reprobated.

"Rotten," he complained.  "What did it matter to any one what the old cat did ?  But I assure you, everybody round me was gloatin' over it. A fellow said to me it was a masterpiece of tragic irony. What's irony, Dick ? I thought it was the tone your commandin' officer adopted, when you had made an ass of yourself, and he showed it by complimentin' you on your intelligence. . . . Oh, by the way, you remember the girl in green we saw at that dancin' place ? Well, I saw her at the show—at least, I'm pretty sure it was she—in a box with the black-bearded fellow. She didn't seem to be takin' much of it in. Wonder who she is and what she was doin' there ? Russian, d'you think ? I believe the silly play was translated from the Russian. I want to see that girl dance again."

The next week was absolutely blank, except for my own perpetual worrying. Medina kept me close to him, and I had to relinquish any idea of going down to Fosse for an occasional night. I longed badly for the place and for a sight of Peter John, and Mary's letters didn't comfort me, for they were getting scrappier and scrappier. My hope was that Medina would act on Kharama's advice, and in order to establish his power over his victims, bring them into the open and exercise it in the environment to which they had been accustomed. That wouldn't help me with the little boy, but it might give me a line on Miss Victor. I rather hoped that at some ball I would see him insisting on some strange woman dancing with him, or telling her to go home, or something, and then I would have cause to suspect. But no such luck. He never spoke to a woman in my presence who wasn't somebody perfectly well known. I began to think that he had rejected the Indian's advice as too dangerous.

Kharama, more by token, was back in town, and Medina took me to see him again. The fellow had left Claridge's and was living in a little house in Eaton Place, and away from the glitter of a big hotel he looked even more sinister and damnable. We went there one evening after dinner, and found him squatting on the usual couch in a room lit by one lamp and fairly stinking with odd scents. He seemed to have shed his occidental dress, for he wore flowing robes, and I could see his beastly bare feet under the skirts of them, when he moved to rearrange a curtain.

They took no more notice of me than if I had been a grandfather's clock, and to my disgust they conducted the whole conversation in some Eastern tongue. I gathered nothing from it, except a deduction as to Medina's state of mind. There was an unmistakable hint of nervousness in his voice. He seemed to be asking urgent questions, and the Indian was replying calmly and soothingly. By-and-by Medina's voice became quieter, and suddenly I realized that the two were speaking of me. Kharama's heavy eyes were raised for a second in my direction, and Medina turned ever so little towards me. The Indian asked some question about me, and Medina replied carelessly with a shrug of his shoulders and a slight laugh. The laugh rasped my temper. He was evidently saying that I was packed up and sealed and safe on the shelf.

That visit didn't make me feel happier, and next day, when I had a holiday from Medina's company, I had nothing better to do than to wander about London and think dismal thoughts. Yet, as luck would have it, that aimless walk had its consequences. It was a Sunday, and on the edge of Battersea Park I encountered a forlorn little company of Salvationists conducting a service in the rain. I stopped to listen—I always do—for I am the eternal average man who is bound to halt at every street show, whether it be a motor accident or a Punch and Judy. I listened to the tail-end of an address from a fat man who looked like a reformed publican, and a few words from an earnest lady in spectacles. Then they sang a hymn to a trombone accompaniment, and lo and behold, it was my old friend, which I had last whistled in Tom Greenslade's bedroom at Fosse. "There is rest for the weary," they sang :

> " On the other side of Jordan,
>     In the green fields of Eden,
>     Where the Tree of Life is blooming,
>         There is rest for you."

I joined heartily in the singing, and contributed two half-crowns to the collecting box, for somehow the thing seemed to be a good omen.

I had been rather neglecting that item in the puzzle, and that evening and during the night I kept turning it over till my brain was nearly addled.

" Where the sower casts his seed in
  Furrows of the fields of Eden."

That was the version in the rhyme, and in Tom
Greenslade's recollection the equivalent was a
curiosity shop in North London kept by a Jew
with a dyed beard.  Surely the two must correspond, though I couldn't just see how.  The other
two items had panned out so well that it was
reasonable to suppose that the third might do the
same.  I could see no light, and I finally dropped
off to sleep with that blessed " fields of Eden "
twittering about my head.

I awoke with the same obsession, but other
phrases had added themselves to it.  One was
the " playing-fields of Eton," about which some
fellow had said something, and for a moment I
wondered if I hadn't got hold of the right trail.
Eton was a school for which Peter John's name
was down, and therefore it had to do with boys,
and might have to do with David Warcliff.  But
after breakfast I gave up that line, for it led
nowhere.  The word was " Eden," to rhyme with
" seed in."  There were other fields haunting me
—names like Tothill Fields and Bunhill Fields.
These were places in London, and that was what I
wanted.  The Directory showed no name like that
of " Fields of Eden," but was it not possible that
there had once in old days been a place called by
that odd title ?

I spent the morning in the Club library, which
was a very good one, reading up Old London.  I

read all about Vauxhall Gardens and Ranelagh and Cremorne, and a dozen other ancient haunts of pleasure, but I found nothing to my purpose. Then I remembered that Bullivant—Lord Artinswell—had had for one of his hobbies the study of bygone London, so I telephoned to him and invited myself to lunch.

He was very pleased to see me, and it somehow comforted me to find myself again in the house in Queen Anne's Gate where I had spent some of the most critical moments of my life.

" You've taken on the work I wrote to you about," he said. " I knew you would. How are you getting on ? "

" So-so. It's a big job, and there's very little time. I want to ask you a question. You're an authority on Old London. Tell me, did you ever come across in your researches the name of the ' Fields of Eden ' ? "

He shook his head. " Not that I remember. What part of London ? "

" I fancy it would be somewhere north of Oxford Street."

He considered. " No. What is your idea ? A name of some private gardens or place of amusement ? "

" Yes. Just like Cremorne or Vauxhall."

" I don't think so, but we'll look it up. I've a good collection of old maps and plans, and some antique directories."

So after luncheon we repaired to his library and set to work. The maps showed nothing, nor did

the books at first.   We were searching too far back,
in the seventeenth and early eighteenth centuries,
when you went fox-hunting in what is now Regent's
Park and Tyburn gallows stood near the Marble
Arch.   Then, by sheer luck, I tried a cast nearer
our own time, and found a ribald work belonging
to about the date of the American War, which
purported to be a countryman's guide to the
amusements of town.   There were all sorts of
information about " Cider Cellars " and " Groves
of Harmony," which must have been pretty low
pubs, and places in the suburbs for cock-fighting
and dog-fighting.   I turned up the index, and
there to my joy I saw the word " Eden."

I read the passage aloud, and I believe my hands
were shaking.   The place was, as I hoped, north of
Oxford Street in what we now call Marylebone.
" The Fields of Eden," said the book, " were opened
by Mr. Askew as a summer resort for the gentlemen and sportsmen of the capital.   There of a fine
afternoon may be seen Lord A—— and the Duke
of B—— roving among the shady, if miniature,
groves, not unaccompanied by the fair nymphs of
the garden, while from adjacent arbours comes the
cheerful tinkle of glasses and the merry clatter
of dice, and the harmonious strains of Signora
F——'s Italian choir."   There was a good deal
more of it, but I stopped reading.   There was a
plan of London in the book, and from it I was
able to plot out the boundaries of that doubtful
paradise.

Then I got a modern map, and fixed the location

on it.  The place had been quite small, only a few acres, and to-day it was covered by the block defined by Wellesley Street, Apwith Lane, Little Fardell Street, and the mews behind Royston Square.  I wrote this down in my note-book and took my leave.

"You look pleased, Dick.  Have you found what you want ?  Curious that I never heard the name, but it seems to have belonged to the dullest part of London at the dullest period of its history." Lord Artinswell, I could see, was a little nettled, for your antiquary hates to be caught out in his own subject.

I spent the rest of the afternoon making a very thorough examination of a not very interesting neighbourhood.  What I wanted was a curiosity shop, and at first I thought I was going to fail. Apwith Lane was a kind of slum, with no shops but a disreputable foreign chemist's and a small dirty confectioner's, round the door of which dirty little children played.  The inhabitants seemed to be chiefly foreigners.  The mews at the back of Royston Square were, of course, useless ; it was long since any dweller in that square had kept a carriage, and they seemed to be occupied chiefly by the motor-vans of a steam laundry and the lorries of a coal merchant.  Wellesley Street, at least the part of it in my area, was entirely filled with the show-rooms of various American automobile companies.  Little Fardell Street was a curious place.  It had one old building which may have been there when the Fields of Eden flourished, and which now seemed to be a furniture repository of a sort, with most of the windows shuttered. The other houses were perhaps forty years old, most of them the offices of small wholesale businesses, such as you find in back streets in the City. There was one big French baker's shop at the corner, a picture-framer's, a watchmaker's, and a small and obviously decaying optician's. I walked down the place twice, and my heart sank, for I could see nothing in the least resembling an antique-shop.

I patrolled the street once more, and then I observed that the old dwelling, which looked like a furniture depository, was also some kind of shop. Through a dirty lower window I caught a glimpse of what seemed to be Persian rugs and the bland face of a soap-stone idol. The door had the air of never having been used, but I tried it and it opened, tinkling a bell in the back premises. I found myself in a small dusty place, littered up like a lumber room with boxes and carpets and rugs and bric-à-brac. Most of the things were clearly antiques, though to my inexpert eye they didn't look worth much. The Turcoman rugs, especially, were the kind of thing you can buy anywhere in the Levant by the dozen.

A dishevelled Jewess confronted me, wearing sham diamond ear-rings.

" I'm interested in antiques," I said pleasantly, taking off my hat to her. " May I look round ? "

" We do not sell to private customers," she said. " Only to the trade."

"I'm sorry to hear that. But may I look round? If I fancied something, I daresay I could get some dealer I know to offer for it."

She made no answer, but fingered her ear-rings with her plump grubby hands.

I turned over some of the rugs and carpets, and my first impression was confirmed. They were mostly trash, and a lacquer cabinet I uncovered was a shameless fake.

"I like that," I said, pointing to a piece of Persian embroidery. "Can't you put a price on it for me?"

"We only sell to the trade," she repeated, as if it were a litany. Her beady eyes, which never left my face, were entirely without expression.

"I expect you have a lot of things upstairs," I said. "Do you think I might have a look at them? I'm only in London for the day, and I might see something I badly wanted. I quite understand that you are wholesale people, but I can arrange any purchase through a dealer. You see, I'm furnishing a country house."

For the first time her face showed a certain life. She shook her head vigorously. "We have no more stock at present. We do not keep a large stock. Things come in and go out every day. We only sell to the trade."

"Well, I'm sorry to have taken up your time. Good-afternoon." As I left the shop, I felt that I had made an important discovery. The business was bogus. There was very little that any dealer would touch, and the profits from all the trade done would not keep the proprietor in Virginian cigarettes.

I paid another visit to the neighbourhood after dinner. The only sign of life was in the slums of Apwith Lane, where frowsy women were chattering on the kerb. Wellesley Street was shuttered and silent from end to end. So was Little Fardell Street. Not a soul was about in it, not a ray of light was seen at any window; in the midst of the din of London it made a little enclave like a graveyard. I stopped at the curiosity shop, and saw that the windows were heavily shuttered and that the flimsy old door was secured by a strong outer frame of iron which fitted into a groove at the edge of the pavement and carried a stout lock. The shutters on the ground-floor windows were substantial things, preposterously substantial for so worthless a show. As I looked at them I had a strong feeling that the house behind that palisade was not as dead as it looked, that somewhere inside it there was life, and that in the night things happened there which it concerned me tremendously to know.

Next morning I went to see Macgillivray.

"Can you lend me a first-class burglar?" I asked. "Only for one night. Some fellow who won't ask any questions and will hold his tongue."

"I've given up being surprised when you're about," he said. "No. We don't keep tame burglars here, but I can find you a man who knows rather more about the art than any professional. Why?"

" Simply because I want to get inside a certain house to-night, and I see no chance of doing it except by breaking my way in. I suppose you could so arrange it that the neighbouring policemen would not interfere. In fact, I want them to help to keep the coast clear."

I went into details with him, and showed him the lie of the land. He suggested trying the back of the house, but I had reconnoitred that side and seen that it was impossible, for the building seemed to join on with the houses in the street behind. In fact, there was no back door. The whole architecture was extremely odd, and I had a notion that the entrance in Little Fardell Street might itself be a back door. I told Macgillivray that I wanted an expert who could let me in by one of the ground-floor windows, and replace everything so that there should be no trace next morning. He rang a bell and asked for Mr. Abel to be sent for. Mr. Abel was summoned, and presently appeared, a small wizened man, like a country tradesman. Macgillivray explained what was required of him, and Mr. Abel nodded. It was a job which offered no difficulties, he said, to an experienced man. He would suggest that he investigated the place immediately after closing time, and began work about ten o'clock. If I arrived at 10.30, he promised to have a means of entrance prepared. He inquired as to who were the constables at the nearest points, and asked that certain special ones should be put on duty, with whom he could arrange matters. I never

saw any one approach what seemed to me to be a
delicate job with such business-like assurance.

"Do you want any one to accompany you
inside ? " Macgillivray asked.

I said no. I thought I had better explore the
place alone, but I wanted somebody within call in
case there was trouble, and of course if I didn't
come back, say within two hours, he had better
come and look for me.

"We may have to arrest you as a housebreaker,"
he said. "How are you going to explain your
presence if there's nothing wrong indoors and you
disturb the sleep of a respectable caretaker ? "

"I must take my chance," I said. I didn't feel
nervous about that point. The place would either
be empty, or occupied by those who would not
invite the aid of the police.

After dinner I changed into an old tweed suit
and rubber-soled shoes, and as I sat in the taxi I
began to think that I had entered too lightly on
the evening's business. How was that little man
Abel to prepare an entrance without alarming the
neighbourhood, even with the connivance of the
police ; and if I found anybody inside, what on
earth was I to say ? There was no possible story
to account for a clandestine entry into somebody
else's house, and I had suddenly a vision of the
ear-ringed Jewess screeching in the night and my
departure for the cells in the midst of a crowd of
hooligans from Apwith Lane. Even if I found
something very shady indoors, it would only be

shady to my own mind in connection with my own problem, and would be all right in the eyes of the law. I was not likely to hit on anything patently criminal, and, even if I did, how was I to explain my presence there? I suffered from a bad attack of cold feet, and would have chucked the business there and then but for that queer feeling at the back of my head that it was my duty to risk it— that if I turned back I should be missing something of tremendous importance. But I can tell you I was feeling far from happy when I dismissed the taxi at the corner of Royston Square, and turned into Little Fardell Street.

It was a dark cloudy evening, threatening rain, and the place was none too brilliantly lit. But to my disgust I saw opposite the door of the curiosity shop a brazier of hot coals and the absurd little shelter which means that part of the street is up. There was the usual roped-in enclosure, decorated with red lamps, a heap of débris, and a hole where some of the setts had been lifted. Here was bad luck with a vengeance, that the Borough Council should have chosen this place and moment of all others for investigating the drains. And yet I had a kind of shamefaced feeling of relief, for this put the lid on my enterprise. I wondered why Macgillivray had not contrived the thing better.

I found I had done him an injustice. It was the decorous face of Mr. Abel which regarded me out of the dingy pent-house.

" This seemed to me the best plan, sir," he said

respectfully. " It enables me to wait for you here without exciting curiosity. I've seen the men on point duty, and it is all right in that quarter. This street is quiet enough, and taxis don't use it as a short-cut. You'll find the door open. The windows might have been difficult, but I had a look at the door first, and that big iron frame is a piece of bluff. The bolt of the lock runs into the side-bar of the frame, but the frame itself is secured to the wall by another much smaller lock, which you can only detect by looking closely. I have opened that for you—quite easily done."

" But the other door—the shop door—that rings a bell inside."

" I found it unlocked," he said, with the ghost of a grin. " Whoever uses this place after closing hours doesn't want to make much noise. The bell is disconnected. You have only to push it open and walk in."

Events were forcing me against all my inclinations to go forward.

" If any one enters when I am inside ? . . ." I began.

" You will hear the sound and must take measures accordingly. On the whole, sir, I am inclined to think that there's something wrong with the place. You are armed ? No. That is as well. Your position is unauthorized, as one would say, and arms might be compromising."

" If you hear me cry ? "

" I will come to your help. If you do not return within—shall we say ?—two hours, I will make an entrance along with the nearest constable. The unlocked door will give us a pretext."

" And if I come out in a hurry ? "

" I have thought of that. If you have a fair start there is room for you to hide here," and he jerked his thumb towards the pent-house. " If you are hard-pressed I will manage to impede the pursuit."

The little man's calm matter-of-factness put me on my mettle. I made sure that the street was empty, opened the iron frame, and pushed through the shop door, closing it softly behind me.

The shop was as dark as the inside of a nut, not a crack of light coming through the closely-shuttered windows. I felt very eerie, as I tiptoed cautiously among the rugs and tables. I listened, but there was no sound of any kind either from within or without, so I switched on my electric torch and waited breathlessly. Still no sound or movement. The conviction grew upon me that the house was uninhabited, and with a little more confidence I started out to explore.

The place did not extend far to the back, as I had believed. Very soon I came upon a dead wall against which every kind of litter was stacked, and that way progress was stopped. The door by which the Jewess had entered lay to the right, and that led me into a little place like a kitchen, with a sink, a cupboard or two, a gas-fire, and in the corner a bed—the kind of lair which a caretaker occupies in a house to let. I made out a window rather high up in the wall, but I could discover no other entrance save that by which I had come. So I returned to the shop and tried the passage to the left.

Here at first I found nothing but locked doors, obviously cupboards. But there was one open, and my torch showed me that it contained a very steep flight of stairs—the kind of thing that in old houses leads to the attics. I tried the boards, for I feared that they would creak, and I discovered that all the treads had been renewed. I can't say I liked diving into that box, but there was nothing else for it unless I were to give up.

At the top I found a door, and I was just about to try to open it when I heard steps on the other side.

I stood rigid in that narrow place, wondering what was to happen next. The man—it was a man's foot—came up to the door and to my consternation turned the handle. Had he opened it I would have been discovered, for he had a light, and Lord knows what mix-up would have followed. But he didn't ; he tried the handle and then turned a key in the lock. After that I heard him move away.

This was fairly discouraging, for it appeared that I was now shut off from the rest of the house. When I had waited for a minute or two for the coast to clear, I too tried the handle, expecting to find it fast. To my surprise the door opened ; the man had not locked, but unlocked it. This could mean only one of two things. Either he intended himself to go out by this way later, or he expected some one and wanted to let him in.

From that moment I recovered my composure. My interest was excited, there was a game to play and something to be done. I looked round the passage in which I found myself and saw the explanation of the architecture which had puzzled me. The old building in Little Fardell Street was the merest slip, only a room thick, and it was plastered against a much more substantial and much newer structure in which I now found myself. The passage was high and broad, and heavily carpeted, and I saw electric fittings at each end. This alarmed me, for if any one came along and switched on the light, there was not cover to hide a cockroach. I considered that the boldest plan would be the safest, so I tiptoed to the end, and saw another passage equally bare going off at right angles. This was no good, so I brazenly assaulted the door of the nearest room. Thank Heaven! it was empty, so I could have a reconnoitring base.

It was a bedroom, well furnished in the Waring and Gillow style, and to my horror I observed that it was a woman's bedroom. It was a woman's dressing-table I saw, with big hair-brushes and oddments of scents and powders. There was a wardrobe with the door ajar full of hanging dresses. The occupant had been there quite lately, for wraps had been flung on the bed and a pair of slippers lay by the dressing-table, as if they had been kicked off hurriedly.

The place put me into the most abject fright. I seemed to have burgled a respectable flat and landed in a lady's bedroom, and I looked forward to some appalling scandal which would never be hushed up. Little Abel roosting in his penthouse seemed a haven of refuge separated from me by leagues of obstacles. I reckoned I had better get back to him as soon as possible, and I was just starting, when that happened which made me stop short. I had left the room door ajar when I entered, and of course I had switched off my torch after my first look round. I had been in utter darkness, but now I saw a light in the passage.

It might be the confounded woman who owned the bedroom, and my heart went into my boots. Then I saw that the passage lights had not been turned on, and that whoever was there had a torch like me. The footsteps were coming by the road I had come myself. Could it be the man for whom the staircase door had been unlocked ?

It was a man all right, and, whatever his errand, it was not with my room. I watched him through the crack left by the door, and saw his figure pass. It was some one in a hurry who walked swiftly and quietly, and, beyond the fact that he wore a dark coat with the collar turned up and a black soft hat, I could make out nothing. The figure went down the corridor and at the end seemed to hesitate. Then it turned into a room on the left and disappeared.

There was nothing to do but wait, and happily I had not to wait long, for I was becoming pretty nervous. The figure reappeared, carrying something in its hand, and as it came towards me I had a glimpse of its face. I recognized it at once as that of the grey melancholy man whom I had seen the first night in Medina's house, when I was coming out of my stupor. For some reason or another that face had become stamped on my memory, and I had been waiting to see it again. It was sad, forlorn, and yet in a curious way pleasant; anyhow there was nothing repellent in it. But he came from Medina, and at that thought every scrap of hesitation and funk fled from me. I had been right in my instinct; this place was Medina's, it was the Fields of Eden of the rhyme. A second ago I had felt a futile blunderer; now I was triumphant.

He passed my door and turned down the passage which ran at right angles. I stepped after him and saw the light halt at the staircase door, and then disappear. My first impulse was to follow, tackle him in the shop, and get the truth out of him, but I at once discarded that notion, which would have given the whole show away. My business was to make further discoveries. I must visit the room which had been the object of his visit.

I was thankful to be out of that bedroom. In the passage I listened, but could hear no sound anywhere. There was indeed a sound in the air, but it appeared to come from the outer world, a sound like an organ or an orchestra a long way off. I concluded that there must be a church somewhere near where the choir boys were practising.

The room I entered was a very queer place. It looked partly like a museum, partly like an office, and partly like a library. The curiosity shop had been full of rubbish, but I could see at a glance that there was no rubbish here. There were some fine Italian plaques—I knew something about these, for Mary collected them—and a set of green Chinese jars which looked the real thing. Also, there was a picture which seemed good enough to be a Hobbema. For the rest there were several safes of a most substantial make ; but there were no papers lying about, and every drawer of a big writing-table was locked. I had not the wherewithal to burgle the safes and the table, even if I had wanted to. I was certain that most valuable information lurked somewhere in that place, but I did not see how I could get at it.

I was just about to leave, when I realized that the sound of music which I had heard in the passage was much louder here. It was no choir-boys' practising, but strictly secular music, apparently fiddles and drums, and the rhythm suggested a dance. Could this odd building abut on a dance-hall ? I looked at my watch and saw that it was scarcely eleven, and that I had only been some twenty minutes indoors. I was now in a mood of almost foolhardy confidence, so I determined to do a little more research.

The music seemed to come from somewhere to the left. The windows of the room, so far as I could judge, must look into Wellesley Street,

which showed me how I had misjudged that
thoroughfare. There might be a dancing-hall
tucked in among the automobile shops. Anyhow,
I wanted to see what lay beyond this room, for
there must be an entrance to it other than by the
curiosity shop. Sure enough I found a door between two bookcases covered with a heavy *portière*,
and emerged into still another passage.

Here the music sounded louder, and I seemed to
be in a place like those warrens behind the stage
in a theatre, where rooms are of all kinds of shapes
and sizes. The door at the end was locked, and
another door which I opened gave on a flight of
wooden steps. I did not want to descend just yet,
so I tried another door, and then shut it softly.
For the room it opened upon was lighted, and I
had the impression of human beings not very far
off. Also the music, as I opened the door, came
out in a great swelling volume of sound.

I stood for a moment hesitating, and then I
opened that door again. For I had a notion that
the light within did not come from anything in the
room. I found myself in a little empty chamber,
dusty and cheerless, like one of those cubby-holes
you see in the Strand, where the big plate-glass
front window reaches higher than the shop, and
there is a space between the ceiling and the next
floor. All one side was of glass, in which a casement was half open, and through the glass came
the glare of a hundred lights from somewhere
beyond. Very gingerly I moved forward, till I
could look down on what was happening below.

For the last few seconds I think I had known what I was going to see. It was the dancing-club which I had visited some weeks before with Archie Roylance. There were the sham Chinese decorations, the blaze of lights, the nigger band, the whole garish spectacle. Only the place was far more crowded than on my previous visit. The babble of laughter and talk which rose from it added a further discord to the ugly music, but there was a fierce raucous gaiety about it all, an overpowering sense of something which might be vulgar, but was also alive and ardent. Round the skirts of the hall was the usual *rastaqouère* crowd of men and women drinking liqueurs and champagne, and mixed with fat Jews and blue-black dagos the flushed faces of boys from barracks or college who imagined they were seeing life. I thought for a moment that I saw Archie, but it was only one of Archie's kind, whose lean red visage made a queer contrast with the dead white of the woman he sat by.

The dancing was madder and livelier than on the last occasion. There was more vigour in the marionettes, and I was bound to confess that they knew their trade, little as I valued it. All the couples were expert, and when now and then a bungler barged in he did not stay long. I saw no sign of the girl in green whom Archie had admired, but there were plenty like her. It was the men I most disliked, pallid skeletons or puffy Latins, whose clothes fitted them too well, and who were sometimes as heavily made-up as the women.

One especially I singled out for violent disapproval. He was a tall young man, with a waist like a wasp, a white face, and hollow drugged eyes. His lips were red like a chorus-girl's, and I would have sworn that his cheeks were rouged. Anyhow, he was a loathsome sight. But, ye gods! he could dance. There was no sign of animation in him, so that he might have been a corpse, galvanized by some infernal power and compelled to move through an everlasting dance of death. I noticed that his heavy eyelids were never raised.

Suddenly I got a bad shock. For I realized that this mannequin was no other than my ancient friend, the Marquis de la Tour du Pin.

I hadn't recovered from that when I got a worse. He was dancing with a woman whose hair seemed too bright to be natural. At first I could not see her face clearly, for it was flattened against his chest, but she seemed to be hideously and sparsely dressed. She too knew how to dance, and the slim grace of her body was conspicuous even in her vulgar clothes. Then she turned her face to me, and I could see the vivid lips and the weary old pink and white enamel of her class. Pretty, too . . .

And then I had a shock which nearly sent me through the window. For in this painted dancer I recognized the wife of my bosom and the mother of Peter John.

# CHAPTER XIV

## SIR ARCHIBALD ROYLANCE PUTS HIS FOOT IN IT

THREE minutes later I was back in the curiosity shop. I switched off my light, and very gently opened the street door. There was a sound of footsteps on the pavement, so I drew back till they had passed. Then I emerged into the quiet street, with Abel's little brazier glowing in front of me, and Abel's little sharp face poked out of his pent-house.

" All right, sir ? " he asked cheerfully.

" All right," I said. " I have found what I wanted."

"There was a party turned up not long after you had gone in. Lucky I had locked the door after you. He wasn't inside more than five minutes. A party with a black top-coat turned up at the collar—respectable party he looked—oldish—might have been a curate. Funny thing, sir, but I guessed correctly when you were coming back, and had the door unlocked ready for you. . . . If you've done with me I'll clear up."

" Can you manage alone ? " I asked. " There's a good deal to tidy up."

He winked solemnly. " In an hour there won't
be a sign of anything. I have my little ways of
doing things. Good-night, sir, and thank you."
He was like a boots seeing a guest off from an hotel.

I found that the time was just after half-past
eleven, so I walked to Tottenham Court Road
and picked up a taxi, telling the man to drive to
Great Charles Street in Westminster. Mary was
in London, and I must see her at once. She had
chosen to take a hand in the game, probably at
Sandy's instigation, and I must find out what
exactly she was doing. The business was difficult enough already with Sandy following his
own trail and me forbidden to get into touch with
him, but if Mary was also on the job it would be
naked chaos unless I knew her plans. I own I
felt miserably nervous. There was nobody in the
world whose wisdom I put higher than hers, and
I would have trusted her to the other side of Tophet,
but I hated to think of a woman mixed up in
something so ugly and perilous. She was far too
young and lovely to be safe on the back-stairs.
And yet I remembered that she had been in
uglier affairs before this, and I recalled old Blenkiron's words : " She can't scare and she can't
soil." And then I began to get a sort of comfort
from the feeling that she was along with me in
the game ; it made me feel less lonely. But it
was pretty rough luck on Peter John. Anyhow,
I must see her, and I argued that she would probably be staying with her Wymondham aunts, and
that in any case I could get news of her there.

The Misses Wymondham were silly ladies, but their butler would have made Montmartre respectable. He and I had always got on well, and I think the only thing that consoled him when Fosse was sold was that Mary and I were to have it. The house in Great Charles Street was one of those tremendously artistic new dwellings with which the intellectual plutocracy have adorned the Westminster slums.

"Is her ladyship home yet?" I asked.

"No, Sir Richard, but she said she wouldn't be late. I expect her any moment."

"Then I think I'll come in and wait. How are you, Barnard? Found your city legs yet?"

"I am improving, Sir Richard, I thank you. Very pleased to have Miss Mary here, if I may take the liberty of so speaking of her. Miss Claire is in Paris still, and Miss Wymondham is dancing to-night, and won't be back till very late. How are things at Fosse, sir, if I may make so bold? And how is the young gentleman? Miss Mary has shown me his photograph. A very handsome young gentleman, sir, and favours yourself."

"Nonsense, Barnard. He's the living image of his mother. Get me a drink, like a good fellow. A tankard of beer, if you have it, for I've a throat like a grindstone."

I drank the beer and waited in a little room which would have been charming but for the garish colour scheme which Mary's aunts had on the brain. I was feeling quite cheerful again, for

Peter John's photograph was on the mantelpiece, and I reckoned that any minute Mary might be at the doorway.

She came in just before midnight. I heard her speak to Barnard in the hall, and then her quick step outside the door. She was preposterously dressed, but she must have done something to her face in the taxi, for the paint was mostly rubbed from it, leaving it very pale.

"Oh, Dick, my darling," she cried, tearing off her cloak and running to my arms. "I never expected you. There's nothing wrong at home?"

"Not that I know of, except that it's deserted. Mary, what on earth brought you here?"

"You're not angry, Dick?"

"Not a bit—only curious."

"How did you know I was here?"

"Guessed. I thought it the likeliest covert to draw. You see I've been watching you dancing to-night. Look here, my dear, if you put so much paint and powder on your face and jam it so close to old Turpin's chest, it won't be easy for the poor fellow to keep his shirt-front clean."

"You—watched—me—dancing! Were you in that place?"

"Well, I wouldn't say in it. But I had a prospect of the show from the gallery. And it struck me that the sooner we met and had a talk the better."

"The gallery! Were you in the house? I don't understand."

"No more do I. I burgled a certain house in

a back street for very particular reasons of my own. In the process I may mention that I got one of the worst frights of my life. After various adventures I came to a place where I heard the dickens of a row, which I made out to be dance music. Eventually I found a dirty little room with a window, and to my surprise looked down on a dancing-hall. I knew it, for I had once been there with Archie Roylance. That was queer enough, but imagine my surprise when I saw my wedded wife, raddled like a geisha, dancing with an old friend who seemed to have got himself up to imitate a waxwork."

She seemed scarcely to be listening. "But in the house! Did you see no one?"

"I saw one man and I heard another. The fellow I saw was a man I once met in the small hours with Medina."

"But the other? You didn't see him? You didn't hear him go out?"

"No." I was puzzled at her excitement. "Why are you so keen about the other?"

"Because I think—I'm sure—it was Sandy—Colonel Arbuthnot."

This was altogether beyond me. "Impossible!" I cried. "The place is a lair of Medina's. The man I saw was Medina's servant or satellite. Do you mean to say that Sandy has been exploring that house?"

She nodded. "You see, it is the Fields of Eden."

"Oh, I know. I found that out for myself. Do you tell me that Sandy discovered it too?"

" Yes. That is why I was there. That is why I have been living a perfectly loathsome life and am now dressed like a chorus girl."

" Mary," I said solemnly, " my fine brain won't support any more violent shocks. Will you please to sit down beside me, and give me the plain tale of all you have been doing since I said good-bye to you at Fosse ? "

" First," she said, " I had a visit from a dramatic critic on holiday, Mr. Alexander Thomson. He said he knew you and that you had suggested that he should call. He came three times to Fosse, but only once to the house. Twice I met him in the woods. He told me a good many things, and one was that he couldn't succeed and you couldn't succeed, unless I helped. He thought that if a woman was lost only a woman could find her. In the end he persuaded me. You said your-self, Dick, that Nanny was quite competent to take charge of Peter John, with Dr. Greenslade so close at hand. And I hear from her every day, and he is very well and happy."

" You came to London. But when ? "

" The day you came back from Norway."

" But I've been having letters regularly from you since then."

" That is my little arrangement with Paddock. I took him into my confidence. I send him the letters in batches and he posts one daily."

" Then you've been here more than a fortnight. Have you seen Sandy ? "

" Twice. He has arranged my life for me, and

has introduced me to my dancing partner, the Marquis de la Tour du Pin, whom you call Turpin. I think I have had the most horrible, the most wearing time that any woman ever had. I have moved in raffish circles and have had to be the most raffish of the lot. Do you know, Dick, I believe I'm really a good actress ! I have acquired a metallic voice, and a high silly laugh, and hard eyes, and when I lie in bed at night I blush all over for my shamelessness. I know you hate it, but you can't hate it more than I do. But it had to be done. I couldn't be a ' piker,' as Mr. Blenkiron used to say."

" Any luck ? "

" Oh yes," she said wearily. " I have found Miss Victor. It wasn't very difficult, really. When I had made friends with the funny people that frequent these places it wasn't hard to see who was different from the others. They're all mannequins, but the one I was looking for was bound to be the most mannequinish of the lot. I wanted some one without mind or soul, and I found her. Besides, I had a clue to start with. Odell, you know."

" It was the green girl ? "

She nodded. " I couldn't be certain, of course, till I had her lover to help me. He is a good man, your French Marquis. He has played his part splendidly. You see, it would never do to try to *awake* Adela Victor now. We couldn't count on her being able to keep up appearances without arousing suspicion till the day of release arrived.

But something had to be done, and that is my business especially. I have made friends with her, and I talk to her and I have attached her to me just a little, like a dog. That will give me the chance to do the rest quickly when the moment comes. You cannot bring back a vanished soul all at once unless you have laid some foundation. We have to be very, very careful, for she is keenly watched, but I think—yes, I am sure—it is going well."

" Oh, bravo ! " I cried. " That makes Number Two. I may tell you that I have got Number One." I gave her a short account of my doings in Norway. " Two of the poor devils will get out of the cage, anyhow. I wonder if it wouldn't be possible to pass the word to Victor and the Duke. It would relieve their anxiety."

" I thought of that," she replied, " but Colonel Arbuthnot says No, on no account. He says it might ruin everything. He takes a very solemn view of the affair, you know. And so do I. I have seen Mr. Medina."

" Where ? " I asked, in astonishment.

" I got Aunt Doria to take me to a party where he was to be present. Don't be worried. I wasn't introduced to him, and he never heard my name. But I watched him, and knowing what I did I was more afraid than I have ever been in my life. He is extraordinarily attractive—no, not attractive—seductive, and he is as cold and hard as chilled steel. You know these impressions I get of people which I can't explain—you say they are always right. Well, I felt him almost super-human. He exhales ease and power like a god, but it is a god from a lost world. I can see that, like a god too, it is souls that he covets. Ordinary human badness seems decent in comparison with that Lucifer's pride of his. I think if I ever could commit murder it would be his life I would take. I should feel like Charlotte Corday. Oh, I'm dis-mally afraid of him."

"I'm not," I said stoutly, "and I see him at closer quarters than most people." The measure of success we had attained was beginning to make me confident.

"Colonel Arbuthnot is afraid for you," she said. "The two times I have seen him in London he kept harping on the need of your keeping very near to him. I think he meant me to warn you. He says that when you are fighting a man with a long-range weapon the only chance is to hug him. Dick, didn't you tell me that Mr. Medina suggested that you should stay in his house ? I have been thinking a lot about that, and I believe it would be the safest plan. Once he saw you secure in his pocket he might forget about you."

"It would be most infernally awkward, for I should have no freedom of movement. But all the same I believe you are right. Things may grow very hectic as we get near the day."

"Besides, you might find out something about Number Three. It is the little boy that breaks my heart. The others might escape on their own account—some day, but unless we find *him* he is lost for ever. And Colonel Arbuthnot says that, even if we found him, it might be hard to restore the child's mind. Unless—unless——"

Mary's face had become grim, if one could use the word of a thing so soft and gentle. Her hands were tightly clasped, and her eyes had a strained, far-away look.

" I am going to find him," she cried. " Listen, Dick. That man despises women and rules them out of his life, except in so far as he can make tools of them. But there is one woman who is going to stop at nothing to beat him. . . . When I think of that little David I grow mad and desperate. I am afraid of myself. Have you no hope to give me ? "

" I haven't the shadow of a clue," I said dolefully. " Has Sandy none ? "

She shook her head. " He is so small, the little fellow, and so easy to hide."

" If I were in Central Africa, I would get Medina by the throat, and peg him down and torture him till he disgorged."

Again she shook her head. " Those methods are useless here. He would laugh at you, for he isn't a coward—at least, I think not. Besides, he is certain to be magnificently guarded. And for the rest, he has the entrenchments of his reputation and popularity, and a quicker brain than any of us. He can put a spell of blindness on the world —on all men and nearly all women."

The arrival of Miss Wymondham made me get up to leave. She was still the same odd-looking creature, with a mass of tow-coloured hair piled above her long white face. She had been dancing somewhere, and looked at once dog-tired and excited. " Mary has been having such a good time," she told me. " Even I can scarcely keep pace with her ardent youth. Can't you persuade her to do her hair differently ? The present arrangement is so *démodé*, and puts her whole figure out of drawing. Nancy Travers was speaking about it only to-night. Properly turned out, she said, Mary would be the most ravishing thing in London. By the way, I saw your friend Sir Archie Roylance at the Parminters'. He is lunching here on Thursday. Will you come, Richard ? "

I told her that my plans were vague and that I thought I might be out of town. But I arranged with Mary before I left to keep me informed at the Club of any news that came from Sandy. As I walked back I was infected by her distress over little David Warcliff. That was the most grievous business of all, and I saw no light in it, for though everything else happened according to plan, we should never be able to bring Medina to book. The more I thought of it the more hopeless our case against him seemed to be. We might free the hostages, but we could never prove that he had had anything to do with them. I could give damning evidence, to be sure, but who would take my word against his ? And I had no one to confirm me. Supposing I indicted him for kidnapping, and told the story of what I knew about the Blind Spinner and Newhover and Odell ? He and the world would simply laugh at me, and I should probably have to pay heavy damages for libel. None of his satellites, I was certain, would ever give him away ; they couldn't, even if they wanted to, for they didn't know anything. No, Sandy was right. We might have a measure of success, but there would be no victory. And yet only victory would give us full success, for only to get him on his knees, gibbering with terror, would restore the poor little boy. I strode through the empty streets with a sort of hopeless fury in my heart.

One thing puzzled me. What was Sandy doing in that house behind the curiosity shop, if indeed it was Sandy ? Whoever had been there had been in league with the sad grey man whom I watched from behind the bedroom door. Now the man was part of Medina's entourage : I had no doubt about the accuracy of my recollection. Had Sandy dealings with some one inside the enemy's citadel ? I didn't see how that was possible, for he had told me he was in deadly danger from Medina, and that his only chance was to make him believe that he was out of Europe. . . . As I went to bed, one thing was very clear in my mind. If Medina asked me to stay with him, I would accept. It would probably be safer, though I wasn't so much concerned about that, and it would possibly be more fruitful. I might find out something about the grey man.

Next day I went to see Medina, for I wanted him to believe that I couldn't keep away from him. He was in tremendous spirits about something or other, and announced that he was going off to the

country for a couple of days. He made me stay
to luncheon, when I had another look at Odell,
who seemed to be getting fat. " Your wind, my
lad," I said to myself, " can't be as good as it
should be. You wouldn't have my money in a
scrap." I hoped that Medina was going to have
a holiday, for he had been doing a good deal
lately in the way of speaking, but he said, " No
such luck." He was going down to the country
on business—an estate of which he was a trustee
wanted looking into. I asked in what part of
England, and he said Shropshire. He liked that
neighbourhood, and had an idea of buying a place
there when he had more leisure.

Somehow that led me to speak of his poetry.
He was surprised to learn that I had been studying the little books, and I could see took it as
a proof of my devotion. I made a few fulsome
observations on their merits, and said that even
an ignorant fellow like me could see how dashed
good they were. I also remarked that they
seemed to me a trifle melancholy.

" Melancholy ! " he said.   " It's a foolish world,
Hannay, and a wise man must have his moods of
contempt. Victory loses some of its salt when it
is won over fools."

And then he said what I had been waiting for.
" I told you weeks ago that I wanted you to take
up your quarters with me. Well, I repeat the
offer and will take no refusal."

" It is most awfully kind of you," I stammered.
" But wouldn't I be in the way ? "

"Not in the least. You see the house—it's as large as a barracks. I'll be back from Shropshire by Friday, and I expect you to move in here on Friday evening. We might dine together."

I was content, for it gave me a day or two to look about me. Medina went off that afternoon, and I spent a restless evening. I wanted to be with Mary, but it seemed to me that the less I saw her the better. She was going her own way, and if I showed myself in her neighbourhood it might ruin all. Next day was no better; I actually longed for Medina to return so that I might feel I was doing something, for there was nothing I could turn my hand to, and when I was idle the thought of David Warcliff was always present to torment me. I went out to Hampton Court and had a long row on the river; then I dined at the Club and sat in the little back smoking-room, avoiding any one I knew, and trying to read a book of travels in Arabia. I fell asleep in my chair, and, waking about half-past eleven, was staggering off to bed, when a servant came to tell me that I was wanted on the telephone.

It was Mary; she was speaking from Great Charles Street and her voice was sharp with alarm.

"There's been an awful mishap, Dick," she said breathlessly. "Are you alone? You're sure there's no one there? . . . Archie Roylance has made a dreadful mess of things. . . . He came to that dancing-place to-night, and Adela Victor was there, and Odell with her. Archie had seen her before, you know, and apparently was much attracted. No! He didn't recognize me, for when I saw him I kept out of range. But of course he recognized the Marquis. He danced with Adela, and I suppose he talked nonsense to her—anyhow, he made himself conspicuous. The result was that Odell proposed to take her away —I suppose he was suspicious of anybody of Archie's world—and, well, there was a row. The place was very empty—only about a dozen, and mostly a rather bad lot. Archie asked what right he had to carry off the girl, and lost his temper, and the manager was called in—the man with the black beard. He backed up Odell, and then Archie did a very silly thing. He said he was Sir Archibald Roylance, and wasn't going to be dictated to by any Jew, and, worse, he said his friend was the Marquis de la Tour du Pin, and that between them they would burst up this show, and that he wouldn't have a poor girl ordered about by a third-rate American bully. . . . I don't know what happened afterwards. The women were hustled out, and I had to go with the rest. . . . But, Dick, it's bad trouble. I'm not afraid so much for Archie, though he has probably had a bad mauling, but for the Marquis. They're sure to know who he is and all about him and remember his connection with Adela. They're almost sure to make certain in some horrible way that he can't endanger them again."

"Lord," I groaned, "what a catastrophe! And what on earth can I do? I daren't take any part!"

"No," came a hesitating voice. "I suppose not. But you can warn the Marquis—if nothing has happened to him already."

"Precious poor chance. These fellows don't waste time. But go to bed and sleep, my dear. I'll do my best."

My best at that time of night was pretty feeble. I rang up Victor's house and found, as I expected, that Turpin had not returned. Then I rang up Archie's house in Grosvenor Street and got the same answer about him. It was no good my going off to the back streets of Marylebone, so I went to bed and spent a wretched night.

Very early next morning I was in Grosvenor Street, and there I had news. Archie's man had just had a telephone message from a hospital to say that his master had had an accident, and would he come round and bring clothes. He packed a bag, and he and I drove there at once and found the miserable Archie in bed, the victim officially of a motor accident. He did not seem to be very bad, but it was a rueful face, much battered about the eyes and bandaged as to the jaw, which was turned on me when the nurse left us.

"You remember what I said about the pug with the diamond studs," he whistled, through damaged teeth. "Well, I took him on last night and got tidily laid out. I'm not up to professional standards, and my game leg made me slow."

"You've put your foot into it most nobly," I said. "What do you mean by brawling in a dance-club ? You've embarrassed me horribly in the job I'm on."

"But how ? " he asked, and but for the bandage his jaw would have dropped.

"Never mind how at present. I want to know exactly what happened. It's more important than you think."

He told me the same story that I had heard from Mary, but much garlanded with objurgations. He denied that he had dined too well—"nothing but a small whisky-and-soda and one glass of port." He had been looking for the girl in green for some time, and, having found her, was not going to miss the chance of making her acquaintance. "A melancholy little being with nothin' to say for herself. She's had hard usage from some swine—you could see it by her eyes—and I expect the pug's the villain. Anyway, I wasn't goin' to stand his orderin' her about like a slave. So I told him so, and a fellow with a black beard chipped in and they began to hustle me. Then I did a dam' silly thing. I tried to solemnize 'em by sayin' who I was, and old Turpin was there, so I dragged his name in. Dashed caddish thing to do, but I thought a marquis would put the wind up that crowd."

"Did he join in ? "

"I don't know—I rather fancy he got scragged at the start. Anyhow, I found myself facin' the pug, seein' bright red, and inclined to fight a dozen. I didn't last for more than one round—my game leg cramped me, I suppose. I got in one or two on his ugly face, and then I suppose I took a knock-out. After that I don't remember anything till I woke up in this bed feelin' as if I had been through a mangle. The people here say I was brought in by two bobbies and a fellow with a motor-car, who said I had walked slap into his bonnet at a street corner and hurt my face. He was very concerned about me, but omitted to leave his name and address. Very thoughtful of the sweeps to make sure there would be no scandal. . . . I say, Dick, you don't suppose this will get into the newspapers ? I don't want to be placarded as havin' been in such a vulgar shindy just as I'm thinkin' of goin' in for Parliament."

" I don't think there's the remotest chance of your hearing another word about it, unless you talk too much yourself. Look here, Archie, you've got to promise me never to go near that place again, and never on any account whatever to go hunting for that girl in green. I'll tell you my reasons some day, but you can take it that they're good ones. Another thing. You've got to keep out of Turpin's way. I only hope you haven't done him irreparable damage because of your idiocy last night."

Archie was desperately penitent. " I know I behaved like a cad. I'll go and grovel to old Turpin as soon as they let me up. But he's all right—sure to be. He wasn't lookin' for a fight like me. I expect he only got shoved into the street and couldn't get back again."

I did not share Archie's optimism, and very

soon my fear was a certainty. I went straight from the hospital to Carlton House Terrace, and found Mr. Victor at breakfast. I learned that the Marquis de la Tour du Pin had been dining out on the previous evening and had not returned.

# CHAPTER XV

## HOW A FRENCH NOBLEMAN DISCOVERED FEAR

I HAVE twice heard from Turpin the story I am going to set down—once before he understood much of it, a second time when he had got some enlightenment—but I doubt whether to his dying day he will ever be perfectly clear about what happened to him.

I have not had time to introduce Turpin properly, and in any case I am not sure that the job is not beyond me. My liking for the French is profound, but I believe there is no race on earth which the average Briton is less qualified to comprehend. For myself, I could far more easily get inside the skin of a Boche. I knew he was as full of courage as a Berserker, pretty mad, but with that queer core of prudence which your Latin possesses and which in the long run makes his madness less dangerous than an Englishman's. He was high-strung, excitable, imaginative, and, I should have said, in a general way very sensitive to influences such as Medina wielded. But he was forewarned. Mary had told him the main lines of the business, and he was playing the part she had set him as dutifully as a good child. I had not done justice to his power of self-control. He saw his sweetheart leading that blind, unearthly life, and it must have been torture to him to do nothing except look on. But he never attempted to wake her memory, but waited obediently till Mary gave orders, and played the part to perfection of the ordinary half-witted dancing mountebank.

When the row with Archie started, and the scurry began, he had the sense to see that he must keep out of it. Then he heard Archie speak his real name, and saw the mischief involved in that, for nobody knew him except Mary, and he had passed as a Monsieur Claud Simond from Buenos Aires. When he saw his friend stand up to the bruiser, he started off instinctively to his help, but stopped in time and turned to the door. The man with the black beard was looking at him, but said nothing.

There seemed to be a good deal of racket at the foot of the stairs. One of the girls caught his arm. " No good that way," she whispered. " It's a raid all right. There's another way out. You don't want your name in to-morrow's papers."

He followed her into a little side passage, which was almost empty and very dark, and there he lost her. He was just starting to prospect, when he saw a little dago whom he recognized as one of the bar-tenders. " Up the stairs, monsieur," the man said. " Then first to the left and down again. You come out in the yard of the Apollo Garage. Quick, monsieur, or *les flics* will be here "

Turpin sped up the steep wooden stairs, and found himself in another passage fairly well lit, with a door at each end.  He took the one to the left, and dashed through, wondering how he was to recover his hat and coat, and also what had become of Mary.  The door opened easily enough, and in his haste he took two steps forward.  It swung behind him, so that he was in complete darkness, and he turned back to open it again to give him light.  But it would not open.  With the shutting of that door he walked clean out of the world.

At first he was angry, and presently, when he realized his situation, a little alarmed.  The place seemed to be small, it was utterly dark, and as stuffy as the inside of a safe.  His chief thought at the moment was that it would never do for him to be caught in a raid on a dance-club, for his true name might come out and the harm which Archie's foolish tongue had wrought might be thereby aggravated.  But soon he saw that he had stepped out of one kind of danger into what was probably a worse.  He was locked in an infernal cupboard in a house which he knew to have the most unholy connections.

He started to grope around, and found that the place was larger than he thought.  The walls were bare, the floor seemed to be of naked boards, and there was not a stick of furniture any-where, nor, so far as he could see, any window.  He could not discover the door he had entered by, which on the inside must have been finished dead

level with the walls. Presently he found that his
breathing was difficult, and that almost put him
in a panic, for the dread of suffocation had always
been for him the private funk from which the
bravest man is not free. To breathe was like
having his face tightly jammed against a pillow.
He made an effort and controlled himself, for he
realized that if he let himself become hysterical
he would only suffocate the faster. . . .

Then he declares that he felt a hand pressing on
his mouth. . . . It must have been imagination,
for he admits that the place was empty; but all
the same the hand came again and again—a large
soft hand smelling of roses. His nerves began to
scream, and his legs to give under him. The roses
came down on him in a cloud, and that horrible
flabby hand, as big as a hill, seemed to smother
him. He tried to move, to get away from it, and
before he knew he found himself on his knees.
He struggled to get up, but the hand was on
him, flattening him out, and that intolerable
sweet sickly odour swathed him in its nauseous
folds. . . . And then he lost consciousness. . . .

How long he was senseless he doesn't know, but
he thinks it must have been a good many hours.
When he came to he was no longer in the cupboard.
He was lying on what seemed to be a couch in
a room which felt spacious, for he could breathe
freely, but it was still as black as the nether pit.
He had a blinding headache, and felt rather sick
and as silly as an owl. He couldn't remember
how he had come there, but as his hand fell on his

shirt-front, and he realized that he was in dress clothes, he recollected Archie's cry. That was the last clear thing in his head, but it steadied him, for it reminded him how grave was his danger. He has told me that at first he was half stifled with panic, for he was feeling abominably weak ; but he had just enough reason left in him to let him take a pull on his nerves. " You must be a man," he repeated to himself. " Even if you have stumbled into hell, you must be a man."

Then a voice spoke out of the darkness, and at the sound of it most of his fright disappeared. It was no voice that he knew, but a pleasant voice, and it spoke to him in French. Not ordinary French, you understand, but the French of his native valley in the South, with the soft slurring patois of his home. It seemed to drive away his headache and nausea, and to soothe every jangled nerve, but it made him weaker. Of that he has no doubt. This friendly voice was making him a child again.

His memory of what it said is hopelessly vague. He thinks that it reminded him of the life of his boyhood—the old château high in a fold of the limestone hills, the feathery chestnuts in the valley bottom, the clear pools where the big trout lived, the snowy winters when the wolves came out of the forests to the farmyard doors, the hot summers when the roads were blinding white and the turf on the downs grew as yellow as corn. The memory of it was all jumbled, and whatever the voice said its effect was more like music than spoken words. It smoothed out the creases in his soul, but it stole also the manhood from him. He was becoming limp and docile and passive like a weak child.

The voice stopped and he felt a powerful inclination to sleep. Then suddenly, between sleeping and waking, he became aware of a light, a star which glowed ahead of him in the darkness. It waxed and then waned, and held his eyes like a vice. At the back of his head he knew that there was some devilry in the business, that it was something which he ought to resist, but for the life of him he could not remember why.

The light broadened till it was like the circle which a magic-lantern makes on a screen. Into the air there crept a strange scent—not the sickly smell of roses, but a hard pungent smell which tantalized him with its familiarity. Where had he met it before ? . . . Slowly out of it there seemed to shape a whole world of memories.

Now Turpin before the War had put in some years' service in Africa with the Armée Coloniale as a lieutenant of Spahis, and had gone with various engineering and military expeditions south of the Algerian frontier into the desert. He used to rave to me about the glories of those lost days, that first youth of a man which does not return. . . . This smell was the desert, that unforgettable, untamable thing which stretches from the Mediterranean to the Central African forests, the place where, in the days when it was sea, Ulysses wandered, and where the magic of Circe and Calypso, for all the world knows, may still linger.

In the moon of light a face appeared, a face so strongly lit up that every grim and subtle line of it was magnified. It was an Eastern face, a lean high-boned Arab face, with the eyes set in a strange slant. He had never seen it before, but he had met something like it when he had dabbled in the crude magic of the sands, the bubbling pot, and the green herb fire. At first it was only a face, half averted, and then it seemed to move so that the eyes appeared, like lights suddenly turned on at night as one looks from without at a dark house.

He felt in every bone a thing he had almost forgotten, the spell and the terror of the desert. It was a cruel and inhuman face, hiding God knows what of ancient horror and sin, but wise as the Sphinx and eternal as the rocks. As he stared at it the eyes seemed to master and envelop him, and, as he put it, suck the soul out of him.

You see he had never been told about Kharama. That was the one mistake Mary made, and a very natural one, for it was not likely that he and the Indian would forgather. So he had nothing in his poor muddled head to help him to combat this mastering presence. He didn't try. He said he felt himself sinking into a delicious lethargy, like the coma which overtakes a man who is being frozen to death.

I could get very little out of Turpin about what happened next. The face spoke to him, but whether in French or some African tongue he didn't know—French, he thought—certainly not English. I gather that, while the eyes and the features were to the last degree awe-inspiring, the voice was, if anything, friendly. It told him that he was in instant danger, and that the only hope lay in utter impassivity. If he attempted to exercise his own will he was doomed, and there was sufficient indication of what that doom meant to shake his lethargy into spasms of childish fear. "Your body is too feeble to move," said the voice, "for God has laid His hand on it." Sure enough, Turpin realized that he hadn't the strength of a kitten. "You have surrendered your will to God till He restores it to you." That also was true, for Turpin knew he could not summon the energy to brush his hair, unless he was ordered to. "You will be safe," said the voice, "so long as you sleep. You will sleep till I bid you awake."

Sleep he probably did, for once again came a big gap in his consciousness. . . . The next he knew he was being jolted in something that ran on wheels, and he suddenly rolled over on his side, as the vehicle took a sharp turn. This time it didn't take him quite so long to wake up. He found he was in a big motor-car, with his overcoat on, and his hat on the seat beside him. He was stretched out almost at full length, and comfortably propped up with cushions. All this he realized fairly soon, but it was some time before he could gather up the past, and then it was all blurred and sketchy. . . . What he remembered most clearly was the warning that he was in grave peril and was only safe while he did nothing. That was burned in on his mind, and the lesson was pointed by the complete powerlessness of his limbs. He could hardly turn over from his side to his back, and he knew that if he attempted to stand he would fall down in a heap. He shut his eyes and tried to think.

Bit by bit the past pieced itself together. He remembered Archie's cry—and things before that —Mary—the girl in green. Very soon the truth smote him in the face. He had been kidnapped like the rest, and had had the same tricks played on him. . . . But they had only affected his body. As he realized this tremendous fact Turpin swelled with pride. Some devilry had stolen his physical strength, but his soul was his own still, his memory and his will. A sort of miasma of past fear still clung about him, like the after-taste of influenza, but this only served to make him angry. He was most certainly not going to be beaten. The swine had miscalculated this time ; they might have a cripple in their hands, but it would be a very watchful, wary, and determined cripple, quick to seize the first chance to be even with them. His anger made his spirits rise. All his life he had been a man of tropical loves and tempestuous hates. He had loathed the Boche, and freemasons, and communists, and the deputies of his own land, and ever since Adela's disappearance he had nursed a fury against a person or persons unknown : and now every detestation of which he was capable had been focused against those who were responsible for this night's work. The fools! They thought they had got a trussed sheep, when all the time it was a lame tiger.

The blinds of the car were down, but by small, painful movements he managed to make out that there was a man in the front seat beside the chauffeur. By-and-by he got a corner of the right-hand blind raised, and saw that it was night-time and that they were moving through broad streets that looked like a suburb. From the beat of the engine he gathered that the car was a Rolls-Royce, but not, he thought, one of the latest models. Presently the motion became less regular, and he realized that the suburban streets were giving place to country roads. His many expeditions in his Delage had taught him a good deal about the ways out of London, but, try as he might, he could not pick up any familiar landmark. The young moon had set, so he assumed that it was near midnight; it was a fine, clear night, not very dark, and he picked up an occasional inn and church, but they never seemed to pass through any village. Probably the driver was taking the less frequented roads—a view he was confirmed in by the frequent right-angled turns and the many patches of indifferent surface.

Very soon he found his efforts at reconnaissance so painful that he gave them up, and contented himself with planning his policy. Of course he must play the part of the witless sheep. That duty, he thought, presented no difficulties, for he

rather fancied himself as an actor. The trouble
was his bodily condition. He did not believe that
a constitution as good as his could have taken any
permanent damage from the night's work. . . .
The night's ! He must have been away for more
than one night, for the row with Archie had taken
place very near twelve o'clock. This must be the
midnight following. He wondered what Mr. Victor
was thinking about it—and Mary—and Hannay.
The miserable Hannay had now four lost ones to
look for instead of three ! . . . Anyhow, the devils
had got an ugly prisoner in him. His body must
soon be all right, unless, of course, they took steps
to keep it all wrong. At that thought Turpin's
jaw set. The rôle of the docile sheep might be
difficult to keep up very long.

The next he knew the car had turned in at a
gate and was following a dark tree-lined avenue.
In another minute it had stopped before the door
of a house, and he was being lifted out by the
chauffeur and the man from the front seat, and
carried into a hall. But first a dark bandana was
tied over his eyes, and, as he could do nothing with
his arms or legs, he had to submit. He felt himself carried up a short staircase, and then along a
corridor into a bedroom, where a lamp was lit.
Hands undressed him—his eyes still bandaged—
and equipped him with pyjamas which were not
his own, and were at once too roomy and too short.
Then food was brought, and an English voice
observed that he had better have some supper
before going to sleep. The bandage was taken off,

and he saw two male backs disappearing through the door.

Up till now he had felt no hunger or thirst, but the sight of food made him realize that he was as empty as a drum. By twisting his head he could see it all laid out on the table beside his bed—a good meal it looked—cold ham and galantine, an omelette, a salad, cheese, and a small decanter of red wine. His soul longed for it, but what about his feeble limbs ? Was this some new torture of Tantalus ?

Desire grew, and like an automaton he moved to it. He felt all numbed, with needles and pins everywhere, but surely he was less feeble than he had been in the car. First he managed to get his right arm extended, and by flexing the elbow and wrist a certain life seemed to creep back. Then he did the same thing with his right leg, and presently found that he could wriggle by inches to the edge of the bed. He was soon out of breath, but there could be no doubt about it—he was getting stronger. A sudden access of thirst enabled him to grasp the decanter, and, after some trouble with the stopper, to draw it to his lips. Spilling a good deal, he succeeded in getting a mouthful. " Larose," he murmured, " and a good vintage. It would have been better if it had been cognac."

But the wine put new life into him. He found he could use both arms, and he began wolfishly on the omelette, making a rather messy job of it. By this time he was feeling a remarkably vigorous convalescent, and he continued with the cold meat, till the cramp in his left shoulder forced him to lie back on the pillow. It soon passed, and he was able in fair comfort to finish the meal down to the last lettuce leaf of the salad and the last drop of claret. The Turpin who reclined again on the bed was to all intents the same vigorous young man who the night before had stumbled through that fateful door into the darkness. But it was a Turpin with a profoundly mystified mind.

He would have liked to smoke, but his cigarettes were in the pocket of his dress coat, which had been removed. So he started to do for his legs what he had already achieved for his arms, and with the same happy results. It occurred to him that, while he was alone, he had better discover whether or not he could stand. He made the effort, rolled out of bed on to the floor, hit the little table with his head and set the dishes rattling.

But after a few scrambles he got to his feet and managed to shuffle round the room. The mischief was leaving his body—so much was plain—and but for a natural stiffness in the joints he felt as well as ever. But what it all meant he hadn't a notion. He was inclined to the belief that somehow he had scored off his enemies, and was a tougher proposition than they had bargained for. They had assuredly done no harm to his mind with their witchcraft, and it looked as if they had also failed with his body. The thought emboldened him. The house seemed quiet ; why should he not do a little exploration ?

He cautiously opened the door, finding it, somewhat to his surprise, unlocked. The passage was lit by a hanging oil-lamp, carpeted with an old-fashioned drugget, and its walls decorated with a set of flower pictures. Turpin came to the conclusion that rarely in his life had he been in a dwelling which seemed more innocent and home-like. He considered himself sensitive to the *nuances* of the sinister in an atmosphere, and there was nothing of that sort in this. He took a step or two down the passage, and then halted, for he thought he heard a sound. Yes, there could be no doubt of it. It was water gushing from a tap. Some one in the establishment was about to have a bath.

Then he slipped back to his room just in time. The some one was approaching with light feet and a rustle of draperies. He had his door shut when the steps passed, and then opened it and stuck his head out. He saw a pink dressing-gown, and above it a slender neck and masses of dark hair. It was the figure which he of all men was likely to know best.

It seemed that the place for him was bed, so he got between the sheets again and tried to think. Adela Victor was here ; therefore he was in the hands of her captors, and made a fourth in their bag. But what insanity had prompted these wary criminals to bring the two of them to the same prison ? Were they so utterly secure, so confident of their power, that they took this crazy risk ? The insolence of it made him furious. In the name of every saint he swore that he would make them regret it. He would free the lady and himself, though he had to burn down the house and wring the neck of every inmate. And then he remembered the delicacy of the business, and the need of exact timing, if the other two hostages were not to be lost, and at the thought he groaned.

There was a tap at the door, and a man entered to clear away the supper table. He seemed an ordinary English valet, with his stiff collar and decent black coat and smug, expressionless face.

" Beg pardon, my lord," he said, " at what hour would you like your shavin' water ? Seein' it's been a late night, I make so bold as to suggest ten o'clock."

Turpin assented, and the servant had hardly gone when another visitor appeared. It was a slim pale man, whom he was not conscious of having seen before, a man with grey hair and a melancholy droop of the head. He stood at the foot of the bed, gazing upon the prostrate Turpin, and his look was friendly. Then he addressed him in French of the most Saxon type.

" Êtes-vous comfortable, monsieur ? C'est bien. Soyez tranquille. Nous sommes vos amis. Bon soir."

# CHAPTER XVI

### OUR TIME IS NARROWED

I LUNCHED that day with Mary—alone, for her aunts were both in Paris—and it would have been hard to find in the confines of the British islands a more dejected pair. Mary, who had always a singular placid gentleness, showed her discomposure only by her pallor. As for me I was as restless as a bantam.

"I wish I had never touched the thing," I cried. "I have done more harm than good."

"You have found Lord Mercot," she protested.

"Yes, and lost Turpin. The brutes are still three up on us. We thought we had found two, and now we have lost Miss Victor again. And Turpin! They'll find him an ugly customer, and probably take strong measures with him. They'll stick to him and the girl and the little boy now like wax; for last night's performance is bound to make them suspicious."

"I wonder," said Mary, always an optimist. "You see, Sir Archie only dragged him in because of his rank. It looked odd his being in Adela's company, but then all the times he has seen her he never spoke a word to her. They must have noticed that. I'm anxious about Sir Archie. He ought to leave London."

"Confound him! He's going to, as soon as he gets out of hospital, which will probably be this afternoon. I insisted on it, but he meant to in any case. He's heard an authentic report of a green sandpiper nesting somewhere. It would be a good thing if Archie would stick to birds. He has no head for anything else. . . . And now we've got to start again at the beginning."

"Not quite the beginning," she interposed.

"Dashed near it. They won't bring Miss Victor into that kind of world again, and all your work goes for nothing, my dear. It's uncommon bad luck that you didn't begin to wake her up, for then she might have done something on her own account. But she's still a dummy, and tucked away, you may be sure, in some place where we can never reach her. And we have little more than three weeks left."

"It is bad luck," Mary agreed. "But, Dick, I've a feeling that I haven't lost Adela Victor. I believe that somehow or other we'll soon get in touch with her again. You remember how children when they lose a ball sometimes send another one after it in the hope that one will find the other. Well, we've sent the Marquis after Adela, and I've a notion we may find them both together. We always did that as children." . . . She paused at the word "children," and I saw pain in her eyes. "Oh, Dick, the little boy! We're no nearer him, and he's far the most tragic of all."

The whole business looked so black that I had no word of comfort to give her.

" And to put the lid on it," I groaned, " I've got to settle down in Medina's house this evening. I hate the idea like poison."

" It's the safest way," she said.

" Yes, but it puts me out of action. He'll watch me like a lynx, and I won't be able to take a single step on my own—simply sit there and eat and drink and play up to his vanity. Great Scott, I swear I'll have a row with him and break his head."

" Dick, you're not going to—how do you say it ?—chuck in your hand ? Everything depends on you. You're our scout in the enemy's head-quarters. Your life depends on your playing the game. Colonel Arbuthnot said so. And you may find out something tremendous. It will be horrible for you, but it isn't for long, and it's the only way."

That was Mary all over. She was trembling with anxiety for me, but she was such a thorough sportsman that she wouldn't take any soft option.

" You may hear something about David War-cliff," she added.

" I hope to God I do. Don't worry, darling. I'll stick it out. But, look here, we must make a plan. I shall be more or less shut off from the world, and I must have a line of communication open. You can't telephone to me at that house, and I daren't ring you up from there. The only chance is the Club. If you have any message, ring up the head porter and make him write it down. I'll arrange that he keeps it quiet, and I'll pick up the messages when I get the chance. And I'll ring you up occasionally to give you the news. But I must be jolly careful, for, likely as not, Medina will keep an eye on me even there. You're in touch with Macgillivray ? "

She nodded.

" And with Sandy ? "

" Yes, but it takes some time—a day at least. We can't correspond direct."

" Well, there's the lay-out. I'm a prisoner—with qualifications. You and I can keep up some sort of communication. As you say, there's only about another three weeks."

" It would be nothing if only we had some hope."

" That's life, my dear. We've got to go on to the finish anyhow, trusting that luck will turn in the last ten minutes."

I arrived in Hill Street after tea and found Medina in the back smoking-room, writing letters.

" Good man, Hannay," he said ; " make yourself comfortable. There are cigars on that table."

" Had a satisfactory time in Shropshire ? " I asked.

" Rotten. I motored back this morning, starting very early. Some tiresome business here wanted my attention. I'm sorry, but I'll be out to dinner to-night. The same thing always happens when I want to see my friends—a hideous rush of work."

He was very hospitable, but his manner had not the ease it used to have. He seemed on the edge about something, and rather preoccupied. I guessed it was the affair of Archie Roylance and Turpin.

I dined alone and sat after dinner in the smoking-room, for Odell never suggested the library, though I would have given a lot to fossick about that place. I fell asleep over the *Field* and was wakened about eleven by Medina. He looked almost tired, a rare thing for him ; also his voice was curiously hard. He made some trivial remark about the weather, and a row in the Cabinet which was going on. Then he said suddenly—

"Have you seen Arbuthnot lately ? "

"No," I replied, with real surprise in my tone. "How could I ?  He has gone back to the East."

"So I thought.  But I have been told that he has been seen again in England."

For a second I had a horrid fear that he had got on the track of my meeting with Sandy at the Cotswold inn and his visit to Fosse. His next words reassured me.

"Yes.  In London.  Within the last few days."

It was easy enough for me to show astonishment. "What a crazy fellow he is ! He can't stay put for a week together. All I can say is that I hope he won't come my way. I've no particular wish to see him again."

Medina said no more.  He accompanied me to

my bedroom, asked if I had everything I wanted, bade me good-night, and left me.

Now began one of the strangest weeks in my life. Looking back, it has still the inconsequence of a nightmare, but one or two episodes stand out like reefs in a tide-race. When I woke the first morning under Medina's roof I believed that somehow or other he had come to suspect me. I soon saw that that was nonsense, that he regarded me as a pure chattel; but I saw, too, that a most active suspicion of something had been awakened in his mind. Probably Archie's fiasco, together with the news of Sandy, had done it, and perhaps there was in it something of the natural anxiety of a man nearing the end of a difficult course. Anyhow, I concluded that this tension of mind on his part was bound to make things more difficult for me. Without suspecting me, he kept me perpetually under his eye. He gave me orders as if I were a child, or rather he made suggestions, which in my character of worshipping disciple I had to treat as orders.

He was furiously busy night and day, and yet he left me no time to myself. He wanted to know everything I did, and I had to give an honest account of my doings, for I had a feeling that he had ways of finding out the truth. One lie discovered would, I knew, wreck my business utterly, for if I were under his power, as he believed I was, it would be impossible for me to lie to him. Consequently I dared not pay many visits to the Club, for he would want to know what I did there.

I was on such desperately thin ice that I thought it best to stay most of my time in Hill Street, unless he asked me to accompany him. I consulted Mary about this, and she agreed that it was the wise course.

Apart from a flock of maids, there was no other servant in the house but Odell. Twice I met the grey, sad-faced man on the stairs, the man I had seen on my first visit, and had watched a week before in the house behind the curiosity shop. I asked who he was, and was told a private secretary, who helped Medina in his political work. I gathered that he did not live regularly in the house, but only came there when his services were required.

Now Mary had said that the other man that evening in Little Fardell Street had been Sandy. If she was right, this fellow might be a friend, and I wondered if I could get in touch with him. The first time I encountered him he never raised his eyes. The second time I forced him by some question to look at me, and he turned on me a perfectly dead expressionless face like a codfish. I concluded that Mary had been in error, for this was the genuine satellite, every feature of whose character had been steam-rollered out of existence by Medina's will.

I was seeing Medina now at very close quarters, and in complete undress, and the impression he had made on me at our first meeting—which had been all overlaid by subsequent happenings—grew as vivid again as daylight. The " good fellow," of course, had gone ; I saw behind all his perfection of manner to the naked ribs of his soul. He would talk to me late at night in that awful library, till I felt that he and the room were one presence, and that all the diabolic lore of the ages had been absorbed by this one mortal. You must understand that there was nothing wrong in the ordinary sense with anything he said. If there had been a phonograph recording his talk it could have been turned on with perfect safety in a girls' school. . . . He never spoke foully, or brutally. I don't believe he had a shadow of those faults of the flesh which we mean when we use the word "vice." But I swear that the most wretched libertine before the bar of the Almighty would have shown a clean sheet compared to his.

I know no word to describe how he impressed me except "wickedness." He seemed to annihilate the world of ordinary moral standards, all the little rags of honest impulse and stumbling kindness with which we try to shelter ourselves from the winds of space. His consuming egotism made life a bare cosmos in which his spirit scorched like a flame. I have met bad men in my day, fellows who ought to have been quietly and summarily put out of existence, but if I had had the trying of them I would have found bits of submerged decency and stunted remnants of good feeling. At any rate they were human, and their beastliness was a degeneration of humanity, not its flat opposite. Medina made an atmosphere which was like a cold bright air in which nothing can live. He was utterly and consumedly wicked, with no

standard which could be remotely related to
ordinary life. That is why, I suppose, mankind
has had to invent the notion of devils. He seemed
to be always lifting the corner of a curtain and
giving me peeps into a hoary mystery of iniquity
older than the stars. . . . I suppose that some
one who had never felt his hypnotic power would
have noticed very little in his talk except its auda-
cious cleverness, and that some one wholly under
his dominion would have been less impressed than
me, because he would have forgotten his own
standards, and been unable to make the comparison.
I was just in the right position to understand and
tremble. . . . Oh, I can tell you, I used to go to
bed solemnized, frightened half out of my wits,
and yet in a violent revulsion, and hating him like
hell. I was pretty clear that he was mad, for
madness means just this dislocation of the modes
of thought which mortals have agreed upon as
necessary to keep the world together. His head
used to seem as round as a bullet, like nothing
you find even in the skulls of cave-men, and his
eyes to have a blue light in them like the sunrise
of death in an arctic waste.

One day I had a very narrow escape. I went
to the club, to see if there was anything from
Mary, and received instead a long cable from
Gaudian in Norway. I had just opened it, when
I found Medina at my elbow. He had seen me
enter, and followed me, in order that we should
walk home together.

Now I had arranged a simple code with Gaudian

for his cables, and by the mercy of Heaven that honest fellow had taken special precautions, and got some friend to send this message from Christiania. Had it borne the Merdal stamp, it would have been all up with me.

The only course was the bold one, though I pursued it with a quaking heart.

"Hullo," I cried, "here's a cable from a pal of mine in Norway. Did I tell you I had been trying to get a beat on the Leardal for July? I had almost forgotten about the thing. I started inquiring in March, and here's my first news."

I handed him the two sheets and he glanced at the place of dispatch.

"Code," he said. "Do you want to work it out now?"

"If you don't mind waiting a few seconds. It's a simple code of my own invention, and I ought to be able to decipher it pretty fast."

We sat down at one of the tables in the hall, and I took up a pen and a sheet of notepaper. As I think I have mentioned before, I am rather a swell at codes, and this one in particular I could read without much difficulty. I jotted down some letters and numbers, and then wrote out a version, which I handed to Medina. This was what he read:

"Upper beat Leardal available from first of month. Rent two hundred and fifty with option of August at one hundred more. No limit to rods. Boat on each pool. Tidal waters can also be got for sea trout by arrangement. If you accept please cable word 'Yes.' You should arrive not later than June 29th. Bring plenty of bottled prawns. Motor-boat can be had from Bergen. Andersen, Grand Hotel, Christiania."

But all the time I was scribbling this nonsense I was reading the code correctly and getting the message by heart. Here is what Gaudian really sent :

"Our friend has quarrelled with keeper and beaten him soundly. I have taken charge at farm and frightened latter into docility. He will remain prisoner in charge of ally of mine till I give the word to release. Meantime, think it safer to bring friend to England and start on Monday. Will wire address in Scotland and wait your instructions. No danger of keeper sending message. Do not be anxious, all is well."

Having got that clear in my head, I tore the cable into small pieces and flung them into the waste-paper basket.

"Well, are you going ? " Medina asked.

"Not I. I'm off salmon-fishing for the present." I took a cable form from the table, and wrote : "Sorry, must cancel Leardal plan," signed it "Hannay," addressed it to "Andersen, Grand Hotel, Christiania," and gave it to the porter to send off. I wonder what happened to that telegram. It is probably still stuck up on the hotel board, awaiting the arrival of the mythical Andersen.

On our way back to Hill Street Medina put his arm in mine, and was very friendly. " I hope to get a holiday," he said, " perhaps just after the beginning of June. Only a day or two off now. I may go abroad for a little. I would like you to come with me."

That puzzled me a lot. Medina could not possibly leave town before the great liquidation, and there could be no motive in his trying to mislead me on such a point, seeing that I was living in his house. I wondered if something had happened to make him change the date. It was of the first importance that I should find this out, and I did my best to draw him about his plans. But I could get nothing out of him except that he hoped for an early holiday, and " early " might apply to the middle of June as well as to the beginning, for it was now the 27th of May.

Next afternoon at tea-time to my surprise Odell appeared in the smoking-room, followed by the long lean figure of Tom Greenslade. I never saw anybody with greater pleasure, but I didn't dare to talk to him alone. " Is your master upstairs ? " I asked the butler. " Will you tell him that Dr. Greenslade is here ? He is an old friend of his."

We had rather less than two minutes before Medina appeared. " I come from your wife," Greenslade whispered. " She has told me all about the business, and she thought this was the

safest plan. I was to tell you that she has news
of Miss Victor and the Marquis. They are safe
enough. Any word of the little boy ? "

He raised his voice as Medina entered. "My
dear fellow, this is a great pleasure. I had to be
in London for a consultation, and I thought I
would look up Hannay. I hardly hoped to have
the luck to catch a busy man like you."

Medina was very gracious—no, that is not the
word, for there was nothing patronizing in his
manner. He asked in the most friendly way about
Greenslade's practice, and how he liked English
country life after his many wanderings. He spoke
with an air of regret of the great valleys of loess
and the windy Central Asian tablelands where
they had first forgathered. Odell brought in tea,
and we made as pleasant a trio of friends as you
could find in London. I asked a few casual
questions about Fosse, and then I mentioned
Peter John. Here Greenslade had an inspiration ;
he told me afterwards that he thought it might
be a good thing to open a channel for further
communications.

"I think he's all right," he said slowly. "He's
been having occasional stomach-aches, but I
expect that is only the result of hot weather and
the first asparagus. Lady Hannay is a little
anxious—you know what she is, and all mothers
to-day keep thinking about appendicitis. So I'm
keeping my eye on the little man. You needn't
worry, Dick."

I take credit to myself for having divined the

doctor's intention. I behaved as if I scarcely heard him, and as if Fosse Manor and my family were things infinitely remote. Indeed, I switched off the conversation to where Medina had last left it, and I behaved towards Tom Greenslade as if his presence rather bored me, and I had very little to say to him. When he got up to go, it was Medina who accompanied him to the front door. All this was a heavy strain upon my self-command, for I would have given anything for a long talk with him—though I had the sense not to believe his news about Peter John.

"Not a bad fellow, that doctor of yours," Medina observed on his return.

"No," I said carelessly. "Rather a dull dog all the same, with his country gossip. But I wish him well, for it is to him that I owe your friendship."

I must count that episode one of my lucky moments, for it seemed to give Medina some special satisfaction. "Why do you make this your only sitting-room?" he asked. "The library is at your disposal, and it is pleasanter in summer than any other part of the house."

"I thought I might be disturbing your work," I said humbly.

"Not a bit of it. Besides, I've nearly finished my work. After to-night I can slack off, and presently I'll be an idle man."

"And then the holiday?"

"Then the holiday." He smiled in a pleasant boyish way, which was one of his prettiest tricks.

" How soon will that be ? "

" If all goes well, very soon. Probably after the 2nd of June. By the way, the Thursday Club dines on the 1st. I want you to be my guest again."

Here was more food for thought. The conviction grew upon me that he and his friends had put forward the date of liquidation ; they must have suspected something—probably from Sandy's presence in England—and were taking no risks. I smoked that evening till my tongue was sore, and went to bed in a fever of excitement. The urgency of the matter fairly screamed in my ears, for Macgillivray must know the truth at once, and so must Mary. Mercot was safe, and there was a chance apparently of Turpin and Miss Victor, which must be acted upon instantly if the main date were changed. Of the little boy I had given up all hope. . . . But how to find the truth ! I felt like a man in a bad dream who is standing on the line with an express train approaching, and does not know how to climb back on to the platform.

Next morning Medina never left me. He took me in his car to the City, and I waited while he did his business, and then to call in Carlton House Terrace a few doors from the Victors' house. I believe it was the residence of the man who led his party in the Lords. After luncheon he solemnly installed me in the library. " You're not much of a reader, and in any case you would probably find my books dull. But there are excellent armchairs to doze in."

Then he went out and I heard the wheels of his car move away. I felt a kind of awe creeping over me when I found myself left alone in the uncanny place, which I knew to be the devil's kitchen for all his schemes. There was a telephone on his writing-table, the only one I had seen in the house, though there was no doubt one in the butler's pantry. I turned up the telephone book and found a number given, but it was not the one on the receiver. This must be a private telephone, by means of which he could ring up anybody he wanted, but of which only his special friends knew the number. There was nothing else in the room to interest me, except the lines and lines of books, for his table was as bare as a bank manager's.

I tried the books, but most of them were a long sight too learned for me. Most were old, and many were in Latin, and some were evidently treasures, for I would take one down and find it a leather box, with inside it a slim battered volume wrapped in wash-leather. But I found in one corner a great array of works of travel, so I selected one of Aurel Stein's books and settled down in an armchair with it. I tried to fix my attention, but found it impossible. The sentences would not make sense to my restless mind, and I could not follow the maps. So I got up again, replaced the work on its shelf, and began to wander about. It was a dull, close day, and out in the street a water-cart was sprinkling the dust and children were going park-wards with their nurses. . . . I simply could not account for my disquiet, but I was like a fine lady with the vapours. I felt that somewhere in that room there was something that it concerned me deeply to know.

I drifted toward the bare writing-table. There was nothing on it but a massive silver inkstand in the shape of an owl, a silver tray of pens and oddments, a leather case of notepaper and a big blotting-book. I would never have made a good thief, for I felt both nervous and ashamed as, after listening for steps, I tried the drawers.

They were all locked—all, that is, except a shallow one at the top, which looked as if it were meant to contain one of those big engagement tablets which busy men affect. There was no tablet there, but there were two sheets of paper.

Both had been torn from a loose-leaf diary, and both covered the same dates—the fortnight between Monday the 29th of May, and Sunday the 11th of June. In the first the space for the days was filled with entries in Medina's neat writing, entries in some sort of shorthand. These entries were close and thick up to and including Friday the 2nd of June ; after that there was nothing. The second sheet of paper was just the opposite. The spaces were virgin up to and including the 2nd of June ; after that, on till the 11th, they were filled with notes.

As I stared at these two sheets, some happy instinct made me divine their meaning. The first sheet contained the steps that Medina would take up to the day of liquidation, which was clearly the 2nd of June. After that, if all went well, came peace and leisure. But if it didn't go well, the second sheet contained his plans—plans I have no doubt for using the hostages, for wringing safety out of certain great men's fears. . . . My interpretation was confirmed by a small jotting in long-hand on the first sheet in the space for 2nd June. It was the two words " *Dies irae*," which my Latin was just good enough to construe.

I had lost all my tremors now, but I was a thousandfold more restless. I must get word to Macgillivray at once—no, that was too dangerous—to Mary. I glanced at the telephone and resolved to trust my luck.

I got through to the Wymondhams' house without difficulty. Barnard the butler answered, and informed me that Mary was at home. Then after a few seconds I heard her voice.

" Mary," I said, " the day is changed to the 2nd of June. You understand—warn everybody. . . . I can't think why you are worrying about that child."

For I was conscious that Medina was entering the room. I managed with my knee to close the shallow drawer with the two sheets in it, and I nodded and smiled to him, putting my hand over the receiver.

" Forgive me using your telephone. Fact is, my wife's in London, and she sent me round a note here asking me to ring her up. She's got the boy on her mind."

I put the tube to my ear again. Mary's voice sounded sharp and high-pitched.

"Are you there? I'm in Mr. Medina's library, and I can't disturb him talking through this machine. There's no cause to worry about Peter John. Greenslade is usually fussy enough, and if he's calm there's no reason why you shouldn't be. But if you want another opinion, why not get it? We may as well get the thing straightened out now, for I may be going abroad early in June. . . . Yes, some time after the 2nd."

Thank God Mary was quick-witted.

"The 2nd is very near. Why do you make such sudden plans, Dick? I can't go home without seeing you. I think I'll come straight to Hill Street."

"All right," I said, "do as you please." I rang off and looked at Medina with a wry smile. "What fussers women are! Do you mind if my wife comes round here? She won't be content till she has seen me. She has come up with a crazy notion of taking down a surgeon to give an opinion on the child's appendix. Tommy rot! But that's a woman's way."

He clearly suspected nothing. "Certainly let Lady Hannay come here. We'll give her tea. I'm sorry that the drawing-room is out of commission just now. She might have liked to see my miniatures."

Mary appeared in ten minutes, and most nobly she acted her part. It was the very model of a distraught silly mother who bustled into the room. Her eyes looked as if she had been crying, and she had managed to disarrange her hat and untidy her hair.

"Oh, I've been so worried," she wailed, after she had murmured apologies to Medina. "He really has had a bad tummy pain, and nurse thought last night that he was feverish. I've seen Mr. Dobson-Wray, and he can come down by the 4.45. . . . He's such a precious little boy, Mr. Medina, that I feel we must take every precaution with him. If Mr. Dobson-Wray says it is all right, I promise not to fuss any more. I think a second opinion would please Dr. Greenslade, for he too looked rather anxious. . . . Oh no, thank you so much, but I can't stay for tea. I have a taxi waiting, and I might miss my train. I'm going to pick up Mr. Dobson-Wray in Wimpole Street."

She departed in the same tornado in which she had come, just stopping to set her hat straight at one of the mirrors in the hall.

"Of course I'll wire when the surgeon has seen him. And, Dick, you'll come down at once if there's anything wrong, and bring nurses. Poor, poor little darling! . . . Did you say after the 2nd of June, Dick? I do hope you'll be able to get off. You need a holiday away from your tiresome family. . . . Good-bye, Mr. Medina. It was so kind of you to be patient with a silly mother. Look after Dick and don't let him worry."

I had preserved admirably the aloof air of the bored and slightly ashamed husband. But now

I realized that Mary was not babbling at large, but was saying something which I was meant to take in.

"Poor, poor little darling!" she crooned, as she got into the taxi. "I do pray he'll be all right—I *think* he may, Dick. . . . I hope, oh, I hope . . . to put your mind at ease . . . before the 2nd of June."

As I turned back to Medina I had a notion that the poor little darling was no longer Peter John.

# CHAPTER XVII

## THE DISTRICT-VISITOR IN PALMYRA SQUARE

DURING the last fortnight a new figure had begun to appear in Palmyra Square. I do not know if Macgillivray's watchers reported its presence, for I saw none of their reports, but they must have been cognisant of it, unless they spent all their time in the nearest public-house. It was a district-visitor of the familiar type—a woman approaching middle age, presumably a spinster, who wore a plain black dress and, though the weather was warm, a cheap fur round her neck, and carried a rather old black silk satchel. Her figure was good, and had still a suggestion of youth, but her hair, which was dressed very flat and tight and coiled behind in an unfashionable bun, seemed—the little that was seen of it—to be sprinkled with grey. She was dowdy, and yet not altogether dowdy, for there was a certain faded elegance in her air, and an observer might have noted that she walked well. Besides the black satchel she carried usually a sheaf of papers, and invariably and in all weathers a cheap badly-rolled umbrella.

She visited at the doctor's house with the brass
plate, and the music-teacher's, and at the various
lodging-houses.   She was attached, it appeared, to
the big church of St. Jude's a quarter of a mile off,
which had just got a new and energetic vicar.
She was full of enthusiasm for her vicar, praised
his earnestness and his eloquence, and dwelt
especially, after the way of elderly maiden ladies,
on the charm of his youth.   She was also very
ready to speak of herself, and eager to explain
that her work was voluntary—she was a gentle-
woman of modest but independent means, and
had rooms in Hampstead, and her father had been
a clergyman at Eastbourne.   Very full of her
family she was to those who would hear her.
There was a gentle simplicity about her manners,
and an absence of all patronage, which attracted
people and made them willing to listen to her
when they would have shut the door on another,
for the inhabitants of Palmyra Square are not a
courteous or patient or religious folk.

Her aim was to enlist the overworked general
servants of the Square in some of the organizations
of St. Jude's.   There were all kinds of activities
in that enlightened church—choral societies, and
mothers' meetings, and country holiday clubs,
and classes for adult education.   She would hand
out sheaves of literature about the Girls' Friendly
Society, and the Mothers' Union, and such-like,
and try to secure a promise of attendance at some
of the St. Jude's functions.   I do not think she
had much success at the doctor's and the music-

teacher's, though she regularly distributed her literature there. The wretched little maids were too down-trodden and harassed to do more than listen dully on the doorstep and say "Yes'm." Nor was she allowed to see the mistresses, except one of the lodging-house keepers, who was a Primitive Methodist and considered St. Jude's a device of Satan. But she had better fortune with the maid at No. 4.

The girl belonged to a village in Kent, and the district-visitor, it seemed, had been asked to look her up by the rector of her old parish. She was a large flat-faced young woman, slow of speech, heavy of movement, and suspicious of nature. At first she greeted the district-visitor coldly, but thawed at the mention of familiar names and accepted a copy of the St. Jude's Magazine. Two days later, when on her afternoon out, she met the district-visitor and consented to walk a little way with her. Now the girl's hobby was dress, and her taste was better than most of her class and aspired to higher things. She had a new hat which her companion admired, but she confessed that she was not quite satisfied with it. The district-visitor revealed a knowledge of fashions which one would have scarcely augured from her own sombre clothes. She pointed out where the trimming was wrong, and might easily be improved, and the girl—her name was Elsie Outhwaite—agreed. " I could put it right for you in ten minutes," she was told. " Perhaps you would let me come and see you when you have a spare

half-hour, and we could do it together. I'm
rather clever at hats, and used to help my
sisters."

The ice was broken and the aloof Miss Outhwaite became confidential. She liked her place,
had no cause to complain, received good wages,
and, above all, was not fussed. " I minds my
own business, and Madame minds 'ers," she said.
Madame was a foreigner, and had her queer ways,
but had also her good points. She did not interfere unnecessarily, and was not mean. There
were handsome presents at Christmas, and every
now and then the house would be shut up, and
Miss Outhwaite returned to Kent on generous
board wages. It was not a hard billet, though,
of course, there were a lot of visitors, Madame's
clients. " She's a massoose, you know, but very
respectable." When asked if there were no other
inmates of the house she became reticent. " Not
what you would call reg'lar part of the family,"
she admitted. "There's an old lady, Madame's
aunt, that stops with us a bit, but I don't see
much of 'er. Madame attends to 'er 'erself, and
she 'as her private room. And, of course,
there's . . ." Miss Outhwaite seemed suddenly to
recollect something, and changed the subject.

The district-visitor professed a desire to make
Madame's acquaintance, but was not encouraged.
" She's not the sort for the likes of you. She don't
'old with churches and God and such-like—I've
'eard 'er say so. You won't be getting 'er near
St. Jude's, miss."

" But if she is so clever and nice I would like to meet her. She could advise me about some of the difficult questions in this big parish. Perhaps she would help with our Country Holidays."

Miss Outhwaite primmed her lips and didn't think so. " You've got to be ill and nervy for Madame to have an interest in you. I'll take in your name if you like, but I expect Madame won't be at 'ome to you."

It was eventually arranged that the district-visitor should call at No. 4 the following afternoon and bring the materials for the reconstructed hat. She duly presented herself, but was warned away by a flustered Miss Outhwaite. " We're that busy to-day I 'aven't a minute to myself." Sunday was suggested, but it appeared that that was the day when the district-visitor was fully occupied, so a provisional appointment was made for the next Tuesday evening.

This time all went well. Madame was out, and the district-visitor spent a profitable hour in Miss Outhwaite's room. Her nimble fingers soon turned the hat, purchased in Queen's Crescent for ten and sixpence, into a distant imitation of a costlier mode. She displayed an innocent interest in the household, and asked many questions which Miss Outhwaite, now in the best of tempers, answered readily. She was told of Madame's habits, her very occasional shortness of temper, her love of every tongue but English. " The worst of them furriners," said Miss Outhwaite, " is that you can't never be sure what they thinks of you.

Half the time I'm with Madame and her aunt they're talking some 'eathen language."

As she departed the district-visitor was given a sketch of the topography of the house, about which she showed an unexpected curiosity. Before she left there was a slight *contretemps*. Madame's latch-key was heard in the door and Miss Outhwaite had a moment of panic. "Here, miss, I'll let you out through the kitchen," she whispered. But her visitor showed no embarrassment. "I'd like to meet Madame Breda," she declared. "This is a good chance."

Madame's plump dark face showed surprise, and possibly annoyance, as she observed the two. Miss Outhwaite hastened to explain the situation with a speed which revealed nervousness. "This is a lady from St. Jude's, Madame," she said. "She comes 'ere districk-visiting, and she knows the folk in Radhurst, where I comes from, so I made bold to ask her in."

"I am very glad to meet you, Madame Breda," said the district-visitor. "I hope you don't mind my calling on Elsie Outhwaite. I want her to help in our Girls' Friendly Society work."

"You have been here before, I think," was the reply in a sufficiently civil tone. "I have seen you in the Square sometimes. There is no objection on my part to Outhwaite's attending your meetings, but I warn you that she has very little free time." The woman was a foreigner, no doubt, but on this occasion her English showed little trace of accent.

"That is very good of you. I should have

asked your permission first, but you were unfortunately not at home when I called, and Elsie
and I made friends by accident. I hope you will
let me come again."

As the visitor descended the steps and passed
through the bright green gate into the gathering
dusk of the Square, Madame Breda watched her
contemplatively from one of the windows.

The lady came again four days later—it must,
I think, have been the 29th of May. Miss Outhwaite, when she opened the door, looked flustered.
"I can't talk to you to-night, miss. Madame's
orders is that when you next came you was to be
shown in to her room."

"How very kind of her!" said the lady. "I
should greatly enjoy a talk with her. And, Elsie
—I've got such a nice present for you—a hat
which a friend gave me and which is too young—
really too young—for me to wear. I'm going to
give it you, if you'll accept it. I'll bring it in a
day or two."

The district-visitor was shown into the large
room on the right-hand side of the hall where
Madame received her patients. There was no one
there except a queer-looking little girl in a linen
smock, who beckoned her to follow to the folding-
doors which divided the apartment from the other
at the back. The lady did a strange thing, for
she picked up the little girl, held her a second in
her arms, and kissed her—after the emotional
habit of the childless. Then she passed through
the folding-doors.

It was an odd apartment in which she found herself—much larger than could have been guessed from the look of the house, and, though the night was warm, there was a fire lit, a smouldering fire which gave off a fine blue smoke. Madame Breda was there, dressed in a low-cut gown as if she had been dining out, and looking handsome and dark and very foreign in the light of the shaded lamps. In an armchair by the hearth sat a wonderful old lady, with a thing like a mantilla over her snow-white hair. It was a room so unlike anything in her narrow experience that the new-comer stood hesitating as the folding-doors shut behind her.

" Oh, Madame Breda, it is so very kind of you to see me," she faltered.

" I do not know your name," Madame said, and then she did a curious thing, for she lifted a lamp and held it in the visitor's face, scrutinizing every line of her shabby figure.

" Clarke—Agnes Clarke. I am the eldest of three sisters—the other two are married—you may have heard of my father—he wrote some beautiful hymns, and edited——"

" How old are you ? " Madame broke in, still holding up the lamp.

The district-visitor gave a small, nervous laugh. " Oh, I am not so very old—just over forty—well, to be quite truthful, nearly forty-seven. I feel so young sometimes that I cannot believe it, and then—at other times—when I am tired—I feel a hundred. Alas ! I have many useless years behind me. But then we all have, don't you think ?

The great thing is to be resolved to make the most of every hour that remains to us. Mr. Empson at St. Jude's preached such a beautiful sermon last Sunday about that. He said we must give every unforgiving minute its sixty seconds' worth of distance run—I think he was quoting poetry. It is terrible to think of unforgiving minutes."

Madame did not appear to be listening. She said something to the older lady in a foreign tongue.

"May I sit down, please ? " the visitor asked. "I have been walking a good deal to-day."

Madame waved her away from the chair she seemed about to take. "You will sit there, if you please," she said, pointing to a low couch beside the old woman.

The visitor was obviously embarrassed. She sat down on the edge of the couch, a faded, nervous figure compared to the two masterful personages, and her fingers played uneasily with the handle of her satchel.

"Why do you come to this house ? " Madame asked, and her tone was almost menacing. "We have nothing to do with your church."

"Oh, but you live in the parish, and it's such a large and difficult parish, and we want help from every one. You cannot imagine how horrible some of the slums are—what bitter poverty in these bad times—and the worn-out mothers and the poor little neglected children. We are trying to make it a brighter place."

" Do you want money ? "

" We always want money." The district-visitor's face wore an ingratiating smile. " But we want chiefly personal service. Mr. Empson always says that one little bit of personal service is better than a large subscription—better for the souls of the giver and the receiver."

" What do you expect to get from Outhwaite ? "

" She is a young girl from a country village and alone in London. She is a good girl, I think, and I want to give her friends and innocent amusement. And I want her help too in our work."

The visitor started, for she found the hand of the old woman on her arm. The long fingers were running down it and pressing it. Hitherto the owner of the hand had not spoken, but now she said—

" This is the arm of a young woman. She has lied about her age. No woman of forty-seven ever had such an arm."

The soft passage of the fingers had suddenly become a grip of steel, and the visitor cried out.

" Oh, please, please, you are hurting me. . . . I do not tell lies. I am proud of my figure—just a little. It is like my mother's, and she was so pretty. But oh ! I am not young. I wish I was. I'm afraid I'm quite old when you see me by daylight."

The grip had relaxed, and the visitor moved along the couch to be out of its reach. She had begun to cry in a helpless, silly way, as if she were frightened. The two other women spoke to each other in a strange tongue, and then Madame said—

"I will not have you come here. I will not have you meddle with my servants. I do not care a fig for your church. If you come here again you will repent it."

Her tone was harsh, and the visitor looked as if her tears would begin again. Her discomposure had deprived her of the faded grace which had been in her air before, and she was now a pathetic and flimsy creature, like some elderly governess pleading against dismissal.

"You are cruel," she sighed. "I am so sorry if I have done anything wrong, but I meant it for the best. I thought that you might help me, for Elsie said you were clever and kind. Won't you think of poor Elsie ? She is so young and far from her people. Mayn't she come to St. Jude's sometimes ? "

"Outhwaite has her duties at home, and so I daresay have you, if truth was spoken. Bah ! I have no patience with restless English old maids. They say an Englishman's house is his castle, and yet there is a plague of barren virgins always buzzing round it in the name of religion and philanthropy. Listen to me. I will not have you in this house. I will not have you talking to Outhwaite. I will not have an idle woman spying on my private affairs."

The visitor dabbed her eyes with a wisp of handkerchief. The old woman had stretched out her hand again and would have laid it on her breast, but she had started up violently. She seemed to be in a mood between distress and fear. She swallowed hard before her voice came, and then it quavered.

"I think I had better go. You have wounded me very deeply. I know I'm not clever, but I try so hard . . . and . . . and—it pains me to be misunderstood. I am afraid I have been tactless, so please forgive me. . . . I won't come again. . . . I'll pray that your hearts may some day be softened."

She seemed to make an effort to regain composure, and with a final dab at her eyes smiled shakily at the unrelenting Madame, who had touched an electric bell. She closed the folding-doors gently behind her, like a repentant child who has been sent to bed. The front room was in darkness, but there was a light in the hall, where Miss Outhwaite waited to show her out.

At the front door the district-visitor had recovered herself.

"Elsie," she whispered, "Madame Breda does not want me to come again. But I must give you the hat I promised you. I'll have it ready by Thursday night. I'm afraid I may be rather late —after eleven perhaps—but don't go to bed till I come. I'll go round to the back door. It's such a smart, pretty hat. I know you'll love it."

Once in the Square she looked sharply about her, cast a glance back at No. 4, and then walked away briskly. There was a man lounging at the corner to whom she spoke; he nodded and touched

his hat, and a big motor-car, which had been
waiting in the shadows on the other side, drew up
at the kerb. It seemed a strange conveyance for
the district-visitor, but she entered it as if she
were used to it, and when it moved off it was not
in the direction of her rooms in Hampstead.

# CHAPTER XVIII

## THE NIGHT OF THE FIRST OF JUNE

THE last two days of May were spent by me in the most miserable restlessness and despondency. I was cut off from all communications with my friends, and I did not see how I could re-open them. For Medina, after his late furious busyness, seemed to have leisure again, and he simply never let me out of his sight. I daresay I might have managed a visit to the Club and a telephone message to Mary, but I durst not venture it, for I realized as I had never done before how delicate was the ground I walked on and how one false step on my part might blow everything sky-high. It would have mattered less if I had been hopeful of success, but a mood of black pessimism had seized me. I could count on Mary passing on my news to Macgillivray and on Macgillivray's taking the necessary steps to hasten the rounding-up; by the 2nd of June Mercot would be restored to his friends, and Miss Victor too, if Mary had got on her track again. But who was arranging all that? Was Mary alone in the business, and where was Sandy? Mercot and

Gaudian would be arriving in Scotland, and telegraphing to me any moment, and I could not answer them. I had the maddening feeling that everything was on a knife edge, that the chances of a blunder were infinite, and that I could do nothing. To crown all, I was tortured by the thought of David Warcliff. I had come to the conclusion that Mary's farewell words at Hill Street had meant nothing : indeed, I couldn't see how she could have found out anything about the little boy, for as yet we had never hit on the faintest clue, and the thought of him made success with the other two seem no better than failure. Likewise I was paying the penalty for the assurance about Medina which I had rashly expressed to Mary. I felt the terror of the man in a new way ; he seemed to me impregnable beyond the hope of assault ; and while I detested him I also shuddered at him—a novel experience, for hitherto I had always found that hatred drove out fear.

He was abominable during those two days—abominable, but also wonderful. He seemed to love the sight of me, as if I were a visible and intimate proof of his power, and he treated me as an Oriental tyrant might treat a favourite slave. He unbent to me as a relief to his long spiritual tension, and let me see the innermost dreams of his heart. I realized with a shudder that he thought me a part of that hideous world he had created, and—I think for the first time in the business—I knew fear on my own account. If he dreamed I could fail him he would become a

ravening beast. . . . I remember that he talked a
good deal of politics, but, ye gods ! what a change
from the respectable conservative views which he
had once treated me to—a Tory revival owing to
the women and that sort of thing ! He declared
that behind all the world's creeds—Christianity,
Buddhism, Islam, and the rest—lay an ancient
devil-worship, and that it was raising its head
again. Bolshevism, he said, was a form of it, and
he attributed the success of Bolshevism in Asia to
a revival of what he called Shamanism—I think
that was the word. By his way of it the War
had cracked the veneer everywhere, and the real
stuff was showing through. He rejoiced in the
prospect, because the old faiths were not ethical
codes but mysteries of the spirit, and they gave a
chance for men who had found the ancient magic.
I think he wanted to win everything that civilization would give him, and then wreck it, for his
hatred of Britain was only a part of his hatred of
all that most men hold in love and repute. The
common anarchist was a fool to him, for the cities
and temples of the whole earth were not sufficient
sacrifice to appease his vanity. I knew now what
a Goth and a Hun meant, and what had been the
temper of scourges like Attila and Timour. . . .
Mad, you will say. Yes, mad beyond doubt, but
it was the most convincing kind of madness. I
had to fight hard, by keeping my mind firm on
my job, to prevent my nerve giving.

I went to bed on the last night of May in something very near despair, comforting myself, I

remember, by what I had said to Mary, that one must go on to the finish and trust to luck changing in the last ten minutes. I woke to a gorgeous morning, and when I came down to breakfast I was in a shade better spirits. Medina proposed a run out into the country and a walk on some high ground. "It will give us an appetite for the Thursday dinner," he said. Then he went upstairs to telephone, and I was in the smoking-room filling my pipe when suddenly Greenslade was shown in.

I didn't listen to what he had to say, but seized a sheet of paper and scribbled a note : " Take this to the head porter at the Club and he will give you any telegram there is for me. If there is one from Gaudian, as there must be, wire him to start at once and go straight to Julius Victor. Then wire the Duke to meet him there. Do you understand ? Now, what have you to tell me ? "

" Only that your wife says things are going pretty well. You must turn up to-night at ten-thirty at the Fields of Eden. Also somehow you must get a latch-key for this house, and see that the door is not chained."

" Nothing more ? "

" Nothing more."

" And Peter John ? "

Greenslade was enlarging on Peter John's case when Medina entered. " I came round to tell Sir Richard that it was all a false alarm. Only the spring fret. The surgeon was rather cross at being taken so far on a fool's errand. Lady Hannay thought he had better hear it from me personally, for then he could start on his holiday with an easy mind."

I was so short with him that Medina must have seen how far my thoughts were from my family. As we motored along the road to Tring I talked of the approaching holiday, like a toadying school-boy who has been asked to stay for a cricket week with some senior. Medina said he had not fixed the place, but it must be somewhere south in the sun—Algiers, perhaps, and the fringes of the desert, or, better still, some remote Mediterranean spot where we could have both sunlight and blue sea. He talked of the sun like a fire-worshipper. He wanted to steep his limbs in it, and wash his soul in light, and swim in wide warm waters. He rhapsodized like a poet, but what struck me about his rhapsodies was how little sensuous they were. The man's body was the most obedient satellite of his mind, and I don't believe he had any weakness of the flesh. What he wanted was a bath of radiance for his spirit.

We walked all day on the hills around Ivinghoe, and had a late lunch in the village inn. He spoke very little, but strode over the thymy downs with his eyes abstracted. Once, as we sat on the summit, he seemed to sigh, and his face for a moment was very grave.

"What is the highest pleasure?" he asked suddenly. "Attainment? . . . No. Renunciation."

"So I've heard the parsons say," I observed.

(2.745)

23

He did not heed me. "To win everything that mankind has ever striven for, and then to cast it aside. To be Emperor of the Earth and then to slip out of the ken of mankind and take up the sandals and begging-bowl. The man who can do that has conquered the world—he is not a king but a god. Only he must be a king first to achieve it."

I cannot hope to reproduce the atmosphere of that scene, the bare top of the hill in the blue summer weather, and that man, nearing, as he thought, the summit of success, and suddenly questioning all mortal codes of value. In all my dealings with Medina I was so obsessed by the sense of my inferiority to him, that I was like a cab horse compared to an Arab stallion, and now I felt it like a blow in the face. That was the kind of thing Napoleon might have said—and done—had his schemes not gone astray. I knew I was contending with a devil, but I knew also that it was a great devil.

We returned to town just in time to dress for dinner, and all my nervousness revived a hundredfold. This was the night of crisis, and I loathed having to screw myself up to emergencies late in the day. Such things should take place in the early morning. It was like going over the top in France; I didn't mind it so much when it happened during a drizzling dawn, when one was anyhow depressed and only half-awake, but I abominated an attack in the cold-blooded daylight, or in the dusk when one wanted to relax.

That evening I shaved, I remember, very carefully, as if I were decking myself out for a sacrifice.
I wondered what would be my feelings when I
next shaved. I wondered what Mary and Sandy
were doing. . . .

＊　　＊　　＊　　＊　　＊　　＊

What Mary and Sandy were doing at that
precise moment I do not know, but I can now
unfold certain contemporary happenings which
were then hid from me. . . . Mercot and Gaudian
were having a late tea in the Midland express,
having nearly broken their necks in a furious motor
race to catch the train at Hawick. The former
was clean and shaven, his hair nicely cut, and
his clothes a fairly well-fitting ready-made suit
of flannels. He was deeply sunburnt, immensely
excited, and constantly breaking in on Gaudian's
study of the works of Sir Walter Scott.

"Newhover is to be let loose to-day. What do
you suppose he'll do ? " he asked.

"Nothing—yet awhile," was the answer. "I
said certain things to him. He cannot openly go
back to Germany, and I do not think he dare
come to England. He fears the vengeance of his
employer. He will disappear for a little, and
then emerge in some new crime with a new name
and a changed face. He is the eternal scoundrel."

The young man's face lighted up pleasantly.
"If I live to be a hundred," he said, "I can't
enjoy anything half as much as that clip I gave
him on the jaw."

In a room in a country house on the Middlesex and Bucks borders Turpin was talking to a girl. He was in evening dress, a very point-device young man, and she was wearing a wonderful gown, grass-green in colour and fantastically cut. Her face was heavily made up, and her scarlet lips and stained eyebrows stood out weirdly against the dead white of her skin. But it was a different face from that which I first saw in the dancing-hall. Life had come back to it, the eyes were no longer dull like pebbles, but were again the windows of a soul. There was still fear in those eyes and bewilderment, but they were human again, and shone at this moment with a wild affection.

"I am terrified," she said. "I have to go to that awful place with that awful man. Please, Antoine, please, do not leave me. You have brought me out of a grave, and you cannot let me slip back again."

He held her close to him and stroked her hair.

"I think it is—how do you say it?—the last lap. My very dear one, we cannot fail our friends. I follow you soon. The grey man—I do not know his name—he told me so, and he is a friend. A car is ordered for me half an hour after you drive off with that Odell."

"But what does it all mean?" she asked.

"I do not know, but I think—I am sure—it is the work of our friends. Consider, my little one. I am brought to the house where you are, but those who have charge of you do not know I am here. When Odell comes I am warned and locked in my room. I am not allowed out of it. I have had no exercise except sparring with that solemn English valet. He indeed has been most amiable, and has allowed me to keep myself in form. He boxes well, too, but I have studied under our own Jules, and he is no match for me. But when the coast is clear I am permitted to see you, and I have waked you from sleep, my princess. Therefore so far it is good. As to what will happen to-night I do not know, but I fancy it is the end of our troubles. The grey man has told me as much. If you go back to that dance place, I think I follow you, and then we shall see something. Have no fear, little one. You go back as a prisoner no more, but as an actress to play a part, and I know you will play the part well. You will not permit the man Odell to suspect. Presently I come, and I think there will be an *éclaircissement*—also, please God, a reckoning."

The wooden-faced valet entered and signed to the young man, who kissed the girl and followed him. A few minutes later Turpin was in his own room, with the door locked behind him. Then came a sound of the wheels of a car outside, and he listened with a smile on his face. As he stood before the glass putting the finishing touches to his smooth hair he was still smiling—an ominous smile.

. . . . . . .

Other things, which I did not know about, were happening that evening. From a certain modest office near Tower Hill a gentleman emerged to seek his rooms in Mayfair. His car was waiting for him at the street corner, but to his surprise as he got into it some one entered also from the other side, and the address to which the car ultimately drove was not Clarges Street. The office, too, which he had left locked and bolted, was presently open, and men were busy there till far into the night—men who did not belong to his staff. An eminent publicist, who was the special patron of the distressed populations of Central Europe, was starting out to dine at his club, when he was unaccountably delayed, and had to postpone his dinner. The Spanish copper company in London Wall had been doing little business of late, except to give luncheons to numerous gentlemen, but that night its rooms were lit, and people who did not look like city clerks were investigating its documents. In Paris a certain French count of royalist proclivities, who had a box that night for the opera and was giving a little dinner beforehand, did not keep his appointment, to the discomfiture of his guests, and a telephone message to his rooms near the Champs Elysées elicited no reply. There was a gruff fellow at the other end who discouraged conversation. A worthy Glasgow accountant, an elder of the kirk and a prospective candidate for Parliament, did not return that evening to his family, and the police, when appealed to, gave curious answers. The office, just off Fleet Street, of the *Christian Advocate* of Milwaukee, a paper which cannot have had much of a circulation in England, was filled about six o'clock with silent, preoccupied people, and the manager, surprised and rather wild of eye, was taken off in a taxi by two large gentlemen who had not had previously the honour of his acquaintance. Odd things seemed to be happening up and down the whole world. More than one ship did not sail at the appointed hour because of the interest of certain people in the passenger lists; a meeting of decorous bankers in Genoa was unexpectedly interrupted by the police; offices of the utmost respectability were occupied and examined by the blundering minions of the law; several fashionable actresses did not appear to gladden their admirers, and more than one pretty dancer was absent from the scene of her usual triumphs; a Senator in Western America, a high official in Rome, and four deputies in France found their movements restricted, and a Prince of the Church, after receiving a telephone message, fell to his prayers. A mining magnate in Westphalia, visiting Antwerp on business, found that he was not permitted to catch the train he had settled on. Five men, all highly placed, and one woman, for no cause apparent to their relatives, chose to rid themselves of life between the hours of six and seven. There was an unpleasant occurrence in a town on the Loire, where an Englishman, motoring to the south of France—a typical English squire, well known in hunting circles in Shropshire — was visited at his hotel by two ordinary Frenchmen, whose conversation

seemed unpalatable to him. He was passing
something from his waistcoat pocket to his mouth,
when they had the audacity to lay violent hands
on him and to slip something over his wrists.

.          .          .          .          .          .          .

It was a heavenly clear evening when Medina
and I set out to walk the half-mile to Mervyn
Street  I had been so cloistered and harassed
during the past weeks that I had missed the
coming of summer.  Suddenly the world seemed to
have lighted up, and the streets were filled with
that intricate odour of flowers, scent, hot wood
pavements and asphalt, which is the summer
smell of London.  Cars were waiting at house-
doors, and women in pretty clothes getting into
them ;   men were walking dinner-wards, with
some of whom we exchanged greetings ;  the whole
earth seemed full of laughter and happy movement.  And it was shut off from me.  I seemed
to be living on the other side of a veil from this
cheerful world, and I could see nothing but a
lonely old man with a tragic face waiting for a
lost boy.  There was one moment at the corner
of Berkeley Square when I accidentally jostled
Medina, and had to clench my hands and bite
my lips to keep myself from throttling him there
and then.

The dining-room in Mervyn Street looked west,
and the evening light strove with the candles on
the table, and made a fairy-like scene of the
flowers and silver.  It was a full meeting—thir-
teen, I think—and the divine weather seemed to

have put everybody in the best of spirits. I had almost forgotten Medina's repute with the ordinary man, and was staggered anew at the signs of his popularity. He was in the chair that evening, and a better chairman of such a dinner I have never seen. He had the right word for everybody, and we sat down to table like a party of under-graduates celebrating a successful cricket-match.

I was on the chairman's right hand, next to Burminster, with Palliser-Yeates opposite me. At first the talk was chiefly about the Derby and Ascot entries, about which Medina proved un-commonly well posted. He had a lot of inside knowledge from the Chilton stables, and showed himself a keen critic of form; also he was a per-fect pundit about the pedigree of racehorses, and made Burminster, who fancied himself in the same line, gape with admiration. I suppose a brain like his could get up any subject at lightning speed, and he thought this kind of knowledge useful to him, for I don't believe he cared more for a horse than for a cat.

Once, during the Somme battle, I went to dine at a French château behind the lines, as the guest of the only son of the house. It was an ancient place, with fishponds and terraces, and there were only two people in it, an old Comtesse and a girl of fifteen called Simone. At dinner, I remember, a decrepit butler filled for me five glasses of different clarets, till I found the one I preferred. After-wards I walked in the garden with Simone in a wonderful yellow twilight, watching the fat carp in the ponds, and hearing the grumbling of the distant guns. I felt in that hour the poignant contrast of youth and innocence and peace with that hideous world of battle a dozen miles off. To-night I had the same feeling—the jolly party of clean, hard, decent fellows, and the abominable hinterland of mystery and crime of which the man at the head of the table was the master. I must have been poor company, but happily everybody was talkative, and I did my best to grin at Burminster's fooling.

Presently the talk drifted away from sport. Palliser-Yeates was speaking, and his fresh, boyish colour contrasted oddly with his wise eyes and grave voice.

"I can't make out what is happening," he said, in reply to a remark of Leithen's. "The City has suddenly become jumpy, and there's no reason in the facts that I can see for it. There's been a good deal of realization of stocks, chiefly by foreign holders, but there are a dozen explanations of that. No, there's a kind of *malaise* about, and it's unpleasantly like what I remember in June 1914. I was in Whittingtons' then, and we suddenly found the foundations beginning to crumble—oh yes, before the Serajevo murders. You remember Charlie Esmond's smash—well, that was largely due to the spasm of insecurity that shook the world. People now and then get a feeling in their bones that something bad is going to happen. And probably they are right, and it has begun to happen."

"Good Lord!" said Leithen. "I don't like this. Is it another war?"

Palliser-Yeates did not answer at once. "It looks like it. I admit it's almost unthinkable, but, then, all wars are really unthinkable, till you're in the middle of them."

"Nonsense!" Medina cried. "There's no nation on the globe fit to go to war, except half-civilized races with whom it is the normal condition. You forget how much we know since 1914. You couldn't get even France to fight without provoking a revolution—a middle-class revolution, the kind that succeeds."

Burminster looked relieved. "The next war," he said, "will be a dashed unpleasant affair. So far as I can see there will be very few soldiers killed, but an enormous number of civilians. The safest place will be the front. There will be such a rush to get into the army that we'll have to have conscription to make people remain in civil life. The *embusqués* will be the regulars."

As he spoke some one entered the room, and to my amazement I saw that it was Sandy.

He was looking extraordinarily fit and as brown as a berry. He murmured an apology to the chairman for being late, patted the bald patch on Burminster's head, and took a seat at the other end of the table. "I'll cut in where you've got to," he told the waiters. "No—don't bother about fish. I want some English roast beef and a tankard of beer."

There was a chorus of questions.

"Just arrived an hour ago. I've been in the East—Egypt and Palestine. Flew most of the way back."

He nodded to me, and smiled at Medina and raised his tankard to him.

I was not in a good position for watching Medina's face, but so far as I could see it was unchanged. He hated Sandy, but he didn't fear him now, when his plans had practically come to fruition. Indeed, he was very gracious to him, and asked in his most genial tones what he had been after.

"Civil aviation," said Sandy. "I'm going to collar the pilgrim traffic to the Holy Places. You've been in Mecca?" he asked Pugh, who nodded. "You remember the *hamelidari* crowd who used to organize the transport from Mespot. Well, I'm a *hamelidari* on a big scale. I am prepared to bring the rank of *hadji* within reach of the poorest and feeblest. I'm going to be the great benefactor of the democracy of Islam, by means of a fleet of patched-up 'planes and a few kindred spirits that know the East. I'll let you fellows in on the ground-floor when I float my company. John"—he addressed Palliser-Yeates—"I look to you to manage the flotation."

Sandy was obviously ragging, and no one took him seriously. He sat there with his merry brown face, looking absurdly young and girlish, so that the most suspicious could have seen nothing more in him than the ordinary mad Englishman who lived for adventure and novelty. Me he never

addressed, and I was glad of it, for I was utterly
at sea. What did he mean by turning up now ?
What part was he to play in the events of the
night ? I could not have controlled the anxiety
in my voice if I had been forced to speak to him.

A servant brought Medina a note, which he
opened at leisure and read. "No answer," he
said, and stuffed it into his pocket. I had a
momentary dread that he might have got news
of Macgillivray's round-up, but his manner reassured me.

There were people there who wanted to turn
Sandy to other subjects, especially Fulleylove and
the young Cambridge don, Nightingale. They
wanted to know about South Arabia, of which at
the time the world was talking. Some fellow—I
forget his name—was trying to raise an expedition
to explore it.

"It's the last geographical secret left un-
riddled," he said, and now he spoke seriously.
"Well, perhaps not quite the last. I'm told
there's still something to be done with the southern
tributaries of the Amazon. Mornington, you know,
believes there's a chance of finding some of the
Inca people still dwelling in the unexplored upper
glens. But all the rest have gone. Since the
beginning of the century we've made a clean
sweep of the jolly old mysteries that made the
world worth living in. We have been to both the
Poles, and to Lhasa, and to the Mountains of the
Moon. We haven't got to the top of Everest yet,
but we know what it is like. Mecca and Medina

are as stale as Bournemouth. We know that there's nothing very stupendous in the Brahmaputra gorges. There's little left for a man's imagination to play with, and our children will grow up in a dull, shrunken world. Except, of course, the Great Southern Desert of Arabia."

" Do you think it can be crossed ? " Nightingale asked.

" It's hard to say, and the man who tried it would take almighty risks. I don't fancy myself pinning my life to milk camels. They're chancy brutes."

" I don't believe there's anything there," said Fulleylove, " except eight hundred miles of soft sand."

" I'm not so sure. I've heard strange stories. There was a man I met once in Oman, who went west from the Manah oasis . . ."

He stopped to taste the Club madeira, then set down the glass and looked at his watch.

" Great Scott ! " he said. " I must be off. I'm sorry, Mr. President, but I felt I must see you all again. You don't mind my butting in ? "

He was half-way to the door, when Burminster asked where he was going.

" To seek the straw in some sequestered grange. . . . Meaning the ten-thirty from King's Cross. I'm off to Scotland to see my father. Remember, I'm the last prop of an ancient house. Good-bye, all of you. I'll tell you about my schemes at the next dinner."

As the door closed on him I had a sense of the

blackest depression and loneliness. He was my one great ally, and he came and disappeared like a ship in the night, without a word to me. I felt like a blind bat, and I must have showed my feeling in my face, for Medina saw it and put it down, I daresay, to my dislike of Sandy. He asked Palliser-Yeates to take his place. "It's not the Scotch express, like Arbuthnot, but I'm off for a holiday very soon, and I have an appointment I must keep." That was all to the good, for I had been wondering how I was to make an excuse for my visit to the Fields of Eden. He asked me when I would be back, and I said listlessly within the next hour. He nodded. "I'll be home by then, and can let you in if Odell has gone to bed." Then with a little chaff of Burminster he left, so much at ease that I was positive he had had no bad news. I waited for five minutes and followed suit. The time was a quarter past ten.

. . . . . . . .

At the entrance to the club in Wellesley Street I expected to have some difficulty, but the man in the box at the head of the stairs, after a sharp glance at me, let me pass. He was not the fellow who had been there on my visit with Archie Roylance and yet I had a queer sense of having seen his face before. I stepped into the dancing-room with its heavy flavour of scent and its infernal din of mountebank music, sat down at a side-table and ordered a liqueur.

There was a difference in the place, but at first I could not put my finger on it. Everything seemed the same ; the only face I knew was Miss Victor's, and that had the same mask-like pallor ; she was dancing with a boy, who seemed to be trying to talk to her and getting few replies. Odell I did not see, nor the Jew with the beard. I observed with interest the little casement above from which I had looked when I burgled the curiosity shop. There were fewer people to-night, but apparently the same class.

No, not quite the same class. The women were the same, but the men were different. They were older and more—how shall I put it ?—responsible-looking, and had not the air of the professional dancing partner or the young man on the spree. They were heavier footed, too, though good enough performers. Somehow I got the notion that most of them were not habitués of this kind of place and were here with a purpose.

As soon as this idea dawned on me I began to notice other things. There were fewer foreign waiters, and their number was steadily decreasing. Drinks would be ordered and would be long in coming ; a servant, once he left the hall, seemed to be unaccountably detained. And then I observed another thing. There was a face looking down from the casement above ; I could see it like a shadow behind the dirty glass.

Presently Odell appeared, a resplendent figure in evening dress, with a diamond solitaire in his shirt and a red silk handkerchief in his left sleeve. He looked massive and formidable, but puffier than ever, and his small pig's eyes were very bright.

I fancied he had been having a glass or two, just enough to excite him. He swaggered about among the small tables, turning now and then to stare at the girl in green, and then went out again. I looked at my watch, and saw that it was a quarter to eleven.

When I lifted my head Mary had arrived. No more paint and powder and bizarre clothes. She was wearing the pale blue gown she had worn at our Hunt Ball in March, and her hair was dressed in the simple way I loved, which showed all the lights and shadows in the gold. She came in like a young queen, cast a swift glance round the room, and then, shading her eyes with her hand, looked up towards the casement. It must have been a signal, for I saw a hand wave.

As she stood there, very still and poised like a runner, the music stopped suddenly. The few men who were still dancing spoke to their partners and moved towards the door. I observed the bearded Jew hurry in and look round. A man touched him on the arm and drew him away, and that was the last I saw of him.

Suddenly Odell reappeared. He must have had some warning which required instant action. I shall never know what it was, but it may have announced the round-up, and the course to be followed towards the hostages. He signed peremptorily to Miss Victor and went forward as if to take her arm. "You gotta come along," I heard, when my eyes were occupied with a new figure.

Turpin was there, a pale taut young man with his brows knit, as I remembered them in tight corners in France. The green girl had darted to Mary's side, and Turpin strode up to her.

" Adela, my dear," he said, " I think it is time for you to be going home."

The next I saw was Miss Victor's hand clutching his arm and Odell advancing with a flush on his sallow face.

" You letta go that goil," he was saying. " You got no business with her. She's my goil."

Turpin was smiling. " I think not, my friend." He disengaged Adela's arm and put her behind him, and with a swift step struck Odell a resounding smack on the cheek with the flat of his hand.

The man seemed to swell with fury. " Hell ! " he cried, with a torrent of Bowery oaths. " My smart guy, I've got it in my mitt for you. You for the sleep pill."

I would have given a fortune to be in Turpin's place, for I felt that a scrap was what I needed to knit up my ragged nerves. But I couldn't chip in, for this was clearly his special quarrel, and very soon I saw that he was not likely to need my help.

Smiling wickedly, he moved round the pug, who had his fists up. " *Fiche-moi la paix*," he crooned. " My friend, I am going to massacre you."

I stepped towards Mary, for I wanted to get the women outside, but she was busy attending to Miss Victor, whom the strain of the evening had left on the verge of swooning. So I only saw bits of the fight. Turpin kept Odell at long range, for in-fighting would have been fatal, and he tried him with his lightning movements, till the professional's bad training told and his wind went. When the Frenchman saw his opponent puffing and his cheeks mottling he started to sail in. That part I witnessed, and I hope that Mary and Miss Victor did not understand old Turpin's language, for he spoke gently to himself the whole time, and it was the quintessence of all the esoteric abuse that the French *poilu* accumulated during the four years of war. His tremendous reach gave him an advantage, he was as light on his legs as a fencer, and his arms seemed to shoot out with the force of a steam-hammer. I realized what I had never known before, that his slimness was deceptive, and that stripped he would be a fine figure of sinew and bone. Also I understood that a big fellow, however formidable, if he is untrained and a little drunk, will go down before speed and quick wits and the deftness of youth.

They fought for just over six minutes. Turpin's deadliest blows were on Odell's body, but the knockout came with one on the point of the chin. The big man crumpled up in a heap, and the back of his head banged on the floor. Turpin wrapped a wisp of a handkerchief round his knuckles, which had suffered from Odell's solitaire, and looked about him.

" What is to become of this offal ? " he asked.

One of the dancers replied. " We will look after him, sir. The whole house is in our hands. This man is wanted on a good many grounds."

I walked up to the prostrate Odell, and took the latch-key from his waistcoat pocket. Turpin and Adela had gone, and Mary stood watching me. I observed that she was very pale.

" I am going to Hill Street," I said.

" I will come later," was her answer. " I hope in less than an hour. The key will let you in. There will be people there to keep the door open for me."

Her face had the alert and absorbed look that old Peter Pienaar's used to have when he was after game. There was no other word spoken between us. She entered a big saloon-car which was waiting in the street below, and I walked to Royston Square to find a taxi. It was not yet eleven o'clock.

# CHAPTER XIX

A LITTLE after eleven that night a late walker in Palmyra Square would have seen a phenomenon rare in the dingy neighbourhood. A large motor-car drew up at the gate of No. 7, where dwelt the teacher of music, who had long retired to rest. A woman descended, wearing a dark cloak and carrying a parcel, and stood for a second looking across the road to where the lean elms in the centre of the square made a patch of shade. She seemed to find there what she expected, for she hastened to the gate of No. 4. She did not approach the front door, but ran down the path to the back where the tradesmen called, and as soon as she was out of sight several figures emerged from the shadow and moved towards the gate.

Miss Outhwaite opened to her tap. "My, but you're late, miss," she whispered, as the woman brushed past her into the dim kitchen. Then she gasped, for some transformation had taken place in the district-visitor. It was no longer a faded spinster that she saw, but a dazzling lady, gorgeously dressed as it seemed to her, and of a remarkable beauty.

" I've brought your hat, Elsie," she said. " It's rather a nice one, and I think you'll like it. Now go at once and open the front door."

" But Madame . . ." the girl gasped.

" Never mind Madame. You are done with Madame. To-morrow you will come and see me at this address," and she gave her a slip of paper. " I will see that you do not suffer. Now hurry, my dear."

The girl seemed to be mesmerized, and turned to obey. The district-visitor followed her, but did not wait in the hall. Instead, she ran lightly up the stairs, guiding herself by a small electric torch, and when the front door was open and four silent figures had entered she was nowhere to be seen.

For the next quarter of an hour an inquisitive passer-by would have noted lights spring out and then die away in more than one room of No. 4. He might have also heard the sound of low, excited speech. At the end of that space of time he would have seen the district-visitor descend the steps and enter the car which had moved up to the gate. She was carrying something in her arms.

Within, in a back room, a furious woman was struggling with a telephone, from which she got no answer, since the line had been cut. And an old woman sat in a chair by the hearth, raving and muttering, with a face like death.

.    .    .    .    .    .    .    .    .

When I got to Hill Street, I waited till the taxi had driven off before I entered. There was a man standing in the porch of the house opposite, and as I waited another passed me, who nodded. "Good-evening, Sir Richard," he said, and though I did not recognize him I knew where he came from. My spirits were at their lowest ebb, and not even the sight of these arrangements could revive them. For I knew that, though we had succeeded with Miss Victor and Mercot, we had failed with the case which mattered most. I was going to try to scare Medina or to buy him, and I felt that both purposes were futile, for the awe of him was still like a black fog on my soul.

I let myself in with Odell's latch-key and left the heavy door ajar. Then I switched on the staircase lights and mounted to the library. I left the lights burning behind me, for they would be needed by those who followed.

Medina was standing by the fireplace, in which logs had been laid ready for a match. As usual, he had only the one lamp lit, that on his writing-table. He had a slip of paper in his hand, one of the two which had lain in the top drawer, as I saw by the dates and the ruled lines. I fancy he had been attempting in vain to ring up Palmyra Square. Some acute suspicion had been aroused in him, and he had been trying to take action. His air of leisure was the kind which is hastily assumed; a minute before I was convinced that he had been furiously busy.

There was surprise in his face when he saw me.

" Hullo ! " he said, " how did you get in ? I didn't hear you ring. I told Odell to go to bed."

I was feeling so weak and listless that I wanted to sit down, so I dropped into a chair out of the circle of the lamp.

" Yes," I said. " Odell's in bed all right. I let myself in with his key. I've just seen that Bowery tough put to sleep with a crack on the chin from Turpin. You know—the Marquis de la Tour du Pin."

I had a good strategic position, for I could see his face clearly and he could only see the outline of mine.

" What on earth are you talking about ? " he said.

" Odell has been knocked out. You see, Turpin has taken Miss Victor back to her father." I looked at my watch. " And by this time Lord Mercot should be in London—unless the Scotch express is late."

A great tide of disillusion must have swept over his mind, but his face gave no sign of it. It had grown stern, but as composed as a judge's.

" You're behaving as if you were mad. What has come over you ? I know nothing of Lord Mercot—you mean the Alcester boy ? Or Miss Victor."

" Oh yes, you do," I said wearily. I did not know where to begin, for I wanted to get him at once to the real business. " It's a long story. Do you want me to tell it when you know it all already ? " I believe I yawned, and I felt so tired I could hardly put the sentences together.

"I insist that you explain this nonsense," was his reply. One thing he must have realized by now, that he had no power over me, for his jaw was set and his eyes stern, as if he were regarding not a satellite, but an enemy and an equal.

"Well, you and your friends for your own purposes took three hostages, and I have made it my business to free them. I let you believe that your tomfoolery had mastered me—your performance in this room and Newhover and Madame Breda and the old blind lady and all the rest of it. When you thought I was drugged and demented I was specially wide awake. I had to abuse your hospitality—rather a dirty game, you may say, but then I was dealing with a scoundrel. I went to Norway when you thought I was in bed at Fosse, and I found Mercot, and I expect at this moment Newhover is feeling rather cheap. . . . Miss Victor, too. She wasn't very difficult, once we hit on the Fields of Eden. You're a very clever man, Mr. Medina, but you oughtn't to circulate doggerel verses. Take my advice and stick to good poetry."

By this time the situation must have been clear to him, but there was not a quiver in that set hard face. I take off my hat to the best actor I have ever met—the best but one, the German count who lies buried at the farm of Gavrelle.

"You've gone off your head," he said, and his quiet considerate voice belied his eyes.

"Oh no! I rather wish I had. I hate to think that there can be so base a thing in the world as you. A man with the brains of a god and living only to glut his rotten vanity! You should be scotched like a snake."

For a moment I had a blessed thought that he was about to go for me, for I would have welcomed a scrap like nothing else on earth. There may have been a flicker of passion, but it was quickly suppressed. His eyes had become grave and reproachful.

"I have been kind to you," he said, "and have treated you as a friend. This is my reward. The most charitable explanation is that your wits are unhinged. But you had better leave this house."

"Not before you hear me out. I have something to propose, Mr. Medina. You have still a third hostage in your hands. We are perfectly aware of the syndicate you have been working with—the Barcelona nut business, and the Jacobite count, and your friend the Shropshire master-of-hounds. Scotland Yard has had its hand over the lot for months, and to-night the hand will be closed. That shop is shut for good. Now listen to me, for I have a proposal to make. You have the ambition of the Devil, and have already made for yourself a great name. I will do nothing to smirch that name. I will swear a solemn oath to hold my tongue. I will go away from England, if you like. I will bury the memory of the past months, and my knowledge will never be used to put a spoke in your wheel. Also, since your syndicate is burst up, you will want money. Well, I will give you one hundred thousand pounds.

And in return for my silence and my cash I ask
you to restore to me David Warcliff, safe and sane.
Sane, I say, for whatever you have made of the
poor little chap you have got to unmake it."

I had made up my mind about this offer as I
came along in the taxi.  It was a big sum, but I
had more money than I needed, and Blenkiron,
who had millions, would lend a hand.

His face showed no response, no interest, only
the same stern melancholy regard.

" Poor devil ! " he said.  " You're madder than
I thought."

My lassitude was disappearing, and I began to
get angry.

" If you do not agree," I said, " I will blacken
your reputation throughout the civilized world.
What use will England have for a kidnapper and
a blackmailer and—a—a—bogus magician ? "

But as I spoke I knew that my threats were
foolish.  He smiled, a wise, pitying smile, which
made me shiver with wrath.

" No, it is you who will appear as the blackmailer," he said softly.  " Consider.  You are
making the most outrageous charges.  I don't
quite follow your meaning, but clearly they are
outrageous—and what evidence have you to support them ?  Your own dreams.  Who will believe
you ?  I have had the good fortune to make many
friends, and they are loyal friends."  There was
a gentle regret in his voice.  " Your story will be
laughed to scorn.  Of course people will be sorry
for you, for you are popular in a way.  They will

say that a meritorious soldier, more notable perhaps for courage than for brains, has gone crazy, and they will comment on the long-drawn-out effects of the War. I must of course protect myself. If you blackguard me I will prosecute you for slander and get your mental condition examined."

It was only too true. I had no evidence except my own word. I knew that it would be impossible to link up Medina with the doings of the syndicate —he was too clever for that. His blind mother would die on the rack before she spoke, and his tools could not give him away, because they were tools and knew nothing. The world would laugh at me if I opened my mouth. At that moment I think I had my first full realization of Medina's quality. Here was a man who had just learned that his pet schemes were shattered, who had had his vanity wounded to the quick by the revelation of how I had fooled him, and yet he could play what was left of the game with coolness and precision. I had struck the largest size of opponent.

" What about the hundred thousand pounds, then ? " I asked. " That is my offer for David Warcliff."

" You are very good," he said mockingly. " I might feel insulted, if I did not know you were a lunatic."

I sat there staring at the figure in the glow of the one lamp, which seemed to wax more formidable as I looked, and a thousandfold more sinister. I saw the hideous roundness of his head, the mercilessness of his eyes, so that I wondered how I had ever thought him handsome. But now that most of his game was spoiled he only seemed the greater, the more assured. Were there no gaps in his defences ? He had kinks in him—witness the silly rhyme which had given me the first clue. . . . Was there no weakness in that panoply which I could use ? Physical fear—physical pain—could anything be done with that ?

I got to my feet with a blind notion of closing with him. He divined my intention, for he showed something in his hand which gleamed dully. "Take care," he said. "I can defend myself against any maniac."

"Put it away," I said hopelessly. "You're safe enough from me. My God, I hope that somewhere there is a hell." I felt as feeble as a babe, and all the while the thought of the little boy was driving me mad.

.          .          .          .          .          .

Suddenly I saw Medina's eyes look over my shoulder. Some one had come into the room, and I turned and found Kharama.

He was in evening dress, wearing a turban, and in the dusk his dark malign face seemed an embodied sneer at my helplessness. I did not see how Medina took his arrival, for all at once something seemed to give in my head. For the Indian I felt now none of the awe which I had for the other, only a flaming, overpowering hate. That this foul thing out of the East should pursue his devilries unchecked seemed to me beyond bearing.

I forgot Medina's pistol and everything else, and went for him like a wild beast.

He dodged me, and, before I knew, had pulled off his turban, and tossed it in my face.

" Don't be an old ass, Dick," he said.

Panting with fury, I stopped short and stared. The voice was Sandy's, and so was the figure. . . . And the face, too, when I came to look into it. He had done something with the corners of his eyebrows and tinted the lids with kohl, but the eyes, which I had never before seen properly opened, were those of my friend.

" What an artist the world has lost in me ! " he laughed, and tried to tidy his disordered hair.

Then he nodded to Medina. " We meet again sooner than we expected. I missed my train, and came to look for Dick. . . . Lay down that pistol, please. I happen to be armed too, you see. It's no case for shooting anyhow. Do you mind if I smoke ? "

He flung himself into an armchair and lit a cigarette. Once more I was conscious of my surroundings, for hitherto for all I knew I might have been arguing in a desert. My eyes had cleared and my brain was beginning to work again. I saw the great room with its tiers of books, some glimmering, some dusky ; Sandy taking his ease in his chair and gazing placidly up into Medina's face ; Medina with his jaw set but his eyes troubled— yes, for the first time I saw flickers of perplexity in those eyes.

" Dick, I suppose, has been reasoning with you,"

Sandy said mildly. " And you have told him that he was a madman? Quite right. He is. You have pointed out to him that his story rests on his unsupported evidence, which no one will believe, for I admit it is an incredible tale. You have warned him that if he opens his mouth you will have him shut up as a lunatic. Is that correct, Dick?

"Well," he continued, looking blandly at Medina, " that was a natural view for you to take. Only, of course, you made one small error. His evidence will not be unsupported."

Medina laughed, but there was no ease in his laugh. " Who are the other lunatics? "

" Myself for one. You have interested me for quite a long time, Mr. Medina. I will confess that one of my reasons for coming home in March was to have the privilege of your acquaintance. I have taken a good deal of pains about it. I have followed your own line of studies—indeed, if the present situation weren't so hectic, I should like to exchange notes with you as a fellow-inquirer. I have traced your career in Central Asia and elsewhere with some precision. I think I know more about you than anybody else in the world."

Medina made no answer. The tables were turning, and his eyes were chained to the slight figure in the armchair.

" All that is very interesting," Sandy went on, " but it is not quite germane to the subject before us. Kharama, whom we both remember in his pride, unfortunately died last year. It was kept very secret for obvious reasons—the goodwill of his business was very valuable and depended upon his being alive—and I only heard of it by a lucky accident. So I took the liberty of borrowing his name, Mr. Medina. As Kharama I was honoured with your confidence. Rather a cad's trick, you will say, and I agree, but in an affair like this one has no choice of weapons. . . . You did more than confide in me. You trusted me with Miss Victor and the Marquis de la Tour du Pin, when it was important that they should be in safe keeping. . . . I have a good deal of evidence to support Dick."

"Moonshine!" said Medina. "Two lunacies do not make sense. I deny every detail of your rubbish."

"Out of the mouth of two or three witnesses," said Sandy pleasantly. "There is still a third . . . Lavater," he cried, "come in; we're ready for you."

There entered the grey melancholy man, whom I had seen on my first visit here, and in the house behind Little Fardell Street. I noticed that he walked straight to Sandy's chair, and did not look at Medina.

"Lavater you know already, I think. He used to be a friend of mine, and lately we have re-sumed the friendship. He was your disciple for some time, but has now relinquished that honour. Lavater will be able to tell the world a good deal about you."

Medina's face had become like a mask, and the colour had gone out of it. He may have been a

volcano within, but outside he was cold ice.  His
voice, acid and sneering, came out like drops of
chilly water.

"Three lunatics," he said.  "I deny every word
you say.  No one will believe you.  It is a con-
spiracy of madmen."

"Let's talk business anyhow," said Sandy.
"The case against you is proven to the hilt, but
let us see how the world will regard it.  The
strong point on your side is that people don't like
to confess they have been fools.  You have been
a very popular man, Mr. Medina, and your many
friends will be loath to believe that you are a
scoundrel.  You've the hedge of your reputation
to protect you.  Again, our story is so monstrous
that the ordinary Englishman may call it un-
believable, for we are not an imaginative nation.
Again, we can get no help from the principal
sufferers.  Miss Victor and Lord Mercot can tell
an ugly story of kidnapping, which may get a
life-sentence for Odell, and for Newhover if he is
caught, but which does not implicate you.  That
will be a stumbling-block to most juries, who are
not as familiar with occult science as you and I.
. . .  These are your strong points.  But consider
what we can bring on the other side.  You are a
propagandist of genius, as I once told Dick, and
I can explain just how you have fooled the world
—your exploits with Denikin and such-like.  Then
the three of us can tell a damning story, and tell it
from close quarters.  It may sound wild, but Dick
has some reputation for good sense, and a good

many people think that I am not altogether a
fool.   Finally, we have on our side Scotland Yard,
which is now gathering in your associates, and we
have behind us Julius Victor, who is not without
influence. . . . I do not say we can send you to
prison, though I think it likely, but we can throw
such suspicion on you that for the rest of your
days you will be a marked man.   You will recognize that for you that means utter failure, for to
succeed you must swim in the glory of popular
confidence."

I could see that Medina was shaken at last.
" You may damage me with your lies," he said
slowly, " but I will be even with you.   You will
find me hard to beat."

" I don't doubt it," was Sandy's answer.   " I
and my friends do not want victory, we want success.   We want David Warcliff."

There was no answer, and Sandy went on.

" We make you a proposal.   The three of us
will keep what we know to ourselves.   We will
pledge ourselves never to breathe a word of it—
if you like we will sign a document to say that
we acknowledge our mistake.   So far as we are
concerned you may go on and become Prime
Minister of Britain or Archbishop of Canterbury,
or anything you jolly well like.   We don't exactly
love you, but we will not interfere with the adora-
tion of others.   I'll take myself off again to the
East with Lavater, and Dick will bury himself in
Oxfordshire mud.   And in return we ask that you
hand over to us David Warcliff in his right mind."

There was no answer.

Then Sandy made a mistake in tactics. " I believe you are attached to your mother," he said. " If you accept our offer she will be safe from annoyance. Otherwise—well, she is an important witness."

The man's pride was stung to the quick. His mother must have been for him an inner sanctuary, a thing apart from and holier than his fiercest ambitions, the very core and shrine of his monstrous vanity. That she should be used as a bargaining counter stirred something deep and primeval in him, something—let me say it—higher and better than I had imagined. A new and a human fury burned the mask off him like tissue paper.

" You fools ! " he cried, and his voice was harsh with rage. " You perfect fools ! You will sweat blood for that insult."

" It's a fair offer," said Sandy, never moving a muscle. " Do I understand that you refuse ? "

Medina stood on the hearth-rug like an animal at bay, and upon my soul I couldn't but admire him. The flame in his face would have scorched most people into abject fear.

" Go to hell, the pack of you ! Out of this house ! You will never hear a word from me till you are bleating for mercy. Get out . . ."

.    .    .    .    .    .    .

His eyes must have been dimmed by his rage, for he did not see Mary enter. She had advanced right up to Sandy's chair before even I noticed her. She was carrying something in her arms, something which she held close as a mother holds a child.

It was the queer little girl from the house in Palmyra Square. Her hair had grown longer and fell in wisps over her brow and her pale tear-stained cheeks. A most piteous little object she was, with dull blind eyes, which seemed to struggle with perpetual terror. She still wore the absurd linen smock, her skinny little legs and arms were bare, and her thin fingers clutched at Mary's gown.

Then Medina saw her, and Sandy ceased to exist for him. He stared for a second uncomprehendingly, till the passion in his face turned to alarm. " What have you done with her ? " he barked, and flung himself forward.

I thought he was going to attack Mary, so I tripped him up. He sprawled on the floor, and since he seemed to have lost all command of himself I reckoned that I had better keep him there. I looked towards Mary, who nodded. " Please tie him up," she said, and passed me the turban cloth of the late Kharama.

He fought like a tiger, but Lavater and I with a little help from Sandy managed to truss him fairly tight, supplementing the turban with one of the curtain cords. We laid him in an armchair.

" What have you done with her ? " he kept on, screwing his head round to look at Mary.

I could not understand his maniacal concern for the little girl, till Mary answered, and I saw what he meant by " her."

" No one has touched your mother. She is in the house in Palmyra Square."

Then Mary laid the child down very gently in the chair where Sandy had been sitting, and stood erect before Medina.

" I want you to bring back this little boy's mind," she said.

I suppose I should have been astonished, but I wasn't—at least, not at her words, though I had not had an inkling beforehand of the truth. All the astonishment I was capable of was reserved for Mary. She stood there looking down on the bound man, her face very pale, her eyes quite gentle, her lips parted as if in expectation. And there was something about her so formidable, so implacable, that the other three of us fell into the background. Her presence dominated everything, and the very grace of her body and the mild sadness of her eyes seemed to make her the more terrifying. I know now how Joan of Arc must have looked when she led her troops into battle.

" Do you hear me ? " she repeated. " You took away his soul and you can give it back again. That is all I ask of you."

He choked before he replied. " What boy ? I tell you I know nothing. You are all mad."

" I mean David Warcliff. The others are free now, and he must be free to-night. Free, and in his right mind, as when you carried him off. Surely you understand."

There was no answer.

"That is all I ask. It is such a little thing. Then we will go away."

I broke in. "Our offer holds. Do as she asks, and we will never open our mouths about to-night's work."

He was not listening to me, nor was she. It was a duel between the two of them, and as she looked at him, his face seemed to grow more dogged and stone-like. If ever he had felt hatred it was for this woman, for it was a conflict between two opposite poles of life, two worlds eternally at war.

"I tell you I know nothing of the brat . . ."

She stopped him with lifted hand. "Oh, do not let us waste time, please. It is far too late for arguing. If you do what I ask we will go away, and you will never be troubled with us again. I promise—we all promise. If you do not, of course we must ruin you."

I think it was the confidence in her tone which stung him.

"I refuse," he almost screamed. "I do not know what you mean . . . I defy you. . . . You can proclaim your lies to the world. . . . You will not crush me. I am too strong for you."

There was no mistaking the finality of that defiance. I thought it put the lid on everything. We could blast the fellow's reputation, no doubt, and win victory ; but we had failed, for we were left with that poor little mindless waif.

Mary's face did not change.

"If you refuse, I must try another way ; " her voice was as gentle as a mother's. "I must give

David Warcliff back to his father. . . . Dick "—
she turned to me—" will you light the fire ? "

I obeyed, not knowing what she meant, and in
a minute the dry fagots were roaring up the
chimney, lighting up our five faces and the mazed
child in the chair.

" You have destroyed a soul," she said, " and
you refuse to repair the wrong. I am going to
destroy your body, and nothing will ever repair it."

Then I saw her meaning, and both Sandy and
I cried out. Neither of us had led the kind of
life which makes a man squeamish, but this was
too much for us. But our protests died half-born,
after one glance at Mary's face. She was my own
wedded wife, but in that moment I could no more
have opposed her than could the poor bemused
child. Her spirit seemed to transcend us all and
radiate an inexorable command. She stood easily
and gracefully, a figure of motherhood and pity
rather than of awe. But all the same I did not
recognize her ; it was a stranger that stood there,
a stern goddess that wielded the lightnings.
Beyond doubt she meant every word she said,
and her quiet voice seemed to deliver judgment as
aloof and impersonal as Fate. I could see creeping over Medina's sullenness the shadow of terror.

" You are a desperate man," she was saying.
" But I am far more desperate. There is nothing
on earth that can stand between me and the
saving of this child. You know that, don't you ?
A body for a soul—a soul for a body—which shall
it be ? "

The light was reflected from the steel fire-irons and Medina saw it and shivered.

"You may live a long time, but you will have to live in seclusion. No woman will ever cast eyes on you except to shudder. People will point at you and say 'There goes the man who was maimed by a woman—because of the soul of a child.' You will carry your story written on your face for the world to read and laugh and revile."

She had got at the central nerve of his vanity, for I think that he was ambitious less of achievement than of the personal glory that attends it. I dared not look at her, but I could look at him, and I saw all the passions of hell chase each other over his face. He tried to speak, but only choked. He seemed to bend his whole soul to look at her, and to shiver at what he saw.

She turned her head to glance at the clock on the mantelpiece.

"You must decide before the quarter strikes," she said. "After that there will be no place for repentance. A body for a soul—a soul for a body."

Then from her black silk reticule she took a little oddly-shaped green bottle. She held it in her hand as if it had been a jewel, and I gulped in horror.

"This is the elixir of death—of death in life, Mr. Medina. It makes comeliness a mockery. It will burn flesh and bone into shapes of hideousness, but it does not kill. Oh no—it does not kill. A body for a soul—a soul for a body."

It was that, I think, which finished him. The

threefold chime which announced the quarter had begun when out of his dry throat came a sound like a clucking hen's. "I agree," a voice croaked, seeming to come from without, so queer and far away it was.

"Thank you," she said, as if some one had opened a door for her. "Dick, will you please make Mr. Medina more comfortable. . . ."

The fire was not replenished, so the quick-burning fagots soon died down. Again the room was shadowy, except for the single lamp that glowed behind Medina's head.

I cannot describe that last scene, for I do not think my sight was clear, and I know that my head was spinning. The child sat on Mary's lap, with its eyes held by the glow of light. "You are Gerda . . . you are sleepy . . . now you sleep" —I did not heed the patter, for I was trying to think of homely things which would keep my wits anchored. I thought chiefly of Peter John.

Sandy was crouched on a stool by the hearth. I noticed that he had his hands on his knees, and that from one of them protruded something round and dark, like the point of a pistol barrel. He was taking no chances, but the thing was folly, for we were in the presence of far more potent weapons. Never since the world began was there a scene of such utter humiliation. I shivered at the indecency of it. Medina performed his sinister ritual, but on us spectators it had no more effect than a charade. Mary especially sat watching it with the detachment with which one watches a

kindergarten play.   The man had suddenly become
a mountebank under those fearless eyes.

The voices droned on, the man asking questions,
the child answering in a weak unnatural voice.
" You are David Warcliff . . . you lost your way
coming from school . . . you have been ill and
have forgotten. . . . You are better now . . . you
remember Haverham and the redshanks down by
the river. . . . You are sleepy . . . I think you
would like to sleep again."

Medina spoke.   " You can wake him now.   Do
it carefully."

I got up and switched on the rest of the lights.
The child was peacefully asleep in Mary's arms,
and she bent and kissed him.   " Speak to him,
Dick," she said.

" Davie," I said loudly.   " Davie, it's about
time for us to get home."

He opened his eyes and sat up.   When he
found himself on Mary's knee, he began to clamber
down.   He was not accustomed to a woman's lap,
and felt a little ashamed.

" Davie," I repeated.   " Your father will be
getting tired waiting for us.   Don't you think we
should go home ? "

" Yes, sir," he said, and put his hand in mine.

.      .      .      .      .      .      .      .

To my dying day I shall not forget my last sight
of that library—the blazing lights which made the
books, which I had never seen before except in
shadow, gleam like a silk tapestry, the wood-fire
dying on the hearth. and the man sunk in the chair.

It may sound odd after all that had happened, but my chief feeling was pity. Yes, pity! He seemed the loneliest thing on God's earth. You see he had never had any friends except himself, and his ambitions had made a barrier between him and all humanity. Now that they were gone he was stripped naked, and left cold and shivering in the wilderness of his broken dreams.

Mary leaned back in the car.

" I hope I'm not going to faint," she said. " Give me the green bottle, please."

" For Heaven's sake ! " I cried.

" Silly ! " she said. " It's only eau-de-cologne."

She laughed, and the laugh seemed to restore her a little, though she still looked deadly pale. She fumbled in her reticule, and drew out a robust pair of scissors.

" I'm going to cut Davie's hair. I can't change his clothes, but at any rate I can make his head like a boy's again, so that his father won't be shocked."

" Does he know we are coming ? "

" Yes. I telephoned to him after dinner, but of course I said nothing about Davie."

She clipped assiduously, and by the time we came to the Pimlico square where Sir Arthur Warcliff lived she had got rid of the long locks, and the head was now that of a pallid and thin but wonderfully composed little boy. " Am I going back to Dad ? " he had asked, and seemed content.

I refused to go in—I was not fit for any more

shocks—so I sat in the car while Mary and David entered the little house. In about three minutes Mary returned. She was crying, and yet smiling too.

"I made Davie wait in the hall, and went into Sir Arthur's study alone. He looked ill—and oh, so old and worn. I said: 'I have brought Davie. Never mind his clothes. He's all right!' Then I fetched him in. Oh, Dick, it was a miracle. That old darling seemed to come back to life. . . . The two didn't run into each other's arms . . . they shook hands . . . and the little boy bowed his head and Sir Arthur kissed the top of it, and said 'Dear Mouse-head, you've come back to me.' . . . And then I slipped away."

# CHAPTER XX

## MACHRAY

A WEEK later, after much consultation with Sandy, I wrote Medina a letter. The papers said he had gone abroad for a short rest, and I could imagine the kind of mental purgatory he was enduring in some Mediterranean bay. We had made up our mind to be content with success. Victory meant a long campaign in the courts and the press, in which no doubt we should have won, but for which I at any rate had no stomach. The whole business was a nightmare which I longed to shut the door on ; we had drawn his fangs, and for all I cared he might go on with his politics and dazzle the world with his gifts, provided he kept his hands out of crime. I wrote and told him that ; told him that the three people who knew everything would hold their tongues, but that they reserved the right to speak if he ever showed any sign of running crooked. I had no reply and did not expect one. I had lost all my hate for the man, and, so strangely are we made, what I mostly felt was compassion. We are all, even the best of us, egotists and self-deceivers, and without a little comfortable make-believe to clothe us we should freeze in the outer winds. I shuddered when I thought of the poor devil with his palace of cards about his ears and his naked soul. I felt that further triumph would be an offence against humanity.

He must have got my message, for in July he was back at his work, and made a speech at a big political demonstration which was highly commended in the papers. Whether he went about in society I do not know, for Sandy was in Scotland and I was at Fosse, and not inclined to leave it. . . . Meantime Macgillivray's business was going on, and the press was full of strange cases, which no one seemed to think of connecting. I gathered from Macgillivray that though the syndicate was smashed to little bits he had failed to make the complete bag of malefactors that he had hoped. In England there were three big financial exposures followed by long sentences ; in Paris there was a first-rate political scandal and a crop of convictions ; a labour agitator and a copper magnate in the Middle West went to gaol for life, and there was the famous rounding-up of the murder gang in Turin. But Macgillivray and his colleagues, like me, had success rather than victory ; indeed in this world I don't think you can get both at once— you must make your choice.

We saw Mercot at the " House " Ball at Oxford, none the worse for his adventures, but rather the better, for he was a man now and not a light-witted boy. Early in July Mary and I went to

Paris for Adela Victor's wedding, the most gorgeous show I have ever witnessed, when I had the privilege of kissing the bride and being kissed by the bridegroom. Sir Arthur Warcliff brought David to pay us a visit at Fosse, where the boy fished from dawn to dusk, and began to get some flesh on his bones. Archie Roylance arrived, and the pair took such a fancy to each other that the three of them went off to Norway to have a look at the birds on Flacksholm.

I was busy during those weeks making up arrears of time at Fosse, for my long absence had put out the whole summer programme. One day, as I was down in the Home Meadow, planning a new outlet for one of the ponds, Sandy turned up, announcing that he must have a talk with me and could only spare twenty minutes.

"When does your tenancy of Machray begin?" he asked.

"I have got it now—ever since April. The sea-trout come early there."

"And you can go up whenever you like?"

"Yes. We propose starting about the 5th of August."

"Take my advice and start at once," he said.

I asked why, though I guessed his reason.

"Because I'm not very happy about you here. You've insulted to the marrow the vainest and one of the cleverest men in the world. Don't imagine he'll take it lying down. You may be sure he is spending sleepless nights planning how he is to get even with you. It's you he is chiefly thinking about. Me he regards as a rival in the same line of business—he'd love to break me, but he'll trust to luck for the chance turning up. Lavater has been his slave and has escaped—but at any rate he once acknowledged his power. *You* have fooled him from start to finish and left his vanity one raw throbbing sore. He won't be at ease till he has had his revenge on you—on you and your wife."

"Peter John!" I exclaimed.

He shook his head. "No, I don't think so. He won't try that line again—at any rate not yet awhile. But he would be much happier, Dick, if you were dead."

The thought had been in my own mind for weeks, and had made me pretty uncomfortable. It is not pleasant to walk in peril of your life, and move about in constant expectation of your decease. I had considered the thing very carefully, and had come to the conclusion that I could do nothing but try to forget the risk. If I ever allowed myself to think about it, my whole existence would be poisoned. It was a most unpleasant affair, but after all the world is full of hazards. I told Sandy that.

"I'm quite aware of the danger," I said. "I always reckoned that as part of the price I had to pay for succeeding. But I'm hanged if I'm going to allow the fellow to score off me to the extent of disarranging my life."

"You've plenty of fortitude, old fellow," said Sandy, "but you owe a duty to your family and your friends. Of course you might get police protection from Macgillivray, but that would be an infernal nuisance for you, and, besides, what kind of police protection would avail against an enemy as subtle as Medina ? . . . No, I want you to go away. I want you to go to Machray now, and stay there till the end of October."

" What good would that do ? He can follow me there, if he wants to, and anyhow the whole thing would begin again when I came back."

" I'm not so sure," he said. " In three months' time his wounded vanity may have healed. It's no part of his general game to have a vendetta with you, and only a passion of injured pride would drive him to it. Presently that must die down, and he will see his real interest. Then as for Machray—why, a Scotch deer-forest is the best sanctuary on earth. Nobody can come up that long glen without your hearing about it, and nobody can move on the hills without half a dozen argus-eyed stalkers and gillies following him. They're the right sort of police protection. I want you for all our sakes to go to Machray at once."

" It looks like funking," I objected.

" Don't be an old ass. Is there any man alive, who is not a raving maniac, likely to doubt your courage ? You know perfectly well that it is sometimes a brave man's duty to run away."

I thought for a bit. " I don't think he'll hire ruffians to murder me," I said.

" Why ? "

" Because he challenged me to a duel. Proposed a place in the Pyrenees and offered to let me choose both seconds."

" What did you reply ? "

" I wired, ' Try not to be a fool.' It looks as if he wanted to keep the job of doing me in for himself."

" Very likely, and that doesn't mend matters. I'd rather face half a dozen cut-throats than Medina. What you tell me strengthens my argument."

I was bound to admit that Sandy talked sense, and after he had gone I thought the matter out and decided to take his advice. Somehow the fact that he should have put my suspicions into words made them more formidable, and I knew again the odious feeling of the hunted. It was hardly fear, for I think that, if necessary, I could have stayed on at Fosse and gone about my business with a stiff lip. But all the peace of the place had been spoiled. If a bullet might at any moment come from a covert—that was the crude way I envisaged the risk—then good-bye to the charm of my summer meadows.

The upshot was that I warned Tom Greenslade to be ready to take his holiday, and by the 20th of July he and I and Mary and Peter John were settled in a little whitewashed lodge tucked into the fold of a birch-clad hill, and looking alternately at a shrunken river and a cloudless sky, while we prayed for rain.

Machray in calm weather is the most solitary

place on earth, lonelier and quieter even than a Boer farm lost in some hollow of the veld. The mountains rise so sheer and high that it seems that only a bird could escape, and the road from the sea-loch ten miles away is only a strip of heather-grown sand which looks as if it would end a mile off at the feet of each steep hill-shoulder. But when the gales come, and the rain is lashing the roof, and the river swirls at the garden-edge, and the birches and rowans are tossing, then a thousand voices talk, and one lives in a world so loud that one's ears are deafened and one's voice acquires a sharp pitch of protest from shouting against the storm.

We had few gales, and the last week of July was a very fair imitation of the Tropics. The hills were cloaked in a heat haze, the Aicill river was a chain of translucent pools with a few reddening salmon below the ledges, the burns were thin trickles, the sun drew hot scents out of the heather and bog-myrtle, and movement was a weariness to man and beast. That was for the daytime; but every evening about five o'clock there would come a light wind from the west, which scattered the haze, and left a land swimming in cool amber light. Then Mary and Tom Greenslade and I would take to the hills, and return well on for midnight to a vast and shameless supper. Sometimes in the hot noontides I went alone, with old Angus the head stalker, and long before the season began I had got a pretty close knowledge of the forest.

The reader must bear with me while I explain the lie of the land. The twenty thousand acres of Machray extend on both sides of the Aicill glen, but principally to the south. West lies the Machray sea-loch, where the hills are low and green and mostly sheep-ground. East, up to the river-head, is Glenaicill Forest, the lodge of which is beyond the watershed on the shore of another sea-loch, and on our side of the divide there is only a stalker's cottage. Glenaicill is an enormous place, far too big to be a single forest. It had been leased for years by Lord Glenfinnan, an uncle of Archie Roylance, but he was a frail old gentleman of over seventy who could only get a stag when they came down to the low ground in October. The result was that the place was ridiculously undershot, and all the western end, which adjoined Machray, was virtually a sanctuary. It was a confounded nuisance, for it made it impossible to stalk our northern beat except in a south-west wind, unless you wanted to shift the deer on to Glenaicill, and that beat had all our best grazing and seemed to attract all our best heads.

Haripol Forest to the south was not so large, but I should think it was the roughest ground in Scotland. Machray had good beats south of the Aicill right up to the watershed, and two noble corries, the Corrie-na-Sidhe and the Corrie Easain. Beyond the watershed was the glen of the Reascuill, both sides of which were Haripol ground. The Machray heights were all over the

3,000 feet, but rounded and fairly easy going, but the Haripol peaks beyond the stream were desperate rock mountains—Stob Ban, Stob Coire Easain, Sgurr Mór—comprising some of the most difficult climbing in the British Isles. The biggest and hardest top of all was at the head of the Reascuill—Sgurr Dearg, with its two pinnacle ridges, its three prongs, and the awesome precipice of its eastern face. Machray marched with Haripol on its summit, but it wasn't often that any of our stalkers went that way. All that upper part of the Reascuill was a series of cliffs and chasms, and the red deer—who is no rock-climber—rarely ventured there. For the rest these four southern beats of ours were as delightful hunting-ground as I have ever seen, and the ladies could follow a good deal of the stalking by means of a big telescope in the library window of the Lodge. Machray was a young man's forest, for the hills rose steep almost from the sea-level, and you might have to go up and down 3,000 feet several times in a day. But Haripol—at least the north and east parts of it—was fit only for athletes, and it seemed to be its fate to fall to tenants who were utterly incapable of doing it justice. In recent years it had been leased successively to an elderly distiller, a young racing ne'er-do-weel who drank, and a plump American railway king. It was now in the hands of a certain middle-aged Midland manufacturer, Lord Claybody, who had won an easy fortune and an easier peerage during the War. " Ach, he will be killed,"

Angus said. "He will never get up a hundred feet of Haripol without being killed." So I found myself, to my disgust, afflicted with another un-authorized sanctuary.

Angus was very solemn about it. He was a lean anxious man, just over fifty, with a face not unlike a stag's, amazingly fast on the hills, a finished cragsman, and with all the Highlander's subtle courtesy. Kennedy, the second stalker, was of Lowland stock ; his father had come to the North from Galloway in the days of the boom in sheep, and had remained as a keeper when sheep prices fell. He was a sturdy young fellow, apt to suffer on steep slopes on a warm day, but strong as an ox and with a better head than Angus for thinking out problems of weather and wind. Though he had the Gaelic, he was a true Lowlander, plain-spoken and imperturbable. It was a contrast of new and old, for Kennedy had served in the War, and learned many things beyond the other's ken. He knew, for example, how to direct your eye to the point he wanted, and would give intelligent directions like a battery observer, whereas with Angus it was always "D'ye see yon stone ? Ay, but d'ye see another stone ? "—and so forth. Kennedy, when we sat down to rest, would smoke a cigarette in a holder, while Angus lit the dottle in a foul old pipe.

In the first fortnight of August we had alternate days of rain, real drenching torrents, and the Aicill rose and let the fish up from the sea. There were few sea-trout that year, but there was a glorious run of salmon. Greenslade killed his first and by the end of a week had a bag of twelve, while Mary, with the luck which seems to attend casual lady anglers, had four in one day to her own rod. Those were pleasant days, though there were mild damp afternoons when the midges were worse than tropical mosquitoes. I liked it best when a breeze rose and the sun was hot and we had all our meals by the waterside. Once at luncheon we took with us an iron pot, made a fire, and boiled a fresh-killed salmon "in his broo"—a device I recommend to any one who wants the full flavour of that noble fish.

Archie Roylance arrived on August 16th, full of the lust of hunting. He reported that they had seen nothing remarkable in the way of birds at Flacksholm, but that David Warcliff had had great sport with the sea-trout. "There's a good boy for you," he declared. "First-class little sportsman, and to see him and his father together made me want to get wedded straight off. I thought him a bit hipped at Fosse, but the North Sea put him right, and I left him as jolly as a grig. By the way, what was the matter with him in the summer ? I gathered that he had been seedy or something, and the old man can't let him out of his sight. . . . Let's get in Angus, and talk deer."

Angus was ready to talk deer till all hours. I had fixed the 21st for the start of the season, though the beasts were in such forward condition that we might have begun four days earlier. Angus reported that he had already seen several stags clear of velvet. But he was inclined to be doleful about our neighbours.

"My uncle Alexander is past prayin' for," said Archie. "He lives for that forest of his, and he won't have me there early in the season, for he says I have no judgment about beasts and won't listen to the stalkers. In October, you see, he has me under his own eye. He refuses to let a stag be killed unless it's a hummel or a diseased ancient. Result is, the place is crawlin' with fine stags that have begun to go back and won't perish till they're fairly moulderin'. Poor notion of a stud has my uncle Alexander. . . . What about Haripol? Who has it this year?"

When he heard he exclaimed delightedly. "I know old Claybody. Rather a good old fellow in his way, and uncommon free-handed. Rum old bird, too! He once introduced his son to me as 'The Honourable Johnson Claybody.' Fairly wallows in his peerage. You know he wanted to take the title of Lord Oxford, because he had a boy goin' up to Magdalen, but even the Heralds' College jibbed at that. But he'll never get up those Haripol hills. He's a little fat puffin' old man. I'm not very spry on my legs now, but compared to Claybody I'm a gazelle."

"He'll maybe have veesitors," said Angus.

"You bet he will. He'll have the Lodge stuffed with young men, for there are various Honourable Claybody daughters. Don't fancy they'll be much good on the hill, though."

"They will not be good, Sir Archibald," said

the melancholy Angus. "There will have been some of them on the hill already. They will be no better than towrists."

"Towrists," I should explain, were the poison in Angus's cup. By that name he meant people who trespassed on a deer-forest during, or shortly before, the stalking season, and had not the good manners to give him notice and ask his consent. He distinguished them sharply from what he called "muntaneers," a class which he respected, for they were modest and civil folk who came usually with ropes and ice axes early in the spring, and were accustomed to feast off Angus's ham and eggs and thaw their frozen limbs by Angus's fire. If they came at other seasons it was after discussing their routes with Angus. They went where no deer could travel, and spent their time, as he said, "shamming themselves into shimneys." But the "towrist" was blatant and foolish and abundantly discourteous. He tramped, generally in a noisy party, over deer-ground, and, if remonstrated with, became truculent. A single member of the species could wreck the stalking on a beat for several days. "The next I see on Machray," said Angus, "I will be rolling down a big stone on him." Some of the Haripol guests, it appeared, were of this malign breed, and had been wandering thoughtlessly over the forest, thereby wrecking their own sport—and mine.

"They will have Alan Macnicol's heart broke," he concluded. "And Alan was saying to me that they was afful bad shots. They was shooting at a big stone and missing it. And they will have little ponies to ride on up to the tops, for the creatures is no use at walking. I hope they will fall down and break their necks."

" They can't all be bad shots," said Archie. " By the way, Dick, I forgot to tell you. You know Medina, Dominick Medina ? You once told me you knew him. Well, I met him on the steamer, and he said he was going to put in a week with old Claybody."

That piece of news took the light out of the day for me. If Medina was at Haripol it was most certainly with a purpose. I had thought little about the matter since I arrived at Machray, for the place had an atmosphere of impregnable seclusion, and I seemed to have shut a door on my recent life. I had fallen into a mood of content and whole-hearted absorption in the ritual of wild sport. But now my comfort vanished. I looked up at the grim wall of hills towards Haripol and wondered what mischief was hatching behind it.

I warned Angus and Kennedy and the gillies to keep a good look-out for trespassers. Whenever one was seen, they were to get their glasses on him and follow him and report his appearance and doings to me. Then I went out alone to shoot a brace of grouse for the pot, and considered the whole matter very carefully. I had an instinct that Medina had come to these parts to have a reckoning with me, and I was determined not to shirk it. I could not go on living under such a menace ; I must face it and reach a settlement.

To Mary, of course, I would say nothing, and I saw no use in telling either Archie or Greenslade. It was, metaphorically, and perhaps literally, my own funeral. But next morning I did not go fishing. Instead, I stayed at home and wrote out a full account of the whole affair up to Medina's appearance at Haripol, and I set down baldly what I believed to be his purpose. This was in case I went out one day and did not return. When I finished it, I put the document in my dispatch-box, and felt easier, as a man feels when he has made his will. I only hoped the time of waiting would not be prolonged.

The 21st was a glorious blue day, with a morning haze which promised heat. What wind there was came from the south-east, so I sent Archie out on the Corrie Easain beat, and went myself, with one gillie, to Clach Glas, which is the western peak on the north bank of the Aicill. I made a practice of doing my own stalking, and by this time I knew the ground well enough to do it safely. I saw two shootable stags, and managed to get within range of one of them, but spared him for the good of the forest, as he was a young beast whose head would improve. I had a happy and peaceful day, and found to my relief that I wasn't worrying about the future. The clear air and the great spaces seemed to have given me the placid fatalism of an Arab.

When I returned I was greeted by Mary with the news that Archie had got a stag, and that she had followed most of his stalk through the big telescope. Archie himself arrived just before dinner, very cheerful and loquacious. He found that his game leg made him slow, but he declared that he was not in the least tired. At dinner we had to listen to every detail of his day, and we had a sweep on the beast's weight, which Mary won. Afterwards in the smoking-room he told me more.

"Those infernal tailors from Haripol were out to-day. Pretty wild shots they must be. When we were lunchin' a spent bullet whistled over our heads—a long way off, to be sure, but I call it uncommon bad form. You should have heard Angus curse in Gaelic. Look here, Dick, I've a good mind to drop a line to old Claybody and ask him to caution his people. The odds are a million to one, of course, against their doin' any harm, but there's always that millionth chance. I had a feelin' to-day as if the War had started over again."

I replied that if anything of the sort happened a second time I would certainly protest, but I pretended to make light of it, as a thing only possible with that particular brand of wind. But I realized now what Medina's plans were. He had been tramping about Haripol, getting a notion of the lie of the land, and I knew that he had a big-game hunter's quick eye for country. He had fostered the legend of wild shooting among the Haripol guests, and probably he made himself the wildest of the lot. The bullet which sang over Archie's head was a proof, but he waited on the chance of a bullet which would not miss.   If a tragedy happened, every one would believe it was a pure accident, there would be heart-broken apologies, and, though Sandy and one or two others would guess the truth, nothing could be proved, and in any case it wouldn't help *me*. . . . Of course I could stalk only on the north beats of Machray, but the idea no sooner occurred to me than I dismissed it.   I must end this hideous suspense.   I must accept Medina's challenge and somehow or other reach a settlement.

When Angus came in for orders, I told him that I was going stalking on the Corrie-na-Sidhe beat the day after to-morrow, and I asked him to send word privately to Alan Macnicol at Haripol.

" It will be no use, sir," he groaned.   " The veesitors will no heed Alan."

But I told him to send word nevertheless.   I wanted to give Medina the chance he sought.   It was my business to draw his fire.

Next day we slacked and fished.   In the afternoon I went a little way up the hill called Clach Glas, from which I could get a view of the ground on the south side of the Aicill.   It was a clear quiet day, with the wind steady in the south-east, and promising to continue there.   The great green hollow of Corrie-na-Sidhe was clear in every detail ; much of it looked like a tennis-court, but I knew that what seemed smooth sward was really matted blaeberries and hidden boulders, and that the darker patches were breast-high bracken and heather.   Corrie Easain I could not see, for it was hidden by the long spur of Bheinn Fhada, over which peeped the cloven summit of Sgurr Dearg. I searched all the ground with my glasses, and picked up several lots of hinds, and a few young stags, but there was no sign of human activity. There seemed to be a rifle out, however, on Glenaicill Forest, for I heard two far-away shots towards the north-east. I lay a long time amid the fern, with bees humming around me and pipits calling, and an occasional buzzard or pere- grine hovering in the blue, thinking precisely the same thoughts that I used to have in France the day before a big action. It was not exactly nervousness that I felt, but a sense that the foundations of everything had got loose, and that the world had become so insecure that I had better draw down the blinds on hoping and planning and everything, and become a log. I was very clear in my mind that next day was going to bring the crisis.

Of course I didn't want Mary to suspect, but I forgot to caution Archie, and that night at dinner, as ill-luck would have it, he mentioned that Medina was at Haripol. I could see her eyes grow troubled, for I expect she had been having the same anxiety as myself those past weeks, and had been too proud to declare it. As we were going to bed she asked me point-blank what it meant. "Nothing in the world," I said. "He is a great stalker and a friend of the Claybodys. I don't suppose he has the remotest idea that I am here. Anyhow that affair is all over. He is not going to cross our path if he can help it. The one wish in his heart is to avoid us."

She appeared to be satisfied, but I don't know how much she slept that night. I never woke till six o'clock, but when I opened my eyes I felt too big a load on my heart to let me stay in bed, so I went down to the Garden Pool and had a swim. That invigorated me, and indeed it was not easy to be depressed in that gorgeous morning, with the streamers of mist still clinging to the high tops, and the whole glen a harmony of singing birds and tumbling waters. I noticed that the wind, what there was of it, seemed to have shifted more to the east—a very good quarter for the Corrie-na-Sidhe beat.

Angus and Kennedy were waiting outside the smoking-room, and even the pessimism of the head stalker was mellowed by the weather. " I think," he said slowly, " we will be getting a sta-ag. There was a big beast on Bheinn Fhada yesterday —Kennedy seen him—a great beast he was— maybe nineteen stone, but Kennedy never right seen his head. . . . We'd better be moving on, sir."

Mary whispered in my ear. " There's no danger, Dick ? You're sure ? " I have never heard her voice more troubled.

" Not a scrap," I laughed. " It's an easy day and I ought to be back for tea. You'll be able to follow me all the time through the big telescope."

We started at nine. As I left, I had a picture of Greenslade sitting on a garden-seat busy with fly-casts, and Archie smoking his pipe and reading a three-days-old *Times*, and Peter John going off with his nurse, and Mary looking after me with a curious, tense gaze. Behind, the smoke of the chimneys was rising straight into the still air, and the finches were twittering among the Prince Charlie roses. The sight gave me a pang. I might never enter my little kingdom again. Neither wife nor friends could help me : it was my own problem, which I must face alone.

We crossed the bridge, and began to plod upwards through a wood of hazels. In such a fashion I entered upon the strangest day of my life.

## HOW I STALKED WILDER GAME THAN DEER

### I

### 9 A.M. TO 2.15 P.M.

OBVIOUSLY I could make no plan, and I had no clear idea in my head as to what kind of settlement I wanted with Medina. I was certain that I should find him somewhere on the hill, and that, if he got a chance, he would try to kill me. The odds were, of course, against his succeeding straight off, but escape was not what I sought— I must get rid of this menace for ever. I don't think that I wanted to kill him, but indeed I never tried to analyse my feelings. I was obeying a blind instinct, and letting myself drift on the tides of fate.

Corrie-na-Sidhe is an upper corrie, separated from the Aicill valley by a curtain of rock and scree which I daresay was once the moraine of a glacier and down which the Alt-na-Sidhe tumbled in a fine chain of cascades. So steep is its fall that no fish can ascend it, so that, while at the foot it is full of sizable trout, in the corrie itself it holds nothing, as Greenslade reported, but little dark fingerlings. It was very warm as we mounted the chaos of slabs and boulders, where a very sketchy and winding track had been cut for bringing down the deer. Only the toughest kind of pony could make that ascent. Though the day was young the heat was already great, and the glen behind us swam in a glassy sheen. Kennedy, as usual, mopped his brow and grunted, but the lean Angus strode ahead as if he were on the flat.

At the edge of the corrie we halted for a spy. Deep hollows have a trick of drawing the wind, and such faint currents of air as I could detect seemed to be coming on our left rear from the north-east. Angus was positive, however, that though the south had gone out of the wind, it was pretty well due east, with no north in it, and maintained that when we were farther up the corrie we would have it fair on our left cheek. We were not long in finding beasts. There was a big drove of hinds on the right bank of the burn, and another lot, with a few small stags, on the left bank, well up on the face of Bheinn Fhada. But there was nothing shootable there.

"The big stags will be all on the high tops," said Angus. "We must be getting up to the burnhead."

It was easier said than done, for there were the hinds to be circumvented, so we had to make a long circuit far up the hill called Clonlet, which is the westernmost of the Machray tops south of the Aicill. It was rough going, for we mounted to about the 3,000 feet level, and traversed the hillside just under the upper scarp of rock. Presently we were looking down upon the cup which was the head of the corrie, and over the col could see the peak of Stob Coire Easain and the ridge of Stob Ban, both on Haripol and beyond the Reascuill. We had another spy, and made out two small lots of stags on the other side of the Alt-na-Sidhe. They were too far off to get a proper view of them, but one or two looked good beasts, and I decided to get nearer.

We had to make a cautious descent of the hillside in case of deer lying in pockets, for the place was seamed with gullies. Before we were half-way down I got my telescope on one of the lots, and picked out a big stag with a poor head, which clearly wanted shooting. Angus agreed, and we started down a sheltering ravine to get to the burnside. The sight of a quarry made me forget everything else, and for the next hour and a half I hadn't a thought in the world except how to get within range of that beast. One stalk is very much like another, and I am not going to describe this. The only trouble came from a small stag in our rear, which had come over Clonlet and got the scent of our track on the hill-face. This unsettled him and he went off at a great pace towards the top of the burn. I thought at first that the brute would go up Bheinn Fhada and carry off our lot with him, but he came to a halt,

changed his mind, and made for the Haripol march
and the col.

After that it was plain sailing.  We crawled up
the right bank of the Alt-na-Sidhe, which was first-
class cover, and then turned up a tributary gully
which came down from Bheinn Fhada.  Indeed
the whole business was too simple to be of much
interest to any one except the man with the rifle.
When I judged I was about the latitude of my stag,
I crept out of the burn and reached a hillock from
which I had a good view of him.  The head, as I
suspected, was poor—only nine points, though
the horns were of the rough, thick, old Highland
type—but the body was heavy, and he was clearly
a back-going beast.  After a wait of some twenty
minutes he got up and gave me a chance at about
two hundred yards, and I dropped him dead with
a shot in the neck, which was the only part of him
clear.

It was for me the first stag of the season, and
it is always a pleasant moment when the tension
relaxes and you light your pipe and look around
you.  As soon as the gralloch was over I proposed
lunch, and we found for the purpose a little nook
by a spring.  We were within a few hundred yards
of the Haripol march, which there does not run
along the watershed but crosses the corrie about
half a mile below the col.  In the old days of sheep
there had been a fence, the decaying posts of which
could be observed a little way off on a knoll.
Between the fence and the col lay some very rough
ground, where the Alt-na-Sidhe had its source,

ground so broken that it was impossible, without going a good way up the hill, to see from it the watershed ridge.

I finished Mary's stuffed scones and ginger biscuits, and had a drink of whisky and spring water, while Angus and Kennedy ate their lunch a few yards off in the heather. I was just lighting my pipe, when a sound made me pause with the match in my hand. A rifle bullet sang over my head. It was not very near—fifty feet or so above me, and a little to the left.

"The tamned towrists!" I heard Angus exclaim.

I knew it was Medina as certainly as if I had seen him. He was somewhere in the rough ground between the Haripol march and the col—probably close to the col, for the sound of the report seemed to come from a good way off. He could not have been aiming at me, for I was perfectly covered, but he must have seen me when I stalked the stag. He had decided that his chance was not yet come, and the shot was camouflage—to keep up the reputation of Haripol for wild shooting.

"It would be the staggie that went over the march," grunted Angus. "The towrists—to be shooting at yon wee beast!"

I had suddenly made up my mind. I would give Medina the opportunity he sought. I would go and look for him.

I got up and stretched my legs. "I'm going to try a stalk on my own," I told Angus. "I'll go over to Corrie Easain. You had better pull this beast down to the burnside, and then fetch the

pony. You might send Hughie and the other
pony up Glenaicill to the Mad Burn. If I get a
stag I'll gralloch him and get him down somehow
to the burn, so tell Hughie to look out for my
signal. I'll wave a white handkerchief. The wind
is backing round to the north, Angus. It should
be all right for Corrie Easain, if I take it from the
south."

"It would be better for Sgurr Dearg," said
Angus, "but that's ower far. Have you the
cartridges, sir?"

"Plenty," I said, patting a side pocket. "Give
me that spare rope, Kennedy. I'll want it for
hauling down my stag, if I get one."

I put my little ·240 into its cover, nodded to
the men, and turned down the gully to the main
burn. I wasn't going to appear on the bare hillside so long as it was possible for Medina to have
a shot at me. But soon a ridge shut off the view
from the Haripol ground, and I then took a slant
up the face of Bheinn Fhada.

Mary had spent most of the morning at the big
telescope in the library window. She saw us reach
the rim of the corrie and lost us when we moved up
the side of Clonlet. We came into view again far
up the corrie, and she saw the stalk and the death
of the stag. Then she went to luncheon, but
hastened back in the middle of it in time to see
me scrambling alone among the screes of Bheinn
Fhada. At first she was reassured because she
thought I was coming home. But when she
realized that I was mounting higher and was

making for Corrie Easain her heart sank, and, when I had gone out of view, she could do nothing but range miserably about the garden.

## II

### 2.15 P.M. TO ABOUT 5 P.M.

It was very hot on Bheinn Fhada, for I was out of the wind, but when I reached the ridge and looked down on Corrie Easain I found a fair breeze, which had certainly more north than east in it. There was not a cloud in the sky, and every top for miles round stood out clear, except the Haripol peaks, which were shut off by the highest part of the ridge I stood on. Corrie Easain lay far below —not a broad cup like Corrie-na-Sidhe, but a deep gash in the hills, inclined at such an angle that the stream in it was nothing but white water. We called it the Mad Burn—its Gaelic name, I think, was the Alt-a-mhuillin—and half-way up and just opposite me a tributary, the Red Burn, came down from the cliffs of Sgurr Dearg. I could see the northern peak of that mountain, a beautiful cone of rock, rising like the Matterhorn from its glacis of scree.

I argued that Medina would have seen me going up Bheinn Fhada and would assume that I was bound for Corrie Easain. He would re-cross the col and make for the Haripol side of the *beallach* which led from that corrie to the Reascuill. Now

I wanted to keep the higher ground, where I could follow his movements, so it was my aim to get to the watershed ridge looking down on Haripol before he did. The wind was a nuisance, for it was blowing from me and would move any deer towards him, thereby giving him a clue to my whereabouts. So I thought that if I could once locate him, I must try to get the lee side of him. At that time I think I had a vague notion of driving him towards Machray.

I moved at my best pace along the east face of Bheinn Fhada towards the *beallach*—which was a deep rift in the grey rock-curtain through which deer could pass. My only feeling was excitement, such as I had never known before in any stalk. I slipped and sprawled among the slabs, slithered over the screes, had one or two awkward traverses round the butt-end of cliffs, but in about twenty minutes I was at the point where the *massif* of Bheinn Fhada joined the watershed ridge. The easy way was now to get on to the ridge, but I dared not appear on the skyline, so I made a troublesome journey along the near side of the ridge-wall, sometimes out on the face of sheer precipices, but more often involved in a chaos of loose boulders which were the débris of the upper rocks. I was forced pretty far down, and eventually struck the *beallach* path about five hundred feet below the summit.

At the crest I found I had no view of the Reascuill valley—only a narrow corrie blocked by a shoulder of hill and the bald top of Stob Coire

Easain beyond.  A prospect I must have, so I
turned east along the watershed ridge in the
direction of Sgurr Dearg.  I was by this time very
warm, for I had come at a brisk pace ; I had a rifle
to carry, and had Angus's rope round my shoulders
like a Swiss guide ; I was wearing an old grey
suit, which, with bluish stockings, made me pretty
well invisible on that hillside.  Presently as I
mounted the ridge, keeping of course under the
skyline, I came to a place where a lift of rock
enabled me to clear the spurs and command a
mile or so of the Reascuill.

The place was on the skyline, bare and exposed,
and I crawled to the edge where I could get a view.
Below me, after a few hundred yards of rocks
and scree, I saw a long tract of bracken and deep
heather sweeping down to the stream.  Medina,
I made sure, was somewhere thereabouts, watching
the ridge.  I calculated that, with his re-crossing
of the col at the head of Corrie-na-Sidhe and his
working round the south end of Bheinn Fhada,
he could not have had time to get to the *beallach*,
or near the *beallach*, before me, and must still be
on the lower ground.  Indeed I hoped to catch
sight of him, for, while I was assured he was pursuing me, he could not know that I was after him,
and might be off his guard.

But there was no sign of life in that sunny stretch
of green and purple, broken by the grey of boulders.
I searched it with my glass and could see no movement except pipits, and a curlew by a patch of
bog.  Then it occurred to me to show myself.

He must be made to know that I had accepted
his challenge.

I stood up straight on the edge of the steep, and
decided to remain standing till I had counted fifty.
It was an insane thing to do, I daresay, but I was
determined to force the pace. . . . I had got to
forty-one without anything happening. Then a
sudden instinct made me crouch and step aside.
That movement was my salvation. There was a
sound like a twanged fiddle-string, and a bullet
passed over my left shoulder. I felt the wind of
it on my cheek.

The next second I was on my back wriggling
below the skyline. Once there I got to my feet
and ran—up the ridge on my left to get a view
from higher ground. The shot, so far as I could
judge, had come from well below and a little to
the east of where I had been standing. I found
another knuckle of rock, and crept to the edge of
it, so that I looked from between two boulders
into the glen.

The place was still utterly quiet. My enemy
was hidden there, probably not half a mile off, but
there was nothing to reveal his presence. The
light wind stirred the bog cotton, a merlin sailed
across to Stob Coire Easain, a raven croaked in
the crags, but these were the only sounds. There
was not even a sign of deer.

My glass showed that half-way down an old
ewe was feeding—one of those melancholy beasts
which stray into a forest from adjacent sheep-
ground, and lead a precarious life among the rocks,

lean and matted and wild, till some gillie cuts their throats. They are far sharper-eyed and quicker of hearing than a stag, and an unmitigated curse to the stalker. The brute was feeding on a patch of turf near a big stretch of bracken, and suddenly I saw her raise her head and stare. It was the first time I had ever felt well disposed towards a sheep.

She was curious about something in a shallow gully which flanked the brackens, and so was I. I kept my glass glued on her, and saw her toss her disreputable head, stamp her foot, and then heard her whistle through her nose. This was a snag Medina could not have reckoned with. He was clearly in that gully, working his way upwards in its cover, unwitting that the ewe was giving him away. I argued that he must want to reach the high ground as soon as possible. He had seen me on the ridge, and must naturally conclude that I had beaten a retreat. My first business, therefore, was to reassure him.

I got my rifle out of its cover, which I stuffed into my pocket. There was a little patch of gravel just on the lip of the gully, and I calculated that he would emerge beside it, under the shade of a blaeberry-covered stone. I guessed right . . . I saw first an arm and then a shoulder part the rushes, and presently a face which peered uphill. My glass showed me that the face was Medina's, very red, and dirty from contact with the peaty soil. He slowly reached for his glass, and began to scan the heights.

I don't know what my purpose was at this time, if indeed I had any purpose. I didn't exactly mean to kill him, I think, though I felt it might come to that. Vaguely I wanted to put him out of action, to put the fear of God into him, and make him come to terms. Of further consequences I never thought. But now I had one clear intention —to make him understand that I accepted his challenge.

I put a bullet neatly into the centre of the patch of gravel, and then got my glass on it. He knew the game all right. In a second, like a weasel, he was back in the gully.

I reckoned that now I had my chance. Along the ridge I went, mounting fast, and keeping always below the skyline. I wanted to get to the lee side of him and so be able to stalk him up-wind, and I thought that I had an opportunity now to turn the head of the Reascuill by one of the steep corries which descend from Sgurr Dearg. Looking back, it all seems very confused and amateurish, for what could I hope to do, even if I had the lee side, beyond killing or wounding him ? and I had a chance of that as long as I had the upper ground. But in the excitement of the chase the mind does not take long views, and I was enthralled by the crazy sport of the thing. I did not feel any fear, because I was not worrying about consequences.

Soon I came to the higher part of the ridge and saw frowning above me the great rock face of Sgurr Dearg. I saw, too, a thing I had forgotten. There was no way up that mountain direct from the ridge, for the tower rose as perpendicular as a house-wall. To surmount it a man must traverse on one side or the other—on the Machray side by a scree slope, or on the Haripol side by a deep gully which formed the top of the corrie into which I was now looking. Across that corrie was the first of the great buttresses which Sgurr Dearg sends down to the Reascuill. It was the famous Pinnacle Ridge (as mountaineers called it) ; I had climbed it three weeks before and found it pretty stiff ; but then I had kept the ridge all the way from the valley bottom, and I did not see any practicable road up the corrie face of it, which seemed nothing but slabs and rotten rocks, while the few chimneys had ugly overhangs.

I lay flat and reconnoitred. What was Medina likely to do ? After my shot he could not follow up the ridge—the cover was too poor on the upper slopes. I reasoned that he would keep on in the broken ground up the glen till he reached this corrie, and try to find a road to the high ground either by the corrie itself or by one of the spurs. In that case it was my business to wait for him. But first I thought I had better put a fresh clip in my magazine, for the shot I had fired had been the last cartridge in the old clip.

It was now that I made an appalling discovery. I had felt my pockets and told Angus that I had plenty of cartridges. So I had, but they didn't fit. . . . I remembered that two days before I had lent Archie my ·240 and had been shooting with a Mannlicher. What I had in my pocket

were Mannlicher clips left over from that day. . . .
I might chuck my rifle away, for it was no more
use than a poker.

At first I was stunned by the fatality. Here
was I, engaged in a duel on a wild mountain with
one of the best shots in the world, and I had lost
my gun! The sensible course would have been to
go home. There was plenty of time for that, and
long before Medina reached the ridge I could be
in cover in the gorge of the Mad Burn. But that
way out of it never occurred to me. I had chosen
to set the course, and the game must be played
out here and now. But I confess I was pretty
well in despair and could see no plan. I think
I had a faint hope of protracting the thing till
dark and then trusting to my hill-craft to get
even with him, but I had an unpleasant feeling
that he was not likely to oblige me with so long a
delay.

I forced myself to think, and decided that
Medina would either come up the corrie or take
the steep spur which formed the right-hand side of
it and ran down to the Reascuill. The second route
would give him cover, but also render him liable
to a surprise at close quarters if I divined his
intention, for I might suddenly confront him four
yards off at the top of one of the pitches. He
would therefore prefer the corrie, which was magnificently broken up with rocks, and seamed with
ravines, and at the same time gave a clear view
of all the higher ground.

With my face in a clump of louse-wort I raked

the place with my glass ; and to my delight saw deer feeding about half-way down in the right-hand corner. Medina could not ascend the corrie without disturbing these deer—a batch of some thirty hinds, with five small and two fairish stags among them. Therefore I was protected from that side, and had only the ridge to watch.

But as I lay there I thought of another plan. Medina, I was pretty certain, would try the corrie first, and would not see the deer till he was well inside it, for they were on a kind of platform which hid them from below. Opposite me across the narrow corrie rose the great black wall of the Pinnacle Ridge, with the wind blowing from me towards it. I remembered a trick which Angus had taught me—how a stalker might have his wind carried against the face of an opposite moun-tain and then, so to speak, reflected from it and brought back to his own side, so that the deer below him would get it and move away from it up *towards him*. If I let my scent be carried to the Pinnacle Ridge and diverted back, it would move the deer on the platform up the corrie towards me. It would be a faint wind, so they would move slowly away from it—no doubt towards a gap under the tower of Sgurr Dearg which led to the little corrie at the head of the Red Burn. We never stalked that corrie, because it was impos-sible to get a stag out of it without cutting him up, so the place was a kind of sanctuary to which disturbed deer would naturally resort.

I stood on the skyline, being confident that

Medina could not yet be within sight, and let the
wind, which was now stronger and nearly due
north, ruffle my hair. I did this for about five
minutes, and then lay down to watch the result,
with my glass on the deer. Presently I saw them
become restless, first the hinds and then the small
stags lifting their heads and looking towards the
Pinnacle Ridge. Soon a little fellow trotted a
few yards uphill ; then a couple of hinds moved
after him ; and then by a sudden and simultaneous
impulse the whole party began to drift up the
corrie. It was a quiet steady advance ; they
were not scared, only a little doubtful. I saw with
satisfaction that their objective seemed to be the
gap which led over to the Red Burn.

Medina must see this and would assume that
wherever I was I was not ahead of the deer. He
might look for me on the other side, but more
likely would follow the beasts so as to get the high
ground. Once there he could see my movements,
whether I was on the slopes of the Pinnacle Ridge
or down on the Machray side. He would consider,
no doubt, that his marksmanship was so infinitely
better than mine that he had only to pick me
out from the landscape to make an end of the
business.

What I exactly intended I do not know. I
had a fleeting notion of lying hidden and surprising
him, but the chances against that were about a million to one, and, even if I got him at close quarters,
he was armed and I was not. I moved a little to
the right so as to keep my wind from the deer.

and waited with a chill beginning to creep over my spirit. . . . My watch told me it was five o'clock. Mary and Peter John would be having tea among the Prince Charlie roses, and Greenslade and Archie coming up from the river. It would be heavenly at Machray now among greenery and the cool airs of evening. Up here there was loveliness enough, from the stars of butterwort and grass of Parnassus by the well-heads to the solemn tops of Sgurr Dearg, the colour of stormy waves against a faint turquoise sky. But I knew now that the beauty of earth depends on the eye of the beholder, for suddenly the clean airy world around me had grown leaden and stifling.

## III

### 5 P.M. TO ABOUT 7.30 P.M.

It was a good hour before he came. I had guessed rightly, and he had made the deduction I hoped for. He was following the deer towards the gap, assuming that I was on the Machray side. I was in a rushy hollow at a junction of the main ridge and the spur I have mentioned, and I could see him clearly as, with immense circumspection and the use of every scrap of cover, he made his way up the corrie. Once he was over the water-shed, I would command him from the higher ground and have the wind to my vantage. I had some hope now, for I ought to be able to keep him on the hill till the light failed, when my superior local knowledge would come to my aid. He must be growing tired, I reflected, for he had had far more ground to cover. For myself, I felt that I could go on for ever.

That might have been the course of events but for a second sheep. Sgurr Dearg had always been noted for possessing a few sheep even on its high rocks—infernal tattered outlaws, strays originally from some decent flock, but now to all intents a new species, unclassified by science. How they lived and bred I knew not, but there was a legend of many a good stalk ruined by their diabolical cunning. I heard something between a snort and a whistle behind me, and, screwing my head round, saw one of these confounded animals poised on a rock and looking in my direction. It could see me perfectly, too, for on that side I had no cover.

I lay like a mouse watching Medina. He was about half a mile off, almost on the top of the corrie, and he had halted for a rest and a spy. I prayed fervently that he would not see the sheep.

He heard it. The brute started its whistling and coughing, and a novice could have seen that it suspected something, and knew where that something was. I observed him get his glass on my lair, though from the place where he was he could see nothing but rushes. Then he seemed to make up his mind and suddenly disappeared from view.

I knew what he was after. He had dropped into a scaur, which would take him to the skyline and enable him to come down on me from above, while he himself would be safe from my observation.

There was nothing to do but to clear out. The spur dropping to the Reascuill seemed to give me the best chance, so I started off, crouching and crawling, to get round the nose of it and on to the steep glen-ward face. It was a miserable job till I had turned the corner, for I expected every moment a bullet in my back. Nothing happened, however, and soon I was slithering down awesome slabs on to insecure ledges of heather. I am a fairly experienced mountaineer, and a lover of rock, but I dislike vegetation mixed up with a climb, and I had too much of it now. There was, perhaps, a thousand feet of that spur, and I think I must hold the speed record for its descent. Scratched, bruised, and breathless, I came to anchor on a bed of screes, with the infant Reascuill tumbling below me, and beyond it, a quarter of a mile off, the black cliffs of the Pinnacle Ridge.

But what was my next step to be ? The position was reversed. Medina was above me with a rifle, and my own weapon was useless. He must find out the road I had taken and would be after me like a flame. . . . It was no good going down the glen ; in the open ground he would get the chance of twenty shots. It was no good sticking to the spur or the adjacent ridge, for the cover was bad. I could not hide for long in the corrie. . . . Then I looked towards the Pinnacle Ridge and considered that, once I got into those dark couloirs, I might

be safe. The Psalmist had turned to the hills for
his help—I had better look to the rocks.

I had a quarter of a mile of open to cross, and
a good deal more if I was to reach the ridge at
a point easy of ascent. There were chimneys in
front of me, deep black gashes, but my recollection
of them was that they had looked horribly difficult,
and had been plentifully supplied with overhangs.
Supposing I got into one of them and stuck.
Medina would have me safe enough. . . . But I
couldn't wait to think. With an ugly cold feeling
in my inside I got into the ravine of the burn, and
had a long drink from a pool. Then I started down-
stream, keeping close to the right-hand bank,
which mercifully was high and dotted with rowan
saplings. And as I went I was always turning my
head to see behind and above me what I feared.

I think Medina, who of course did not know
about my rifle, may have suspected a trap, for he
came on slowly, and when I caught sight of him
it was not on the spur I had descended, but farther
up the corrie. Two things I now realized. One
was that I could not make the easy end of the
Pinnacle Ridge without exposing myself on some
particularly bare ground. The other was that to
my left in the Ridge was a deep gully which
looked climbable. Moreover, the foot of that gully
was not a hundred yards from the burn, and the
mouth was so deep that a man would find shelter
as soon as he entered it.

For the moment I could not see Medina, and I
don't think he had yet caught sight of me. There

was a trickle of water coming down from the gully
to the burn, and that gave me an apology for cover.
I ground my nose into the flowe-moss and let the
water trickle down my neck, as I squirmed my
way up, praying hard that my enemy's eyes might
be sealed.

I think I had got about half-way, when a turn
gave me a view of the corrie, and there was Medina
halted and looking towards me.  By the mercy of
Providence my boots were out of sight, and my
head a little lower than my shoulders, so that I
suppose among the sand and gravel and rushes I
must have been hard to detect.  Had he used his
telescope I think he must have spotted me, though
I am not certain.  I saw him staring.  I saw him
half-raise his rifle to his shoulder, while I heard my
heart thump.  Then he lowered his weapon, and
moved out of sight.

Two minutes later I was inside the gully.

The place ran in like a cave with a sandy floor,
and then came a steep pitch of rock, while the sides
narrowed into a chimney.  This was not very difficult.  I swung myself up into the second storey,
and found that the cleft was so deep that the back
wall was about three yards from the opening, so
that I climbed in almost complete darkness and in
perfect safety from view.  This went on for about
fifty feet, and then, after a rather awkward chockstone, I came to a fork.  The branch on the left
looked hopeless, while that on the right seemed to
offer some chances.  But I stopped to consider,
for I remembered something.

I remembered that this was the chimney which I had prospected three weeks before when I climbed the Pinnacle Ridge. I had prospected it from above, and had come to the conclusion that, while the left fork *might* be climbed, the right was impossible or nearly so, for, modestly as it began, it ran out into a fearsome crack on the face of the cliff, and did not become a chimney again till after a hundred feet of unclimbable rotten granite.

So I tried the left fork, which looked horribly unpromising. The first trouble was a chockstone, which I managed to climb round, and then the confounded thing widened and became perpendicular. I remembered that I had believed a way could be found by taking to the right-hand face, and in the excitement of the climb I forgot all precautions. It simply did not occur to me that this face route might bring me in sight of eyes which at all costs I must avoid.

It was not an easy business, for there was an extreme poverty of decent holds. But I have done worse pitches in my time, and had I not had a rifle to carry (I had no sling), might have thought less of it. Very soon I was past the worst, and saw my way to returning to the chimney, which had once more become reasonable. I stopped for a second to prospect the route, with my foot on a sound ledge, my right elbow crooked round a jag of rock, and my left hand, which held the rifle, stretched out so that my fingers could test the soundness of a certain handhold.

Suddenly I felt the power go out of those fingers. The stone seemed to crumble and splinters flew into my eye. There was a crashing of echoes, which drowned the noise of my rifle as it clattered down the precipice. I remember looking at my hand spread-eagled against the rock, and wondering why it looked so strange.

The light was just beginning to fail, so it must have been about half-past seven.

## IV

### 7.30 P.M. AND ONWARDS

Had anything of the sort happened to me during an ordinary climb I should beyond doubt have lost my footing with the shock and fallen. But, being pursued, I suppose my nerves were keyed to a perpetual expectancy, and I did not slip. The fear of a second bullet saved my life. In a trice I was back in the chimney, and the second bullet spent itself harmlessly on the granite.

Mercifully it was now easier going—honest knee-and-back work, which I could manage in spite of my shattered fingers. I climbed fever-ishly with a cold sweat on my brow, but every muscle was in order, and I knew I would make no mistake. The chimney was deep, and a ledge of rock hid me from my enemy below. . . . Pres-ently I squeezed through a gap, swung myself up with my right hand and my knees to a shelf, and saw that the difficulties were over. A shallow gully, filled with screes, led up to the crest of the ridge. It was the place from which I had looked down three weeks before.

I examined my left hand, which was in a horrid mess. The top of my thumb was blown off, and the two top joints of my middle and third fingers were smashed to pulp. I felt no pain in them, though they were dripping blood, but I had a queer numbness in my left shoulder. I managed to bind the hand up in a handkerchief, where it made a gory bundle. Then I tried to collect my wits.

Medina was coming up the chimney after me. He knew I had no rifle. He was, as I had heard, an expert cragsman, and he was the younger man by at least ten years. My first thought was to make for the upper part of the Pinnacle Ridge, and try to hide or to elude him somehow till the darkness. But he could follow me in the transparent northern night, and I must soon weaken from loss of blood. I could not hope to put sufficient distance between us for safety, and he had his deadly rifle. Somewhere in the night or in the dawning he would get me. No, I must stay and fight it out.

Could I hold the chimney ? I had no weapon but stones, but I might be able to prevent a man ascending by those intricate rocks. In the chimney, at any rate, there was cover, and he could not use his rifle. . . . But would he try the chimney ? Why should he not go round by the lower slopes of the Pinnacle Ridge and come on me from above ?

It was the dread of his bullets that decided me. My one passionate longing was for cover. I might get him in a place where his rifle was useless and I had a chance to use my greater muscular strength. I did not care what happened to me provided I got my hands on him. Behind all my fear and confusion and pain there was now a cold fury of rage.

So I slipped back into the chimney and descended it to where it turned slightly to the left past a nose of rock. Here I had cover, and could peer down into the darkening deeps of the great couloir.

A purple haze filled the corrie, and the Machray tops were like dull amethysts. The sky was a cloudy blue sprinkled with stars, and mingled with the last flush of sunset was the first tide of the afterglow. . . . At first all was quiet in the gully. I heard the faint trickle of stones which are always falling in such a place, and once the croak of a hungry raven. . . . Was my enemy there ? Did he know of the easier route up the Pinnacle Ridge ? Would he not assume that if I could climb the cleft he could follow, and would he feel any dread of a man with no gun and a shattered hand ?

Then from far below came a sound I recognized —iron hobnails on rock. I began to collect loose stones, and made a little pile of such ammunition beside me. . . . I realized that Medina had begun

the ascent of the lower pitches. Every breach
in the stillness was perfectly clear—the steady
scraping in the chimney, the fall of a fragment of
rock as he surmounted the lower chockstone, the
scraping again as he was forced out on to the
containing wall. The light must have been poor,
but the road was plain. Of course I saw nothing
of him, for a bulge prevented me, but my ears
told me the story. Then there was silence. I
realized that he had come to the place where the
chimney forked.

I had my stones ready, for I hoped to get him
when he was driven out on the face at the over-
hang, the spot where I had been when he fired.

The sounds began again, and I waited in a
desperate choking calm. In a minute or two
would come the crisis. I remember that the
afterglow was on the Machray tops and made a
pale light in the corrie below. In the cleft there
was still a kind of dim twilight. Any moment I
expected to see a dark thing in movement fifty
feet below, which would be Medina's head.

But it did not come. The noise of scraped rock
still continued, but it seemed to draw no nearer.
Then I realized that I had misjudged the situation. Medina had taken the right-hand fork. He
was bound to, unless he had made, like me, an
earlier reconnaissance. My route in the half-light
must have looked starkly impossible.

The odds were now on my side. No man in
the fast-gathering darkness could hope to climb
the cliff face and rejoin that chimney after its

interruption. He would go on till he stuck—
and then it would not be too easy to get back. I
reascended my own cleft, for I had a notion that
I might traverse across the space between the
two forks, and find a vantage point for a view.

Very slowly and painfully, for my left arm was
beginning to burn like fire and my left shoulder
and neck to feel strangely paralysed, I wriggled
across the steep face till I found a sort of *gendarme*
of rock, beyond which the cliff fell smoothly to
the lip of the other fork. The great gully below
was now a pit of darkness, but the afterglow still
lingered on this upper section, and I saw clearly
where Medina's chimney lay, where it narrowed
and where it ran out. I fixed myself so as to
prevent myself falling, for I feared I was becoming
light-headed. Then I remembered Angus's rope,
got it unrolled, took a coil round my waist, and
made a hitch over the *gendarme*.

There was a smothered cry from below, and
suddenly came the ring of metal on stone, and
then a clatter of something falling. I knew what
it meant. Medina's rifle had gone the way of
mine and lay now among the boulders at the
chimney foot. At last we stood on equal terms,
and, befogged as my mind was, I saw that nothing
now could stand between us and a settlement.

It seemed to me that I saw something moving
in the half-light. If it was Medina, he had left
the chimney and was trying the face. That way
I knew there was no hope. He would be forced
back, and surely would soon realize the folly of

it and descend.  Now that his rifle had gone my
hatred had ebbed.  I seemed only to be watching
a fellow-mountaineer in a quandary.

He could not have been forty feet from me, for
I heard his quick breathing.  He was striving
hard for holds, and the rock must have been
rotten, for there was a continuous dropping of
fragments, and once a considerable boulder hurtled
down the couloir.

"Go back, man," I cried instinctively.  "Back
to the chimney.  You can't get farther that way."

I suppose he heard me, for he made a more
violent effort, and I thought I could see him
sprawl at a foothold which he missed, and then
swing out on his hands.  He was evidently weakening, for I heard a sob of weariness.  If he could
not regain the chimney, there was three hundred
feet of a fall to the boulders at the foot.

"Medina," I yelled, "I've a rope.  I'm going
to send it down to you.  Get your arm in the
loop."

I made a noose at the end with my teeth and
my right hand, working with a maniac's fury.

"I'll fling it straight out," I cried.  "Catch it
when it falls to you."

My cast was good enough, but he let it pass, and
the rope dangled down into the abyss.

"Oh, damn it, man," I roared, "you can trust
me.  We'll have it out when I get you safe.
You'll break your neck if you hang there."

Again I threw, and suddenly the rope tightened.
He believed my word, and I think that was the

greatest compliment ever paid me in all my days.

"Now you're held," I cried. "I've got a belay here. Try and climb back into the chimney."

He understood and began to move. But his arms and legs must have been numb with fatigue, for suddenly that happened which I had feared. There was a wild slipping and plunging, and then he swung out limply, missing the chimney, right on to the smooth wall of the cliff.

There was nothing for it but to haul him back. I knew Angus's ropes too well to have any confidence in them, and I had only the one good hand. The rope ran through a groove of stone which I had covered with my coat, and I hoped to work it even with a single arm by moving slowly upwards.

"I'll pull you up," I yelled, "but for God's sake give me some help. Don't hang on the rope more than you need."

My loop was a large one, and I think he had got both arms through it. He was a monstrous weight, limp and dead as a sack, for though I could feel him scraping and kicking at the cliff face, the rock was too smooth for fissures. I held the rope with my feet planted against boulders, and wrought till my muscles cracked. Inch by inch I was drawing him in, till I realized the danger.

The rope was grating on the sharp brink beyond the chimney and might at any moment be cut by a knife-edge.

"Medina"—my voice must have been like a wild animal's scream—"this is too dangerous. I'm going to let you down a bit so that you can traverse. There's a sort of ledge down there. For Heaven's sake go canny with this rope."

I slipped the belay from the *gendarme*, and hideously difficult it was. Then I moved farther down to a little platform nearer the chimney. This gave me about six extra yards.

"Now," I cried, when I had let him slip down, "a little to your left. Do you feel the ledge?"

He had found some sort of foothold, and for a moment there was a relaxation of the strain. The rope swayed to my right towards the chimney. I began to see a glimmer of hope.

"Cheer up," I cried. "Once in the chimney you're safe. Sing out when you reach it."

The answer out of the darkness was a sob. I think giddiness must have overtaken him, or that atrophy of muscle which is the peril of rock-climbing. Suddenly the rope scorched my fingers and a shock came on my middle which dragged me to the very edge of the abyss.

I still believe that I could have saved him if I had had the use of both my hands, for I could have guided the rope away from that fatal knife-edge. I knew it was hopeless, but I put every ounce of strength and will into the effort to swing it with its burden into the chimney. He gave me no help, for I think—I hope—that he was unconscious. Next second the strands had parted, and I fell back with a sound in my ears which I pray God I may never hear again—the sound of a body rebounding dully from crag to crag, and then a long soft rumbling of screes like a snowslip.

.     .     .     .     .     .

I managed to crawl the few yards to the anchorage of the *gendarme* before my senses departed. There in the morning Mary and Angus found me.

THE END

PRINTED IN GREAT BRITAIN AT
THE PRESS OF THE PUBLISHERS.